"They got her," someone said. Zann turned and stared hard at the speaker, who lowered his eyes. Red Wing. The eight people who crowded around Zann's board ignored her studiously. They knew, they all knew. The White Wing took no prisoners. And they were never taken in battle. Never. Not one capture in two hundred years.

The violet staining the holo crept out farther and deepened. The white fleck appeared to move slightly, to sink into it. Tractor beams might be notoriously slow, but they were impossible to break once they drained a ship's power.

The blood thundered in Zann's ears. She felt as if the entire staff of Battle Op could hear it pound, and she wanted to curse it for giving her Wing away. Almost imperceptibly the staff of Battle Op shifted position, without even the echo of a scuffle. Zann found herself shifting with them. They were all standing at attention.

"Battle Op, record. This is Maryam of White Wing, to Gregory, squad leader. I request the privilege of the Mercy of the Wing."

GORDON KENDALL
WHITE WING

TOR

A TOM DOHERTY ASSOCIATES BOOK
NEW YORK

This is a work of fiction. All the characters and events portrayed in this book are fictitious, and any resemblance to real people or events is purely coincidental.

WHITE WING

Copyright © 1985 by Gordon Kendall

Lines from "An Irish Airman Foresees His Death" on page 83 reprinted with permission of Macmillan Publishing Company from *The Poems* by W.B. Yeats, edited by Richard J. Finneran. Copyright © 1919 by Macmillan Publishing Company, renewed by Bertha Georgie Yeats.

All rights reserved, including the right to reproduce this book, or portions thereof, in any form.

A Tor Book
Published by Tom Doherty Associates, Inc.
49 West 24th Street
New York, N.Y. 10010

Cover art by Janny Wurtz

ISBN: 0-812-51770-9

First printing: July 1985

Printed in the United States of America

0 9 8 7 6 5 4 3 2

Acknowledgments

I would like to acknowledge with gratitude the advice of Captain Robert K. Irvine, USN (Ret.), regarding tactics and weapons systems.

I would also like to thank BEA Associates for the use of computer time.

GORDON KENDALL (who likes to say he was born in Ohio, just like John Glenn and Neil Armstrong) studied in France and England before entering Harvard University, where he majored in Applied Mathematics and Near Eastern Studies. In 1978, he received his Ph.D. from Yale University in Government. Though he is often out of the country on business, Kendall calls MacLean, Virginia, home. He is an avid science fiction reader since he was nine; this is his first novel. When neither writing nor working, Kendall's interests include music, aviation, and badgering NASA for a seat on the Space Shuttle.

CHAPTER 1

Crosshatched on Yuri's scan, the Sejiedi fighter turned for an attack run. Adrenaline flooded Yuri's veins. The hum of his comm, crackling into life with terse orders from the Wingleaders, only emphasized the silence about him, the absolute silence that was battle. In that eternal quiet, Yuri forgot the heatrush of adrenaline, the sweat prickling his flightsuit, and entered the monozone that was fight-concentration. The Sejiedi knifed straight at him, making only slight evasive maneuvers, the merest pretense of a feint. Yuri held his stingfighter—a delta-winged shell surrounding life-support, weapons, and enormous engines— steady. The Sej would be low on energy. He had to be. It had to be infrared.

"Come on, baby . . . infrared," he murmured.

There would be time, there would be time . . . just enough time . . . there! The barest sparkle on the Sejiedi's underbelly alerted him. His fingers played a fugue on the control board at double speed, and the tiny stingfighter began to spin rapidly. The infrared hit but never landed long enough to burn.

His squad wouldn't like that. He shouldn't take those kinds of risks, not even when he knew they were the best part of Sejiedi psychology. The Sej never bluffed. Neither would he. He hesitated for a moment. Maybe this was one fight where he ought to call for backups. *Caution be vaporized!* he thought, then opened the throttle full out for a breakneck approach. He felt his skin go taut as the a-gravs compensated for the thrust. Around him glittered the blasts of battle. Starlight and silent explosions glared off sleek, polished hulls. They were only light to him now. A faint memory told him those lights were friends and comrades, committed and struggling for their lives—as he was. Now each of those silent battles, that blue-white flare of a dying ship glancing off his portside, were only the backdrop of his own encounter. His concentration grew: he couldn't even hear himself breathe now. The universe narrowed to that one Sejiedi ship out there. It was his.

The Sejiedi tried the old trick of turn and dive, but Yuri was ready for it. The Sejiedi pulled that one too often for it to be a surprise. Two centuries of war on a front half a galaxy wide had taught the League that much. He knew where that ship would show up on the scope once it pulled out, if this pilot flew true to form. If it didn't, well, then his own tactics and, quite incidentally, he himself, would be blown. Even before the Sejiedi turned up again on the scope, he fired a scatter-burst to the area where it should appear, filling it with lances of ravening light. Momentarily the lights grew ragged as the Sejiedi came around to attack position, and collided with them.

Yuri turned to view the wreckage. It wasn't enough just to see the ship's death on scan. There, on the black field, motes of light danced fiercely on shards of Sejiedi hull. Clean kill. Single kill. His. Then which kill this was hit him and he whooped in excitement.

"That's ten," he yelled into the comm. "My tenth!"

"Could have done a more elegant job," Judith's voice replied.

Yuri smiled beneath the visor of his flight helmet, although Judith, assisting at a kill a thousand kilometers away, wouldn't see it. Judith was right, of course. A really elegant kill reduced an enemy ship into a subtle fall of stardust. But he didn't care. This was ten, his tenth kill in single combat. Ace! He could already feel the fine white silk of the scarf and hear the noises of the party where the other aces in his squad would drape it around his neck.

"Good going!" Maryam's voice came excitedly into his ear.

"Too much chatter," said Gregory, the senior pilot of the squad. But Yuri could hear the congratulations in his voice, and he practically glowed. He looked around for other ships, feeling time stretch out again, back to normal. Ace! He was hot. Well, there was one call he could make that wouldn't be chatter. He raised his command ship.

"Battle Op, mark it down," Yuri said, trying to keep the excitement from his voice. "Zann? This is Yuri. Tenth kill."

"Good going," said Suzannah, standing at the comm board. If Battle Op hadn't been dark, someone might have noticed the smile that spread across her face.

Battle Op was darker than the space surrounding the command ship. Only the dull violet and green and red lights of various boards monitoring the battle pierced it. They glowed with far less light than the laser traces of the stings and Sejiedi ships. The silence quivered with palpable concentration, far more intense than the hush of thought. There was none. There didn't have to be. Monitoring battles was what they had done forever. The bodies of comm and security officers became human statues, took on alien, frozen dimensions as the murky light accented faces and bodies with strange, hard angles.

Suzannah's white uniform shimmered eerily in the multihued night of Battle Operations. She was being observed, and she knew it. Someone was always staring at White Wingers, and she—out of all of them—had had plenty of practice ignoring it. Earthers had only been part of the League—as refugees, clients tolerated for their fighting abilities and their taxes—for two centuries. Even she didn't know how many centuries it would take for the League to accept them as full citizens . . . and full humans. Humans! She would have snorted if she hadn't known her reaction would be watched and analyzed. Even the alien members of the League, who had retreated from their human allies, uninterested in and appalled at the war for human-habitable real estate, had more acceptance. She could feel the eyes on her back, stronger by far this time than the usual anger or morbid curiosity. The watcher kept well back in the shadows away from the boards, and that was proper. This was clean combat; Intelligence's place was to skulk on the fringes till the battle was over.

She wore two comm plugs in her ears: one for the general frequencies that everyone in Battle Op monitored; the other a frequency restricted to the White Wing. She was the only one who wore the unrelieved white of the Earther Wing in this assembly. The bleeding tints of the boards only stressed how alien she was among these others, who outwardly looked so much like herself.

Humans. But not *Earth*-humans. They had homes, even a homeworld. Zann didn't. No Earther had, not for two hundred years, since the Sejiedi blasted Earth and its orphans joined the League of Known Worlds on sufferance. As always, she spared an instant to wonder just why the planet-hungry Sej had destroyed Earth. After all, they'd annexed all the other planets that had fallen to them in the early decades of the war. But that information had a higher classified status than anything they'd ever let her access. *One of these days, I'll find out,* she promised herself as she did every few months. She was an eidetic, and she was in Intelligence; data deprivation was like taking away food or water—and more infuriating. Then she shook herself back to total concentration. She had her Wing and her Wing's honor. They were more than enough.

"Yuri got one, and I'm going to get myself one too." Maryam's voice came clearly over the comm and pierced into her brain.

Suzannah's heart froze. *Oh no, not now. Not Maryam. Not this time.* The darkness in Battle Op was complete enough that no one noticed the tension twisting her face. Not Maryam. Maryam always took too many risks. She flew for the love of it, and the danger alone. And she had no caution at all. Tau-void was what other pilots called it. Their stings had no trans-light capability. As they reached the sightless, timeless barrier between normal space and the faster-than-light blankness of tau, they strained, then blew. All pilots dumped tau, taking risks that non-pilots regarded as insane. But a tau-void pilot was practically a flying suicide until that inevitable moment when he (*or she,* Zann thought with a shudder) became a statistic. Tau-void? Sense-void was the way Suzannah defined it for herself. Maryam was still alive only because she was so very, very good. She had made her ace's rating, her tenth ship-to-ship kill in single combat, only three years out of training. That alone was enough to make everyone in the Wing worry. Every time Maryam flew, Zann felt her stomach clench. And this time. . . .

Zann took a deep breath to settle herself. Words tumbled through her head. "We cry for Your unfailing Grace for those in peril deep in space,'' she mouthed silently, and shuddered. Then rationality returned. Maryam was a fine pilot. And she, Zann, was a comm officer, she was Intelligence, and she was on duty. She could hide her fear in any one of those things—couldn't she?

"I'm going in to cover,'' came Gregory's voice, seemingly cool and unconcerned. "Judith, fly wing for me. Yuri, get back in formation. Sibs, could you close up for us?''

Zann knew the squad all too well, knew that Gregory's voice was too light and too controlled. He was shaky, probably cursing under his breath so she couldn't hear it, his hands stone steady on the instrument board. His hands were always unnaturally still when there was trouble.

It was Judith he had taken out with him, the best team pilot in the whole Wing, just about. Judith didn't go in for theatrics and single kills. She only took credit for getting more pilots back alive than anyone else. Knowing that, at least, was some relief. And Yuri was safely flying with the formation. Smart of Gregory to order it that way. Yuri was too high, too hot, right now. He would do something rash, and then—

Zann's fingers tightened convulsively. *No*, she thought, *no. Maryam's flown dozens of tasks, she's an ace. Not this time. Please let it not be this time.*

It had been almost a year since the Mercy had happened. Not to Maryam, that time, although that idea gave the whole squad nightmares. Not that, above all, not that. Judith would fly her out of it. Judith had flown more pilots out of the Mercy than from under Sejiedi cruisers.

She could feel the eyes again, boring into her neck. Damn, damn, damn! What kind of sadistic Intelligence Director would pick *now* to spring a new Intelligence chief on her? Another test? Zann wanted to bare her teeth at

Security's passion for testing its own operatives . . . White Wingers especially. The war was crammed with watchers. One of them, Federico Hashrahh Kroeger, half-Earther, half not, was watching her right now. With an act of will, she relaxed her jaw muscles. No one was going to see a White Winger go tense. Maryam was flying solo, glory-high, tau-void . . . pure energy. Gregory was chasing her, but Maryam was far ahead. There was little chance that he and Judith could catch her before she did something stupid and maybe wonderful. But there were outsiders here, who weren't Wing. They would never see.

She carefully composed her features and stretched to keep her muscles from locking. But she never took her eyes from the tracking holos. In two hundred years, since Earth died, the honor of the Wing had never been broken, not by a capture, not by so little as a concerned look. Zann was White Wing. It wasn't the Colors' place, those smug other Wings, to see her fear for the chase they were all watching.

"Yummy. A nice, fat Sejiedi cruiser just sitting there . . . mine . . ." Maryam sounded hushed and hungry, poised for the kill. Zann could see her face, flushed red and glowing, her eyes wide and her fingers tensed against the control board. Maryam always smiled when she closed in for a fight, the delighted smile of a precocious child, innocent and alert. Maryam only came alive when there was danger, when she was flying and fighting. It was all she could do. It was what she was.

"You're in range," Gregory informed her, as if Maryam's comp wouldn't be spitting out the same information, with an alarm added. From the quiet of his voice, Zann knew that he was at least as distressed as she herself was, probably more so. They'd flown together for years.

The last time Maryam had flown against the Sejiedi in

an engagement of this size, she had taken out two in single combat and at least four more in assists. And all six of them had been well in the danger zone, certainly at least as close as she was now. Helplessness washed over Zann like the bloody lights of Battle Op. Judith and Gregory were out there, tiny white lights steady on her screens, while all she could do was watch.

They were coming around now, Judith glued to her position just a little behind and to the left of Gregory. They began to arc out in a cutting sweep. Zann plotted their course, her eidetic brain racing the computers to reach its verdict: no intercept possible. Maryam was way out there, and the Sejiedi she was hunting was no lone fighter but a cruiser.

How many times Zann had heard the pilots talking about taking out a Sejiedi cruiser. It had happened once or twice, as much from blind stupidity and sheer luck as from brilliant tactics, no matter what they said. It was rare that pilots came back from a cruiser-kill, but when they did, there was no glory like it. The Wing would celebrate for weeks, would earn even harder stares and more cold anger from the other Colors. *The joy of it,* she remembered Maryam saying, her eyes bright. But Maryam had only been talking the way they all talked, even Judith, drawing diagrams, overloading their wristcomps as they calculated probabilities and speculated on tactics that could bring the numbers down to something an ace might risk—and survive. But how could a sting take out a cruiser?

Maryam was coming out from under and behind at an angle, the holoboards showed clearly. That was the only possible approach, Zann remembered the pilots declaring, before they got too high on the idea to do more than daydream. Her hands froze on the board. Then she recognized the pattern, and she wanted to shake. It was her curse to recognize such patterns seconds before anyone else in Battle Op. Maryam was just mad enough, tau-void enough, to try it. There wasn't a pilot in the White Wing who hadn't speculated on the best way to try it, in the same spirit that Valentina, her squad's comp-hacker, played with conjectures, for the sheer intellectual challenge. Suzannah's own fascination with math had almost drawn her into the net of this ultimate, preposterous risk. She'd helped calculate odds. But only Maryam, their own Maryam, would have the idiocy to try it.

Both of Zann's earplugs went silent. She felt a warmth start about her, and flashed a glare around. The entire staff of Battle Op had gathered around the flashing red, white, and green of her board. Some silent alarm, even perhaps the silence itself, had drawn them all to that single, focal fight. They wanted to be in at the kill.

"The sheer courage of . . ." someone whispered. Zann didn't turn. It sounded admiring, but she knew better. The other Colors watched to see what the White Wing would do. She didn't want to know which one of the scavengers had said it.

The general-frequency plug went from empty noise to opacity in her ear, then switched off. Zann knew that the fight was being piped into the room. Everyone would want to hear what was going on out there. She removed the useless plug, and left the Wing communications gear in place. There was no chatter out there, and knowing the pilots involved, there wasn't going to be any.

The small white sting was closing in on the Sejiedi cruiser. Maryam positioned her sting so that its main forward lasers would be perfectly aligned to blast the cruiser's central power ganglia. Zann cursed herself for having helped the pilots obtain engineering specs on the latest Sejiedi craft. And to think she'd enjoyed doing it, a gift for Maryam and all the other crazy pilots of her Wing. One good bolt into just the right place, and the cruiser would cease to function. It wouldn't be an elegant kill, but this was a cruiser. It was big. The tiny stingfighter barely showed a disk against the bulk of that hull.

Maryam's ship corrected minutely. She was drawing into position. Back in Battle Op the holo spewed out a deep violet field, surging out to engulf the tiny white fleck of Maryam's ship. Violet tractor-emissions.

The silence around Suzannah yawned deeper than the eternity of space. She could see Gregory's sting closing in, Judith at his side, hopeless. Zann felt despair wash through her. She realized that she had forgotten to breathe, and inhaled raggedly, burying the pain of that breath somewhere deep in her mind with the stiffness and the fear and all the other pains. All there was now was Maryam and the cruiser, married by the violent incandescence deepening between them.

"They got her," someone said. Zann turned and stared hard at the speaker, who lowered his eyes. Red Wing. The eight people who crowded around Zann's board ignored her studiously. They knew, they all knew. The White Wing took no prisoners. And they were never taken in battle. Never. Not one capture in two hundred years. Anger merged with grief in Zann until the lights on her board blurred. Those Colors around her, in their blue and yellow and green and red and orange, what did they know? When Earth's orphaned fighters had come into the League, they'd been handed their no-color—League-wide, the color of mourning—and ordered to make the best of it. They'd turned it into a glory. So now, after all these years, did the Colors actually think that they would actually get to watch the first capture of a White Wing ship? Contempt for them filled her, and she made the lights around her focus again. Nothing had changed. Only seconds had elapsed.

"I've tried auxiliary power." Maryam's light voice, controlled now, piped into Battle Op. "I've tried manual override, I've tried laser reroute. Power's below critical."

"Have you tried atmospheric thrusters?" some anonymous pilot asked.

A moment of silence. "Affirmative. No response."

"Hard-fuel boosters?" came from another pilot. Zann understood. Maryam was asking anyone, everyone, for help. They were all trying. She didn't recognize the voices. Some must be pilots from other Colors. Regardless of Wing color, they were all pilots, and Zann had the urge to kiss the whole insane lot of them. Her heart ached for Maryam, for her stupidity and her bravery. She sounded as calm as if she were discussing the weather.

"Copy," Maryam said. There was a pause. "No response."

"Abandon ship!" came a cry.

"No response from the ejectors."

"Have you tried the self-destruct?" Gregory suggested it as evenly as if he were commenting on the food in the wardroom.

"No response."

The violet staining the holo crept out farther and deepened. The white fleck appeared to move slightly, to sink into it. Tractor beams might be notoriously slow, but they were impossible to break once they drained a ship's power. Zann felt as if this Sejiedi cruiser were sitting on her chest.

The blood thundered in Zann's ears. She felt as if the entire staff of Battle Op could hear it pound, and she wanted to curse it for giving her Wing away. Almost imperceptibly the staff of Battle Op shifted position, with-

out even the echo of a scuffle. Zann found herself shifting
with them. They were all standing at attention. It was the
least honor they could give. Zann could feel terror and
exhilaration flowing from the people who crowded around
that fatal holo display.

"Battle Op, record. This is Maryam of White Wing, to
Gregory, squad leader. I request the privilege of the Mercy
of the Wing."

CHAPTER 2

Numbly, Suzannah analyzed the numbers flying by underneath the holoboard. She could see it, see Gregory, the lines around his mouth hardening as he switched to manual control. He would be in visual contact with Maryam's sting and the bulk of the Sejiedi cruiser. One sequence would lock power into the main forward lasers; simultaneously his left hand would activate the targeting scope. He knew every millimeter of the sting's shell, every board and circuit lying beneath its skin. Beneath the twin thrusters just aft of the fuel tanks was the central power converter. It would be clean.

Gregory's eyes would be fixed on target, unblinking. His long fingers would unconsciously caress the weapons console and Maryam's tiny, vulnerable fighter would remain precisely positioned in the scope's bull's-eye. Then, so rapidly that an observer might miss it, he would activate the three heat-sensitive keys.

Brilliant frequencies from the visible into ultraviolet surged forward into one narrow beam to flare hungrily through the sting's titanium hull, into the heart of his squadmate's sting.

Violet light flared against the purple haze of the tractor beam on Suzannah's board. When it died, the white fleck that had been Maryam's ship was gone. Zann shut her eyes briefly, a luxury she could allow herself for the instant that the others, mesmerized by the lethal choreography, were blinded by the flash of the Mercy.

Good-bye, Maryam.

Suzannah activated scanners to check that area. Radiation, a few stray metallic atoms: Gregory's aim had been flawless.

"Elegant, indeed," she whispered to herself. Maryam was gone. What a damned rotten waste. And the worst of it was that Zann wasn't the least bit surprised. Since the moment Maryam had joined the squad, they had anticipated this day, dreaded it. But Maryam had been worth it, she decided, as she had decided every time the pilots went out.

"We're finishing out the scramble," came Judith's voice as calmly as if she hadn't just watched Maryam die. Zann shook herself. She had been too far away, in the cockpit of a stingfighter with her helmet's blastshield blocking out most of the laser's glare, savage as the core of a star. How had Gregory described the perfect kill? Just a tease of a starlight, a red glow shifting over a spray of dust.

Zann could hear the mutters starting up again behind her back. The eyes started burning into her again. She replaced her earplug, grateful to have two: one for her own Wing, the other for general frequencies—and right now, both for a merciful deafness. In a moment, she could slip into a trance of decryption, reading the pulse of cipher the way other people scanned printouts. She could escape into the serenity of mathematics the way, half a system distant,

Gregory, Judith, and Yuri would slip into the monozone of fighting concentration.

The Wing was flying tight formation, the sibs keeping Yuri well covered, Zann observed. He hadn't gotten to enjoy being an ace for long.

"Why don't they come in?" she heard a young commtech from Red Wing whisper despite the earplugs.

Gregory and Judith were wheeling, diving like needles below the ecliptic to escape the scatter of Sejiedi ships as they rejoined their Wing.

Zann opened the in-ship frequencies. "Life-support?" There were others to notify.

"Life-support, aye."

"Joao?" She could visualize her two squadmates down there: Valentina, monitoring her screens on her wristcomp if nothing better were available; Joao, the squad's comfortingly huge, solid medic, awaiting the summons to the flight deck just in case there were casualties. Usually there weren't. Either people were vaped or they made it back whole.

"Here, Suzannah," came Joao's imperturbable voice.

"Maryam," she said quietly. "Gregory gave her the Mercy."

"On my way to flight deck."

"Not now," Zann told him. "They're finishing out the fight."

She broke contact and turned her attention back to the holo. Gregory and Judith had rejoined the Wing. The sib squads hovered protectively around them.

"Let me clear!" Gregory ordered, and reluctantly they made a way for him. His stingfighter leapt forward, Judith and Yuri flying point for him, guarding one another.

With agonized approval, Zann watched them wheel to starboard and "up," heading for where the fighting was most vicious, where the White Wing always fought. There were no theatrics now, no glory-riding. Even Yuri was flying by the book, carefully calibrating his cover-fire, assisting kills.

Close-packed diamonds and colored triangles—red, yellow, blue—began to pull away, arcing back to their base cruisers. Only the white lights still pressed forward, the rearguard, vaporizing Sejiedi ships too damaged to flee them.

"Animals!" Zann heard someone say in the darkness of Battle Op. She smiled thinly as the cub was hushed. The White Wing took no prisoners. They had a battle to clean up after, picking off crippled Sejiedi ships. Their cruisers would only abandon them anyway. Actually, the Wing was doing the Sejiedi a favor, giving them a death almost as clean as the Mercy. But you couldn't expect the Colors to understand that.

She wondered if the Sejiedi did. Her own operatives had brought in reports that emphasized their fanatic obsession with honor, with duty. They even seemed to have a military caste. Maybe the Wing was fighting on the wrong . . . she turned her thoughts away from that idea once again and recited the litany of wrongs that all White Wingers learned from their first days in the training schools. The Sejiedi had destroyed Earth, they took slaves, they tortured prisoners, they grew rich off drugs that leached whole planets of vital resources, then tried to seize the planets of the League. The human-habitable planets. Easier to steal them than to find them. And, given the Sej, easier to get appropriations for military action than for exploration. Her memory conjured up pictures, memories of data glowing on-screen, actual printouts.

She had been well into her teens before she realized that very few people shared her ability to recall so perfectly.

The psychtechs had a word for it: Suzannah was eidetic. It was cause for jubilation. And so the tall, skinny girl, who'd dreamed, like all her year, of becoming a pilot, even an ace (but who was prepared to settle for being the best comm officer in the Wing) was tapped for Intelligence. It was hard; it meant more contact with the Colors than any Winger really liked. And now she had to work with a man whose eyes took in her every move, every flash of the holoboard, every pulse of life-support. Her new chief . . . what a time to have to meet him!

The holos went dark as the League ships and the Sejiedi disengaged totally. The battle was over. Now the only lights that shone were the ruddy back-glow of the Battle Op panels, flecked with tiny white gems, each of them a White Wing ship coming home. They wheeled and dived in formation, stunning catenary curves that brought them closer and closer to the League cruisers. At the perigee of their dives, they pulled out fast. You could almost see the parabolas the maneuver defined.

She bet her new chief could tell precisely what equation would describe that dive. The aliens who had trained him had done their job well, she knew from the man's dossier. Federico Hashrahh Kroeger. Three names. Odd. Hashrahh—that was no human name. She supposed he'd chosen it when he completed training, just as she had chosen her own adult name. Suzannah—an odd change from the endless Sallies and Valentinas, the Svetlanas and Judiths so many women in the Wing selected. Most people chose names borne by old Earth fliers. Zann hadn't. It was just as well, seeing that she wasn't a pilot. Maryam's had been exotic. Like the woman herself, Zann thought. The others— Yuri and Judith, Gregory, Valentina . . . even Joao was no more than a variant on the name John. Many White

Wingers chose that name in memory of one of Earth's first
orbital fliers.

Zann shut down her board. Her watch was over. The
White Wing would be last in, as it had been first out. She
hoped that the sibs had already landed. She was going to
have to go down there and greet her squad with all those
hostile eyes from every Color searing into her. The only
thing that could matter was that they would think she
didn't care.

That was the illusion she had to create. She was White
Wing, and the Wing didn't plead for sympathy, didn't
walk naked amid enemies all the more bitter for bearing
the name of ally. Ally! Sure, the Earthers had been allowed into the Wings. Sure, the League had granted them
a Color. The Blues were from Arthan-controlled worlds,
rich in water; the Purples—as rotten fighters as they were—
drew their color from the gems that were their system's
prized export; and the Reds, with typical bravado, equated
their color with courage. The entire Fleet was alive with
that kind of garish heraldry. Even though Zann's Wing had
been tossed white more because it was about the only
shade left than because it was a color of mourning, now it
was a saying throughout the Fleet that even, after two
hundred years, the Wing still hadn't put off wearing it for
their dead world. It was the sort of respect you might give
a tame predator that served you well—from a distance.
White Wingers were refugees, not quite citizens, never
quite equals, and never allowed to forget it. Ha! The
Colors had been proud enough to adopt the White Wing's
tradition of ten single kills making an ace and the long
white silk scarf that aces traditionally wore.

Zann stood up and walked over to her new chief. He
was a tall man, lean, somehow seeming dried out, as if his
soul had been left to blow in a high hot wind for too long.

Parched, that was the word. He wore the gray of civilian service and was almost perfectly nondescript until you looked at his eyes. Those eyes gleamed with the enthusiasm of the eidetic, for whom perception meant more than life itself.

"Request permission to report to the flight deck, sir," she said crisply. Kroeger was silent, letting the silence drag out until Zann felt her words echo in Battle Op as if she'd screamed them. He was observing her, perhaps trying to goad her into a response that would mean more data for him. She would bet her life that he had been assigned as much to watch the Wing as to coordinate Intelligence activity in this sector.

Zann was not naive. Intelligence work had taken care of that long ago. She knew the rumors, and more than rumors, about the recent capture of an enemy agent in the civ section of Yellow Wing. The agent had died before he had said much. Something about that triggered a warning in Zann. Definitely, this was not business as usual.

A loud buzz came over the Battle Op speakers, indicating that the airlocks were opening off the flight deck. Now they would all be coming in. Zann fumed silently. She had to get down there. She couldn't leave Gregory, Yuri, and Judith to face that barrage of hateful eyes alone. What would convince this gray chief that she was as duty-bound and heartless as he?

"I have to debrief the squad and get Gregory's report for Wing archives," she told him.

"I shall accompany you," the Intelligence chief decided.

Zann inclined her head. "Sir," she said, and stood aside so he could precede her. The doors of Battle Op whispered open, counterpoint to the susurrus of shocked whispers that attended their exit.

Red glare from the panels swept across Suzannah's tall,

white-suited body, staining it with bloody light. Federico Hashrahh Kroeger slitted his eyes against the increasing brightness of the passage leading toward the tubes. He felt an unusual urge to shudder at the sight of the White Wing officer, imperturbable in the stain. He shrugged it off, striving to equal the woman's cold-blooded hauteur. She was, after all, White Wing. Half-Earth though he was, a sterile outcast from the gene pools that had spawned him, he didn't wholly understand the Wing. That was an admission he rarely had to make. He had hoped that this new task would give him another line of sight, more data on the enigma. He knew that Comm Officer Suzannah was an eidetic like himself. But what had he expected? Someone to play n-dimensional chess with? That was preposterous. Eidetics were solitary, and she was a White Winger besides.

He had started out inhumanly bright, and the alien training of his intelligence and temperament had completed his estrangement. The White Wing had a point: fight, fight hard and clean, and forget to feel. There was the intersection. They had their ships, and he had his databanks and his files of emotionless memory kept at absolute zero and filling far too rapidly with alarming indications of Sejiedi espionage. The Service was riddled with it, he was certain. He had been present at Astun Koda's interrogation, the only person able to understand when the man broke and began babbling in Sej. Before they'd finished brainstripping him, he had given them two Sejiedi names. Bikmat and Aglo. The prospect of unwinding the whole rotten skein appealed to him, and he had two names to work from.

In the end, it hadn't been Kroeger's operatives who had killed Koda. Triggers in the Sejiedi conditioning had been responsible. Kroeger had regretted it. Even though Koda had held only a minor civ post in Yellow Wing, his death had robbed Kroeger of precious data. That was almost as bad as his treachery.

The tube's panel slid aside for them. Suzannah stayed to his left and three steps behind, punctilious, deferential, unknowable. Was it possible, he wondered, that she and her Wing shared the taint of the others? Very likely. According to some of the civilians with political contacts and expensively equipped lobbies, the White Wing was the source of the sabotage, the security leaks, and the bleeding away of Force morale. As much as he deplored amateurs meddling in Intelligence, those people knew people who controlled appropriations, so he had to listen to them. And in any case, even after two hundred years, White Wingers were still strangers in the League. That alone could make them alienated and dissatisfied.

Were they dissatisfied enough to turn traitor? That was the question Federico Hashrahh Kroeger had to answer for himself, a question important and intricate enough to fill him with an emotion as close to joy as he ever got. Between the White Wing and the clues from Astun Koda, he was facing the first real challenge in his professional life, and he relished it.

Perhaps if there hadn't been a White Wing, if Earthers had assimilated totally into League culture . . . he broke off that line of thought. There had been a time when he too had dreamed of the Wing, but his half-Earther blood wasn't enough. He was a League citizen, as his father had become by taking the prerogative offered him upon his marriage to a citizen. Earth Standard was not Kroeger's mother tongue. He was as alien in the Earther enclaves as he had been among the Sikkahhad.

It wasn't everyone who got to study with the Sikkahhad. It wasn't everyone who wanted to. Ever since the Sejiedi had encroached into League space, the aliens in the League had held aloof. The planets that the Sejiedi wanted were of little interest to them, save that they belonged to human allies who could definitely defend themselves. The League had gotten far more help from the White Wing it despised than from its civilized alien brothers.

Spies, dissension on the League's capital worlds, and on the White Wing's base, impenetrable by tradition and treaty, who knew? Federico Hashrahh Kroeger meant to. The Mercy that had staggered Battle Op with its clean ruthlessness, the dignity of the woman beside him, and what lay ahead on the flight deck were all raw data to him.

The tube slowed. Used to its shifts in pressure and its tricky gravity, he swallowed and bent his knees, automatically compensating. It opened onto the gleaming sweep of the flight deck. Deck Nineteen, populated by squads of all the Colors, was a pointillist's paradise. Here all the Colors of the Service intermingled, relieved and accented lightly by a few white silk scarves that invariably fell to the wearers' knees. These were the ace pilots, focal points on deck. Clusters converged around them and regrouped in obscure patterns. The deck was crowded. The fliers loitered about, waiting for the last ships to arrive, waiting to see the pilots emerge from their strings wearing their no-color.

CHAPTER 3

Stings and shuttles still moved from the airlocks into docking bays. Mechanics and pilots of all Colors swarmed over the ships, checking for damage to the fighters as they shimmered under the bright lights. Squads huddled together, surrounded by squads from different Wings, offering comfort until the medics could carry out all the fighters suffering from burns and broken bones or those shaking with reaction.

It had been a rough fight. Many ships had not come back. Two squads had lost fliers to the Sejiedi tractor beams; the people on deck clustered most thickly about these people. What *did* the Sejiedi do to prisoners? Kroeger knew what the League did, had participated in many interrogations. Sejiedi treatment of prisoners was worse, he knew. How much worse? That was classified. If people knew for sure, they might think that the White Wing had some justification for the Mercy. As it was, however . . .

A rattling and a buzz accompanied by lights flashing across the flight deck indicated that the airlock was cycling again. An entire wall slid aside to reveal silent, glistening stings, patterned with the markings of various squads, flights, and Wings. In the last rank stood a neat row of stings whose winglights glowed as the ships powered down and were the only colors about them.

One by one the white stings came to full rest. Eight hoods opened and the crowd of pilots drifted forward, self-righteous indignation masking their curiosity. Kroeger didn't understand why they felt the need to conceal it. They knew what they would see. Some of them had even been present at this scavengers' ritual before. He could guess that the younger, the less experienced of them were hoping it wasn't true; for the others, it was what they had lingered for. They had come to see.

"Damn them all," said a short woman in a purple jumpsuit. She wore the white ace's scarf, its fringes just brushing her calves. Canopies swung back from eight of the ships, and the fliers hauled themselves out, moving with easy grace despite the strain of battle and the long, cramped hours in the tiny cockpits. With a casualness Federico mistrusted, they ranged themselves between the onlookers from the other Colors and the three ships that had not yet cracked their hatches. They were clad in unrelieved white, with no masks of rank or honor, no patches or tags, no namebands printed neatly on the left breast, to break the hard, glacial monotony. There had to be aces among them, though they wore no scarves. Their faces, bearing all the colors and features of a dead world, were identical masks: smooth skin; hard, impenetrable eyes; firmly set mouths. Those masks and their slightly aggressive stance were all they needed. No one had ever seen a White Winger look any different.

In a wardroom or a bar, or somewhere on a base ship between victory and defeat, they invariably looked that way. Occasionally they smiled at a joke, but their smiles touched only their lips. And their eyes remained opaque.

The comm officer beside Federico walked toward the eight, lengthening her stride to cover the broad expanse of flight deck. Two more White Wingers entered the area from a small, human-sized door. She nodded at them: an immensely tall man with the copper skin of a, yes, the Earther word was *mestizo*, he remembered with satisfaction. The other was tiny, a woman whose ebony face was so lovely that he could scarcely believe that she was not the creation of some sculptor who had had a lucky image of perfection. The other members of Suzannah's squad, these must be, he concluded. Joao and Valentina, medical and computer officers.

Federico could hear mutters rippling out like rocks flung into a dark pool. "The Mercy." "They kill each other off as easily as they kill the Sejiedi." "Butchers . . . robots." He catalogued each response. It would be interesting if the other Colors turned on them. It would indicate just how bad matters had become.

Several White Wingers turned aside and flickered their eyes contemptuously over the Colored figures. An edge of aggression, a sort of quiet menace charged them, heightened by their very anonymity.

Like the three White Wingers who now accompanied him, his eyes never left the sealed stings.

The three remaining pilots climbed out of their ships. Now it was time to see, if there were anything to see.

Kroeger heard a snatch of conversation coming from his left.

"That tall, blond one is the squad leader. He's the one who did it," said an even taller man clad in blue and wearing an ace's scarf to a younger pilot. "And that one who looks like Genshiro Taki, who owns the art gallery in the Earther quarter back home, that's Yuri. He won his scarf today.''

''But the big one, the one who killed his squadmate, he doesn't even look like, well, like anything. I mean, look at his face. He could have just come from a lecture at the War College.''

The older pilot nodded. ''You've never flown with the White Wing before, have you?'' He spat out his words with contempt. ''They're savages.''

''I'd like to go and . . .'' replied another voice.

''Don't even think it,'' warned a pilot in white.

''Neil,'' Suzannah said quietly, identifying the man for Kroeger's benefit. ''He's a senior pilot. He and Gregory were in flight test together.'' Kroeger scanned the man's face, pale skin under black hair, close-cropped to fit under the white, visored helmet.

Seeing their comm officer, the three pilots moved into a lead-and-point formation and stood at ease as she walked over to them. The other two, Joao and Valentina, simply took up guard positions around them.

Suzannah turned to Kroeger and came to attention. ''Sir, may I present the pilots of my squad?''

At his nod, they stepped forward, ranked precisely enough to satisfy any drillmaster. They stood at attention, each holding a helmet in the crook of the arm.

''Senior Pilot Gregory.'' Tallest and oldest, this was the man who had killed his companion. Wisps of sandy hair stuck to his brow and his pale blue eyes gazed beyond Federico to his squadmate. Many years an ace, he lacked the scarf that the other Wings' fliers wore proudly into each scramble. The White Wing reserved them for dress occasions. The man nodded sharply at Kroeger, half-bow, half-salute.

''Yuri.'' The new ace. Slighter than Gregory and sallow

under the violet-tinged lights; with an epicanthic fold to the heavy lids of his dark eyes, he had a look of taut nerves about him.

"Judith." She had to be the most unlikely flier he had ever seen. A little under average height but with the figure of a much taller, riper woman, she had fine features which gave away no more than those of her colleagues. The incongruous vanity of her hair, dark and heavy, coiled into a crown of braids, framing that callous face, was something Federico stored away.

"This is my superior, Federico Hashrahh Kroeger," Suzannah said.

The three came to attention and saluted crisply. Federico quickly concealed his surprise.

"Because of the . . . irregularity today," Suzannah continued in a businesslike fashion, "it will be necessary for you to report at length, Gregory. Are you prepared?"

Her voice was low, but in the hush of watchful, hostile people, it echoed across the flight deck.

"I am." Gregory's words fell evenly.

A knot of fliers from Yellow Wing pushed forward, to be confronted by several silent figures in white. Neil and two other pilots, one a woman whose name Federico had never heard, jerked their chins at yellow-clad figures with clusters indicating senior rank on their high collars. The gesture was a rebuke, and the rankers flushed, hastening to restrain their subordinates.

"White Winger or not," Kroeger heard one woman grumble, "that Maryam was a sweet kid. It's a bleeding shame she had to pick icicles like these to fly with."

There were mutters of agreement which Suzannah and her squad ignored. She nodded a brief thanks, it seemed, at the other White Wingers. Without a backward glance, she pivoted in precise, military style and returned to the door, flanked by her squadmates. Despite her composure she moved so swiftly that Federico all but had to break into an awkward lope to catch up. They paused at the battered metal desk next to the door as Gregory, with perfect calm, picked up the hard-copy log and thumbprinted it. Behind them, other white-clad figures watched them go and, by the force of their own calm, compelled the onlookers' restraint.

Fliers were gaudy, quick to laugh, quick to anger, Federico had always assumed. It came, they said, of having such brief lives . . . half-lives, they called them. Like that Maryam. Federico had heard of her before. She had been unusual in many ways, apparently, including her popularity with other Wings. Federico, following the squad out, found his scalp prickling with tension and resented it. Who were these people, from the same stock as he, with their dignity and their arrogance, their single names and their stubborn refusal to claim rank? They seemed like some legendary religious order, anonymous in their whites, lacking family, lacking friends, their only identity their Wing and their squads. Damn them for that inflexible aloofness and sheer arrogant skill that had made them the focus of systems-wide jealousy and suspicion.

Federico remembered a pilot talking too much in a bar once. The man had been drunk enough that he would willingly talk to a civ about how his Wing, the Red, loved and hated to fly with them. And despised them. "Damn them," the Red Winger had mumbled. "They fight like demons out of hell. Who d'they think they are, anyway? No one . . . no one's going to avenge a whole world or take out a fleet, but you think they believe it?" Kroeger remembered how the man's eyes had lit with awe and anger. Then they filled with tears. Like Maryam's courage, the White Wing's nerve was admired and even a little loved. The Red Winger had told him that he'd have been able to put up with a Wing that produced more heroes, more aces, and more kills than any other, even if they *were* mere refugees. "If those damned frozen-faces would only look at us!" the man had said, running fingers through wildly disheveled hair. Federico, as always, remembered it correctly. "They don't even talk to us!"

The coldness and isolation—that was what people hated. That, and the pride of a people who should know their place, who should express their gratitude for the charity that had given them any place at all.

Perhaps if the Wing weren't so conspicuous, he too might have been able to fade away into pure research instead of the lovely ambivalences of safeguarding the very people among whom he had never felt at home. They were a cipher he had never cracked.

He too had been called cold-blooded, but he wouldn't allow himself any reaction that might bias his perceptions. There were the data, only the data, which formed enticing, intricate patterns, challenging him, forming his life.

The Wing, the silent squad he walked with, even the act he had witnessed not long before—these were data too. As was the hiss he heard before the doors of the flight deck slid shut behind him.

"White Wingers? Might as well call them Death-Wingers. They've got vacuum in their veins."

CHAPTER 4

Federico followed the squad down the long metal corridors leading to their quarters. All White Wing members were housed in a single block, he knew. Invariably—and to the great displeasure of ships' officers—they refused to be separated. He could see no breakdown of discipline as they marched home, no instance of a single look, or a wince. No chatter. They seemed too perfect to be human, androids programmed for military duties.

Their behavior would make this investigation even harder. And it was already a tough one; the Director of Intelligence had made that abundantly clear when he had assigned Kroeger to the job. *Set an Earther to watch Earthers, was that it? Trust them not to know—or not acknowledge— that Kroeger was no Earther. Or was it a reminder that Kroeger's Sikkahhad training had made him, like the Wing, only half-human?* The Intelligence chief's motives hardly mattered; either the psychtechs could guarantee his stability, or he wouldn't hold that post.

What did matter was Kroeger's fascination with this

assignment. To pierce a spy ring and—in the bargain—to learn more about an enigma two centuries old. Call it human archeology. It would be useful in terms of revitalizing the Fleet. The other Wings and Ground Control always mentioned their insularity and protested vehemently their practice of killing off all crippled Sejiedi. Kroeger himself didn't like it either; it deprived him of too many possibilities to break Sejiedi in his own offices, to pry data from them.

He glanced at his companions, and a wry smile almost reached his lips. As an eidetic, Comm Officer Suzannah ought to share his passion for data. If she were reliable, she would be a valuable ally. He wondered if she had another name, if any of them did. Rumors had it that the personal names they used were the only ones they had. He meant to find out for certain. Sejiedi used one name too. Bikmat and Aglo. He would find them if he had to interrogate the sector. This time no one would be permitted near a brainstripper; that method was clumsy and wiped as much data as it produced.

It was even harder to track down Sejiedi operatives since they were of the same genetic stock as the Wings they infiltrated. Genetic stock—that was one of the most cruel (and most highly classified) uses Sejiedi made of their prisoners before discarding them.

And the White Wing used no indications of rank, not in dress, address, or behavior; their salutes to him must have been a propriety granted to an outsider with power over one of their own. Then there was the question of their home, such as it was. They lived on a moon, generously ceded to them in recognition of their service to a League that was not their own. It was said that a substantial part of any appropriations that the Wing got went to transforming their base from a dome settlement to a habitable world.

By treaty, White Wing controlled access to that moon—forbade access was more accurate.

They would make good operatives, Kroeger mused. Take them out of uniform, and who'd recognize them? Then he watched them marching before him, the tall mestizo moderating his pace to the others, and thought again. Their expressions, their body language marked them more clearly than any uniform.

It seemed as if they marched through kilometers of corridor. The maze led them farther and farther from the clamor at the flight deck. But there was no release here, nothing that would make them pause for even a step. Several others, both Battle Op staff and ship's crew, passed them and gave way. Looks of shock sometimes crossed faces if the passersby had heard about the events of the day's battle, as surely everyone on board had by now. The six squad members seemed oblivious to the stares that followed them.

After what seemed like a suspension of eternity, they came to their own quarters, a private wardroom with adjoining suites. The medic, Joao, placed his palm against the lock and stood aside for the pilots to enter first. A glance inside told Federico that their quarters were as impersonal and plain as their uniforms. He waited to be asked in to observe the debriefing. Gregory's report would be highly informative.

Then he met Suzannah's eyes. "More data. That's what you want," she said. There was no need, of course, to make it a question. "Don't even try it . . . sir."

The door slid closed behind her, and Federico was left staring at an expanse of cold metal bulkhead. She would not share privileged information, was that it? Or had she simply refused to allow an outsider to be present? It didn't matter. She would have to make her own report. With something akin to fatalism, Kroeger made his way back to Battle Op. Suzannah would know where to find him.

The door whispered decently closed behind them. Gregory made it one step farther into the wardroom before his knees buckled. Still clutching his flight helmet, he sagged against Valentina.

"My God, we've lost her," Joao whispered. Then Gregory moaned in loss and guilt, and the big medic knelt beside him.

"Maryam!" Valentina wailed.

Zann turned around to see Judith and Yuri, the remaining pilots, still standing by the door. Their hands were locked, and there was a sort of horror and abandonment in their eyes. Zann ran over to them, and Yuri clutched her and Judith to him. Tears ran down Judith's face and she turned her face into Yuri's shoulder.

"I shouldn't have done it," he sobbed over and over. "It was my fault. I shouldn't have gone for . . ."

"I killed Maryam," Gregory whispered. "*I* killed her."

"We knew it was going to happen," Joao said softly, more for his own benefit than for Gregory's. "We knew it when we married her. She was always risky. Well, we had her for a while, and she was happy. Remember how happy."

Gregory sobbed hoarsely, and Joao gathered him and Valentina into his arms. "We said it would be worth it," he reminded them all. Then his voice broke and he bent his head.

"I didn't know what it would feel like. I didn't know it would be me."

Who else could it have been? Zann thought. Gregory was senior, and he had that protective streak . . . he had helped Yuri through the critical time when no one knew whether a pilot would "achieve mass"—become stable enough not to throw his life away tau-void and glory-riding. But he couldn't pull Maryam through. That failure would probably haunt him the rest of his life.

For the first time in Zann's life, she cursed the mind that refused to let her succumb to grief, that stubbornly went on processing. Like that Kroeger.

She felt her whirling brain begin to slow, to power down, felt the tears beginning to come.

"Gregory?" It was Judith's voice, calling as if the older pilot could somehow make things better. His head rose, responding to the plea. Then his eyes filled with horror, and he turned away, hiding his face against Valentina's cropped hair.

Zann couldn't remember how time passed. The next thing she knew, she was sitting on the floor, her head on Yuri's knees. Joao had somehow disentangled himself from Gregory, and had raided their private supplies for a large bottle of brandy. His, and a luxury they had been saving for their next leave. Silently, he poured out large glasses for each of them.

"I don't want to get drunk," Yuri protested, pushing away the glass.

"Drink it, or so help me, I'll put you out on nepenthine, and you'll be unfit to fly for the next ten days. I'm not threatening this time, Yuri. That goes for all of you."

Yuri took the glass, spilling a little on his hand.

"We're widowed," Judith said, unbelieving. She stared into the amber liquor, then took deep, dutiful swallows.

"Zann." Suzannah looked up at Joao. They were older than Judith, Yuri, and Valentina . . . they were older than Maryam too, who would never age now in their memories. She'd always be red-haired, laughing, too young and too crazy for them to keep for long.

"I'll have to report."

"Later, Zann. Later." She took the drink, since Joao wouldn't leave until she did, and she wanted him to get back to Gregory. She gulped it, then gasped and put her head down, hoping she wouldn't be sick. Every once in a while, Maryam's death would hit her as something new. Then Joao would be there with the brandy.

She heard herself talking, her words coming as if from very far away. "Maryam wouldn't drink this. She liked sweet drinks, but said they were too fattening. She always worried about that, even the night we ended up in the brig. There won't be any more low-calorie candy around the place, no more horrible protein drinks to watch out for. No more nights in lockup. And there was Shore Patrol, and they all watched her."

"I used to hide her candy when she'd cheat," Yuri confessed, wiping at her eyes.

"We all did, love," Judith said.

The grief was gentler now, quieter, shared. They were silent, remembering. Zann had a sudden overview of them: *this is a widowed family*. She wondered if the others, the first refugees, had felt this way when Earth died, and wondered how they could have survived. A whole planet!

Interesting. If she scraped her nail along the carpet, it made a different sort of line than if she simply rubbed her thumb against it. It must be the light on the fibers . . . the light hurt her eyes . . .

She fought escaping from her grief into data by peering at Gregory. She hoped he could get through this, and saw Joao watching him closely. He had an ongoing fight with any pilot who believed—and they all did—that nothing was more important than flying. He'd probably have to drug Gregory out; he was a bad drunk, mean or remorseful as his moods shifted. Today it was, it had to be, remorse.

Gregory, Gregory, Zann thought. Part of what made him such a fine leader, part of what she valued in him, was his loyalty, his trust in what was: pilots flew, pilots protected their Squad and their Wing. Today he'd had to give a squadmate the Mercy. It had been his duty and her last request.

They had all loved her, but he had killed her. It didn't matter that he'd had no choice.

Zann wanted to go to him. If her tongue hadn't been so thick, she thought she might have said something, something profound drawn from the complexities of her kind of thought. But there seemed no point in it right now. She came back to awareness to find Judith's hand stroking her hair.

"You've got that report to do, Zann," Judith reminded her.

"Oh God, I don't want to do it, go up there with all the Colors watching," Zann whispered.

"He'll wonder . . . we could have him down here."

That was a terrible thought. Then Zann had another. "I'll ask him to approve our leave. We have to get home."

There was silent assent. "I'll comm Wing Command," Valentina offered through a haze of alcohol and tears.

Suzannah forced herself up and turned on the recorder.

"Keyboard it," Valentina said dully. "We don't want that outsider to hear. He has to have the facts but . . ."

Gregory reached out and squeezed Valentina's hand. Zann hauled herself up to the console and began, very slowly, to write. Her hands were shaking. Judith and Yuri sat together, clutching one another. He didn't want to look at them. He had killed Maryam, but there were two more pilots in his squad. He couldn't face them.

The comp beeped. Zann hit the function keys first for

cipher, then for printout, and waited for the hard copy to emerge, sealed in its case, awaiting either a reader . . . or an eidetic like Kroeger who didn't need one.

Taking the copy, she rose and looked at the rest of her family. She wanted to hold them. She didn't want to return to Battle Op and face Kroeger. She didn't want to face anyone but her squad. For the time it took to deliver her report, she would be alone, and they would be doubly bereft.

She sighed. "Better move it," Joao whispered.

With drunken care, she made her way to her own quarters, then to the head and ran the water until it was ice. Peeling off her crumpled white jumpsuit, she forced herself to stand under it until her head was clear and she thought she'd removed all traces of redness from her face. There were eyedrops and alcodote in the cabinet. She used both, dressed hastily, and looked at herself in the mirror. Water had condensed on it, but she could see herself well enough. Zann never cared how she looked or what she wore. She knew she was well enough—chin-length hair of no particular brownish color, hazel eyes, tall and (Maryam had never quite forgiven her) slender. But Maryam had been striking. Valentina was beautiful. Judith was lovely. Zann was . . . just Zann. Though she had no particular vanity, she rifled through the cabinet until she found someone's—Judith's or Maryam's—cosmetics and used them to hide her pallor and the darkness under her eyes. Not bad. Her actions were mechanical. The Colors would be watching her.

When she emerged, Joao looked up. "They'll never guess," he told her. "Look at Zann, everyone. Doesn't she do the Wing proud?"

The honor of the Wing . . . doing it proud had forced them to kill Maryam, to keep themselves in strict discipline until they were alone. She had seen that Blue squad practically collapsed all over the flight deck because one of them had hit a tractor beam and they were all too civilized to protect him from the Sejiedi prisons. Oh God, if they only knew! They'd adopt the Mercy as quickly as they'd taken up the white scarf for ace pilots.

Gregory nodded and raised his right thumb in a gesture probably as old as the homeworld they'd lost. He approved. That would have to get her through the interview with Kroeger (and that icicle had damned well better keep it short!) and the journey through the ship's corridors past a barrage of curious stares. She squared her shoulders, picked up her report, and headed for the direct tube to Battle Op.

The overhead lights were back on in Battle Op. Constant chatter came in through the speakers from other parts of the ship. Those on watch stood quietly, without the attention of the scramble earlier that day. Someone wearing Green stood at Zann's board. She glanced around the bright, chattering place before she found Kroeger draped in one of the three chairs of the installation. He seemed encased in his own shell of privacy, but the eyes were watching as she walked over to him. Someone muttered something about "Kolatolo's going to love this," and she sniffed inwardly. Ag Kolatolo really ought to stick to his multiplanetary investments, not meddle in League politics: he hated the White Wing, and let it show. Today's Mercy . . . Zann turned her attention instead to her superior.

Wordlessly, she handed him her report.

"Hard copy?" He raised one eyebrow.

"It's regulation."

"You took your time about it." Her face was expressionless, and Kroeger resigned himself, for the time being, to no further input on that particular subject.

"Request immediate leave for myself and my squad. Grounds: compassionate leave. We need to get to the Wing Moon for Maryam's Memorial. The pilots have to recuperate."

Kroeger leaned forward and activated the "privacy" circuits in the chair's control panel. Blankness surrounded them as a charged field shielded them from the rest of Battle Op. This wasn't anything he expected. The Wing, as far as he had heard, didn't have any compassion. Its pilots seemed tireless.

Leave for this officer and her squad might have its advantages for him, depending on how much she wanted it. If she were willing to agree to his terms . . .

"Granted on two conditions," Kroeger said evenly. She watched him carefully, not even looking for an invitation to sit down. "First, I want confirmation from White Wing Command." He was willing to wager money that confirmation had already been transmitted and was awaiting his attention. "Second, on your way home, I want you and the rest of the squad to manage a few nights out, listening to what other officers are saying. Civilians too. You've done this before."

Zann nodded sharply in reply. It took all her control to hold herself in check. She wanted to take his neck in her hands and squeeze until blood ran out of his eyes. Of course the squad had prowled the bars before, carefully following her instructions, even more carefully not asking her any questions. When Maryam had been alive, in a strange way, those bar-crawls had even been enjoyable. But now, to go out to bars and try to pick up information before they had even had the Memorial . . . even Wing Command itself, famed for its harsh standards, would never order that. Of course, Wing Command understood what Maryam had been to her squad; Zann doubted that this alien eidetic understood anything about people at all.

"Another thing," Kroeger added almost lazily, watching her. "I'm heading in the same direction myself, deeper into this sector. Astun Koda didn't tell much before that hemorrhage took him out, but we do know that his orders were coming from near the core worlds. At least the ones we could track were. And we know another thing: two names. Bikmat and Aglo. Ever hear them?"

"I don't know much Sej, sir," Zann said. She had a bad idea of what Kroeger was leading up to.

"Sejiedi names mentioned by Koda. I've become very interested in those names, since the transmissions we followed contained them. So I'll be traveling with you."

If Zann had wanted to kill before, now she wanted to torture and mutilate. She knew that Kroeger was manipulating her, perhaps even punishing her for her refusal to let him attend Gregory's debriefing. For a wild, self-destructive moment she had the urge to refuse this second condition. Then she thought of the rest of the squad. She remembered Yuri's strained weeping and knew how close to the edge his nerves could bring him. And Gregory . . . he couldn't even look at the pilots of his squad. How could he face all the other prying eyes? With the best intentions in the world, Zann couldn't and wouldn't shield him from the public outcry about Maryam's death that was bound to filter into the Wings. He needed to heal before he had to confront it. Agreeing to Kroeger's terms would give him precious time.

She would include this in her own private report to Wing Command, she swore to herself. Kroeger had no idea of how to manage his operatives. The Wing's procedures—officially recognized mourning and special status—helped.

Kroeger activated his screens, showing her which in-bound ship they could transfer to. She saw with relief that two of her sib squads would be on it. Sally's and Werner's families, close-sibs indeed. They had been witnesses at her marriage. Suddenly Zann longed desperately for the Wing Moon, for their home, where no outsiders were permitted, and where they would be helped and held until they could face themselves again. Especially Gregory. He had to be gotten home. Her willingness not to contest Kroeger's terms for a chance of home-leave out of the squad's regular rotation made her realize just how anxious she was for Gregory.

CHAPTER 5

"You don't look happy, Bikmat. Did the demonstration down the block give you trouble?"

"A few insults, sir. That's not trouble," Bikmat said. He glanced around the secondhand store where they were meeting, shabby like every contact point he'd ever had. Useful too. The taped music functioned effectively as white noise, and the narrow aisles, crowded with ancient tapes and back-model hardware, baffled directional listening devices.

The hunger was on him, or he wouldn't have given a second thought to the hostiles down the street. He could feel the beginnings of nausea in the pit of his stomach.

"You should be very proud, Bikmat. That Wing of yours has become our number one priority."

Bikmat kept silent. He never gave his contacts more than the minimum necessary to report and escape them. The Sej had trained him that way.

"We have identified six potential leaders in your Wing. Report what you know about each of them. *Record*." The contact activated an ancient recorder. By long-trained reflex, Bikmat fiddled with it as if he considered buying it, and spoke rapidly in an undertone.

"Hold yourself in readiness. Your assignment will be made shortly."

Bikmat handed the recorder to his contact, scooped up a packet from the counter, and drifted away. His contact took the recorder to the front of the store to pay for it.

Zann grimaced at the crowds streaming down the walkways of Central. The Colors were bad enough; if they hated the White Wing, at least they were familiar antagonists. But this press of civilians, their faces and bodies bearing the genetic stamps of most of the humanoid races in the League and a few of the aliens'—this was too much. They were undisciplined, unpredictable, and they were all watching her and the other six . . . *it was five now,* she remembered with a wrench too agonizing to be as familiar with it as she was.

For the tenth time that evening she regretted taking Federico Hashrahh Kroeger up on his offer to provide transportation to the Wing Moon in return for help in his interminable, sadistic datahunts. Bikmat and Aglo: whoever the Sejiedi were pretending to be, they didn't have a prayer. She'd apologized herself hoarse to the squad for the roundabout course he'd chosen. No military transport was available, and standby status on the usual direct runs seemed to have become overcrowded by methods Zann would have called almost magical if she hadn't been familiar with Kroeger's tactics. Of course, their papers had been held up too. So, from base to station, from station to world they traveled—and no chance to hide out and mourn properly in their quarters. Kroeger had them on the prowl almost every evening. Evenings they didn't go out, he ran simulations or delicately interrogated the squad. They were all strained now from the effort to hold their grief in check. And, as they headed farther into the capital systems of the League, matters grew worse.

The last stop on Central was like all the others, precisely calibrated to elicit maximum information both from the squad and anything they would use as an informant. Kroeger saw Sejiedi spies lurking beside every Winger and every civ in the League. Zann and her family agreed. Kroeger wasn't being deliberately cruel; it simply did not occur to him that the squad might prefer to head home to the Wing Moon without this deliberately protracted journey.

Why quarrel with a good cover? Zann thought ironically. *He treats us as if we don't have feelings because that's precisely what we want him to see. Besides, it's something he's used to.*

Joao, she knew, was muttering about how haggard most of them were looking.

You know why Joao isn't a pilot? Maryam's wispy, laughing voice slipped inside her mind and flicked the usual anguish into active pain. *Because he'd need two stings to carry him!* He'd lost weight, Yuri was in a continual state of low-grade jitters, and Gregory wasn't sleeping. Zann had good reason to know that.

And these interminable bar-crawls! The last thing any of them wanted to do was act out the part of a squad on a gaudy night out before going on leave. This charade was murderous. But judging from Kroeger's simulations, things were so bad that she hadn't even tried to intercede for the squad. It was hard to hate Kroeger when you shared his duty-fix.

Now they marched along, six aloof White Wingers and their exceedingly unlikely companion. From bar to bar.

Yuri recognized a store he'd visited years ago, and raised eyebrows.

"The Blue Angel," said Judith. "You know. It's home space. Meet us there." Yuri vanished inside.

"Home space?" Almost before Kroeger asked the question, Zann had her answer ready. "Earther-owned."

"I see no reason in your seeking information in an Earther bar," he replied.

"Well, I call that friendly," Gregory muttered. "First time he hasn't looked at us as if *we* were spies."

"Gregory, hush," Judith said under her breath as Joao shook his head.

"Will you look at that crowd?" Zann pointed, drawing Kroeger's attention. She was glad to distract the civ, but she would have picked another sort of disturbance. She'd seen signs of this on board various cruisers; it wasn't just increased hostility to the Wing. People actually seemed to distrust all Earth-humans. She thought she could put a name to this phenomenon, and it wasn't xenophobia. Not unless Ag Kolatolo was a xenophobe. It was fine public relations—carefully artless references to growing Earther wealth in the many speeches and articles circulated under his name, subtle advertising, and whispers about just how "uncivilized" Earthers were, and why. Apparently refugees were marginally acceptable only when they were poor. Zann should have made herself listen to those whispers, but some of them—involving what actually had happened to her race's homeworld—had driven her from the area before she broke cover. Demonstrations were a logical outgrowth.

Outside the Blue Angel people milled and grumbled. They carried printed kites, glittering, flying high, painted with symbols: SUPPORT LOCAL MERCHANTS. WHITE WING = DEATH-WING, and worst of all, on an eight-meter kite: WHITE WING GO HOME . . . IF YOU HAVEN'T VAPED IT.

These in-system civs took greater risks with the Wing than the other Colors dared. Pampered, protected—in part by the very refugees they hated—they had the luxury and ignorance to express what the Colors masked with chill, civilized correctness and the formality of regulations. For the thousandth time, Zann considered the League's policy of trusting itself to a Wing of client-soldiers, not citizens, and decided it was folly—with any other Wing but hers. White Wing could be trusted. Perhaps that was one reason these civs felt safe enough to riot. The idea gave her bleak satisfaction.

"We're really going to go in there?" Valentina inquired wryly.

"Either that or let them see they turned us back," Gregory said. He strode ahead, shoulders squared. Federico Hashrahh Kroeger walked just behind him, looking into people's faces. He paused as if he wanted to ask a few questions.

"Come *on*, sir," Zann hissed.

"That's the squad that did it . . . that's *him*, I recognize him from the broadcasts . . ."

"They murder one of their own and then go celebrate?" The voice rose and twisted in disgust.

"I just want to ask—"

"It just got worse," Joao told Zann in an undertone. "Commcrews. D'you see their fliers?"

Zann actually dared to tug at her superior. "Just how much publicity do you want?" she asked him.

But it was too late; the crews were out and swarming. Three men blocked Gregory's path.

"Tell me, pilot, how do you feel about the—I believe it's called the Mercy of the Wing . . ."

"Isn't it hard just to turn on a—"

Gregory shouldered the crew aside without a word and made for the Blue Angel's gleaming doors. One of the men fell hard and cried out, a sharp noise which gathered an ominous, rumbling echo. Kroeger was moving away from the squad, toward the increasingly angry crowd.

"They're going to turn ugly, can't you feel it?" Zann asked. She saw Joao move into position, preparing to drag him inside.

"This crowd's angry, won't listen to reason," Joao soothed Kroeger. "Maybe later they'll feel more like talking. Come on, Federico Hashrahh Kroeger."

The double doors were locked, and that cost the squad a few bad seconds until Valentina hit the night buzzer, and the barkeep himself opened up to them.

"Can't say I think much of your neighborhood," Valentina commented, and walked in. "Are your games still rigged?" Not waiting for an answer, she walked over to the small, garish arcade at the entrance, muttering about Yuri's having most of the change on him, and began to play. She would lose herself in the fight simulations, maybe take away some of the truculence Zann had lately noticed in her.

Gregory disappeared down a small corridor. Kroeger raised eyebrows as he saw his tame hunting pack evaporate, but Judith and Joao eased him along.

"I recognized several of the ringleaders," Zann told Kroeger in an undertone. He nodded, surprising her. She did not think he would concede the possibility that that demonstration (or the others like it) had been carefully staged. *Kolatolo again,* she decided. Why couldn't he stick to investments instead of turning League politics into his personal hobby? He seemed to own half the votes in the Assembly.

The barkeep came up to Zann and murmured, "First round's on the house." Zann blinked at him, and swallowed before thanking him. The bartender at the Blue Angel wasn't the stingiest thing in the League of Known Worlds, but he came close. This was sympathy, so tactfully offered it could even be accepted.

He pointed at a booth in the corner. "I'll bring them over when you get settled."

Judith stared around her. The Blue Angel, local color, if "local" meant a planet two centuries dead. Judging from all the tapes, it was authentic. She looked down at all the props that made non-Earthers find the place fascinating, and made it seem like home (wherever it was) to White Wing. Her shredded cocktail napkin was reflected in the smoky glass table; under the glass slab, she could see her legs and feet. She thought she ought to look around. It was better than staring at the ring under her glass, and at least Kroeger couldn't assume she was moping.

Across from her she could see Federico Hashrahh Kroeger in his gray civ suit. He was leaning back so she couldn't see his face. She was glad. He was talking to Zann, and that was cause for distress; Judith sensed that Zann was reaching the limits of her endurance; she was the one stuck dealing with the operative most of the time. At least he wasn't trying to draw her, Judith, out. Now he had fallen silent, and was studying her. She turned away casually. He was an annoyance and she wished he would evaporate.

He was right about one thing: he wouldn't get much here. The Blue Angel was home-space, safe. With any luck, only other White Wingers would be in the bar, and their gray shadow would have to let them be. She saw several white uniforms and felt relief. She couldn't make

out faces, but it was a small place, and the mirrors that
lined one wall didn't go far to making it seem larger.

In the mirrors, the blue carpeting that went up to the
ceiling looked cleaner and less worn than it did when you
sat near the wall. The polished copper bar was distorted by
the glass into a molten river flowing across the rich blue.
In it, Joao and Suzannah's figures, as they ordered drinks,
seemed to waver. Judith didn't like watching that. Behind
the bar, bottles were prominently displayed, a frame for the
human barkeep who was the place's chief status symbol
and tourist attraction.

*Used to be you went to Earther places to get away from
the Colors*, she thought. *Now they may hate us, but they've
decided that Earther civs are quaint.* The word made her
want to spit.

Joao and Zann had gathered up an insane number of
drinks between the two of them and were turning toward
the table. Judith wondered why Gregory was so long in the
washroom, and thought she could come up with a few
good guesses. *He doesn't want to look at any of us,* she
thought. At the back of her mind where she could almost
ignore it came a whispered addition. Gregory especially
couldn't bear to look at the other pilots who survived. Not
her. Not Yuri. It was easier to assume the rest of the truth,
that he couldn't stand having Federico Hashrahh Kroeger
around all the time either. More than the rest of them,
Gregory couldn't stand these nights out. By rights he
should, they all should, be protected. She noticed with
satisfaction that the barkeep had resealed the doors. There'd
be security around in a few moments, she suspected, but
not to deal with that crowd.

Valentina was still by the games at the entrance. Playing
alone, and she preferred to win against human opponents.
Usually she would have several reluctant victims, or she'd

sit and coax until someone volunteered to be loser. Tonight she was using the games to escape from poor Zann's
strange superior. Judith envied her. If she hadn't hated the
games even more than she hated being shadowed, she'd
have joined her.

A noise from a side table drew her attention. Against the
mirrors stood two very drunk Red Wingers. They were
laughing raucously, toasting each other with ribald hoots,
then laughing again at the Earther custom of tapping glasses
together. Several broken ones lay in puddles of liquor that
smelled to deep space even across the room. She turned
her eyes away with disgust. She supposed as long as they
were only obnoxious, the barkeep wouldn't throw them
out. From the corner of her eye, she saw a familiar face.

So, obviously, did the Red Wingers. "Hey, come over
and have a drink with us!" one called out in a thickened
voice. "You fought with us at Capra Six. Didn't we just
give the damned Sejiedi a run for it?"

"Hey, I remember this one," said the other Red pilot.
"White Winger. You. You took one in single combat,
didn't you? We owe you a drink, brudder. What's your
name . . . lemme see . . . 's Dusty, isn't it?"

Judith winced and made her way over to the corner.
They should know better than to use short-names for anyone in the White Wing. It was a serious insult, though the
Red Winger meant to be friendly. She hoped that this
Wingmate of hers whose face seemed so familiar would
have the sense to turn his back. Then Judith got a closer
look at the man—not as tall as Gregory and more slender,
with almost the same sandy hair. Amber eyes she remembered as being aloof . . . but they snapped with anger
now. *Dusty.* She knew who he was now, and winced
again. He'd be keyed up from coping with the mob outside, in any case. And this particular Winger . . . there

wasn't a chance he'd be sensible, not if it came to a matter of Names.

The White Winger stood utterly still, then took three deliberate steps that placed him directly in front of the two drunken pilots in Red. "The name," he said, softly and evenly, "is Dustin." His fists balled and he swung at the man nearer the mirrors. "Dustin."

The Red Wing pilot was already off-balance, too drunk to expect it. The single blow propelled him back the half-meter into the mirrors.

"Hey?" The other Red Winger seemed bemused. Dustin took him by his high collar and tossed him contemptuously on his comrade. As the second pilot hit the wall, Judith heard a tearing sound, and several of the mirror tiles crashed down around the three. The two Red Wingers— *luck of the drunk!* Judith thought—were unhurt. One of the mirrors had glanced across Dustin's hand, lacerating it.

Dustin didn't notice. He bent over and tried to pull one of the pilots to his feet, the better to continue the fight.

Maryam would have loved this. For once her memories made Judith almost giggle and sent her racing over to Dustin.

"Dustin," she cried over the din, "it's me, Judith. From flight test class, remember? Come on now. Stop it. Drop that idiot." She pulled him away from the corner. With what seemed like real regret, he dropped the drunken pilot into the nearest chair. The man's head dropped until he hunched over the table, narrowly missing the liquor and shattered glass.

"That was a stupid thing to do," she hissed. "They were trying to pay back. You could at least be gracious."

She glanced quickly in the surviving mirrors. Yes, there they were, she hadn't been mistaken. She heard the night buzzer which had gotten her squad past the doors, saw the

barkeep move, and knew that the Shore Patrol would be
entering the place any moment. She could see the shadows
of their brilliant gold tunics against the plate glass set into
the bar. If she hadn't been on the lookout . . . Maryam
had loved a good brawl. For Judith, one night in lockup
had been too much entirely.

"What?" Dustin asked.

"Shut up! It's Shore Patrol. Come sit with us. No one's
going to notice you if there are a bunch of white uniforms
all together. They say we all look alike."

She took him firmly by the arm and steered him over to
the table, now cluttered with drinks. Joao sat on one side,
as far from Federico Hashrahh Kroeger as he could po-
litely get. Zann didn't have that option. Judith gestured
Dustin to a seat by Joao.

"Shore Patrol," she said softly. Joao and Zann glanced
at one another. Then Zann scanned the mirror. The two
SPs in their gold were already past the games where
Valentina was so absorbed she didn't even bother to look
up. Joao shoved a drink into Dustin's good hand as they
came closer.

"Assault and battery," Federico Hashrahh Kroeger observed. "You're obstructing justice. And there's the broken mirror to pay for."

"Put the mirror on Security's expense account," Zann
said evenly.

"They used a *nickname*," Judith said firmly. "He had
every reason."

"Every reason for what?" asked Federico Hashrahh
Kroeger, his eyes flashing. Judith could have groaned as
she realized what this fight had done: just one more bit of
data, intimate details of the customs of a highly insular
group.

"We don't use nicknames," Zann said, making each

word deliberate. "Have we ever given you less than the honor of your full name, Federico Hashrahh Kroeger?"

Kroeger half-smiled.

"I think he suspected we were being insulting," Joao whispered to Judith, diverted. "Now he's got a new fact and is happy with it."

"This man's still guilty of assault," the operative began, then trailed off. One look at the White Wingers about him had to indicate even to him that he wouldn't get far with this line of reasoning.

"Consider it this way, sir," Zann said. "Pilot Dustin has staged this demonstration for the benefit of your files. Therefore, it can be charged to Intelligence . . . or to the Red Wing," she added slyly.

Valentina came over to the table and sat down. She eyed the Shore Patrol, now inspecting the shattered mirrors, shrugged, and reached for a clear drink. Then she saw the thick green concoction next to it—*Maryam favored those vile things called grasshoppers, whatever* they *were*—picked it up, and downed it so rapidly Judith hadn't even time to gag.

Judith watched Dustin, enjoying his surprise. Valentina's beauty generally had that effect and Judith always liked watching it. Valentina was so used to it that she didn't even notice. A long time ago it ceased even being a bore.

"Those games malfunctioned," she stated flatly. "One owes me another free game, and it went down."

"Are you sure it's the game? Aren't they programmed to crash after you win five or so games off them?" Joao asked.

Valentina shrugged. It was a point of honor with her never to pay for more than a single game. Joao passed the clear drink over to her, and she sipped it demurely. She might look like a fragile doll, but she could drink most of the squad under a table.

"What are *they* doing here?" she asked, gesturing with her pointed chin at the Shore Patrol. "They know they're not wanted in home-space."

"In case you hadn't noticed, we've become popular," Dustin said. "Notorious, even."

Valentina blinked. "What else would you expect refugees to do but open ethnic restaurants? Become mercenaries?"

Dustin almost choked on his drink.

Satisfied with his reaction, Valentina studied him. Judith nudged her under the table. The smaller woman nodded, a sign she recognized Dustin and would play along.

Again Judith studied the mirror. The Shore Patrol was going from table to table, questioning people, civs and Colors alike, about the altercation.

"Used to be they wouldn't come in here," she muttered. "Why . . ."

Zann, bless her, had the words right out of Federico Hashrahh Kroeger's mouth. "It used to be quite a tidy arrangement. We wouldn't make trouble; they would stay out. Then Ag Kolatolo . . . in three years he's undone two centuries of reasonably peaceful coexistence between Earthers and the League."

"Not 'the rest of the League'?"

Zann shrugged.

"How did you learn that this . . . arrangement . . . had come to an end?"

"Easy enough. We got into a fight."

"Someone called Suzannah a spook and used her nickname," Judith spoke out. Zann was family, not a spook. But this Kroeger character, now . . .

"And of course you couldn't let this go unchallenged . . ." he goaded.

It had been Maryam who'd launched herself gleefully at the Blue Winger's knees, Maryam who'd gotten the first punch in and who'd gotten very nearly flattened until the rest of them joined in, except for Joao, who tried to make them all listen to reason in a bellow that was completely unreasonable in and of itself. Someone standing on a chair threw a wild punch and that set him off . . . until the Shore Patrol smugly carted them all off. Judith had groused almost all night. They had separated the men and the women, the place was cold and cheerless, and once the drinks and excitement wore off, she was starving. Maryam, despite her own hunger (she had decided to break another of her diets), had chuckled most of the night.

No, that memory was too tender for Federico Hashrahh Kroeger to feast on.

Dustin wasn't a friend, had always been more reserved than most. But he was White Wing and therefore due their protection. She tried to catch the barkeep's eyes, but he was ostentatiously busy pouring drinks and wiping glasses fresh out of the sterilizer, pretending that the place hadn't been invaded by the gold uniforms no one liked.

From out of the crowd, Gregory materialized and went to stand at the opposite end of the table from Federico Hashrahh Kroeger, who stared at him as if wondering what had taken him so long.

"I was reading graffiti," he said outrageously. "It doesn't seem to like Ag Kolatolo. Well, isn't that what you expect of us?" Gregory's face was insultingly blank.

"I was watching Security clear up that mess outside," came Yuri's voice. It was a little too cheerful. "I found a real bargain!" Yuri never could resist a bargain, and his ideas of cheap were everyone else's idea of lavish. As he flung himself into the nearest seat, he handled the package under his arm with the care he would have given a baby. No, more.

Dustin had risen at Gregory's approach. He stood almost at attention, a respect to the senior pilot that the White Wing normally didn't use.

"Sit down," Gregory said, his face still lifeless.

He dropped back down into his seat. The Shore Patrol was talking to the barkeep now. Reluctantly he started to lead them to the table.

"Gentlemen," the man said, eyeing the SPs nervously, "you can see for yourselves that there are seven here, a full squad. You know that there aren't any loners in the Wing."

That wasn't true, Judith thought. Dustin was a loner. And Gregory had retreated so thoroughly into some fastness within himself that he might as well be classed as one too.

"You just ask those people if they can tell which one of these White Wingers is the one who hit that gentleman over there."

Dustin slid his good hand over the bloody one, concealing it.

The two members of the Shore Patrol looked at one another. All they'd been told was that the assailant had been a White Winger, alone.

"I'll tell you," said the barkeep in a low, conspiratorial voice, "they'd had a lot to drink, all of them in that corner. They'd been here since, oh, I'd say since eighteen-hundred hours, and really kicking it back. Stygians and blasters . . . that sort of stuff. And you know, 'Never mix, never worry.' But Stygians and blasters, I mean, can you just think of a worse combination?"

Obviously the two SPs couldn't. "Do you want to press charges?"

The bartender smiled blandly. "No. A little damage is an occupational hazard in this business." The two Shore Patrol officers turned to leave. As the barkeep buzzed them out, he winked broadly at the squad.

Federico Hashrahh Kroeger turned to Zann.

"Elucidate," he said.

"The bartender's an Earther," Zann said simply, as if explaining elementary quadratics to a backward child. "We take care of our own. And they're proud of us."

"Do you know something, Federico Hashrahh Kroeger?" Valentina said. "Except for one round here that the barkeep provided, we've paid out of pocket for all the drinks tonight, just as if we were out having fun, not tracking your pet Sejiedi. And you're on an expense account, but you haven't bought one drink."

"What?"

"It's an Earth custom," Joao explained. "Each person takes a turn buying drinks for all the others at the table. At the end of the evening, it should come out even."

"Quite a set of customs you have," Kroeger observed. He was becoming highly intrigued, Judith could see. Zann would probably say that that showed how little his Earther blood could be counted on.

"Yes, don't we? I enjoy studying intercultural communications and traditional differences," Joao replied. "For example, your experiences among the Sikkahhad. You must have had quite a fascinating time of it."

The man actually appeared pleased! "Why yes," he said. "I never felt as if I were quite able to function in their society. It was quite different from ours; I always felt I was missing nuances."

"But you do agree that one should try to adapt to the

customs of the majority group insofar as one is able and it does not violate your own ethics?'' Valentina asked. She was baiting him, was playing with Joao the game she used to play with Maryam. *How Maryam would have enjoyed this!*

''Of course.''

Valentina favored him with a dazzlingly guiltless smile. ''Then, Federico Hashrahh Kroeger, in accordance with Earther custom, you must now buy each of us a drink.''

Kroeger stood. He seemed mildly perplexed. Judith could almost follow that convoluted reasoning of his: was this squad trying to dig deeper into his expense account, or—well, he had been drinking with them all evening and they had indeed bought every drink. Had the man ever been out drinking with anyone? Judith suddenly wondered. She tried to catch Gregory's attention, share the joke with him but he was avoiding everyone, as if he were angry. Why? Then she looked about and saw Dustin.

As Kroeger made his way to the bar, Zann caught the barkeep's eye and nodded. He winked at her with perfect understanding. Of course a squad of seven—six and one—wouldn't want to be interrupted. Kroeger would have a hard time getting served.

''Let me see that hand, Dustin,'' Joao said in something a little warmer than his usual doctor-voice. ''Looks as if there's been enough bleeding to wash out any glass fragments,'' he murmured more to himself than anyone else. ''And this would have to happen when I don't have my bag.''

He pulled out a rather generous handkerchief—trust Joao to enjoy that affectation!—and dipped one edge into his drink, muttering about the pitiful waste of fine spirits, then washed the wound. Dustin didn't flinch.

Joao used the handkerchief as a bandage. ''Get in to a

Wing medic tomorrow for collagen packing, will you?'' he ordered.

Dustin smiled and looked down, inspecting the bandage. His eyelashes were quite long, Judith noticed irrelevantly, and felt a stab of guilt.

"Still flying single?" she asked. "You had quite a reputation for loving and leaving 'em in our class. But I thought, last I heard, you were going with Charles and Anna . . .''

"I like to fly free," Dustin said. Judith remembered what else she had heard. Anna was a close friend. When John, one of her squad's other pilots, bought it, they'd flown with Dustin so often they thought they might as well marry him, but he'd refused.

Dustin shrugged and glanced around the table. Judith noticed that they were all observing him, except for Gregory, busy shredding his napkin. Of course he had heard of them, had heard of Maryam's death. Who hadn't . . . even civs? And now, here he was, alone with them. It couldn't be anything but embarrassing. Sure enough, he was flushing, but he didn't look displeased. Why should he? They were a good squad. Gregory was one of the finest pilots in the Wing.

Yuri looked over at Dustin. "You know," he said a little hesitantly, "we're under strength. We wouldn't mind some help now and then. If you want to fly with us some time . . .''

Gregory looked hard at Yuri, who suddenly found that making figure eights with the straw in his drink was unfathomably fascinating.

Gregory used to call Judith and Yuri twins. They really were thinking in tandem about this. "You know, Gregory," Judith said softly, "we're going to have to pick up a solo. Dustin's pretty good."

"He's as different from Maryam as you could get, I suppose." Gregory shrugged.

They were all quiet. Judith knew what they were remembering: Maryam's quick jokes, her arm-wrestling matches. She'd have commented on Dustin's eyelashes for sure. No one wanted to think of someone taking her place, not even for one flight. No one could.

Without a fourth pilot, it would be difficult to interface with their sibs as a complete combat unit. Three sibs to a unit, with ten to fourteen pilots, at least one medic, one comm officer and two maintenance techs, made a functional complement in the Wing. Each triad was responsible for maintaining fighting strength. If her squad didn't have a fourth pilot, the sibs would have to pick up the slack. Grudgingly. And she could fly with Dustin, had done so several times in training. He wasn't a total glory-rider, and she could vouch for his cool head and teamwork. No one had ever worried about his attaining mass the way they had about Maryam.

Gregory's feelings were too obvious from his hunched shoulders, averted eyes, and busy hands. Did he want to give it all away to anyone who happened to see them? Sure, it was a little intimate to ask someone to fly with you. But what did Gregory want?

Dustin glanced at Gregory and flushed again. "Look," he said, "no need to rush things. You need time. I'm filling in here and there. If you decide you need me, I'll be around. Now . . . I'm on line at 05:00, so I'd better get back." He smiled a bit sadly and rose. Minutes later he was out the door.

"We haven't even had Maryam's Memorial yet, and you . . ." Gregory started to sputter. Zann grabbed his hand.

"Are you saying you're the only one here with feelings?

Do you think that the rest of us don't hurt the way you do? But we're responsible for finding a fourth pilot." Zann lowered her voice, and Judith leaned forward to listen. Zann, she could tell, was about to be devious, and Judith always enjoyed that. What a family she had!

"Listen, Gregory, if we have a regular, the sibs won't be pushing us to remarry fast. You know what can happen. And this one's somebody Judith's flown with. He's protection for us. And we can use it."

"I don't think Dustin will take it the wrong way," Judith added. Gregory spared her a glance. "I don't think he really is looking to settle down. He's flown with lots of families in situations like ours; he knows the rules. And he's still solo. Anna told me that her family thought of marrying him when John got vaped, but he said no. He told them that they needed time and space, that he loved flying with them, but that he couldn't fill John's place and wasn't going to try. They still like him a whole lot. He's a sib to them."

Joao looked up and cleared his throat. Federico Hashrahh Kroeger had finally been served and scrounged himself a tray. Now he was making his way over from the bar with eight varicolored glasses jouncing about precariously. Without thinking, the squad smoothed their features into the blank, uncommunicative countenances fit for outsiders to view.

"I apologize for the delay," Kroeger stated, setting down the tray. "I don't know why anyone prefers to pay more in order to have a live bartender. Programmables are much more efficient."

The six squad members took their drinks. They were glad that he'd been away so long. Judith didn't want her drink. She wanted to go home, but it would have been rude to refuse the offering. Kroeger was right; they'd found no leads here. Poor Zann, who would probably hear it from him later.

Kroeger seated himself between Judith and Joao. "Where did that other pilot—the aggressive one—go?"

"He had an early call," Joao said smoothly. "Look, when we finish this round, let's call it a night. The crowd's thinned out; nothing's going to happen now."

They all drank rapidly. Judith met Zann's eyes, and realized that the taller woman would see that Kroeger put the correct interpretation on this evening: that many in the Wing felt uneasy around the shadow world of Intelligence. They were all very quiet as they set down empty glasses and rose to leave.

"Are you returning to quarters?"

Did he really think they'd abandon him and go on to a fourth bar? He was hopeless, hopeless.

Judith merely looked at him. "Of course."

"Then I'll meet you at Slick Four tomorrow, 08:00."

They all nodded wearily. Zann pleaded exhaustion to his idea of running simulations or checking the files for known paid agitators for the rest of the evening. *Let her rest!* Judith wanted to shout. *Let her, let all of us go home and cry.*

When they left the Blue Angel, the crowd was gone, and the lights of Central's nightspots were casting their usual garish aurora into the sky. A crumpled kite lay abandoned outside the bar. GO HOME was all Judith could read. Metallic powder from the letters had collected in a crease in the fabric; red light glittered over it. Gregory winced, then shook himself and set the pace back to their quarters.

CHAPTER 6

They had spent too many furloughs away from the Wing Moon, Zann mused. In their absence, the ecologists had managed to create clouds; the dome looked almost like a real planetary sky. She sat down outside her home, and leaned back against a slender tree. It had sprung up nicely since Maryam had planted it . . . how many years ago? She ought to remember. Yes, it was five years. Some of the sibs must have come over to tend the gardens that each Wing squad, with the connivance of the Moon's agronomists, maintained. The trees and flowering plants looked lusher than she remembered.

Maryam would know for certain. She had always taken delight in the way that the Moon was developing from a domed settlement into a real world, painstakingly seeded with all the plants of a vanished Earth. It had been strange to make the approach to the Moon without her, stranger still to sit here on the lawn into which Maryam had sprinkled seeds of wildflowers, tiny hints of orange and yellow.

"In a little bit!" she called in response to a wave from

the windows. She could see the others moving about the enormous, windowed kitchen.

But she didn't want to go inside, not just yet. It was better to stare at Maryam's wildflowers, at the iris that Valentina had set out or Gregory's favorite garish annuals. Judith's roses hadn't gone wild; Zann would have been astounded if anyone here would have allowed that. They combined with the scent from the lilac bush she had planted shortly after they married her. It was too sweet.

But it was near sunset. In a little while, there would be a night wind; she decided to wait for it. The garden was where she felt Maryam's presence most strongly. She used to cut flowers and set them out on every available flat space. She always had bouquets in her room. Zann turned her thoughts away. "I'm coming!" If she didn't, Joao would probably come and fetch her. She could smell Yuri's inevitable pot of coffee; the first thing he always did when they came home was brew up a big pot "to make the place smell lived in." She was color-mad; they all were, whenever they came home, as an antidote to all that pristine white.

Zann steeled herself and made for the front entrance, walking along the stone path Yuri had laid out.

As she entered the living room disorientation washed over her. For a moment, she couldn't place it, and then she remembered. It was always this way when they came back. The place was too neat to belong to them. All the cassettes were neatly stacked, and the floor wasn't cluttered with Valentina's projects that involved trailing wires, stacks of boards, and semiconductors rolling about to endanger everyone's neck. The screens were still dark, and Yuri hadn't had time to scatter printouts all over.

The deep polished grain of the tables shone clearly, reflecting the shining antique glass they were all so proud of. There was no dust: in their absence, the place was sealed against it. Pale blue, violet, and yellow cushions lay neatly across the backs of sand-colored sofas, instead of wherever someone had tossed them. The living room was calm and orderly, full of color and life. It was home, but it wasn't complete.

She headed toward her room to change from her uniform. Someone had come in while they were gone and shut the door to Maryam's room. Usually they left doors open, but she thanked whomever had closed that one; she didn't want to look at it. Maryam's favorite oranges and yellows would mock her.

Zann's own room was restful; Yuri had suggested deep blues and peach. She didn't let it register as she peeled off her uniform and tossed it into the cleaner, then rummaged about for something roomy and homelike to throw on. There it was!—the giant caftan Joao had given her as an anniversary gift two years ago. She dived into it. Badly worn, with a stain that had never come out and a few small never-mended gaps where the stitching had come undone, it was her favorite. Suddenly she felt scared. She was too far from the others, too close to being totally alone for the first time since they had left Kroeger at the last stop.

She tore out of the room, not bothering to check how she looked.

She walked into the dining area and reached for a mug before sitting in her usual place around the oval table that had been laser-hewn from a chunk of the Moon itself. The others had gathered there too, but it was all wrong. No one was talking. There were seven chairs, but only six of them. Yuri had his spreadsheets, was calculating credits and debits, even after the residence tithe each squad paid toward terraforming their base. He began to speak of salary, and fell silent before he had to mention survivors' benefits.

The others looked up. Now that the businesslike monotone had stilled itself, they missed it. Darkness came rapidly; the atmospheric layer was still too thin to allow for long twilights. Valentina turned on the lights.

"We ought to eat something," Judith said dully.

No one jumped up. No one replied. Zann hadn't thought of food. After a time, Joao muttered something, but even he couldn't face the idea, not here, not now.

She had thought that things would be easier at home, when they could relax Wing discipline.

Gregory slipped forward, resting his head on the cool stone of the table, his arms covering his face.

It was so lonely with only the six of them! Tears trickled down Zann's face, but she didn't bother to wipe them away. In assorted ships' berths and planetside quarters, with Kroeger trailing them and gossip to sift through, it had been less real.

Suddenly, it was dawn. Zann didn't know if she had slept or dozed, or passed the whole night in some kind of meditative trance like the ones she used for really tough decryptions. No one had moved from the table.

Outside, birds sang in Judith's lilacs, and golden light spread in a buttery puddle on the burnished stone. Maryam would say that the color made her hungry. It didn't feel as if a whole night had passed. Pretty soon that door would slide open and Maryam would rush in, laughing. The thought startled Zann into full wakefulness. Her mouth tasted bad and her head felt fuzzy. She rose and stretched painfully.

"Anyone for coffee?" The dregs in the pot smelled vile, and she tapped in an order for a fresh one. She brought it over to the table, and the others took it because it was there.

The door slid aside and they all started, looking at one another. Maybe that was Maryam now.

Of course it wasn't. Gus, Ghermann, Svetlana, and Rhea came in carrying covered platters. "Breakfast," Rhea said quietly and placed the food on the table. Zann could hear the rest of that squad, their closest Moonside neighbor's, in the other room. "Come on in where it's more comfortable," they said, gently compelling Zann and her family back into the living room where they let the squad in on the news of the Wing.

"I think we ought to offer another language besides Earth Standard in the training schools," Rhea said.

"Fine," Zann commented. "Make it Arthan. Then we can apply to the Arthan Assembly for aid and use it for the dome instead." Arthan was Ag Kolatolo's homeworld; it would be bitterly amusing to try just that.

"You hear about his Institute for Spacers' Orphans? Educates them, just the way he wants 'em to be. Maybe we could try convincing . . ."

"Try breathing vacuum instead. We're better off taking care of our own. No quotas for 'poor Earther refugees' that way."

Joao shook his head at her, but had no time to comment. Gus had started off on his favorite hobby: gardening. He was deep in a highly technical conversation on fertilizers for fruit trees. Joao knew nothing about the subject but made polite noises.

The place was getting crowded. More sibs arrived, and neighbors, and sibs of their parent squads. There were old classmates, even people who had lived down the hall in the Batch. There was a dizzying variety of foods. Then the door slid open fast and a midshipman ran in breathlessly.

She flung herself down beside Gregory, tried to compose herself, and burst into noisy sobs.

Pam. The first time they were trusted to play parent squad to a homeless kid in junor training, and this had to happen.

"Pam, Pam girl," Gregory said softly and put his arm around her shoulders.

"You just watch!" she cried. "Just watch me. I'm going for pilot training, and when I get out, I'm going to pick the name 'Maryam.' She'll be so proud . . ." and then tears fell as she realized anew that Maryam would never be proud of anything again.

Gregory's face went stark white and his arm went limp on the trainee's shoulders. Gently, Ghermann drew her away. "I didn't want to, you know," Gregory told her back. "I wish it had been me."

Joao had hoped that here at least Gregory might break. After that first passionate outburst on board the base ship, he had been too calm, had moved almost in a trance unless someone angered him, like the commcrews outside the Blue Angel. And he had clung to Suzannah, Valentina, and Joao himself rather than turning to the other pilots in his squad. Pam couldn't know what she'd said . . . but Gus was droning on about mulch or something equally unappetizing, and seemed to expect a reply. It was good that Ghermann could take care of the girl.

A buzzer sounded and Zann jumped, murmuring something as she activated the computer. She turned her back to the rest of the room, placed her palm on the screen, then leaned forward for retinal scan. What had Federico Hashrahh Kroeger come up with now? Her eyes went wide, which meant she was concentrating on the screen, lines and lines of cipher. Valentina had long since cannibalized the decoder Zann never used.

Judith's friend Anna patted her shoulder and whispered something.

"You are?" Judith's head came up. "When's the birth?"

"That's why I took a ground assignment. I'm on day 160 now."

Joao looked at Anna carefully. Female pilots had the lowest pregnancy rate in the Wing because of Wing Command's insistence on their taking Base or ground assignments: they'd risk one pilot, the line ran, but not two. Maryam now . . . she'd have had to be pulled out of her sting.

"That's wonderful," Judith breathed, smiling through tears.

"Oh, Judith, I just wish it were John's child too! Except for memories, there's nothing left of him."

The women hugged one another. Joao nodded approval across at Charles, another member of Anna's squad. Two people were gently forcing Valentina to eat. Just as well: she didn't pack any excess kilos. Someone else was replacing Yuri's coffee mug with fruit juice. Good.

Charles walked over to Gregory, knelt beside him and handed him something; Joao couldn't quite make out what. The two senior pilots spoke together in an undertone. Charles patted Gregory's shoulder, and then walked over to help Ghermann comfort the squad's foster daughter. Joao wished he could join him, but his body felt as if he were under heavy acceleration.

They would be all right, that crazy, wonderful squad of his, even if he couldn't take care of them right this moment. That was what the others were for. As it always did, the Wing had come around, making the calls he had made too often both as a friend and as a medic. He knew that those calls were therapeutic for everyone, but knowing it didn't dull his grief. At least no well-meaning oaf had mentioned remarriage yet. They would have to discuss it sometime, though. Perhaps, as Yuri and Judith thought, that solo pilot—his name was Dustin, Joao recalled. Smart of Yuri to think of a solo as a way of buying time.

Zann joined him and Gus. Discouragement as well as sadness marked her features. "More of the same," she said. "Gripes about inefficient security. And Kolatolo's lobbying to cut the Moon's appropriations."

"Again?" That took Gus' mind off trees temporarily. The two of them started the usual discussion about League politics, and Joao was free to look around.

Each time the door opened, all six of them turned to it by instinct. It was ridiculous. *He* had known from the minute that Battle Op had paged him on the base ship.

Gus tried to draw his attention, and Joao knew why. Over on the table between two couches, Ghermann was setting up the little Memorial which would remain there for seven days after the memorial service itself.

Too bad it wasn't going to work on him. Though Zann deliberately looked away, and Gus tried to get him to turn around, he watched. "It's all right," he assured Gus. "The rituals help make it seem real to me."

Gus nodded and tried to interest Zann in gardening.

Even though some crazy part of him still wanted to cling to the fantasy of Maryam alive, Maryam coming home, having a mourning table made the truth that much more inescapable. But it was very good that the tradition was old, dating back into pre-space times, times before there were even holos. The two-dimensional picture on the table bore so little resemblance to the quicksilver Maryam he loved.

Rhea came by with a plate of small meat pies, and made him take one. He held it absently as he scanned the room. Everything wasn't as it should be, his instincts told him, just as they did whenever a patient took a turn for the worse.

He excused himself and went down the hall. Gregory's door was shut, and that worried him. No one could blame Gregory for wanting to get away from the crowd for a moment, but the closed door was a bad sign.

"Gregory?" he called into the annunciator grid. No answer. Then he knocked. If he had to, he'd force the door panel. Instead it opened to him.

Gregory was sitting on his bed, and didn't acknowledge him.

"What is it, Gregory?"

He kept looking down at something in his hands. "I can't stand that table or the picture there for everyone to stare at. It's a cruel custom. We should take it down."

"Eat this." Joao handed him the pie. As Gregory took it, Joao saw that his other hand was cupped around a holo. He got a quick glimpse of a blaze of red hair and shut his eyes for a second.

"Do you think that's smart?" Joao gestured at the holo.

Gregory rubbed his thumb tenderly over it and shrugged.

"You have to come back." Joao tried another tack. "We should be with the others. They'll wonder about it."

"Give me a couple more minutes," Gregory said. For the first time, he focused on Joao. "I can't stand the way they look at me."

Joao raised his eyebrows. *Keep him talking*. But night after night he'd kept Gregory talking, trying to get him to talk out all his grief, and succeeded instead in exhausting both of them.

"It's such a jumble. I wish it were tomorrow. I wish it were next year. It wasn't real till we came back home."

"Come on, Gregory." Using gentle force, Joao pulled Gregory up from the bed. As he rose, Joao noticed the

small package in its plain wrapper that Charles had brought.
He decided not to mention it and led Gregory back into the
living room.

Gregory looked once, hard, at the mourning altar, and
then sat down so his back was toward it. No one commented. Svetlana drifted over to him, sat down, and began
to tell stories about junior training. She could always make
Gregory smile; half her escapades were things Gregory had
shared.

Gregory woke, feeling groggy. He reached for his cabin's light control, then realized that he was on the Wing
Moon and it was still dark. With that realization came
knowledge of what day it was. The grogginess burned
away. He wondered if any of the others were up yet.
Despite what Joao had said about isolating himself, Gregory had preferred to sleep alone. His hand curled about the
holo of Maryam he had kept with him, and he gazed deep
into it, as if into the living woman's eyes.

She was in uniform; full-dress, with the ace's scarf
whipping around her legs. Her smile was almost a grin.
Her body seemed to strain against the holo, wanting to run
and jump up and move fast, as she always did. Her eyes
twinkled with laughter, and her blazing hair settled around
her face like a soft cloud.

Maryam. She had always teased and joked with him,
calling him the old man until he proved he wasn't. When
Maryam was around, he always felt like he had just gradu-
ated, was eighteen again. He remembered funny, personal
things: her passion for sweet drinks, Joao's revulsion at the
waste of fine liquor, his laughter each time he found out
she'd pilfered his private stock. And her arm-wrestling
trick of angling the opponent's wrist. He'd never learned
it. He remembered the first day Yuri had brought her

around. They had arm-wrestled; she had won, and then laughed. And he had been lost since then. He remembered Maryam's voice, chattering and light and too wispy and childlike for a pilot.

Nothing about that static, treacherous holo warned him that Maryam was dead, that he had killed her, that she was no more than billions of sub-elementary particles drifting in space.

The room began to fill with light. Gregory made a savage effort, put down the holo, and heaved himself out of bed and into a robe. The bathrooms were empty. Perhaps Joao had been right; he usually was. Perhaps it had been stupid to spend the night alone.

I wasn't alone. I was with Maryam, he told himself stubbornly.

After he showered, he stared at his chin in the mirror, not quite sure it was his own. He felt the heavy stubble on his face, winced, and then rubbed depilatory cream on his face. Even after he washed it off, he still looked like he was convalescing from some strange illness.

He returned to his own room. Still no noises from the rest of the squad. Carefully he put on his dress uniform. Strangeness entered him. One rarely wore dress uniform at home. It felt strange, lighter-weight and softer-textured than the working uniforms and flightsuits he usually wore.

When he could no longer avoid it, he lifted the long white scarf from his dresser and draped it around his neck. It fell evenly to his knees, the long tassels brushing against his legs. Unconsciously his fingers rubbed the date embroidered just above the hem, the date of the battle in which he had won his ace's rating.

He hefted the small package Charles had brought over the day before. Why didn't it burn his hands? Poor Yuri.

No use delaying it. He walked slowly over to the living room.

Yuri was there before him, slumped on the sofa, staring deep into the mug he held. Gregory wondered how much coffee he had put away. He started to move across the room, to take the mug from Yuri, when the younger pilot stirred.

"It's full dress," Gregory said softly, displaying the package in his hands. He peeled back the wrapper, exposing the white silk. Yuri rose.

Scarves were always awarded ace to ace. He remembered how he and Maryam had laughed and planned how they would drape the scarf around Yuri with all their family and sibs watching. He remembered the lavish display of off-world flowers he had ordered for Maryam when she had made ace. Yuri would have no such party.

Gregory whipped the scarf from its wrappings and displayed the length of it before he doubled it between his hands. Yuri turned back the edges and found the embroidered date.

"Not much of a party," Gregory said.

Yuri shrugged and touched the white silk. "I don't want a party," he said.

Feeling awkward and terribly alone, Gregory arranged the scarf on Yuri. Maryam, laughing Maryam, should have been here to assist. Then the two of them would have admired the new ace, turned him to face the assembled family, sibs, and friends. No one would laugh and clap and exclaim for Yuri. There would be no first-year flight students to rub him for good luck, no festivities to mark this occasion that they all had looked forward to for so long. He could almost hear Maryam saying, "Yuri, what *took* you so long?" and then standing on tiptoe to kiss them both.

"I'm sorry," was the best Gregory could come up with.

"No problem," Yuri said. "I'd prefer to do Maryam proper honor than wait for a better time." He glanced over at the mourning table, then went over and brought Gregory a mug of coffee.

Valentina came in, noted Yuri's scarf, then walked over and kissed him on the cheek without cracking a smile. She sat demurely on the edge of the nearest easy chair, looking too much like a holo to be real.

Zann came in and just smiled at Yuri as she sat down. It seemed like she didn't trust her voice. Joao offered congrat-ulations and a warm smile. Judith, last of all but Maryam (who had always been last to get up), walked in, paused, noticed Yuri's scarf, and then ran over to hug him hard, as if reassuring herself of his living presence.

"We should go," Joao said finally. They piled into the light transport. Valentina took the controls and they skimmed from the residential enclave into Center.

The chapel wasn't large enough for the entire Wing. After all, how often were the two thousand of them home on leave at the same time? It stood neatly to the side of the Block, that complex of Wing Command, school, and the youngest students' dorms. Around it ranged another ring, with the dorms of the older students, several mess halls (where they ate when they were too lazy or too broke to cook at home), and Bachelor Officers' Quarters, commonly known as the Batch. Alone in a planted glade, balanced by the Officers' Club, stood the chapel.

It was serene here, Gregory mused. He imagined that the chapel on old Earth had looked this way when people had first built it, centuries before pilots had soared in the skies, when they had sailed, rather than soared.

They had all lived here from the age of fourteen until they married, had partied, had studied. The chapel was austere with its backless benches of imported blond wood. Gregory remembered the days when attendance was compulsory.

People were waiting, sibs in the next to front row, their familiar faces grave. It felt strange when Gregory sat down on the first bench. Usually it was reserved for the Commander.

On the plain white altar rested Maryam's plaque, a heavy stone, smoothed from the living rock of the Moon and carved with Maryam's name, the dates of her birth and death, and beneath the words and numbers, the wings of a pilot yoked with the five-pointed star of the ace. After the service, they would bring it home. It would rest on the mourning table for six days. Then they would select a place in the park, and nestle it into the ground.

Behind him, Gregory heard the shuffle of people arriving and taking their places. He played with schedules and leave rotations as the chapel filled and the waiting stopped.

The Commander approached the lectern and Gregory felt time yawn around him. The old man looked no different than he had when Gregory had finished training, no different than he had the year Gregory had passed flight test at the head of his class, no different, even, than the time Gregory and the others had married Maryam. He had shaken his head when they had told him, but no one had laughed louder or drunk more at the reception.

Even the smells were the same.

"Let us pray," said the Commander, words older than the Wing Moon, words remembered from lost Earth. He joined in them without thinking of the contents. Then the old officer spoke very briefly about Maryam. The Commander wove Maryam's life into a morality tale for the Wing, especially the young students sitting in the back. That angered Gregory—reducing Maryam to a hero-story like that. And yet it was good too, not to display her in public. After another prayer, Charles came to the front and read a poem. It hadn't been so long ago that he had been sitting on this same bench.

That must have been Judith's idea. She and Maryam both had always liked Charles' poems, the ones he wrote, and the old ones he unearthed from civilian and Wing archives. Compassion flowed from Charles' voice, and Gregory listened to the last lines.

> *A lonely impulse of delight*
> *Drove to this tumult in the clouds;*
> *I balanced all, brought all to mind,*
> *The years to come seemed waste of breath,*
> *A waste of breath the years behind*
> *In balance with this life, this death.*

Charles had found a really old poem this time. Even as Maryam asked for the Mercy, her voice had held hidden laughter. Only the flying had been truly real to her. No, that wasn't true; she loved them, didn't she? But if she did, how could she have asked him to . . . Gregory shook his head.

Kind of Charles, Gregory thought, and kind of Judith to think of this. He'd have to think of something to say to her. Only it was so hard to make the right words come!

Music, voices this time, not ancient tapes, swelled around them. Gregory rose. The song was incredibly old. It had been sung for pilots back on Earth, and before that for sailors on their lost world's prodigious, vanished oceans.

> *''Eternal Father, strong to save,*
> *Whose Hand o' errules the starry maze,*
> *Who keeps all galaxies on course*

> *And governs their destructive force.*
> *We cry for Your unending Grace*
> *For those in peril deep in space."*

Gregory let the strong, solemn music and the ancient words flow over him, shield him in their calm and dignity. Then the Commander pronounced the benediction. It was all over. The squad rose and walked slowly from the chapel. One of the sibs would bring the stone from the altar back to the house. This time, only the closest sibs would be there. And their "daughter." Pam was holding up well.

Gregory paced down the aisle of the chapel. Friendly, comforting faces surrounded him on all sides. Each was someone he knew well.

Just before they got to the door, Gregory saw someone not quite as familiar as the others. He turned it over in his mind. Then he remembered. Dustin.

CHAPTER 7

The dying Sejiedi fighter spiraled toward the base ship. As Joao watched the board in Life Support, he flinched although he knew he would never feel it. Spinning sick and dizzy, the fighter plunged toward the ship and the alarm shrieked. If that thing got through the grav fields, there would be casualties, old-style, messy ones on board. The shell was too fragile, and the shields had never been designed to take that kind of intrusion. Joao looked at the stretchers, at the surgical field generators and laser scalpels, the carefully laid out anesthetic sprays, and hoped that they would go unused.

"Here comes eight," he heard over his Wing comm and cringed inside again. That was Dustin, counting off kills. What was getting into the damned fool? Since this wasn't Battle Op, he couldn't speak to the pilots of his Wing or hear the rest of the Colors, but his own Wingmates' frequencies were, as always, open to him.

He watched the White sting on the board as it spun around the toroid of the base ship. The Sej had already tried one suicide run. The alarm shrieked and buzzed throughout the deck and echoed off the steel bulkhead.

Damn it, Dustin! Stay with the flight! His silent order was useless. Dustin was flying crazy again. The Sejiedi would pierce the force zone soon, and then they would see, but the ship was moving on sheer inertia now, and spinning faster than it could fly. Even with the best shooting Joao had ever heard of, Dustin couldn't bring ship's lasers to bear on the thing. And now there were flashes of motion behind him, at the very periphery of the board.

That had to be the rest of the flight, closing up. But Dustin was dumping mass, flying tau-void out there, hurling himself at the crippled ship and cursing the limitations of the sting that held him back. The dying Sej fighter changed colors as its a-gravs faltered. Twenty, forty, an incredible four hundred gravities . . . the pilot was long dead, and better so, Joao thought. Even if he *were* Sejiedi. The soundless explosion was almost a relief.

A rainbow seared across the screen as the alarm brought the deck into full alert.

"Shit!" Dustin's voice came over the comm, hungry and frustrated. "He was already dead. No fight at all. I'm stuck at seven."

"Get back in formation," Joao heard Zann order softly.

He promised himself that he'd break Dustin's neck if he happened to bring it back, safe and sound. Then he glanced at the holoboard again. It wasn't the rest of the flight he had spotted there, but something red—not the brilliant color of Red Wing, but the sullen, darker crimson of the Sejiedi.

There were medics from the other Colors watching the board and watching Joao too. He steadied his breathing, not wanting to betray himself, just the way he had done each time Maryam had flown and before Yuri had achieved mass. He had hoped that that was all behind him now. Not Dustin. Not him too. The Sej flying lead was good, curving around, keeping ten degrees left and "up," between the tail and the stabilizer: perfect attack position. It was one of the few spots where a sting was almost blind and where firepower couldn't easily cover. Dustin would have to turn to evade, assuming he had time. The Sejiedi was accelerating cautiously, getting just inside firing range.

Stings could practically turn in an airlock, but Joao felt his hands chill. Even that might be too much space for Dustin now. He was turning, neat and fast, but the Sej moved with him. He had to know now that there was someone on his tail. Damn all pilots!

Light blazed across the board and Joao shut his eyes, dying a little inside. When it subsided, he dared to look again. The Sej was gone, and a Blue sting flashed over the bulk of the base ship. *Saved by a Blue Winger, worse luck,* Joao thought. It would *have* to be a Blue Winger. The Blues would be feeling good tonight, and at the Wing's expense. And the story would get around, probably be transmitted all over the sector, not to mention all the way to Arthan, Blue Wing's homeworld.

It was, it had to be a lucky shot. The Blue sting was well out of range. Only a weapons expert or a combat virgin deserved to land that kind of shot. The two medics in Blue whooped, glancing triumphantly over at Joao, who kept his features carefully expressionless. The medics weren't responsible for their pilots' achievements, least of all in Blue Wing where medics were scarcely more than warrant officers. They barely knew the fliers they treated.

Dustin's sting yawed slightly as he corrected and headed back for the rest of the flight. The alarm shut down.

A cone of White stings appeared. The flight was out, flying near max, their formation tight. Joao made quick adjustments to his wristcomp. That new solo—her name was Elizabeth—Charles' squad had picked up was just out of training, had never flown in actual combat before. From the look of her med readout, she wasn't doing all that well. Heart and respiration were way up. So were Yuri's, but then he always ran a bit to the high side of the scale. But the kid was not in good shape, Joao thought. None of them were. Not now. They'd been flying too hard, watch on watch, without a respite.

If Colors hadn't been around, he would have sworn out loud or crashed one giant fist against the holoboard's controls. Now the nose of the cone's formation was detaching. The board glowed brighter, the white blips turning faintly scarlet. Gregory, Yuri, and Dustin, with Neil and Glennis just behind, were pushing their a-gravs to capacity, beyond tested limits. *This isn't flight test,* Joao wanted to storm. He remembered the Sejiedi ship and how its gravs had burned out. The red tinge grew stronger, pushing into red, as light itself receded for his squad's stings. They weren't true starships. They were meant to fight, and that meant sublight capability. At near-light speeds, they were unstable and they couldn't jump tau.

Now the laser flares showed up only as blue-green, aquamarine, an ocean of silent flame against blackness. Gregory fired, then fired again. Joao shut his eyes against the explosion of Sejiedi ships.

"Wish you'd let me have that one," Dustin complained.

"Get back here," Neil said hoarsely.

"Save the chatter for the Sej," Gregory ordered.

The formation, now strung out across the board, wheeled again, cutting a tight curving loop around and "up." Joao could see what Gregory had already spotted: Green and Yellow squads in trouble as a full flight of Sejiedi poured around them on all three axes. His sting started to shade crimson on the board again; Yuri and Dustin strained to keep pace. Judith had dropped back beside Charles, covering Elizabeth. Lasers erupted intermittently, and Joao slitted his eyes. The rest of the flight was a good six thousand kilometers behind.

"They're pushing their gravs into the red zone," someone said behind Joao.

"White Wing to the rescue?"

"Of course. Glory-riding, as always. Not that they'll say anything; they never do. But they'll look, and you know how they can."

Joao did.

"I'm demanding an immediate meeting of the flight." He heard Neil's voice over the comm, steady, not as if he had just broken every one of the Wing's traditions by calling a meeting in the middle of a fight. Now there'd be a meeting, and Joao didn't want to think about the outcome. Even before they had left Wing Moon, Gregory had been called down by the Wing Commander for the way he was dumping tau. The Commander had chewed him out royally, Judith had reported, and she rarely exaggerated. Gregory and Yuri had both walked small for days afterward. But not long enough.

"What the hell's going on?" one of the medics in Blue asked Joao. "They've called a regroup, the Sej are withdrawing, but your Wing's still blasting away."

Joao turned a cold face to him. "Cleanup," he replied. "As always." He watched a few minutes longer, until he saw the white blips regroup into the tight cone and begin the long loop back home. The holo looked like the calyx of a lily, as the shining motes described clean, brilliant arcs on their way back home. Joao turned away from the board, and palmed a hypo of nepenthine before heading for a tube to the flight deck.

Damn! This had been coming for too long. Joao glared at the tube's readout. How long did it have to take to get to the flight deck? The tubes were too slow. Everyone on board must be wandering around, and the hell with battle stations. That suicide mission must have taken a bigger bite out of the ship's power than anyone had reported. That figured too. He'd ask Valentina to run a check on power when he got back to quarters. Zann would want that data for Kroeger, probably.

After all these years, Joao fumed. Gregory had achieved mass early, stabilized shortly after graduation into one of the finest pilots the Wing had produced in years, the sort who looked made to lead a flight, who could be promoted . . . "Say, Gregory, how'd you like to be commander one of these years?" Maryam used to tease him. "Keep flying straight, and you will." How many pilots had he shepherded through the danger stage? Four? Five? In all those years, he had lost only two: John, vaped as he covered a retreat, and Maryam.

Was that it—he was following her? The trouble had started during compassionate leave. Even while mourning, the squad had flying time to get in. Some of Gregory's maneuvers had been so risky that the Commander had threatened to put the whole squad on report, pilots and nonpilots alike. Gregory had taken his own chewing-out quietly; but the Commander's threat had infuriated him.

It actually made sense. If your own squad couldn't keep you in line, who could? Joao remembered how Judith had pleaded with Maryam to slow down, to stick with the flight, not to chase off after single kills or dream of taking out a cruiser. Gregory had always backed her.

"In case you've forgotten," he would say, "we're here to win a war, not make single kills . . . as much fun as it is."

Maryam had always promised to slow down, more because Judith was in tears and she hated to upset her family
than for any other reason. And then there'd be an alert,
and she'd start to grin, all her good intentions forgotten.

Today Gregory had accounted for two stings. Dustin
had taken out one, not to mention the kills he and Yuri had
assisted at. Joao began to rehearse what he'd say when he
got those pilots of his back to quarters.

The tube slid to a halt, and Joao strode onto flight deck,
passing the usual military rainbow without a nod. Gregory
was thumbprinting the log. An outsider wouldn't notice it,
he thought wryly, but Joao could see the strain in his
flight. Neil was a little too taut, Gregory too challenging.
They avoided each other's eyes the way they had in the
academy after a particularly mean argument. The new kid
looked scared out of her mind, but she was hiding it well.
Joao was pretty sure she could keep the mask on till they
got back to quarters. It would shame all of them if he had to
put her out right here in front of all the Colors.

Dustin nodded to Joao. Then, looking like the most
arrogant Winger who ever wore white, he strolled over to
a man in blue whom Joao recognized. Not only did he
wear the scarf of an ace pilot, but his flightsuit gleamed
with evidence of his skills. Pilot. Weaponsmaster. The
strip across his breast read TreMorion, Haral. Joao groaned
inwardly. Why did it have to be this Blue who had rescued
Dustin?

"Thanks," Dustin told TreMorion in a hush so profound that the simple word echoed in the cavernous flight
deck.

"It means more to you than it does to me," TreMorion
replied and turned his back abruptly. One Red Winger
hissed under his breath, but the pilots flanking TreMorion,
Blues, with a smattering of Yellows and one Green, seemed

to approve. Joao could hear them snickering. Before long the news that TreMorion had saved a White Wing pilot and even gotten a thanks out of him—probably the first time that had ever happened—would be all over the base ship.

Dustin rejoined the group. "What'd you have to do that for?" Yuri whispered.

Dustin, his face reflecting nothing, cocked his head slightly to the right. "Be kind to the animals," he answered lightly.

Both Dustin and Yuri were a little too cocky. Yuri's hands gave him away; blue veins throbbed prominently under sallow skin. The new solo, shadowed by Charles, was standing at one side. If her training hadn't been so rigorous, she'd have been cowering by now.

Gregory led the way back to White Wing territory, ten pilots and one medic crowding the corridors, grimly pleased at the way the other Colors hugged the walls.

The tension continued unabated, even in the blessed privacy of quarters. Zann and Shannon, Michael and a few of the others were waiting there. Joao came up behind Elizabeth and eased her onto a chair. She tried to smile at him, but she was shivering and her breathing came in shallow gasps. Quickly he injected her with the nepenthine he had kept palmed.

"Nepenthine. By the time she's flight-ready again, she'll have forgotten most of this," he reassured Charles. Flight regs forbade pilots to fly for ten days after that junk got into their system. Mostly Joao used it as a threat when pilots didn't get their proper rest. This time he was using it to protect a very junior pilot who felt she couldn't fly anymore.

Zann produced a robe that Joao recognized as Yuri's, a big, warm thing. As he wrapped it around the young woman, he felt something rolling in a pocket and reached for it. Caffeine tablets.

Joao felt the blood rushing through his neck into his temples. He wanted to slam Yuri onto the deck. An addict, that's what he was becoming. Carefully he brought his fury under control. It would be too easy to lash out, and things were bad enough already. The pressure was getting to him too. Usually he kept that temper of his leashed.

"Charles, get Elizabeth settled, will you?" he asked softly. He barely trusted his voice. "Zann, where's Valentina? Still playing with those codes for Kroeger? Get her down here."

Charles lifted Elizabeth against his shoulder gently. "Come on now, Beth," he whispered. "Easy, baby." He disappeared into a room off the wardroom.

Zann activated the terminal's comm. "Valentina? We're in L-50W. No, I don't care how productive Dustin's last hunch was. Are you Wing, or Cryptology? Get down here on the double."

Charles reentered the wardroom and all hell broke loose.

"Do you want to scare her out of the sky?" he accused Gregory. "You too, Dustin. You and Yuri. You never used to fly this way. What kind of crazy tau-dumping contest are you getting into?"

"Why'd you take on that Sej? It was way out of our zone, and we weren't nearly close enough to cover you," Neil shouted at Yuri.

The smaller pilot flinched. Neil could be too rigid. When he got really angry, he could terrorize all of them. But he was far likelier to take out a beaten-up old guitar and start a crazy midshipman song than to chew out a fellow ace in the middle of a crowded wardroom.

"Look," Yuri said, trying to keep his voice light, "it was just calling to me. Practically got down on its knees and begged, 'Vape me, vape me.' Couldn't leave the poor thing in pain, could I? So I vaped 'em.''

Gregory turned away sharply. Judith's cheeks flushed deep red. Joao could barely stop from grimacing in disgust and anger.

"You know it's that way." Judith's voice penetrated his revulsion. She could always read him. "We don't talk about it, but it's like that."

Something in him froze. If even Judith, lovely, gentle Judith, felt that way . . . All pilots were crazy. They had to be. That was why every White Wing medic was also a psychtech. They had to be.

The hatch whispered open, and Valentina appeared. She found her usual place on the ungainly regulation-issue chair beside the terminal. They all sat, gingerly, the way they had had to sit at meals their first years in the academy, as they still sat when invited to do so by the Commander, spines erect, not touching the back of their chairs. The posture was too serious, too formal. Joao wanted to pick Gregory up and shake him. Didn't he know what he was doing to the whole flight?

"Let's get this started," Joao said.

Neil flashed a glance at Valentina. Joao nodded. "Valentina, this one's on the record."

"Neil, you called for this meeting in the middle of a battle. So I assume you have a statement to make."

"My squad doesn't like the risks Gregory's been taking," Neil said as dispassionately as if there had been Colors present. "He's putting the whole flight in jeopardy."

"You were flying team back there," Gregory pointed out heatedly. "We took no casualties. None of the flights did, and I call that a damned fine day's work. How many other Wings escaped today?"

"Just Purple," Zann reported.

Even Neil had to snort at that one.

"And did they make any kills?" Judith feigned innocence.

"One," Zann said calmly. Valentina was smiling, but Joao had no heart for the usual joke that Purple had both the lowest casualty record and the lowest number of aces in the Fleet, and that there was a direct correlation.

This meeting wasn't for sly jokes at the Colors. It was on the record. A copy would be transmitted to Wing Command, and Gregory'd already been reprimanded once. Another serious violation would relieve him of command of the flight. Another infraction after that, and he'd be grounded. Joao had known Gregory long enough to know that it would be kinder to break both his legs than to ground him. Command would pass to Neil, then to Anna, assuming she was back on duty. And Neil didn't want command. The sib had made it perfectly clear on more than one occasion.

"That's not what I mean," Neil said. "Gregory, you, Yuri, and Dustin are flying wild. Dustin had to be rescued by that damned arrogant Blue. Gregory, you know perfectly well what the a-gravs are capable of, and you were pushing too hard. I'm not saying you're glory-riding, but you are taking insane risks. And you're senior, Gregory. If you get vaped, what happens to the rest of us?"

Judith put one hand to her mouth.

"What happens if all three of you get it?" Charles asked. "This has been a rocky year for all of us." Joao noted that he looked haunted. First John, then Maryam. "We've lost a few. Anna's on ground assignment, and now . . ." He gestured at the empty space beside Judith and his lips almost trembled.

Charles' eyes kept slipping over to Dustin, Joao noticed. Dustin had been stable, Judith had said, had achieved mass early and easily, had never been accused of glory-riding.

Yet in the months he'd been flying with the squad, he had achieved three single kills and was pushing hard for more. Sure, he was spending a lot of time with Yuri, but where Yuri went, Judith came too, and Dustin and Judith were very, very close these days.

"Do you want to see my flight tapes?" Gregory asked.

Zann glanced over at her wristcomp. Probably Kroeger again, Joao thought. With the way their luck was running, he'd be waiting outside their quarters.

"I'm sure they're in top shape," Neil replied. "I know how good you are. Why do you think we all still follow you? That's part of your problem, Gregory. You can pull stunts other people can't get away with. One of these days, someone with less experience is going to make a mistake, and then where will we all be? Didn't you pick up that one reason Charles is so worried about Elizabeth is that they're thinking of making her permanent?"

Charles nodded. "About that," he said softly. "I want this on the record too. You don't look like you have any intention of marrying up to strength. It's good to have someone to cover for the flight, but it's got to be squad, or things won't fall out right. It's been six months since Maryam, and none of you have shown any signs of doing anything about it."

Dustin had almost married into that squad, Joao remembered. He didn't look away as Charles' eyes met his, almost as if Charles were trying to do his best by a friend.

"Agreed," Neil said softly. "We haven't wanted to say much about this, but it's getting to be time. You've got to think about remarriage, or this flight just won't settle down."

A treacherous part of Joao wanted to agree. He had often dreamed that if they were seven instead of just six, Gregory would be himself again.

But this stranger-Gregory's face was as cold as deep space. "Do you want to make a formal complaint about my flying, or my leadership of this flight?" he asked in a voice that could freeze hydrogen.

"Let's call it a warning, for now," Neil replied.

Joao looked at the pilots around him. Neil's anger had been spent. Now his eyes seemed to plead with Gregory to fly sanely again. Charles, his face down, kept glancing back to the closed door of the room where Elizabeth was resting. Yuri's eyes were lowered, a sign he was ashamed of himself. Judith seemed more concerned about the flight than anything else. That stood to reason though. She had the most mass of any of them. Dustin was looking over at Gregory, and Joao's heart sank at the look. His face was full of hero worship. Couldn't Gregory see that all Dustin wanted was approval, or even simple recognition?

"Anything to add?" Joao asked. Silence was the only response. "Then this meeting's adjourned."

They all rose. Charles headed in to look at Elizabeth. Neil and Glennis returned to their own squad for comfort. Zann, Valentina, and Dustin disappeared to that den of Kroeger's down by Life Support. All three of them were so caught up in cracking Kroeger's codes that Joao had started to worry about that too. Intelligence was getting a little too popular in the squad, cutting in on their limited sleeptime.

As Yuri started to leave, Joao went over and laid a hand on his shoulder. "I want to talk with you," he said. "In my quarters."

Joao's cabin was small, consisting only of a bunk, a chair, and a terminal. Joao took the chair, forcing Yuri to stand. His eyes flickered all over the place, but found nothing to hold their attention.

Joao opened his left fist. The white vial of caffeine tabs

with their neat label glared against his cinnamon-colored palm.

"Where'd you get them, Yuri? You've really got a choice this time. Either you tell me, or I'm making sure you don't fly for at least ten days. I thought you were cutting down."

Yuri met Joao's eyes evenly. "You know I don't usually use caffeine or any of the other stims. Hell, before I fly, I don't even drink coffee. But the past few weeks, well, Neil's right. Gregory's flying crazy. And we're all too tired. It's not just no R and R in six months. That'll be coming up on rotation. But we've been standing double watches, even on off days, and we haven't stood down for a long time. Joao, the Sej are trying to wear us down. We're under strength and I don't mean just this flight. I haven't had more than four hours sleep at once for two weeks. We haven't stood down for more than three. Everyone's on something. We all need a night's sleep and a real meal, not just whatever you push at us in between scrambles. It's been too long, and we still haven't gotten reinforcements. Hell, we even ran out of chaff two days ago."

Joao looked at Yuri. His slanting eyes had dark circles under them, and his head was nodding as if it were an effort to hold it up.

"Judith?" Joao asked.

"She's as bad off as the rest of us," Yuri replied. "Only she uses cosmetics to cover it up." Suddenly his face went hard and furious. "The damned thing is, there're plenty of Blues around here. They're on rotation, standing regular watches."

Joao nodded. He'd heard about that. He decided he should talk to Zann. Something seemed a little strange, and Yuri wasn't just tense and overwrought. All the pilots were practically passing out on their feet. Was it exhaustion that was warping Gregory's judgment? That was too easy. Fatigue might be making matters worse, but they were all too edgy. Someone was going to make a mistake, the way Dustin had that afternoon. Joao had never thought he'd be grateful to a Blue. Only an expert like TreMorion could have pulled off that shot.

He closed his hand around the caffeine tablets. "Get some sleep now, while you can," he told Yuri. "Let me keep these. But if you need them, you just tell me, all right?"

Yuri nodded and staggered off to his own quarters. Joao watched him leave and wondered if he should try to talk to Gregory now. Knocking him out for a few days might be his best answer. Unfortunately, given their shorthandedness, it wasn't acceptable. They'd need him for the next flight. Devoutly Joao cursed the entire League. It would be just like them to waste Earther lives and protect their own.

But they were due for leave very soon now, he thought, trying to calm himself enough to sleep. Very shortly, they came up on rotation, and then they could go home. Then they would be able to help Gregory and heal themselves. Joao yawned and lay down. Medic though he was, he wanted to cling to the idea that all that crazy squad of his needed was a little rest and a safe haven. He pulled that dream down with him into sleep.

CHAPTER 8

For privacy, Federico Hashrahh Kroeger had wangled office space and quarters deep in the bowels of the base ship. His rooms were slipped in between a utility closet and Life Support's drug synthesizers—about as far away from the glossy corridors that other people out on temporary duty from Central preferred as he could get. The place was, he reflected, somewhat of a demilitarized zone between Engineering and Medical, with a few vague hackers floating around when anyone at all was there. Usually the cul-de-sac off an unfrequented corridor was quiet, forgotten by almost everything except the maintenance robots. Down here no one would notice a gray shadow or his associates.

Shabby as it was, the place pleased Kroeger. Since no one else wanted it, it had been easy to secure. Nothing on the door betrayed its purpose. His office had the mismatched look of scrounged back-issue pieces. None of the chairs matched. His conference table was a slab of faded orange plastic with more than a few telltale rings and splashes on it. Recently the color had been mercifully hidden under a mountain of printouts that threatened to topple like the legend of lost Atlantis, wherever that was. The walls were badly in need of polishing. Even the terminal was in a condition that a very polite antique dealer might have described as distressed.

But that was where the makeshifts ended. The battered housing cased one of the most powerful and reliable computers ever produced. Kroeger had secured that computer and passworded it so stealthily that no other computer on or off board could detect its presence, much less interface with it.

He had covered the dingy walls with huge maps of Sejiedi and League space. There was neither room nor money for accurate holos. But Kroeger didn't need them. Quite possibly he didn't need even the maps. He had them all in his head.

Now he was impatient. Intelligence Officer Suzannah would join him shortly after whatever White Wing business she had to attend to. He spared a thought to wonder what that business was. One of these days he must investigate the inner workings of the Wing, just to gratify his own curiosity: this wasn't the right time, however. Kroeger glanced at the chrono and sighed. What were they finding to talk about? White Wingers always seemed to be in accord. Suzannah had told him emphatically that this meeting was important. This using subordinates who had a dual function was inefficient, but she was far more valuable to him than regular Intelligence personnel. Their uniformity of approach made his own brand of analysis almost impossible. He much preferred to rely on the tall comm officer who could be trusted—to his level of satisfaction—to input data and remember it.

Though he had pulped the message from Central Intelligence Coordination hours ago, it still lay clear in his mind: veiled innuendoes about his reliance on a White Wing squad, and not just any squad, but the one so recently made notorious for killing one of its own pilots. Well, it was his risk, and his career. A lot of people at Central, perhaps including the Chief of Intelligence, would be glad if he were forced to resign. Half-Earther, half-alien. Citizenship was supposed to be all that mattered, but they never forgot his background.

Kroeger far preferred the squad's indifference to external matters such as bureau politics. And he loved their competence. He had been dubious at first when Suzannah suggested that her squad's computer officer be cleared for cipher work. There was no one from Cryptology aboard (an oversight about which he had had plenty to transmit, and for which a few people would pay); and she had mentioned that a good mathematician or two might just uncover things before they could be transmitted back to Central. Unspoken, of course, was their understanding that such a mathematician might catch things that the orthodox types at Central could miss.

He believed that there had been some minor security fracas about a decoder that Engineering Officer Valentina had "put to unauthorized uses," but the better the computer officer, the more pieces of miscellaneous equipment that he, she, or it usually cannibalized. And Valentina was very, very good. Clearance had come through rapidly after that.

Ever since the war broke out, Intelligence had been trying to crack Sejiedi codes. Even with planetary computer hookups, cracking one of the diabolical prime number codes could take centuries. Adding generalists with a flair for mathematics and linguistics and guessing right cut away at that time. So did bringing in people like Valentina.

To Kroeger's way of thinking, she added a further advantage: unorthodoxy. She was completely unprejudiced and fascinated by the process of developing methods of decoding. Game theory, Kroeger knew, was a highly abstract and arcane field of mathematics, an area that the water-walkers in Cryptology considered to be the strict preserve of academics on planets like Sikkahhad. For Valentina, it was a preferred off-duty activity. Her approach was a little weird, but if she got results by thinking of decoding as "winning," Kroeger was all for it.

She had begun with some of the less complex codes, one that Intelligence had long since cracked. After mastering their structures, she studied methods of transmission. She seemed to regard the Sejiedi's habit (which League Intelligence shared) of changing black boxes every so often as a personal insult. That was an opinion Kroeger encouraged.

The transcription she had completed just that morning lay on top of Kroeger's pile of printouts. Like several others received over the past few weeks, it detailed atmospheric disturbances on three Sejiedi worlds. Since these were sites of the slave-labor camps that grew hathoti, this was important data. He knew that most of the higher-ups in League Intelligence simply called the hathoti drug-lilies. The fighting Wings—apart from White Wing—painted them on the underbellies of their stings: one kill, one lily.

Drug traffic on the Sejiedi worlds was all-pervasive, and it was spreading. Two former League representatives had accepted bribes. When it was discovered, they had met with unfortunate accidents and impressive funerals at government expense. Much of the drug traffic was left to system-wide security. It was a matter for police, not Intelligence. But in border systems like Taluri, the traffic had created an entire shadow economy. In one community that

Kroeger could name, hathoti resin had been introduced into the water supply.

Hathoti depleted the soil of the worlds on which they grew. They didn't respond well to artificial fertilizers, could not be grown hydroponically, and their effect could not be synthesized by any known process. Kroeger shook his head. He had no logic to make everything come clear. The Sej didn't appear to be running out of room fast enough to justify recent attacks. Wars were expensive. Basic research on planetary ecologies and pharmacology came a great deal more cheaply. Drugs alone weren't forcing the Sej to fight the way they did.

Some soft science idiots on Central had suggested that a Sejiedi warrior ethic drove them. Published it too. Kroeger was more inclined to write off any warrior ethic as a system of mores designed to provide suitable meat for enemy lasers whenever and wherever the ruling castes decided.

There was something else, a key piece missing somewhere. Perhaps it was locked up in those tantalizing military codes that no one had broken yet. Kroeger had intercepted one transmission when Koda was hauled in. Brainstripping him had resulted in a few lines of clear text. He had turned the tape over to Valentina on the chance she would have more luck or skill than his usual staff. He smiled thinly. It would please him to see their faces when they realized that an Earther hacker and a half-Earther spook had done what they failed to do.

He glanced again at a chrono and wondered why Suzannah hadn't simply left the flight's meeting on some pretext or other. Briefly he toyed with the idea of asking Wing Command to detach her for temporary duty exclusively with Intelligence. That would be extremely productive.

But if he left that squad short-handed, then he might just lose Valentina's skills.

Although he had no need to do so, he began sorting out the well-remembered heap on the hideous orange table. A few half-decoded reports about a scientific conference on one of the Sejiedi prime worlds. A high population world, at that. Three noted spectroscopists were to attend. Security was tight. There were even references to the Planetary Council. This had to be important. Kroeger could feel it, just the way he had felt the break coming before Koda's cover had been pierced.

He had set his limited staff two tasks: to find researchers capable of duplicating Sejiedi technology in spectroscopy, and to try to get a transcript of the meeting. Military Intelligence had balked at appropriations (and possible risk of personnel) for "irrelevant nosing about after garbage." Well, there were three kinds of intelligence: machine intelligence, human intelligence, and military intelligence . . . if you wanted to dignify it by the name. A little relabeling and some creative bookkeeping had solved the problem of appropriations rather neatly.

Valentina's work was really promising. She had two traits he respected. She knew where to start work and she trusted her hunches. The League had missed superb material by keeping the White Wing in isolation. Why, the creativity of this one squad alone was amazing. Even that backup pilot they had acquired—Dustin, the belligerent young man from the Blue Angel—meshed well. He had seen the flier speaking with Valentina, and Suzannah informed him that Dustin's work had guided Valentina to the right answer more than once. Magnificent raw talent: who would have thought to turn a pilot loose on codes? No one in Military Intelligence had even gotten pilots to use their "black boxes" on board the stings because, the fliers griped, transmissions were far too slow for combat communications.

For a brief moment, Kroeger imagined the lecture he would never get a chance to give at Intelligence Central. "The White Wing offers a different line of sight," he would say. After all, line of sight was data too; anyone who drew information from only one source or by only one means ran into the danger of biased data. Well, if he were ever Director of Intelligence himself . . . *What would you do, Federico? Teach the basic introduction course? You'd be bored. But face it, passing on your data is the only immortality you'll ever have.* He was living proof that Earther and Reykskjoldar could crossbreed. But his line would end with him. Sterile . . . it hadn't mattered. He wasn't a man for a family; his own mixed clan hadn't been such a success that he wished to replicate it. There always was, had to be, one outcast in a family, someone a little different, a little too bright, an embarrassment in a clan as upwardly mobile as his was. He was used to it.

A discreet tone brought him out of his unproductive reverie. Suzannah was at the door, he could tell; he had rigged the system so that each individual was identified by a tone associated with fingerprints: he could choose whom to admit. He pressed the "enter" button, and she walked in.

"Sir?"

Kroeger pointed to a chair upholstered in blue plastic patched with gray. She sat, her face unreadable.

"Have you searched that quartermaster's inventory?" he asked, disdaining preliminary greetings.

"No, sir," the Wing officer replied calmly. "The flight meeting ended just now. I came directly from it."

"Tell me what you make of this," he said, laying a stack of printouts in front of her.

"Hmm," she said as she scanned. "Some petty pilfering; that's common enough. But some of this stuff looks like it wasn't signed for . . ." Her eyebrows went up and she ran a hand through tousled hair that glinted amber in the overhead lights.

"Yes?" he encouraged her.

Suzannah laid aside the hard copy and called records to the screen, flicking from file to file with a speed only Kroeger, of all the operatives he knew, could duplicate. She split the screen and marked critical items with a glowing pencil. "Five hundred grams of radioactives from Ordnance. Detonator components. I'm no arms officer, but this looks like it would work very tidily. Someone put some very careful effort into these thefts. Look, they're all from different sectors and widely varied times. Never enough disappears at once to call attention to it. See? Inventory 9.97—three hundred sixteen timers. 9.99—three hundred fifteen. This could be simply a counting error." She tapped her stylus on the terminal. "But there are too many counting errors here. They add up. Besides, Ordnance is audited too carefully. No one could make that mistake twenty different times in twenty different places. This is deliberate, and it's been concealed."

The confirmation relieved Kroeger. "Do you think Bikmat or Aglo are on board?" he asked.

"That's the logical conclusion," she replied quietly. "I hope so. I wouldn't like to find out that we've been even more deeply infiltrated than we think now. The only people with access to these supplies are weaponsmasters rated 5.7 and above." She looked up expectantly.

"I find no flaw in your reasoning. That gives us six people, doesn't it? They seem like the logical place to start." Kroeger smiled almost pleasantly, and cleared the table with a sweep of his arm. Printouts scattered onto the deck. They didn't matter; soon they'd be so much recyclable pulp. The data were all safely locked inside his head and Suzannah's now. On the clear plastic surface, he arranged six dossiers. "Let's begin, shall we?"

When the bell chimed again, they were so deeply engrossed that only years of training kept them from leaping out of their seats. Valentina's signal, Kroeger observed with satisfaction.

"Have you got any coffee?" Valentina asked, dumping herself into the red-painted chair closest to the battered computer housing. "Dustin and I flipped over who would come down here. I was the lucky winner." She stretched luxuriously. "Just as well. I've stood down three watches in the past thirty-six hours, and that's getting off light, considering what a few of the others are stuck with. Thanks." She accepted a disposable cup from Kroeger. "I hope you coded it extrastrength." Then, seeing his raised eyebrow, "Even Earthers get tired sometimes. Don't you?"

"What did you get?" Kroeger asked, his eyes shining with anticipation.

"Take a look. You can thank another one of Dustin's crazy hunches."

She slammed a tape into the drive and a series of numbers marched over the screen. Kroeger had seen similar series before. By their format they were stellar coordinates. But they were unfamiliar.

"Sejiedi?"

"Well, it's not Central or the Wing Moon," Valentina replied. "Assuming we got it right. Look here."

The screen blurred, then resolved itself again. Most of it was still filled with a garble of codes. But two words shone clear. What was "predictive spectroscopy?"

Hunger glittered on Kroeger's face, which looked pale,

and starvingly intent in the readout's livid gleam. Embedded somewhere in that gibberish had to be the answer he was looking for, the piece that would make the puzzle fall into place, lock, and create a unified whole.

The League had never penetrated into the three core Sejiedi worlds. Their coordinates weren't known as more than a matter of educated speculation. Just the numbers here might convince that damned desk pilot in Naval Intelligence that this venture was more useful than he had thought. Make Federico Hashrahh Kroeger resign indeed!

If this could be cracked . . . predictive spectroscopy. Was there an unstable star . . . perhaps near the Sejiedi capital worlds? He felt himself start to shake with joy.

"Finish decoding this," he ordered.

"No, sir," Valentina replied, with all military precision. "With respect, sir, I'm standing watch in half an hour. Technically Dustin is still on watch, too."

They seemed always to be on watch, Kroeger thought. He looked from Valentina to Suzannah and back again. They were tired. Then the data came back to him, teasing, shimmering at the edges of his awareness. He had to think about this, wanted time to himself to coax the data to the surface of his mind, seduce them into giving him a more complete understanding. It was this technique, above all others, that he'd learned with the Sikkahhad in all those patient, lonely years.

He regarded the two Earther women, tawny and dark, tall and tiny, but so stiff, so alike in their white uniforms. They were intruders now. He had to be alone with his beloved data.

"Dismissed," he said as he turned back to the screen. He never even heard them leave.

*   *   *

Zann stood under the hot spray that pelted from the shower nozzle at the highest pressure available. Even though it was recycled water, it felt great against her back. As usual she had hunched too long over Kroeger's workbench. Joao would chew her out if he knew. She felt sorry for Val, standing watch over the furiously paced machines in CompCenter, but not sorry enough not to be glad of the shower and the time to rest.

She soaped herself luxuriously with whatever she could reach quickest, and found herself basking in the scents of heady spices and fragrant woods. She smiled as she identified Judith's very special soap. She turned off the spray, scooped up her uniform and tossed it into the cleaning chute, then wrapped the large, soft robe Yuri had given her one year ago around her. The feel of the soft fabric pleased her. Briefly she toyed with the idea of hunting out Joao and asking him to rub her down. Then she yawned and gave up the idea. She needed sleep—just sleep—desperately. That bunk was going to feel so good!

She padded down the hall to her own quarters. The shower had almost washed her mind clear of the data clogging it. Briefly she envied computers. You could wipe their memories or power them down. Eidetics didn't have that option. They either learned self-discipline or worked themselves into exhaustion. Until the medics had figured out how to cope with them, they'd had a high burnout rate.

Sounds . . . she tried not to let them impinge on her consciousness; she didn't want more information to process just now. Still . . . that was sobbing she heard. Coming from where? Zann was tired enough to imagine anything. Nevertheless, she stood still and tracked the sound. She was sure of it now. The door to Gregory's room was shut. The weeping was coming from in there.

That was Judith's voice. Zann sighed. She had been

hoping for a peaceful night. Well, if Judith needed help
talking Gregory back into sanity . . . hell, it seemed like
all she and Joao did at night, try to talk Gregory into
seeing reason. She couldn't leave Judith to cope alone, not
if there were anything she could do.

She pushed the door aside and walked in. Gregory was
nowhere in sight. Judith, a flowing sweep of wine silk and
black hair, was curled up on his bed, her face buried in it,
sobbing.

Zann sat down on the edge of the bunk, caught Judith
by one shoulder, and turned her. "Where's Gregory?"

"How should I know?" Judith replied between hacking
breaths. "The only time I see him is when we're at meals
or on duty. At night, he's always . . . I haven't . . . and
when I decided to come here tonight, hoping he'd be
here . . ." Tears welled up in her dark eyes and she scrubbed
them away. Lowering her voice, she added, "Zann, he
hasn't touched me . . . Touched me? That's a joke. He
hasn't so much as looked at me since Maryam died."

Zann brushed Judith's hair, falling free below her waist
to beguile Gregory, back from her hot face. She could
smell the traces of the perfumed soap on Judith's shoulder
where the robe slipped away.

"Not since Maryam?" Zann asked softly, playing for
time. "And Yuri?"

"Not him either. It's as if he can't bear to look at us.
And he's with you, or Valentina, or Joao, as if we don't
exist, or we're just sibs or something. It's so lonely and
. . . and . . ."

She started weeping. Zann cradled the smaller woman
against her shoulder and rocked her. Computations flashed
through her brain. Gregory couldn't bear the company of
his own squad's pilots. Interesting: Dustin looked a lot like

Gregory, and he paid both Yuri and Judith a good deal of attention.

"Dustin?" Zann asked even more delicately.

"Charles talked to me, too," Judith said. "Everyone knows now. Dustin would turn himself inside out for a kind word, even. But Gregory can't face him because he isn't Maryam. Oh, I know what you're thinking. It's not so. Yuri and I aren't encouraging Dustin because he's a pilot and we're pilots, and we just happen to feel like a pair of burned-out reactors. Dustin is . . . Anna was right, Zann. Dustin's special people. Friendly, kind, even a little shy. And we're all so scared." Judith gulped and half-choked again.

"Let me take you back to your room, Jude," Suzannah said, helping her to rise. "You'll rest better there. You could use it. Tell me: what are you afraid of?"

"Don't you know?" Judith asked, her eyes wide. At the flight's meeting, Elizabeth's eyes had looked like that before Joao put her out, dilated, focused on horror that she couldn't turn away from.

"Yuri and I . . . Dustin too . . . we're all scared that one of these days, Gregory's going to dump so much tau that he can't get back and we can't bring him back. And, Zann, none of us wants to give him the Mercy."

CHAPTER 9

Dustin squinted at the board, his face strained and pale in its glow. "Try to use the frequency this was sent at for the constant in the equation and see what comes up," he suggested to Valentina.

Suzannah watched as her tiny squadmate's fingers played over the keyboard. Valentina punched the "Print" key for the tenth time.

"Here goes nothing . . . wait a moment! That did it, all right." She relaxed, almost purring. "But, Zann, this is just a lot of junk about food riots. Part of a city burned off. I don't know what good this can do you."

She punched the key for cipher, and sat back as it printed out. Zann walked over and picked up the printout. "Do you really want to know?"

"Not as long as we get away on leave," Valentina said.

Zann smiled at Valentina's earnestness and hefted the printout. There were times when it seemed that Military Intelligence didn't want to know either. "Good work, you two. I really mean it."

Valentina shrugged. Dustin tried to smile, but it turned into a grimace. The skin at the corner of his left eye ticced.

"You don't look good," Zann said. She remembered seeing this before.

"My usual headache," he replied. "Comes from too much close work. Besides, this board is a little hard on my eyes. Maybe we could pick up an amber shield for it," he finished lamely.

"You're just wiped out because you can't keep up," Valentina said in a brittle, bantering tone. "We were only playing until oh-two-hundred. Or were you getting a headache calculating how you're going to spend your winnings?"

Zann glanced sharply away from her printout. "How much did you lose, Val?" she asked.

The smaller woman shrugged. "Not all that much. They threw us out pretty early. Couple of Blues said we were hogging the machines, and I was too tired for a fight. So we went back to Dustin's quarters, and there I did win a few."

"Wait a minute," Dustin interrupted. "I thought *I* won."

Valentina laughed softly. "Care to lay a bet on that?"

Zann groaned, then started to hoist herself up. "I'd better get this down to Kroeger," she said and ran a finger over the seam that sealed the package against anything but her or Kroeger's thumbprint. She hesitated. Piece by piece, the information about the Sejiedi was coalescing into a pattern, something like a puzzle that needed the definition of its proper border. But she had no model, no picture to follow, and her information was so uneven! She needed more, and she knew Kroeger would demand more, too.

But as much as she needed data, she needed rest more. Not just a night's uninterrupted sleep, though the lack of that showed in every member of the squad and Dustin too. What she needed was freedom, detachment from the constant, nagging wearing-down of the squad's inner reserves, their sense of perspective. She knew with an ache so strong it was almost anger that if she could simply get clear for a day, even for a few hours, that the patterns would resolve themselves.

Facts were facts, though. She had no way to get free.

"Hey, Zann," Valentina said softly, scanning her face, "look, I can take that thing down to Kroeger. I've got to get back to CompCen anyhow."

She laughed feebly. Zann wanted to hug her, to comfort her for the unreasonable hours all of them were being forced to work. "We're going home tomorrow," she offered as compensation.

Valentina's face blazed into a dazzling smile. "I know. Oh-eight-hundred. Thank God." Years of weariness seemed to drop from her as she picked up the sealed transcript and darted out the door.

Color was returning to Dustin's face. He logged off, then launched himself from the table to flop down near where Zann sat, files of notes spread across her lap. She closed the files and smiled up at him.

"You've got a real talent for codes," she told him.

The pilot grinned. "It's just math. I like it, like the challenge. Don't tell Valentina, but I like it better than the computer games. Still, I'll be more than glad of a rest." For a moment, he turned serious. "I'm looking forward to my own leave. I really do want to thank you . . . it was kind of Judith and Val to ask me to join you. You're sure you don't mind?"

Zann offered to swat him with a folder, then let it drop into her lap again. "I figure it's the least we owe you," she laughed. "After practically flying you into the ground, working you ragged on these code groups, not to mention whatever unspeakable stuff you've been up to when you're off-duty—which hasn't been for about three weeks or so, if I'm right (and I am), well, we all owe you. And I'll be glad for the chance to get to know you better."

"I'm not sure Gregory's too happy about it," Dustin said wistfully.

Zann sighed. She wasn't going to tell him how furious Gregory had been when the idea came up. They had all been huddled together in Joao's quarters. Valentina had stretched out on the floor, and she herself had sat, at Gregory's insistence, on the bunk between him and the other pilots. She had felt strange, like a barrier, between them.

"For God's sake, does he have to live with us too?" Gregory had raged.

"Would that be so bad?" Joao had asked him. "Let's face it, the pressure's on. He likes us. He has to, or he wouldn't spend his free time with us. He certainly wouldn't volunteer for extra duty working on code for you—don't think I haven't seen the headaches it gives him. I'd like to get him under my scanners and check him out. Most of us are fond of him. What's he ever done to you, Greg, except not be Maryam?"

Gregory had snarled. For a moment it looked as if he were going to swing at the big medic, something he'd never tried, not even the time Joao had grounded him for broken ribs. He'd almost taken that one as a joke: put one over on the medic if you can. If you can't, at least you tried. But getting cleared for flight was one thing. Marrying up to strength was entirely another order of business.

Maryam's name, finally, was what silenced Gregory and earned his grudging consent.

Zann remembered that she couldn't look at Gregory. Instead, she found herself staring at Yuri, Judith, and Val. Their eyes were fixed on her and she knew that they wanted Dustin with them, that they thought that if anyone could bring Gregory around, she could.

Once it had been Maryam or Judith or Yuri who could coax him into doing what they wanted. Now Maryam was dead, and he wouldn't look at the other pilots.

She drifted back to the present, saw Dustin watching her anxiously. "Gregory will come around," she said softly and saw him nod. She shut her eyes. The data were swarming in front of her, dancing and squealing like devils that refused to be exorcised. Food riots, crop failures, predictive spectroscopy—they all clamored into one massive chant that never quite resolved into a central theme. The core Sejiedi worlds were heavily urbanized, whole planets built over into cities haunted by wolfpacks from the underclass.

Well, if they put more acreage into food crops, less into hathoti, they wouldn't have food riots that resembled minor wars. At least that kept the military busy, reduced population . . . no, she wouldn't think that. Perhaps the riots, with their wholesale slaughters and punishments, kept the urban populations stable, but she refused to think of that as a good. Even for Sejiedi. No matter what people said about Intelligence operatives, she had that much honor left.

What *did* Kroeger think he would get from all this? Again the demons began in her brain, then faded out as she yawned. All he was going to get was a ruined career. Military Intelligence openly sneered at his findings, despite Val's success at cracking codes that had baffled them for generations. *Try working on something useful for a change.* That had been the entire text of his last message from them. She herself had recommended that they try for one solid breakthrough in Military Intelligence, something they could appreciate. *You'd think I was backing him in a power grab,* she thought with weary amusement. *All I want is to go home.* For all she cared, Kroeger could become Director of Intelligence for the sector, for the entire damned League, just so long as they all left her and her family in peace.

The door hissed open, breaking into her reverie. Gregory stood just inside the wardroom. His eyes, red-veined, raked over Dustin.

"What's up?" Dustin asked.

Gregory shook his head. "Full-force meeting. Have to change into dress uniform. All of us flight leaders agreed. Let the Colors see us in scarves for a change." He laughed harshly.

"Wait a minute," Zann said. "I want to know what's going on."

"It's very, very simple," Gregory said. A hint of bitterness crept into his voice. "We were just going over the checklists on our stings, like the rotation said, when Alexei told me. Some Red leaked it to him, and he passed it on. Otherwise none of us would have known. There's a meeting of all flight leaders on this base ship in fifteen minutes, allegedly to work out work schedules. I suspect there's also going to be some formal complaints about how low we are on vital resources like reinforcements, chaff, long-range power ammunition—little amenities like that. Funny, don't you think, that Alexei didn't get any official notification. Neither did I. When I happened on Kathryn on the way back here, she hadn't been notified either. We've been passing the word. Kathryn's comming Yelena and Robert, and I told Virgil when I ran into him in the tube. So if they had the bright idea that the six flights of the Wing don't care to be represented *despite* all their intensive efforts to find us, well, they're in for a shock.''

Dustin whistled between his teeth. Zann blinked as Gregory vanished into his quarters. So they'd tried to leave the six White Wing flight leaders out of a full-force meeting. That stood to reason, the way they were trying to make reason operate. Since the Wing didn't use rank, the Colors could just say that the meeting was for, oh, say, only lieutenant commanders and above. It had happened before.

Now, when everyone was short staffed, Zann could just see the scheduling they would do. Had done before. Rage filled her.

Gregory reemerged in a uniform even more severe than his usual flightsuit. Zann got up and gave a light tug to his scarf, making it fall evenly. Then she gestured ''thumbs up'' and smiled into his eyes.

He squeezed her hand, and even managed a sharp grin at Dustin.

''Tomorrow at this time we're going to be on our way home. No matter what those bloodsuckers do, we're going home.'' Gregory rushed out again, as if galvanized by the thought of their leave.

Dustin reached over and tugged the folder Zann still held. ''Don't open . . .'' She started to warn him just as he deposited it, still closed, on the nearest table.

''You want to shred your notes yet?'' he asked.

''Not yet.''

''I think we've earned a break,'' he said. ''Especially you. I don't envy you, working all day among the Colors.''

''What about you?'' Zann asked. ''You're a solo, and you're working watch on watch—on our projects. Don't think I don't know how much of this decryption is yours. Valentina's told me how good you are. You've got a real flair for cryptography. Why'd you ever become a pilot?''

Dustin laughed easily, amber eyes crinkling warmly up at her. ''Tell me, Suzannah,'' he asked teasingly, ''when you started Basic, what was the first thing you thought of as a specialty?''

''Flying, of course.'' Every child in the Wing schools dreamed of being a pilot. As they grew older, other fields opened up, and they found out that engineers and comm officers and medics—all the other fields—did vital work too. Only a minority ever really did develop a real feel for flying, for weapons and for strategic intuition. These were the ones who went into flight training in earnest. Fewer still possessed the calm logic and almost imbecilic disregard for danger that helped them survive.

She grinned at him.

''I just never grew out of it, is all. Never grew up, maybe.''

Zann chuckled. She felt good, better than she had in days. It felt right to have him around, to relax with him here in the squad's quarters. He was a brilliant flier, fast enough to keep pace with Gregory and stable enough to advise against some of the other pilots' madder schemes. She was glad he was going home with them. Otherwise some squad might realize what a good thing they had in him and try to latch on.

''What's Gregory like to fly with?'' she asked abruptly.

Dustin's eyes widened and warmed. ''Spectacular,'' he said simply. ''I've never flown with anyone like him. He's smart, confident, and he makes you feel excited and safe at the same time.'' Admiration for the senior pilot glowed in his eyes and in his voice and he stared out into the distance.

"Why didn't you become a pilot after all, Zann?" he asked. "That was a pilot's sort of question. You've got the speed, the flair . . ."

"Flair's precisely what I haven't got, friend," Zann said. "No glamor. Don't laugh at me. All you pilots are a pretty glamorous lot. You know you are. You're romantics, all of you, down to those long white scarves you all risk your necks to win. How many more kills till you make ace, Dustin?"

"Two," he responded automatically.

"You see? You're surprised that I don't know it. You don't even have to think about it. None of you do. Except maybe Judith, and even her, with that long, long hair . . . Me, I'm just Zann. I do my work, and go on my way. I like it. And it makes me a good operative too. I fit in, as much as anyone in White Wing can. I need to, in order to work with Kroeger and all the Colors . . ."

Dustin was so easy to talk to, Zann thought in wonder. She realized she was close to pouring it all out in a way she hadn't wanted to for years. She'd learned better. Before her marriage, she'd been heartsick to realize that some people wanted her because they found her Intelligence work exotic and exciting. She didn't want that, and she had started to withdraw, might have pulled back totally as some eidetics did, if it hadn't been for Joao, first, then the others—her crazy squad where the others were the colorful ones: Yuri with his fondness for archaic, expensive objects; Gregory, whose off-duty clothing consisted of *things* (Zann refused to call them shirts) that screamed at three hundred decibels; Valentina's outrageous beauty; Judith's charm; Joao's sensuality. *"Ever wonder where Joao learned all the useful, fun things he knows?"* Maryam's wispy, laughing voice teased its way unbidden into her consciousness. *"In medical school!"*

What could she tell Dustin? That she was Intelligence because it was her best way to protect her Wing and her family, and that nothing in all the worlds was more important to her? It sounded so sickly sweet, but she thought he'd understand—maybe without her even having to say it. Dustin had no squad—yet—but his loyalty to the Wing was ferocious.

Still, because their half-lives were so brief, pilots were a gaudy, adventurous lot. Intelligence officers grew old and gray in the Service. Like Kroeger. She sighed, depressed by the idea.

"Zann?" Dustin asked. "What did I say? I want to know about what you are, not particularly what you do. Besides," he laughed, "I've done a good deal of it myself these past months. Enough classified stuff!"

"Why do you want to know?"

"Would you believe I'm curious about you?"

"I'd believe you had plenty of practice with that line." Her defense was automatic.

"No fair, Zann," Dustin said softly. "I wouldn't take leave with the squad if I were just practicing. I've never spent more than one night in any family's house." Dustin drew closer to her and pulled her against his shoulder. "You're tired. I can feel it in you." He began to rub her neck gently. "Feel good?" he murmured into her hair.

"I'm going to call you 'Joao,' " she said wryly and leaned against him, warming under his hands. What had Judith said—that Dustin had quite a reputation for loving and leaving them? Somehow she couldn't see him that way. His touch was practiced, surely, but very gentle, new to her. Lately Gregory had been fiercely passionate and he had been taking up a lot of her nights . . . well, when they had nights. A smile crossed her face briefly. Dustin seemed tender, almost shy.

"Why didn't you marry Anna's squad?" she asked. "They're good."

"Yes, they're good," Dustin agreed. His hands moved down her back and probed at the knot between her shoulder blades. She purred and shifted to let him have more room to work on her. "But they didn't feel quite right. I never thought they really wanted me for me, just as John's replacement. From some of the things they said, I reminded them of him. And, once or twice, well . . ."

"Yes?" Zann asked, cautious at the hesitancy of his words.

"Nothing. It's nothing, Zann. One morning, it was very early. A few of us weren't really up yet. Charles called me 'John.' That's when I left."

"They should have known better," Zann said softly. "It makes good sense for a squad to replace a man with a woman and vice versa. The reason for that custom's obvious. They shouldn't have tried."

"It's not important. Especially not now. They didn't mean anything by it. Maybe I'd have done the same," Dustin said. "But now, well, I don't know, I'm hoping this time . . . I feel at home with your squad, Zann. Maybe one day even Gregory will come around and— would you like it?"

Abruptly Zann's thoughts crystallized. She liked this man with the charm of a practiced flirt, but whose voice rang with sincerity and an undercurrent of loneliness. He was one of those dashing hell-raisers that everyone in the Wing admired, but that voice made him vulnerable, open to her. She moved against his shoulder and raised one hand to stroke his cheek.

"Suzannah?" He brushed a kiss into her palm, then turned her face toward his with gentle fingers. They kissed, and she smiled against his mouth.

Much later she was still smiling as he murmured her name against her throat. "What is it?" she asked drowsily.

"I want you to know. You may not be glamorous, but you're one wonderful woman. And *I* think you're beautiful."

"Get Joao to check out your vision, flier." Zann laughed to take the sting out of her words. She hugged him and drifted peacefully into sleep.

"We know what you're doing in there!" Yuri's voice called out just beyond the door.

Dustin woke, startled, and moved away from Zann in a half-crouch, protectively putting his body between her and the door.

"Let's ignore him, and he'll go away," Zann whispered. "Or just lie here like good little spooks and eavesdrop." He stroked her and she started to pull him down against her again.

"Don't tell me you've forgotten that we're going home in two and a half hours?" Yuri asked.

"Home!" Zann rose, tugged on a robe and hurried into the wardroom, Dustin trailing behind her. Yuri was already dressed, or perhaps he'd never been to bed at all. He had cups of coffee steaming on the table, the smell and steam rising to wake her fully.

"You want to know the best part of it?" Judith greeted them. "I checked as soon as I woke up, and our transport's ready. Of course, it would have to be that Blue TreMorion on duty, but I don't care. Guess what we've got! Luxury of luxuries, a private shuttle, no passengers except the seven of us, and a straight shot home!"

"I wonder what we did right to rate private transport," Joao asked mildly. His hair was still glistening wet.

"Who knows, you pirate," Yuri asked. "Who cares? At this point, I wouldn't care if they sent us cargo."

The computer beeped irritably, and Valentina groaned.

"Now what's it want?" she asked no one in particular, then went to the board. Her face turned a dull gray.

"What's up, Val?" Joao asked, impatient.

Valentina shook her head as if trying to shake clear of a bad dream. A single tear slid down her cheek.

"Hey, baby," Joao whispered as she buried her face against his chest.

"Oh, *shit*!" Judith, who only cursed when she was furious, hissed.

Gregory crossed the narrow room in four long strides and read the message off in a cold voice. " 'Leave canceled until further notice by order of Intelligence Chief Federico Hashrahh Kroeger. Cipher follows immediately.' That bastard!" Gregory slammed his fist against the steel housing of the machine, which blinked once, then returned to normal. "Can he do that, Zann? Tell him he can't do this to us!"

Zann looked down, not wanting to say anything. Gregory knew perfectly well that Kroeger could keep them here as long as he wanted. But the rage in the senior pilot's face scared her. Then the Wing mask dropped into place, sealing the fury off from his squad, and that scared her even more.

When he spoke again, his voice was calm and steady. His hands rested motionless on the board, as if it were the control panel of his sting. "Well, then. Dustin, Val, get to work on this thing fast. I suppose the next squad on rotation's been contacted already. Very well. Joao, Judith,

Yuri, get some sleep. At least we don't have any duty assignments set yet. I'm getting hold of Wing Command. Throw Kroeger his bone and cross your fingers, all of you. Maybe we can override this thing.''

"I'm sorry," Zann said in a small voice. She didn't want Gregory to kill Kroeger. She wanted to do it herself. She watched dully as Valentina and Dustin took their accustomed places.

"Lousy damned codes," Valentina muttered. "Just when we're ready to go home, Kroeger has to land us with this new junk. Military transmissions, no less, and he just has to have this new one right away. Where's he intercepting these from, his head?"

"Come on, Val," Dustin said wearily. "You going to bitch, or you going to work? The sooner we get this stuff transcribed, the sooner we can get out of here."

"Working and bitching are not mutually exclusive," Valentina informed him haughtily. They began to work intently.

Feeling guilty, Zann showered and dressed quickly. Gregory would still be trying to raise hell and Wing Command simultaneously, and she wished him luck on both counts. But she knew, they all knew, that there were simply times when they couldn't be spared.

Kroeger again. Couldn't he understand that people needed rest to work efficiently? Or did he even care? When she returned to the wardroom, Val and Dustin were as she'd left them, swearing softly from time to time. Yuri was pacing up and down the length of the room and finishing off everyone's coffee. Judith and Joao were playing a game of chess in which rooks tried to commit suicide, but the bishops and queens weren't paying attention.

A soft chime made everyone jump.

"I don't need any more news today," Joao groused.

Zann shrugged and activated the door. What else could she do? In stepped Guy and Amelia, perfect in their white uniforms. As soon as they dropped the requisite Wing expressions, their faces struggled with joy and pity.

"We . . . we wanted to tell you that, really, we're sorry that your leave got canceled out from under you."

Zann grimaced. "Blind luck," she said. She felt awkward saying much to these two. For twenty years they'd been part of a good fighting squad. Soon they would retire to the Wing Moon.

"You've got a trainee now, haven't you?" Amelia went on. "I think I know her, from the same year as our Jim. Listen, we'll have her over to dinner."

"Thanks," Zann said. "Tell her we miss her." She felt like crying. *Their Jim.* She remembered Pam's telling them that Jim was their real child, born—not assigned—to them; she wondered what Anna's baby looked like. She'd hoped to see it on this trip. "Have a great time."

"Look." Guy said. "We, well, we'll try to make it up to you somehow."

"It's not you, it's Command," Val interrupted from the computer. "Nothing to make up."

Guy and Amelia left soon after, and Zann didn't blame them. They would want to join the rest of their squad, and they had barely an hour before the transport was scheduled for takeoff. And they were uncomfortable.

"Thanks, Val," Zann said.

"What for? I've finally learned to be circumspect, thank you very much."

Gregory stalked back into the wardroom. No need to ask him how his talk with Command had gone.

"Try substituting this code group here, why don't you?"

Dustin suggested. "See, it repeats. Let's get a readout. Ag
. . . Ag . . . Aglo?"

"Give that to me!" Zann ordered. Dustin leaned over
hcr shoulder. Seconds later they both turned so pale that
Joao reached involuntarily for his mediket. Dustin winced,
then straightened.

"When did you say this transmission was intercepted?"
he demanded.

"Oh-four-hundred hours. No!" Zann had started adding
up the clues. "That ship . . . oh, it works. It works all
right. The thefts from Ordnance . . . there was a detonator
too . . . and now this! *Aglo*. We've got to get to the flight
deck right now. Maybe they haven't boarded yet. That
ship's a flying bomb!"

The words erupted from Zann without conscious thought
and then she was flying out the door, Gregory and Yuri at
her heels.

"I'll raise Kroeger," Valentina called after them. "Can't
run as fast as the rest of you."

They ran. It seemed like forever to the tube, years until
they got access, an agony before they managed to get to
the flight deck. Blue Squad controlled flight operations
today, but Zann didn't give one single damn if all the
Colors saw them arrive sweaty, panting, and undignified
on the deck. What did that matter, compared with the life
of an entire squad? There was no trace of Guy or Amelia
or the rest of them, no chance that they'd be late. The
chrono read 7:52.

A tall Blue in an ace's scarf, weaponsmaster rating and
rank glittering on his collar, materialized from behind
master controls. Zann read disdain on the pale face. She
knew it well: Haral TreMorion, the pilot who had saved
Dustin, one of the weaponsmasters whose dossiers she and
Kroeger had scrutinized.

He flicked a sharp glance at Dustin as if hoping for the chance to snub him again. Dustin looked away. Gregory strode up to the Blue ace and began arguing in a low, controlled voice.

Blues practically breathed by the book, Zann thought. Gregory's persuasiveness would be wasted. Their only hope was for Valentina to get through to Kroeger. He could declare an emergency, get the flight halted, or make the ship's captain halt it.

Ahead of them, the transport shuttle turned, rotated on the airlock's movable disk. Doors clashed shut behind it.

"PREPARE FOR TAKEOFF . . ."

"I'm telling you, we have strong evidence . . ." Gregory's words were interrupted by Zann's: "That ship's sabotaged. We just intercepted a transmission. Classified. I've notified Intelligence. My chief will send authorization. If you won't abort takeoff, put the launch sequence on temporary hold—"

"AIRLOCK DEPRESSURIZING . . ."

"What's going on?" Kroeger demanded as he erupted onto the deck. "When Valentina contacted me, I came as quickly as I could. You say those latest signals mean . . ."

"They mean we've figured out why there have been thefts from Ordnance, sir. Please halt the takeoff before I report!"

Kroeger turned to TreMorion. "I'm Federico Hashrahh Kroeger, Deputy Director of Intelligence in this sector. Abort launch on my authority."

"Sorry, sir, I'll need more confirmation than that. Besides, the sequence from now until lift-off is automatic."

Zann caught the glint of a smile in his eyes. She could practically hear him thinking aloud, wondering why he should even bother listening to a civ spook, let alone take his orders.

Zann stepped up to the big board and tapped rapidly on the keys. The gray screens sprang to life, pictures from outside so vivid that it was hard to realize that these weren't viewports. "You're going to watch what you've just done," she said, her voice quiet and deadly.

Gregory reached for the comm. "Senior Pilot Gregory of White Wing to transport. Do you copy?"

"Affirmative."

"Transport, we have reason to believe that there's been some . . . tampering on board."

Incongruous laughter filtered briefly over the comm, then was suppressed. "You really do want to go home on leave, don't you, Gregory?"

"Gregory to transport. *This is no joke*. Scan your systems. I suggest you start with the main drive."

"Report. Negative."

"It wouldn't show up in the automatic launch sequence." Valentina slid onto the flight deck and spoke up at Gregory's elbow. "Check main operating system."

"Testing now."

Seven people, Zann thought, functioning as a superbly integrated whole, could run checks on the drive, on life support, on the entire vessel, and still have time to report back calmly before takeoff.

Kroeger turned to the Blue Winger again. "I'm going to pass the word for the Captain to come down here," he declared. "I can claim emergency override, and I will, unless you bring that ship back in."

"Sir, if that ship's sabotaged, I may not bring it in. My standing orders prohibit endangering the integrity of the base ship." TreMorion seemed almost pleased to defy Kroeger by quoting his sacred regulations.

"Transport, this is Gregory. What have you turned up?"

"We found it, all right. Small fusion bomb, tied into the main drive. The minute we accelerate, the bomb goes off. Tidy."

"Can you deactivate it?" Gregory asked, his voice as smooth as when he had given Maryam the Mercy.

"Our engineer's on it right now. I'll patch you through."

Zann glanced over at Kroeger, now calling the Bridge. Haral TreMorion stood nearby, surrounded by several subordinates who tensed, as if awaiting a fight. Zann eyed him critically. He was an outsider, but he had helped them out once. She hated asking, but there was an entire squad at stake. "Can you help them deactivate it?" she asked.

"Now you want to know, White Winger? I can try." He shouldered Gregory aside roughly and demanded specifications, details of the sabotage. Then he turned away. "The bomb's tied into the main drive, true enough. Keyed into the acceleration sequence. But if the drive isn't activated within a given period, the timer's keyed to blow life support."

"Transport," Gregory said huskily, "if you can't get that thing deactivated before the drive cuts in, suit up and abandon ship." He gestured to Dustin, Yuri, and Judith, who watched him closely. "The pilots of my squad—correction, the pilots of my flight—will pick you up."

"Negative, Gregory, negative. We can't halt the automatic cut-in. Even if we abandon ship, the buffeting would take us out . . . and you with us. Seven is enough to lose on this piece of work."

Refusing assistance was almost as bad as the Mercy, Suzannah thought. And yet the squad was together. None of them would be left, widowed and grieving. It would be a quick death—but such a waste that it would dishonor the whole Wing unless they found their killers and avenged them.

Chillingly, data fell into place for Zann. The postpone-
ment had come so fast that there had barely been time to
notify the next squad on rotation. The transport had been
private. Then she knew: her squad had been set up to be
vaporized.

She didn't want to face it. Somewhere between her
stomach and the marrow of her bones, Zann knew that she
was responsible for this. Blame it on her Intelligence
work, or on the coding she had roped Val and Dustin into:
they'd become targets . . . unless this was some Sejiedi
logic she didn't know how to follow yet.

"At least let's *try*," she heard Dustin pleading with
Gregory in an undertone.

"There isn't anything to try," Gregory admitted. He
reached out to clasp Dustin's shoulder, his hand rock-
steady. "You heard."

"He could be wrong."

"That Blue. Hardly. He's too damned good to be wrong
about this. Judith! Try to talk some sense into your friend
here, will you?" Gregory turned away and walked over to
Joao.

The senior pilot regarded the medic for a moment. "Get
Wing Command. We're offering to take responsibility for
that squad's children and trainees."

"They have sibs who may dispute that."

"I said we're offering. That . . ." Gregory bit off the
rest of the sentence, but it didn't take an eidetic's mind to
know what was in his thoughts. *That could have been us.
That should have been us.*

"You can't blame yourself for this."

"I don't. But I'm going to have someone to hang it on,
if I have to tie Kroeger to a computer. At least he'll be
good for something, do something for us for a change."

Zann walked over to the comms where the Blue was still working with the doomed transport. Finally he stood away. "It's useless. Drive-activation sequence cuts in in two minutes. It'll take at least an hour to remove that device."

The man showed no human warmth. In fact, he acted as much like what people said White Wingers were as anyone not actually wearing their uniform. Zann thought of seven vibrant, happy people suddenly learning that their lives were to be snuffed out by chance and malice. She wanted to get on that comm, or get Joao—with his wisdom and compassion—on it, and offer them some comfort, some promise. She knew she could not. The Colors were listening. Besides, what promise could she make? That their children would be cared for? That they would be avenged? They knew that already.

Zann hadn't known Guy, Amelia, or any of that squad particularly well, but she wanted revenge for them so badly she shook. Fury, primitive and blazing, rose in her. She wanted to catch that saboteur and see him addicted to hathoti, then taken off it suddenly. She'd watch his convulsions and laugh.

Distantly, she saw Dustin walk up to Joao. "I heard you offering to take on the squad's family obligations. Let me help. It's the least we can do."

"We?" Gregory asked from behind.

"Yes, dammit, we. If you'll let me."

The sabotaged transport looked fine.

It maintained perfect attitude; its vanes were extending for drive cut-in, and as always with the fast, sleek vessel, it seemed poised to spring into action. Perfect . . . and perfectly fatal.

"I wish we'd deciphered that transmission just a few minutes earlier," Valentina muttered.

"We've got it now." Zann was surprised at the hunger for revenge in Kroeger's voice, too. "I'm going to find out who set that ship up and you're going . . ."

"THIRTY SECONDS . . ."

Zann slapped a hand on the comm, shutting off the recorded countdown. It was macabre enough to watch the ship tense toward the acceleration that would blast it out of space without having a computer voice wrenching at everyone's nerves. The Blue Wingers turned aside and headed for the flight log. They had a report to file.

The comm crackled once. "Thanks for trying," Zann heard. "You did your best. Transport out."

In the huge overhead screen the ship appeared to pause, to waver, then to leap into full speed . . .

. . . an enormous, soundless fireball filled the screen, exploding, seething then expanding outward in a blaze of violent blue, white, and orange light . . .

Zann glanced away in time from the silent fury and threw out a hand to secure herself against the nutrino buffeting that followed.

After it died, she looked about. The others were staring into the nothingness on the screen, their faces blank, feral with hunger. Kroeger, one hand across his eyes, sprawled on the deck, and Zann reached over to pull him to his feet, to tug him into a corner where it was safely dark.

"Joao will have drops for your eyes," she said. "You caught the fireball, but the screens are filtered; you won't lose your sight."

"Stupidity," he muttered, but didn't withdraw his hand from hers.

"Joao!" Zann called. "Can you get Kroeger back to his quarters?"

"I don't need to lie down. I've got work to do."

"So do I," Joao murmured. "That squad's flight medic was on board. Someone's got to break the news . . ."

"Your face is wet," Kroeger said, daring to test his sight.

"It's the fireball," Joao told him glibly. "You won't be seeing straight for a couple hours."

"Captain on deck," Zann warned everyone, alerted by a glimmer of braid emerging from the tube.

They turned to confront him and saluted. Zann was pleased to observe that there was hunger in the Captain's eyes too, hunger that wouldn't be sated by anything less than a full investigation and complete disclosure.

CHAPTER 10

By the time the base ship achieved orbit around Corvynem, Bikmat knew two things for certain. The hunger was on him, forcing him in to report. This time, he was too tired to fight it off. Fortunately it seemed like everyone else was tired too. League security was never lax, least of all on board a base ship, especially after an "accident" like the one which had taken out that White Wing transport. But for someone trained as exhaustively and as ruthlessly as he had been, getting onworld wasn't a matter of detection, but of logistics.

It had amused him to acquire the coverall of a low-rank Blue. Even though a Sejiedi operative should consider all Leaguers equally as enemies and sources of information, Bikmat especially disliked the Blues who aped Sejiedi ways and were arrogant enough to think they had invented them. But it was just as well. No one would look at a junior Blue tech, barely a step up from mechanic. The coverall's attached hood would help him leave the ship unnoticed, just one of a number of enlisted people taking advantage of a day's pass down to Corvynem to smell real air and walk in real gravity for a change.

Bikmat shut his eyes, waiting for the hypnotic cues that had guided him the last time, eight months back, he had been commanded to report. Something at the back of his skull squirmed and protested. Pain squeezed his temples, and he flinched, almost reeling against the woman seated next to him in the transport.

"They make you stand watch on watch?" she asked. "Well, that's what we're here for, anyway. Won't it be wonderful to have reinforcements? And stand regular watches, have regular duty rotations once again? I could kiss that whole Base downworld."

He muttered something and bit his lip, turning to the port. He couldn't stand her chatter, breaking in and disorienting him. He watched her reflection as she shrugged at her silent seatmate and absorbed herself in the tapes she carried. Then the hunger came on again, stronger, beating aside the pain and feeble resistance.

Bikmat remembered the hunger. Beating waves of hunger brought back the memories, and made him too weak to push them aside.

He was four. They were always hungry, his mother and his brothers and sister and himself. He couldn't remember a time when they weren't. But then it got worse. He remembered their street in the arcology on Nahi II, the hard-packed dirt just outside the complex where nothing ever grew, where the children laughed and taunted and called him names.

"Changeling, changeling," they sang around him. He knew he looked different from his mother and the rest of his family, but he couldn't say quite how. He was small, but he was only four. He wondered if "changeling" meant someone who was supposed to be dumped outside the walls to starve to death, or someone locked out of the complex at night. That was when the hungries came out, the older boys and girls with their shaved heads and tattooed shoulders and long, glittering knives. It was a game far more deadly than the pack wars in the arenas. Bikmat had seen the skeleton of one of the people that the hungries had found. His brother said that he ought to be food for the hungries, but his mother said he was too little and not fat enough.

It had made Bikmat afraid of the night, of the hoots and cries and occasional screams he could hear through the shoddy walls of the complex, the hungries out hunting with their long knives like the ones that workers used to cut hathoti with.

The street was always gray. But one evening it turned red, with beautiful soft red and orange clouds floating through the alleys of the complex. He had cried out in wonder, and his mother had come and hugged him. He could feel her shaking as they watched. Outside, as the red clouds touched them, people wriggled and fell down. Bikmat asked what would happen to those people, but he already knew the answer. The hungries would get them. He was scared, but his mother made him watch anyway. But he didn't cry. He might be only four, but he knew that Sejiedi never cried.

Then his mother started packing their things into great kerchiefs and trying to contact her man, drafted for the Guard, before they had to flee. A little later Bikmat's family was among the survivors as their block too was sealed and gassed. He knew that the hungries would come in after them.

He remembered the refugee camp and how they had all had to report to the tall, well-fed officers at the camp's

crude school. One by one, children and their parents registered, produced their identification. Then it was their turn.
No problem with his brothers and sister. Then the tall
officer pointed at him. "That one. That's the one we
want." The officers took him away, and fed him. At
first that was enough. But he never saw his mother again.
Gradually he learned to hope she was relieved at having
one less to feed. She hadn't cried when they took him
away from her.

"We could have let you starve. We saved you from the
hungries." Night after night the hypnoreels droned it into
him. Bikmat knew that was true. He would have been
grateful if anyone had just smiled at him. At least no one
called him a changeling anymore.

Later he began to learn more. He learned the languages
of the League in which he would work, even the language
of the Earther refugees that the warrior-born seemed to
hate with an especial poison. He learned how to kill, with
weapons or whatever he could improvise from wire or pipe
or garbage heap. He learned math, codes, gymnastics, the
sociology of the League cultures. And every night the
hypnoreels sang through his brain.

He learned that he was being trained for Intelligence, to
seem to serve the League, to fight the Sejiedi in battle, to
blend into the fighting Wings that didn't have proper
warrior-borns. But he would wait. One day orders would
come and it would be time to use the skills they were
giving him. They often said that the waiting was the
hardest part.

Finally he learned he wasn't Sej at all. No wonder the
other children had called him a changeling. He was older
now, and he knew what the word meant. The woman he
had called mother hadn't been his mother. She'd simply
been paid to raise him until he was old enough to train, if

he proved he was worth it by having the will to survive in the pits of Nahi II and keep free of the hungries. They only wanted the ones with the will to survive . . .

There were three of them then: Bikmat, Idris, and Aramin. It was their field-survival exercises, their last test before assignment. He was glad to be with them. Aramin was smart and Idris, at least, was a friend.

Bikmat could smell the hathoti growing in ordered hectares in the valley below. He was only glad he couldn't smell the sweat of the gangs working there. He'd been drafted for punishment detail only once or twice. Not even Aramin could match that record. Now they were all hungry, and their food had run out. Still, they had to make it back to camp across terrain their instructors had designated as hostile. Rumor had it that the volcanic ridges were mined and that there would be fliers out, with lasers to fry anyone stupid enough to travel in the open.

As they hiked across the rough, lightless night, Idris stumbled into a tangle of wire. Bikmat thought he had probably broken an ankle. Aramin said it didn't matter, to keep on walking. But the pain and hunger drove Idris a little crazy, and he gobbled all the potent, crude hathoti tincture meant as a painkiller. By midnight he writhed in convulsions, froth and animal noises bubbling from his lips.

"Can't you shut him up and stop that thrashing?" Aramin hissed. "If they hear him . . ."

Bikmat tried to tie him down, and was almost bitten. He hadn't realized that Idris was that strong.

"I can't," he whispered. "What if he bites me? I need two good hands."

"Then we leave him. We have to. Come on! Or do you want them to catch us?"

"But he'll die!" Bikmat protested. He was four again, watching the hungries gorge after the red clouds had passed.

"He ate the hathoti 'cause he couldn't stand the pain. He was weak. If that's all he valued his life, then why should we value it? Come *on*, Bikmat." Aramin already had her pack on and was heading down the slope.

He'd had only two charges left in his sidearm, and he used one of them on Idris. He was eleven.

The next year, when he was twelve, he was out of training among the Sejiedi, already a full-fledged operative for them, training for a career in the League. Before he left, the hypnoreels had run at triple intensity for weeks. His instructors had reminded him, "In all the years we've been routing the League animals, not one operative has ever failed us. Many have died—honor to their names— but not one has betrayed us."

His instructors knew he'd find temptation. And he found it. He liked the people in whose schools the Sejiedi had planted him. They thought Sej, with that fierce loyalty to their kind and their families that separated Sej from animals. They were worthy of honor—and they were also kind.

At first just the simple fact of liking them had brought on severe headaches, but they held him, comforted him even when he vomited up precious food. They brought him to medics to be cared for. After a time, he learned to control his headaches.

Then the hunger started. When he could no longer fight it off, he had to come in and report. Since he was twelve, he had done it many times, and he cursed the memory of each one of them, cursed the Sej for making him two people at war within himself. One day the fighting inside him would go wild, and people would get hurt. So he tried to keep aloof, but he was so hungry for more than food . . .

"Wake up, fellow." The woman prodded him. For a moment Bikmat thought Aramin had come back to goad him into action. What had happened to her anyhow? "We're landing."

Bikmat smiled carefully at her, then hurried away from the shuttle. Corvynem. He checked his wristcomp. Time to make the contact he knew was waiting for him. Following both the maps blazoned across blank walls and the hunger-guide within him, Bikmat made for the Old Town, farthest from the League Base and the landing slicks. A light drizzle was falling, alien and alarming to a man used to the no-weather of the vast base ships. Overhead the town's shields flickered violet as the rain touched them. Occasionally they crackled into brilliant blue as something alive—a flight of bugs or some other creatures—blundered into them. Corvynem was marshy, dank. Half its original population had died of fever, and the survivors still took precautions against its carriers. By now they were probably immune, but they had that base quartered here, too big a prize in revenues and taxes to risk losing it to bugs.

Corvynem. Pain twisted in his skull again. Did he really want to remember where the contact point was? For an endless moment the Sejiedi Bikmat fought with the other part of himself, the man whose loyalty and training tied him to League service. Then the hunger throbbed again, and he knew that the walkby point was down this street, where the shops were cramped and their goods were shoddy. He walked into one of them, made a small purchase for cash, not credit—his cards would betray his League identity and he was still too useful to discard—and said a few words to the woman at the counter.

Slipped into the package was a capsule. He darted into an alley, flicked the capsule open, and found the street coordinates he needed to report to. Carefully he sealed the capsule into his coverall's breast pouch.

Glancing at the gleaming street map, Bikmat traced the coordinates. If anyone were watching him (and someone who would file a report later probably was) all he would see was a slender man in a coverall dark with rain, a man in too much of a hurry to activate the map's "Find" display. Walking no faster than such a man might be expected to walk, Bikmat headed to a more populous area, but not a more prosperous one. Here the struggling streets of second- and third-class businesses were not strictly licensed. Or strictly legal.

Or even—as Bikmat knew for a fact—completely under the control of the League. He knew now whom he was going to meet, not by name but by code. His contact was an illegal, a Sejiedi with forged papers who actually ran his operation with the money he made working some sort of small business—in this case, a computer-repair service. Bikmat permitted himself a nod of professional approval. No one would question the proprietor of such a place if he acquired slightly unusual equipment. It would be expected, even approved of.

He paused outside the store to read the newscreen carefully maintained as a public service. He clicked his tongue in exasperation at the way the war news was slanted. Information content: about nil. Semantic content: revoltingly cheerful. Local news. Editorial comments by representatives not just of the press, but by multiplanetary executives lobbying to raise appropriations, or cut them, or whatever it was at the moment.

The hunger swept over him and turned him giddy. Before he could stagger, leaving himself open to arrest for what looked like drunkenness, he turned and went inside.

Most of the boards displayed were old models, of little

interest to him except as he needed to pretend. He strolled from one to another, occasionally tapping out a word to see it glow on the screen. Finally he reached the board he knew he would find. Once again he tapped out what looked like a word. In actuality the character string registered his presence and identification to the Sejiedi who would take his report.

"May I help you, sir?"

Bikmat turned around rapidly, but not so rapidly that he would appear threatened—or actually give a threat to the operative he expected to face.

Only careful training kept the surprise from showing on Bikmat's face. Sejiedi residents were chosen from official-level families, the warrior-born. Only the wiliest, the toughest, and the most security-clear got these dangerous assignments. But this man didn't look Sej at all. He looked fat and soft. The hawklike features Bikmat had expected had blurred into a countenance that nearly left him gaping. The man's nose was bent, his cheeks weathered with a faint tracing of tiny blood vessels broken by exposure to Corvynem's weather. At first the eyes appeared half-shut and bleary, but the expression in them caught and held his attention. Bikmat would have been willing to bet that beneath the rolls of fat bulking out the man's cheap jumpsuit-and-jacket combination there was strength.

"I'm interested in configuring a keyboard like this to a late-model memory," Bikmat said.

"You've got the memory system?"

"Let's say I'm looking for more storage, or I'll have to dump records."

The man gestured him toward a back room. Bikmat noticed the door was keyed not only by a palm lock, but by a beam of light that checked the proprietor's retinal patterns. He raised one eyebrow at the precaution. "We've had robberies in this neighborhood,'' the man said. For a Sejiedi, that was positively garrulous. As he realized it, he glared at Bikmat, angry at his self-revelation, even angrier at Bikmat for his slenderness, his height, and the taut strength of his carriage, despite the hunger that drained the strength from him. As the illegal had to know, he was no true Sejiedi, but he looked more like one than this specimen of the warrior-born who had had to call him "sir."

He sank into a padded chair and waited slightly too long before waving Bikmat into a metal one Bikmat was glad enough to take.

"Quite a while since your last report, isn't it?'' he remarked.

"Eight months, sir,'' Bikmat responded crisply. Just give the Sej the facts, any facts he could scramble together without betraying the people who had been kind to him, people who seemed more his own kind than those who had gassed the only home he had ever known, then robbed him of the right to call it that. Just give them as little as possible. Only Bikmat knew that one day it would come. They would assign him and he would flare up, like the others they had trained.

Human time bombs, wired, and carefully welded into place . . . that's what the foreign operatives were to the Sej. Bikmat knew that come assignment time he would be completely expendable.

The Sejiedi leaned back. One hand made minuscule adjustments to the chair arm, and Bikmat assumed he was not only under observation, but under a potential weapon. No Sejiedi would ever trust one of the moles, despite whatever Training said about their inability to switch sides. After all, a man who would betray his second loyalty might try to betray the first, especially since the second was also his own genetic heritage.

He knew the man thought he was despicable, just as any warrior-born thought that other Sej were beneath notice, and that non-Sej were beneath contempt. And the moles like him were the most despicable of the lot, not worthy of any honor no matter how well they performed, traitors to their own, born and trained to be traitors.

"Pay attention, Bikmat," the Sejiedi snapped, slamming his hand flat on the desk. "If you think you've done well, let me tell you, you're wrong. What have you got for me?"

Bikmat pulled out the message capsule. Safer to dispose of it here than anywhere else. From within the stolen blue coverall, he pulled a disk loaded with daily reports of his Wing. None of it was anyone else's business, but except for that, it was innocuous. The man gestured.

"On the table."

Carefully, so he wouldn't think Bikmat was going to jump him, he tossed the disk down.

"Is there anything else in addition?"

Bikmat tried to say no, to refuse, but the hypnoreels had droned their way into his mind for too long, too deeply. Shaking inwardly, he found himself nodding curtly.

The Sej regarded him closely and took from a cabinet what Bikmat knew was a state-of-the-art recorder. It didn't just input information; it monitored the identity and, some claimed, the veracity of the speaker. Optical scan and life-support readings were recorded as well as speech. Bikmat leaned forward to stare into the screen. Before the light flashed into his eyes, he could see himself. His face was a little paler than usual below the fine, light hair, now a little tousled from the coverall's sodden hood. His amber eyes were a little reddened. He looked unfamiliar, alien to himself in blue. Ever since he was twelve and the

Sejiedi had slipped him into the Wing schools, his uniforms had all been white.

"Pilot Dustin," said the Sejiedi. The Earther name sounded vile and trivial coming from him, and Bikmat/ Dustin had the urge to slap it from his mouth. Earned and chosen, it was the only thing he had that was truly his, except for the kills that went with it.

"I wouldn't try it, Dustin. Or you'll wish that Wing of yours vaped you along with your parents. Believe me. So tell me about Kroeger and the codes."

He knew when he was being humiliated. And he knew about his family. The Sejiedi had made it very clear to him when he was still young. They had been in a life-support craft, fleeing from a system the Sej were annexing. Someone had managed to jettison him before the White Wing attacked the fleeing vessel that was just about to fall into the Sej's hands. He remembered. *"Earther, we saved you."*

And what if they were lying to him?

It was like the Mercy, wasn't it? He had seen the slaves working the hathoti fields, some mind-dead. The Wing had done right, he knew. And then he didn't know, not really. Bitterness filled him, as it did all the times he'd had to report. It might have been better for him if the Wing had blasted him too. Facing the fat Sej, he wished for that with all his heart. There was the squad—his, if only they'd have him—still grieving because Maryam had received the Mercy.

For the first time he wondered if the fliers who fired on civilians had felt grief.

He was glad to see that his face, reflected in the screen, was almost impassive. A tiny muscle jerked at the corner of his right eye. He recognized the sign. Within half an hour, he was going to have a ferocious headache.

"Look into the screen," the heavy man ordered him. Dustin looked.

"Now, tell me what they've got on the codes."

Dustin was glad to be able to answer with the full truth. "Cracked a word or two. Kroeger says that breaking MI primes depends on luck as much as anything else. And I don't think he's an especially lucky man."

"What about his staff?"

"Suzannah's no cryptologist. Valentina works with her, but mostly on other projects, technical material, not military. They've had some success there." The headache intensified, combining nauseatingly with the hunger. *He didn't ask about me. I haven't betrayed anything important. Nothing Kroeger doesn't suspect they already know. And he hasn't asked about my part in it. I don't have to answer what I haven't been asked.*

"A question, Pilot. Why haven't you joined this squad? You're very close to it, so very close . . . you needn't look bland, Pilot; we've known for years what the Wing squads are to themselves. You are supposed to get as close to the center of power as you can, and the squads are the center of your Wing. Besides, this Gregory of yours is very interesting to us."

The truth blazed in Dustin's head: *because they haven't asked me. I'm scared of hurting them if they do, and even more scared that they won't.* Dustin forced their faces out of his memory. He had them with him, all of them, wrapped in his luck, the much-worn handkerchief that Joao had used to bandage his hand at the Blue Angel. Ever since, he'd flown with it tucked into his flightsuit.

He forced ice and reason into his next words. "If . . . my squad is so valuable to you, why did you try to destroy it? We were scheduled for that transport that blew."

The Sej held up a hand. "One way or another, your squad makes a difference. That was one way."

Dustin suppressed a shiver. He supposed it made sense: expend one operative to take out six. What was it that the people on board the doomed shuttle had said? *Seven is enough to lose on this piece of work.*

"You should be very glad. There is a mission for you. Your assignment has been made."

Every muscle in Bikmat/Dustin's body tensed. It was the time he had dreaded. Now they would ask him to do more than feed them with useless reports, things he could hide behind. It took an act of will to keep from screaming, raging, launching himself across the desk and squeezing the fat man's neck until the blood came out of his eyes, just as they had taught him in Training so very long ago.

"Your assignment," said the Sejiedi, revealing no awareness of the change in Dustin's mood, "is to get into that squad. Your target is its senior pilot. He isn't to be killed. Those people don't need another martyred hero. Instead, in any way possible, you are to discredit him."

Dustin almost risked closing his eyes against the recorder's probe. Gregory. To be aimed against Gregory, when all he wanted. . . .

"We would like to eliminate the White Wing as a threat," the Sejiedi continued. "As far as the League is concerned, Gregory is already under somewhat of a cloud for giving his squadmate the Mercy. Don't be surprised we know the term; we're not fools. It has been decided that he should survive and rise to the position of which others generally feel him capable. Which means that by the time he is in any position of real authority as far as the inner command of the Wing goes, he will be so unpalatable to the League that the very fact of his existence will motivate it to cut all appropriations for the Wing. Perhaps even your

Moon will be appropriated for another, more reliable group. In any case, we eliminate the White Wing as a fighting unit.''

Of course. Dustin understood perfectly. In Sejiedi terms, Gregory's honor was perfect. That was part of what had drawn Dustin to him in the first place. There were times when he wasn't sure if the Wing thought Sejiedi or the Sejiedi thought Wing. Pilot and operative started wrestling within him again. He heard the Sej chuckle sarcastically and knew that the life-support readings had betrayed him. Now he could be expected to show weakness, he thought. For one blessed moment he let himself sag, then resumed his rigid stare into the recorder. That too was expected.

The rest of the debriefing went like what he could remember of all the other times. After exhaustive examination, part of which, Dustin was sure, was designed to catch him in any lies or weaknesses, he was ready to lay his head down on the crowded desk and sleep, or be sick, whichever happened first. His head felt as if a spiked strap were wound about it and tightened by the man across from him, and then pulled. And the hunger—

The Sej reached out and switched off the recorder. A whining, almost imperceptible except to Dustin's anguished senses, died away. The man went to a cupboard and returned with packages Dustin remembered from his days in training on Nahi II. Sejiedi field rations. They tasted of iron and the soil in which they had grown. Hathoti pulp had been added, making them simultaneously nourishing and addictive.

''Eat,'' said the Sej.

Hating himself, Dustin ate. It was all he could force himself to do to eat with propriety and at a decent speed. He wanted to rip open the packs and devour the russet-colored cakes the way the hungries. . . . But as he ate, the hunger subsided. Now it was gone, but he still had one more chunk to go. The smell was as loathsome now as it had been enticing before. He forced himself to choke the thing down, gagging a little on the last bite. They had always been punished if they didn't eat everything set before them. Food was a privilege, not a right.

"Ate too fast," he apologized.

"Be careful." It wasn't a warning about table manners.

Expressing both dismissal and contempt, the operative turned his back on Dustin. He was free to go, and he strode rapidly out of the back room, walking fast and far away from the store where the power he was trying to fight against had brought him to heel once again, and all too rapidly.

CHAPTER II

The shriek of a low-flying craft heading for the landing slicks drowned out the sound of occasional ground vehicles, passersby, and the steady, hushed fall of rain, hissing against the blue of the screens. Dustin looked up. It troubled him that he could not immediately tell what sort of craft made that noise. By the time he had identified it, he had recovered some awareness, a sense of something beside the desperate humiliation his encounter with the warrior-born Sej had left him with.

He was near the city limits of Corvynem. He didn't like the street where he found himself wandering; it looked too much like Nahi II. But he could hear the sea, and it drew him. It was the work of a few moments to head for the perimeter, to create a momentary breach in the screens, and to slip outside. Easy work, considering his training. Dirty work.

The beach lay before him. Beyond lay an abandoned wharf, several derelict boats rubbing against its piles. Rain pelted Dustin, dripping down his hair and puddling beneath his collar and in the hood he had forgotten to pull up. He stared at the wet sand. He was going to have to leave footprints, but he had to make it to the darkness beneath that wharf. Perhaps the rain and the tide would sweep the beach clean again.

Dustin clenched his teeth against a sudden wave of pain and stepped out onto the sand. His head was throbbing and his stomach heaved from the drugged rations. Ever since puberty, hathoti had hit him that way. He'd never have survived on Nahi, not with the food available for the likes of him. Hathoti made him so sick that given the chance of a medical test before combat, there'd be no trace of the rotten stuff left in his system. Another thing to be grateful for.

Almost reeling, he made his way down under the rotten pilings. It was drier there, but the stench of rot and refuse was overpowering. Rags, bottles, and less savory objects littered the darkness which dragged his memory back to the back alleys of Nahi where he'd dodged hungries. Dustin had devoured those rations like a hungry who roamed the streets with a big knife, waiting for some stupid wanderer in the night. They had made a hungry of him! All the combat kills of a lifetime wouldn't make up for that.

The hathoti hit him hard then, brought him retching to his knees for a long, long time. By the time his sickness shuddered away into dry heaves, Dustin wanted to die. To use Gregory that way, Gregory of all people. What he wouldn't give to have half of Gregory's honor, his coolness, his coaxing hands with a sting. And Gregory was loyal beyond loyal. He wouldn't accept a replacement for a dead squadmate when his flight demanded it. He'd even had the courage to kill her when it would have hurt less to kill himself.

Was there a reason beyond loyalty that Gregory treated him like an enemy? Maybe he suspected that Dustin was rotten. Pilot on the outside, Sej within—if Gregory learned that, Dustin thought he'd kill himself.

But it wasn't only Gregory; it was the whole squad. Dustin's orders were to betray the entire Wing into the hands of its enemies, League and Sej alike.

The Wing schools were so right. Earthers could trust only their own. Look how far Kroeger's precious citizenship had taken him! It wasn't simply blind prejudice. The Wing schools had taught him something of it, but it was worlds like these where he really saw it. The League was afraid of them, of all Earthers.

Walter, his favorite in the parent squad they'd assigned him when he entered the Wing, had explained it strangely, in that slow, precise way that engineers always had. Once there'd been a type of insect no one liked. They hated them, killed them by the millions, but there were always more. The people found more and more efficient ways to kill them, but the insects developed immunities and kept on going. Nothing could stop them. Nothing could destroy them. They were invincible.

Face it, Dustin, you're more Wing than anything else. You know it. You're Earther, man, he told himself as he always did. *They couldn't have lied about that. It's impossible to modify somatic type, gene patterns enough for anyone to pass as Earth human . . . isn't it?*

He scrambled out of the blue coverall, buried it deep in the sand, and then kicked the wet, muddy stuff over the place where he had retched. Brushing grit from his white uniform, he emerged out from under the wharf into the rain again.

Staring deep into the gray waves, he considered his options, such as they were, just as he did each time the damned Sej snapped his leash on him. He could continue fighting, turning in inadequate reports to the Sejiedi, and hoping that his headaches wouldn't turn into something fatal. Or he could end it right now, before he betrayed . . . it was *his* squad now, more precious to him than his own life. Easy enough to keep on walking. He was weak from hunger, strain, and his recent nausea. The water was cold. That would probably kill him before the water finally dragged him down and filled his lungs. He had heard that freezing to death was like drifting gently into sleep. It was soft, peaceful.

He spat and turned away. If he had to die, he was damned if he'd do it anywhere except in a clean fight, with his squad and his sibs about to give him honor. He wouldn't simply disappear, leaving them to wonder why he had abandoned them and what weakness in them had made them take up with a deserter. There'd never been a deserter in the Wing. He had no choice. He had to go on fighting. It was what Gregory would respect, what Gregory would do.

He walked up from the beach where the rain was already blurring his footsteps toward the town. In an instant, no one would ever know he had passed by. A checkpoint materialized out of the mist and this time he showed his papers, then wandered back into the warren of streets. He still had a few hours to kill before his pass was up, and he had to work out an account of how he had spent his day.

The streets in this quarter were narrow and twisting, built, probably, before the rest of the place was laid out in the usual meticulous grid. The rain fell harder. He was getting soaked again. Joao would be furious when he returned to the ship. When he saw a sign for a café farther down, half-heartedly he headed for it. The idea of ordering food made him gag a little, but he had to get in, had to replace what the hathoti had stolen from him.

"Sir . . . sir . . ."

For a moment, Dustin kept on walking and ignored the childish voice. He didn't know anyone on Corvynem, and he didn't want to.

"Please . . . *mister* . . ."

The old Earther title spun him around to look down at a boy with dark curls plastered against his head by the slanting rain. He glanced up at the signs again. So Earthers had settled on Corvynem too. Sure enough, this quarter had signs of home space. It looked like all of the others that dotted many of the poorer worlds in the League.

"What is it?" Dustin smiled to reassure the boy.

"Please, sir, my mother saw you from the window. She sent me down to ask you to please come in out of the rain."

As Dustin started to open his mouth to refuse, to tell him he wouldn't trouble the boy's family, the child spoke up again. "I'm supposed to say we'd be honored, sir. We would, really. It would be great! And you could get dry."

Clearly the boy was ready to stand here arguing in the rain. He'd only get wetter, and he might get sick—fine repayment to the people who had sent him out here with their invitation. For a moment, Dustin wondered if it were a trap. How much did the Sej know about the relations between Earther Wing and Earther civs? The refugees were proud of their Wing and showed it in small, friendly ways. Like this.

"Lead on," Dustin gestured. As the boy ran ahead, he quickened his pace. *Fraud*, he told himself, *exploiting these people's kindness*.

But Earthers had a right to expect certain things, a certain graciousness from the Wing. The least he could do was to play the part. And it was raining very hard indeed now.

"Come on over this way, please."

"This way" meant a shabby entryway and a scrupulously clean tube that jolted him and the boy up eight floors into a scrubbed hallway. Dustin had a moment's embarrassment at the way he was dripping water all over as he entered the apartment before he was "this way'd" into a bathroom.

"There's a dryer attached to the laundry unit, sir," he heard as the door scraped behind him. "It's pretty primitive, but it works."

It was fine, he thought, and peeled off the flightsuit. At least the rain had washed the sand from it. As he waited for it to cycle through clean to dry, he got under the shower and adjusted it for as hot as he could stand to warm the sickness from him.

Half an hour later, he emerged clean and almost shy. The boy was sitting on the floor across from the door.

"You weren't waiting for me?" Dustin asked, shocked.

"My mother said to bring you . . . come on, sir. She's fixed a real special supper for you."

Dustin entered a family room about the size of his squad's wardroom. A table had been drawn out, and spread with a cloth and covered dishes. In a room beyond it, he could hear the soft clinking of metal utensils, and someone walking toward him. He was abashed. He wasn't worth this trouble . . . this expense, he realized, taking in the age and plainness of his surroundings. They were willing to share food with a stranger! Bikmat was shocked into silence.

Dustin hadn't had the time to look before. Now he noticed that the floor was plastic tile, patterned once, but now mottled yellow-gray. The walls were decorated with old pictures, probably family heirlooms, and artwork that the boy must have brought home from school. He noticed that the cheerful plastic chairs and cloth had been expertly patched.

Everything had been cheap, or used, to start out with and was showing hard wear. Except for the late-model terminal on a desk by the wall. Like the rest of the apartment, it was scrupulously polished. A sudden, horrible thought struck him, and he walked over to inspect the machine. He hoped that these Earthers hadn't bought it from his contact. It might please the Sej's humor to sell them inferior goods.

"Do you like that computer?" came a man's voice from the hall. "Three families in the building pooled funds to buy it for the children. We've got a few who're studying for the Wing exams, and we thought they'd need something better than school issue. I suppose that by your standards, it's not much."

"Military hardware is superior, yes," Dustin answered truthfully. "But on the Wing Moon, the trainees don't have better than this. You chose well."

"Come, sit down," the man said, smiling at the compliment. "It's really thrilling to have you here. Let me get you a plate. My wife will be in shortly."

"There's no need for all this trouble . . ."

"Trouble? Don't talk nonsense. You're one of the Wing. For my money, you deserve the best there is. I was delighted when Ammie spotted you down there, getting soaked. It's the least we can do. Besides, my own daughter is taking the exam this year. I'd hope that someone . . ."

Dustin smiled warmly and sat down. He was afraid he couldn't eat at all, much less handle the mountain of food the man was heaping on the plate. But it was warm and wholesome—fresh stew brimming with large chunks of vegetables and soft, boiled grains. There was hot bread, and its smell satisfied more than just physical hunger. He basked not just in the warmth of the food, in the taste of the coffee, laced with the contents of an old bottle that was produced in triumph and dusted off with reverence. Their pride in him, in being able to offer him hospitality, warmed him even more deeply than the liquor.

"Tell me, sir . . ."

"Please," he said carefully. "My *name* is Dustin."

They nodded acceptance, thanks, knowing how White Wingers prized their Names.

"Are many of the people in your squad . . . did they come in via the exams?" the man asked, concern creasing his face.

It's not really my squad, he wanted to admit, but he knew that would only confuse them. Besides, something in the man's concern touched Dustin. Of course the father wanted to know what it would be like for his daughter if she were accepted. He cared. Telling him might make it easier for him. He wouldn't just turn his child over to the authorities and walk away.

"Some," he said. "Yuri, I think . . . and I did, of course. You know, I'm not sure about the rest. It really doesn't make much of a difference. When you come in, you're assigned to a dorm and a parent squad that sort of looks after you. Mine made us write home every week— that is, those of us that had homes. There aren't that many of us, you see. Some of the younger officers played big brother and sister to us. My parent squad made a big thing out of all our birthdays, especially when I was eighteen. That's when you're commissioned and can start specialized training. Anyway, they invited everyone in my year, and our big brothers and sisters, and all their friends. First time they ever let me have bourbon.'' Dustin permitted himself to smile at the memory, and the curiosity he saw in the man who had served him. ''I asked rather loudly why I only got such a little glass. Then my friends chased me around the room with whipped cream . . . well, that was sort of a tradition our year. We managed to get all the adults.''

''If Gwen passes, we know we'll lose her,'' her mother said. ''But it's such a chance for her. And it's ours, not like the university here.''

''I just heard that they're tightening the quota on Earthers at the university,'' the father said. ''Again.''

''Interesting, isn't it, that the universities that tightened up the most have just gotten huge grants from . . . let's not mention names,'' said Ammie.

''Gwen . . . is this the young lady who's studying for the Wing examination?'' Dustin looked around for an eleven-year-old girl. Anything he could do for a child . . .

''She was too shy to come out,'' the little boy said. ''I told her I wasn't scared, and I won't be, when I take the exams. I've already got a Wing name picked out. It's Gordon. You can call me Gordo if you want to.''

''I'd rather earn the privilege,'' Dustin replied as gravely as if he spoke to another Wingman. ''And I'd like to meet Gwen.''

When she entered, he rose and shook her hand with formal, adult courtesy that made her blush and stand even straighter. She was a thin girl with thoughtful green eyes and cropped dark hair.

''So, you're taking the Wing exam,'' Dustin said. ''What do you want to do when you get there?''

''What's your specialty, sir?'' the girl asked calmly. She didn't seem shy at all, only quiet and watchful.

"I'm a pilot," Dustin said, and heard them exclaim softly.

"That's what I want too. My teachers tell me I shouldn't aim quite so high . . ."

"She takes dancing and gymnastics to improve her balance, and her math's in the top one percentile on Corvynem," her mother interrupted. "I tell her she has to try. The surest way not to do something is not to try for it."

"You're right," Dustin said. Then he turned his attention back to Gwen. "I hope you make it."

"Thank you," she replied. "Was it very difficult when you took it?"

Dustin thought back to the stories he'd heard in training. "The worst part," he said, "was waiting for the scores. Wing Command considers a lot more than just the exams, however. They're just the first cut."

The young girl nodded gravely. "Yes, I saw the material they sent. Interviews and psych tests. All that stuff. I just try not to think about it too much."

"That's the best thing," Dustin agreed.

"What worries me," her father cut in, "is all this stuff I've seen on the newspads. Seems like there's another campaign to cut your appropriations again."

"I think it's that Kolatolo character. He's just an Eartherhater all the way," countered his wife. "Unfortunately, he's got more money than he knows what to do with, and too many friends at the top. I suppose it's easier to own the Assembly than run for it."

"Kolatolo! For sure, he's the worst of the lot!" chimed in a neighbor who stepped in unannounced, three other people with him. "Heard you and Ammie had some company, Jim." He turned to Dustin. "I'm Kyu, and this is Leah and Jason. Paul's telling the rest of the building you've got one of the Wing visiting."

Dustin rose and shook hands with all of them. He was embarrassed; he knew he'd never remember all the names, especially if more people came. *Suzannah would never have that problem*, he thought wryly. And she wouldn't have trouble with the unfamiliar words, the shifts in sounds and meanings these people had acquired in years of living among outsiders, variations in the language so carefully preserved on the Wing Moon. He tried to remember them to tell her; the Sej had seen to it that he was good at languages.

"What I'd like to know is, why's Kolatolo have it in for us so bad? Do you know if there's been riots in other places? Here they came in and busted some of the windows a bit, then painted slogans all over the school. All of a sudden, like. I mean, they didn't have any kind of reason I could see. And then, down at The Park . . ."

"Don't," said Dustin's hostess. He was pleased he could remember at least her name. Ammie.

"No, please," Dustin said softly. "I need to know. We hear rumors, but we don't get much information about local events on the base ships."

"Wait a minute," someone else said. "I read that there were all kinds of fights on the big ships. That the Wing claimed credit for the Colors' actions . . . no one around here believed it, you can bet on that, but there were fights breaking out all over."

"Well," Dustin said slowly, "we're not exactly drinking buddies with the other Wings. We keep to ourselves. But we all answer to military discipline. Anyone getting caught throwing a punch, or returning one, winds up in the brig to think it over."

"Way I see it," Jim said, "a lot of the problem's that Kolatolo character. He owns half the press on Corvynem, and we don't count for a whole lot. Those student groups at the university, the ones that are real big on cutting down Earther enrollment, they seem to have lots of money. Ever see one of their 'casts? Real slick, real professional. Kolatalo's always showing up on them too—deep-space hookups, and you know what that costs. Now you *know* that those kids don't have that kind of money.''

"I don't know what's all behind it," Kyu said. "Only I've been going down to The Park for sim games every week for ten years. Just like that they told me I wasn't welcome. Said it wasn't me. Just that they'd gotten this message that they'd be trashed if any more of us were allowed in.''

"That owner has a yellow streak a klick wide," Gordon spoke up.

The boy's father pretended to cuff him, while the others nodded.

"Higgledy, piggledy, ad-man incarnate/Ag Kolatolo has media news./All in a huff about Earther activities./Better start moving or we're going to lose," Gwen recited.

"Where'd you steal that from?" Ammie asked.

The girl just shrugged thin shoulders. "In the gym. It's all right. We're all Earthers there."

"That's great, I like that," Kyu said.

"Gwen, why don't you get your father's guitar?" Ammie said quickly. "More folks will be here soon, and I don't want . . . get the guitar, Gwen."

So it was that bad. You couldn't talk on Nahi either.

"The thing is," one of them—Leah—spoke in a hushed voice, "they don't even try to get us just because we're Earthers. There's rumors going around that because we're not citizens, we side with the Sej. Who denied us citizenship in the first place, that's what I'd like to know? It's a setup!''

"So if there's a lot of us in one place," Ammie cut in softly, "well, it's better not to talk about politics too much. If anyone asks how come you're here, you can bet he's not one of ours. You tell him you're Jim's cousin. You've got about the same coloring.''

Dustin nodded thanks for the advice. He couldn't wait to get this information to Zann. She had access to more data than he did, and she had that unbelievable brain . . . perhaps this would be of use to someone back home, someone besides Kroeger . . .

The guitar appeared. At first there were a few songs that he didn't know, local ones, maybe. Then the old songs started. Dustin joined in heartily, and was surprised to see the mixture of shock and pleasure he brought the others. They didn't think that people in the Wing sang, did they? They sang one he had sung many times, one of Neil's favorites, about pilots who fly out to die in the morning. Plenty of times on this long haul, Neil had pulled out a battered old guitar and turned the cold, functional wardroom into home. But somehow this was more. Here, the song was a treasure, something to offer Dustin. They were staring at him and at Gwen almost in awe.

He had a feeling Gwen would pass. He'd keep an eye out for her. If he lived.

The last chords died. Dustin glanced at the window. Only the faintest touch of vivid crimson glared at the horizon. The brightness and warmth in the shabby room had hidden night from him.

"Last shuttle leaves at eighteen-hundred." Gwen caught his glance. "You have plenty of time."

"Yes, I suppose so," Dustin said. He hadn't meant to be gone this long, had never dreamed that the whole ghastly day could have been redeemed by anything. He even had an irreproachable cover story. "I can't thank you enough. But I'd better check in with my squad now. May I . . . ?"

"Over here, sir." Jim led Dustin to an anteroom where a chair stood next to a messager. Dustin pulled out his ID to debit his account for the call to the base ship. Jim shoved the card back at him.

"You are our *guest*, Pilot Dustin. Believe me, it's our pleasure to do this for you."

The man waited till Dustin sealed the card away again, then left him to make his call in private.

Joao answered when the call was patched through to Wing quarters. "Suzannah's been looking for you. Have you been downworld all day?"

"Went into the Earther quarter. I'm calling from a private line; can't talk long. I'll be up on the eighteen-hundred shuttle . . . no . . . nothing's wrong . . . I just didn't have sense to come in when it started raining . . . I'm fine, Joao . . . yes, we'll talk about it when I get back."

CHAPTER 12

For the third time Gregory ran over all the reasons he ought to be pleased as though they were a maintenance checklist he didn't trust. They'd picked up a large contingent of reinforcements—even one flight of White Wingers—on Corvynem. They were taking on supplies. For almost a week now, he'd only stood one duty shift per day, and that situation was likely to continue for the forseeable future. Neil and he hadn't had a single fight all this week; the other pilot had even volunteered to report that their earlier problems had been the consequence of overwork and severe supply shortages.

Just wonderful. He should feel good. He should be happy. The rest of them were. Outside the door of his own quarters, he could hear his squad chattering away in the wardroom. Judith's laughter rippled brightly through the bulkhead (*Damn! I thought these things were soundproofed!*), and he flinched away from the sound.

He wanted Zann. Zann knew how to talk to him and take the pain away. Of all of them, only Zann and Joao

could make him feel almost like his old self. But Joao
analyzed too much, like all medics, and lately he'd been
looking at him in a way that had Gregory worried. He'd
gotten the feeling recently that Joao thought he was crazy,
or nearly so. If Joao thought that, he could ground him.
Better to find Zann, who'd listen and keep her thoughts to
herself.

Maybe it was just idleness. Ever since that strategic
regroup back to Corvynem, he really hadn't had enough to
do. That was the problem. It always happened. No sooner
than he'd catch up on sleep than he'd get restless, start to
itch at the waiting, at the boredom of routine patrol. He
was sick of having the Colors around everywhere, sick of
wondering whenever he looked at any of them, *did* you *kill
that squad?*

In school once, he'd had to read a story, something
about how waiting too long for revenge could drive someone mad. He would go crazy, cooped up here, waiting and
thinking. How could Zann put up with it? Maybe she
could because she was doing something, solving the puz-
zles rather than just waiting for the order to strike. When
he was in pilots' training, no one had ever warned him
about that part of a pilot's life, all the interminable waiting.

But Zann would laugh deep in her throat and reassure
him that they were getting closer. Then she'd move closer
to him and remind him of how crazy they'd been when
they had just met, the night that he, Zann, and Joao had
painted the Old Man's flier with leftovers from the Officers' Club. Before he had met Maryam or the rest of . . .

He palmed the door open and entered the bleak space
that his family's presence made so warm. They'd dimmed
the lights to something not suited for work, but that was
restful at the end of a long day.

There Zann was . . . with Dustin sitting beside her, an

arm draped over her shoulder, and telling the rest, " . . . and there I was in the middle of this party, and we were singing just like Neil does. Only the guitar was in even worse shape."

"Not possible," Valentina commented, and everybody laughed.

"But you should have seen the food. I mean, I know we've got fresh provisions now, but this stuff was *hand-cooked!*"

That drew another laugh, and Gregory knew he couldn't stop himself. He could feel the anger rising in him, and he knew he should either sit down and listen to the rest of the story or leave. But the days of inactivity and that other, more potent feeling combined, driving his temper to critical mass.

He wanted Dustin out. Dustin, that intruder. Even Joao approved of him now. That galled him. So did the sight of the younger pilot sitting there just as if he belonged with them off duty, so relaxed, and with his arm around Zann so possessively . . .

"What's *he* doing here?" Gregory kept his voice cool as he pointed with his chin at Dustin.

"Dustin is *my* guest," Zann replied, looking away from Gregory to smile at Dustin. He thought he caught her dart a look at Joao. Data—was that all he meant to her now?

"Stop acting like a kid, Gregory," Joao said, a double meaning in his eyes.

Gregory hesitated for a moment. He knew what Joao meant. When they had first met, he and Joao had skirmished jealously over Zann. Working it out had taken them a long time, longer for him, he knew Joao believed, because of his stubbornness. But this time he wasn't jealous, he was angry. His anger grabbed him before he knew what he was doing. He was rushing, ready to swing, when the medic's huge hand flattened against his chest, and pushed him into a chair so hard that his jaw snapped shut and all his teeth rattled.

"I think maybe I'd better . . ." Dustin started to say.

"Don't go," Zann said to Dustin so softly Gregory could almost make himself believe he hadn't heard it. Then she took the man's hand and brushed her cheek against it, and he knew he had.

"It's gone on too long, Gregory," Joao said. "People can say it's exhaustion and overwork and a whole lot of other things. People do say that. You've fooled Neil. But I . . . we . . . we know better. This has got to stop, Greg. Now."

Gregory frowned. He'd thought Joao might understand. Gregory hadn't been any different than usual, except for the empty times.

"You're hurting everyone here," Joao continued. "You won't even give Dustin a chance. When you're not working the same shifts, you barely talk to him."

"I just want my own family," Gregory replied stiffly. Didn't they all know that Maryam was still here? She was still part of them, even if they wanted to put some stranger in her place.

"Really?" Judith asked.

Gregory felt the mood shift around him. He couldn't make sense of the undercurrents. Something strange was going on here, almost as if they'd all been drilled in it. But this was not a drill.

"Your family?" Judith asked again. "Gregory, look at me."

He looked. She stood up and moved the three steps to the chair in which Joao had planted him. She'd opened her jumpsuit at the throat and unbound her hair. It swung freely about her hips. As she approached, it nearly brushed his face.

"What am I to you, Gregory? A sib?"

"Hardly," he said.

"Then why have you avoided me ever since Maryam died?" she demanded harshly. Dropping onto the arm of his chair, she leaned so close that he could feel the texture of her heavy hair and smell the fragrance of flowers and woods that always seemed to rise from her skin. He didn't want to want her.

"I haven't avoided you," he defended himself. He reached out to brush her hair from his shoulder.

"That's the first time you've touched me in over eight months."

He pulled away from her slightly. It wasn't Judith he wanted, but Zann, Zann who was safe, who wouldn't go out in a sting one morning and get herself killed. Zann, whom he would never have to kill. "What's going on?" he asked.

"Besides the fact that you've been known to be nicer to Blues than to Judith, Yuri, and Dustin, nothing," Valentina said.

"So you've all decided to gang up on me, is that it?"

"Don't listen to any of them, Gregory," an almost sinister voice hissed from the shadows. "Listen to *me*."

Gregory turned and saw Yuri leaning insolently against the wall. Despite his languid posture, his body was tense, the way it was before combat. Gregory felt the menace in him.

"No, they don't know," Yuri went on. "I do. It's how you feel when you're flying. When you're dumping tau, glory-riding. When you know you're hot. And one of those slim Sej fighters comes into your scans, and it's only the two of you. You're all alone, and you can feel your own power, and you can feel his. You're so very close, you and that stranger.''

Gregory stiffened. He knew. Yuri was right, Yuri did know, and he could feel it. Fear closed around him. The serpent in Yuri was taking over, and he was going to talk about the thing no pilot ever wanted to mention. The others ought to be spared the knowledge, but he couldn't ask Yuri to stop. Now he could feel the controls slick beneath his fingers, see the Sej, relive that one moment of freedom, of purity, the moment that was both living and dying.

''You're so close that opening fire is just a tease, pulling him closer to you. And you're half-glad when he evades. Then you evade too, slipping just barely to the side, playing with him, laughing. So you match each other, shot for shot, fire for fire, and the rhythm of the battle is your pulse beating out. And you slip into combat and you fire, cool like the smell of the oxygen. And you evade and you breathe and you fire again, and it burns and feels good like old whiskey going down smooth. You know. You're wide open, feeling with him, breathing with him, matching him beat for beat. And you forget it ever started, and you forget it has to end.

''Then someone makes a mistake, and you report another kill. And you feel cold and sad because he was good, and he was pushing you to the last. You're sorry he's gone, and you never knew him. And he would have killed you if you'd given him half a chance.

''That's what you felt with Maryam, that power in the lasers, surging in the lines like the last breath of a kiss. You hate it, don't you, that you went on a glory-high when you gave her the Mercy? But don't you see that you were closer to her than you'd ever been? When you're fighting, you're only whole because the enemy is there.

Only this time, it was Maryam who made it whole. She knew, too. It wasn't killing her you enjoyed. It was that she was so completely yours for that fragment of a second. Gregory, listen to me. I mean this. There's nothing evil here.'' Yuri's low voice went husky and broke. ''Let me tell you, Gregory, if you had to do that for me, I'd be glad it was you and not some Sej who was closer to me than my own skin in that game.''

Gregory gulped for air. Tears were burning in his eyes, and he found himself clutching Judith tight against his shoulder. Then he was sliding down until his head lay in her lap, and she was stroking his hair. His throat was tight, too tight. He couldn't speak. He could only nod as Yuri came over and dropped beside them both.

He wanted to hate Yuri, who knew the secret and told them all. But he'd needed Yuri to show him that he wasn't guilty, that he wasn't evil. Because Yuri was right, and more honest than Gregory would ever let himself be. Gregory had never let himself look in that place, had turned away from it many times. Yet now it all fell together and he had to admit it was true. He had never touched Maryam so deeply as when he'd had to kill her. He was unutterably relieved to know that it was the touch, not the death, that had stirred him so.

He looked up. Of the others in the wardroom only Dustin's eyes glowed with response, understanding. Tactfully, Dustin broke free of the moment and turned back to Suzannah.

Joao seemed shocked, and his face went haggard with pain. ''I think the three of you have some making up to do,'' he said, his voice heavy with unwanted understanding.

Gregory pitied him. He pitied all of the others who'd gotten a glimpse of the thing that most pilots hid, even from themselves. He rose, pulling Judith with him, one arm around her slim waist. Something wasn't right yet. He turned and faced Dustin. The solo rose.

"I'm sorry," Gregory told him.

"I know." Dustin's voice was hoarse. "Forget it."

Relief washed over Gregory. Dustin understood, and he wasn't about to drag it out in the open in front of the others. For the first time in over six months, the tension that hardened the back of his neck unclenched, and he felt good. The secret was out. No one had turned away from him.

"Come on, you two," he said, ushering Judith and Yuri back to his own cabin. "I've got some good bourbon I was saving for a special occasion. And this is pretty special."

Dustin couldn't believe the change in Gregory, in the entire squad. He remembered the times he'd stayed with his parent squad on Wing Moon, remembered the cheerfulness and ease that had made the days flow smoothly.

There hadn't been much time for code work lately, or perhaps Kroeger hadn't intercepted anything new. As long as Dustin avoided it, avoided any confrontation between his two halves, he could forget or at least push it to the back of his mind and lock it away. He belonged now. The squad felt right. Anna was back on duty. Neil and Charles had stopped hinting to Gregory about the squad's marrying up to strength. Dustin thought he knew what that meant, but he didn't really want to hope too much. He didn't dare.

Just as well. The work was piling up as they left Corvynem's orbit, heading to the Mahalir system where the Sej were besieging the two habitable planets. Tactical meetings, briefings, and drill added constant background noises to their lives. All over the ship, morale was high. A

Yellow tech had passed on some information to him about the fuel reserve levels, an unusual occurrence.

Suzannah was rarely around. She was cooped up with Kroeger doing *something*. Dustin both devoutly wished he knew what it was, and didn't want to. What he didn't know, he couldn't tell.

He was scared again. Of all of them, Zann was likeliest to find him out. Obviously the name *Aglo* had meant something to her beyond its designation as the agent who'd taken out the White Wing transport. Maybe . . . probably . . . she'd heard the name *Bikmat* too. He tried not to think about it.

When he checked out his sting, he found Hangar Deck 16 in chaos. Steaming tubes and hoses snaked across the gratings where rank on rank of battle-worn stings crouched. Technicians in every Color of the force carried tools Dustin could easily visualize as implements of—call it interrogation. Engineers, identifiable by their portable readouts on which ships' specs glowed amber, talked to techs and made notes in every language of the League. Red techs worked on Blue stings; from time to time pilots from Green and Yellow strode over to watch. That was Valentina, clambering over an Orange sting right now. Joao knelt beside a Blue corpsman, supervising as the man worked over a tech who'd taken a shock. The jumble of equipment and Color produced a vitality all its own. Even the presence of gold-uniformed security officers couldn't damp Dustin's exhilaration.

He'd only rarely seen it before. Savoring it now, he understood why the Sej, for all their need and tenacity, had never been able to invade deep into League space and stay there. This wasn't just the Wings of the Known Worlds; it was the united Fleet.

The plain White stings of the flight stood together,

dotted with brilliant color as three Reds and a Green scrambled over them, opening their bellies and pulling out boards.

"This one yours, sir?" one of the techs asked. A red scarf kept her hair from tumbling onto her forehead.

Dustin nodded.

"Well, sir, you've got a new set of a-gravs going in now. You'd nearly burned away the old ones. And the converter's been scrubbed down so you could eat dinner off it. Begging your pardon, sir, but how was the forward port laser acting? Sluggish?"

"Yes."

"Thanks," the Red tech said. "Hey, Famne, you were right!" she yelled at the tech in Green. "Set this one up for laser refitting." She turned back to Dustin. "Now that won't trouble you anymore. Anything else you want, sir?" She eyed him hopefully.

"No, it looks like you've caught it all." Dustin hesitated a moment. "Thanks, anyhow," he said.

The woman grinned and went back to work as Dustin watched.

"Shame that White Wingers never break the regs on fraternization, isn't it?" he heard her say. "Did you *see* that one?"

Dustin heard a chuckle and wheeled abruptly to find Gregory standing at his shoulder. "I love this part of it, don't you?"

"Come on," said Gregory. "We've got at least ten minutes before the briefing. Want some coffee?"

Dustin nodded briefly and followed Gregory back across the deck into the "closet," the smaller ready-room with its scrounged chairs and battered hot-drinks dispenser. It was deserted.

"We've been talking, all of us," Gregory began. "I

asked to be the one to say it, since, well, I . . . Anyway, I do like to fly with you. So do Judith and Yuri. But you know that. If you want, if you'd be willing, well, we'd like to make it official.''

Startled, Dustin sank into a chair. "You're sure? Everyone agreed?" he asked softly, not quite believing it. He could feel a flush starting at his toes and working its way up to his face.

"I wouldn't be here if we hadn't."

The flush hit Dustin's face about the same time as a wide smile. "Hell, *yes!*" he said so loudly that he startled himself. By reflex he and Gregory both glanced at the door. Dustin wanted to whoop or to hug Gregory. And a small, very private corner of him wanted simply to go off by himself and cry.

"Would tomorrow be too soon?" Dustin asked hesitantly. "I mean, I know it's not home, but it may be a long time till we get leave again and . . ."

He didn't intend to get himself vaped. But it would be so . . . so *good* to go into battle as part of a family, not a solo, even a well-liked one.

Gregory smiled warmly at Dustin's eagerness. "How does today after the briefing sound? Zann finally got all the documents back from Wing Command, and Judith's reserved Deck 30 rec room. But I forgot. Did you want any coffee?"

Dustin shook his head, trying to stop grinning. How was he going to look impassive at the briefing? "That's going to be the longest, dullest briefing in the history of the Fleet, you know? At least for me it is. And speaking of which . . ."

Throughout the briefing Dustin struggled with the presence of Colors, with keeping cool, arrogant, when what he really wanted was to laugh and sweep Judith up for a long kiss. Instead he sat bolt upright and pretended to look at the holos and listen to the low-voiced discussions that followed. He only hoped that someone in the flight was taking down this stuff. A pity Zann wasn't a pilot. He watched Gregory gesture sharply to a nodding Green and even to one Blue flight leader, and he wanted to grin. *That's my flight leader!*

Only . . . only he wished that there weren't the other part, the Bikmat part lurking back there in his mind.

Go away, he told it. *After the briefing, I'm going to do just what you've assigned me to do.* Marry in and set himself up in a position where he could damage Gregory and the squad. They had raised and trained—and fed—him so he could do it. Bikmat. He forced it from his mind.

He'd been solo for years, had despaired of ever finding a family of his own, not really sure he deserved to try. If they ever found out about Bikmat, they'd hate him. Gregory would want to kill him, and he'd want to die. But for this one moment, Dustin was about to get everything he ever wanted.

If only the Sejiedi task were a bad dream . . . his head started to ache, and he cursed silently. *For this one day,* he wished the throbbing in his head, *for just this once, let me be.* His wish and the demand of his Sejiedi masters were the same; the headache ought to let him alone.

After the briefing the four pilots headed back to quarters and found the rest of the squad waiting for them.

"You did say yes?" Valentina asked, running to Dustin as soon as the hatch was safely sealed.

Dustin picked her up and hugged her, swinging her about. His family crowded about, and Dustin couldn't remember when he had ever felt so wanted, so much at home.

"Better get changed," Yuri said at last. "The sibs will be here to witness in a few minutes."

"Too bad we aren't home," Valentina said. "The Old Man always gets drunk at weddings."

They laughed and separated. As Dustin changed into dress uniform, he found himself trembling. Outside, he heard the sound of people filing in, joking, shuffling about. The wardroom would be crowded with the full flight and sibs.

When he emerged, he smiled, embarrassed, and took one of the seats. Judith reached over and squeezed his hand. Sibs crowded in to stand behind them. Before them, on the large worktable (cleaned off, he noticed, for the occasion), lay a large, elaborate document. Underneath lay three more, these on green fax that would be filed with Command. These were hard copy. One of the techs was waiting to send the transmission that would record their agreement.

Neil picked up the important legal document that they would keep for always and read from it. "As evidenced by their signatures on this document, Dustin, Gregory, Joao, Judith, Suzannah, Valentina, and Yuri, officers of the White Wing, residents on Wing Moon, publicly acknowledge and legalize their marriage in accordance with the laws and the traditions of the Wing Moon of the peoples of Earth."

In the order Neil mentioned them, they signed the documents, thumbprinting the green forms that would be kept on file. Then their sibs squeezed by to sign and print the second column for witnesses. The entire ceremony took less than four minutes.

Dustin found himself surrounded, being kissed and congratulated by sibs on all sides.

"Hey, wait a minute," Neil interrupted, "by *old* Earth

traditions, you're not really married until after the party. Let's get moving!''

Deck 30's rec room was filled with every White Winger on board—seven full flights. Somehow the squad had snatched time from combat preparations to arrange for three tables laden with food, even including exotic fresh fish from Corvynem. Was this one of the reasons Zann had been so quiet lately? She was good at secrets.

Another table held an ancient holdover from the days of lost Earth itself, an enormous multi-tiered cake. Yuri produced something that he and a chem engineer vowed was exactly like old Earth champagne. Everyone drank enthusiastically, if not with much appreciation.

''Don't want to hurt their feelings,'' Gregory muttered to Dustin and Judith, ''but when I *do* drink, I prefer bourbon.''

''Do you think the transmission's arrived yet?'' Anna asked.

''Ten minutes ago,'' Zann replied.

''Then,'' Charles said, raising his glass, ''here's to the official transmission!''

A half-whisper of sound made everyone snap back into their Wing masks of expressionlessness before the door slid fully open. Dustin didn't dare to look. Three Blue Wing officers examined the group, their eyebrows raising. Dustin recognized the ace who had saved him so long ago and clenched his jaw against hot words.

''This is a private party,'' Alexei told them calmly. ''You must not have seen the sign. The rec room on Deck 32 is free, I think.''

The three Blues said nothing for a moment. TreMorion stepped past Alexei and walked over to the tables of food. He stared at the cake a moment. ''I didn't know you ever had anything to celebrate," he commented, then walked quietly out.

When the door sealed itself again, Judith ran over to Dustin. "I'm so sorry, I told those clowns before that this was private . . ." She shook her head and muttered a curse under her breath.

Dustin smiled at her and kissed her lightly. "It's not important, Judith. You are. All of you."

"Hey, Neil, how about it?" Someone was passing him the guitar.

Dustin sprawled out on a sofa, Judith and Valentina beside him. For a few minutes he watched Elizabeth with Charles, Anna, and the rest of that squad. They were a good squad; the kid would have a good life as a part of it. But they weren't his squad.

Yuri gave him more champagne and then food, more of it than he could possibly eat. His squad. They really did belong to him now. He'd find a way around the Sej. He always had before, and now he had so much more reason to.

Anna brought him out of his fog by looking up and saying, "We've only got seven hours to tau for Mahalir." Now only their flight remained in the room. The others drifted back to quarters to get some rest. Neil was still strumming away, reminding Dustin of the many times he'd sat on the floor in that squad's house, learning songs and eating pastry.

"Dustin, someone just slipped this under the door. It's for you." Yuri poked an envelope with Dustin's name on it into his hands. He tore it open and scanned the message, written in a firm, angular hand in symbols no language of Earth or the League used. He crumpled the note and threw it into the nearest waste chute.

"What was that?" Yuri asked.

"Love letter," Dustin answered, keeping his voice even.

"That should have stopped at ten-hundred hours," Zann observed to a general yell of laughter.

"You should have seen the techs today," Gregory said, and told her.

Yuri shrugged. Dustin closed his eyes and tried to pretend he hadn't seen the note. No one would question him. After all, there were always jokes at weddings. And his class had been particularly good—or bad—at practical jokes. Yuri and the others would think that one of his classmates had decided to be obnoxious. He'd done the same thing himself often enough.

They returned to their own quarters. Dustin's personal effects had already been transferred there by the sibs—without, he hoped, playful additions. The marriage contract still lay on the wardroom table. Dustin stared at it. Try as he could, he couldn't stop seeing the image of the Sejiedi writing, and the single line of the note he'd received. *Nice work, Bikmat.*

As he touched the document, Joao came over. "I'm glad we're a real family again," the medic said. He paused for a moment, studying Dustin. "Headache?"

Dustin smiled weakly. "Don't tell Yuri, but I can live without that champagne of his."

Hangar Deck 16 was lonely. The techs had finished with their overhauls and the stings looked new and polished.

Tomorrow they'd fight Sej, Gregory thought. Adrenaline hit him hard, and he ran his hand caressingly over the smooth hull of his sting. Five days in tau were enough. Tomorrow at oh-five-hundred, they would arrive in Mahalir, and they would fight.

He was content. The empty place that Maryam's death had gouged out of him had closed up, and he felt a security and confidence he'd never hoped to have again. He patted his sting once more, and turned across the vast deck, uninhabited except by the ranks of fighter craft. He walked quietly, but his footfalls echoed in the darkness of the launch bays.

A shadow moved softly, and Gregory froze. He had heard too many of Zann's stories, had thought too much about security lately. Wishing for a sidearm, he crouched, ready for a fight. The shadow dislodged itself completely from the wall and resolved into a tall gray figure that cast its lanky shadow across his path.

Kroeger.

Gregory sighed in relief and let himself relax minutely. What the hell did Kroeger want with him? He moved to stand under one of the few functioning lights and waited, letting Kroeger come to him, observing how the spook kept his hands away from his body.

"I didn't want to use a messager," he said. "Suzannah said I'd find you here. Would you come with me, please."

He turned and, without waiting to see if Gregory would follow, led the way from the hangar deck. Puzzled and excited at the same time, Gregory strode after the Intelligence chief. He had no doubt that something very strange was going on, had been since Corvynem. Now he was about to find out what it was, and he wasn't sure if he wanted to.

He had barely spoken to Federico Hashrahh Kroeger before, and only when he had no other choice. He'd never hidden from Suzannah that he disliked her chief, and he especially disliked her chief's particular interest in their squad.

They took the tubes down to a section of the ship where Gregory had never been before. He'd never had any reason to go down to Engineering or Medical Supply. If he'd had, he would never have chosen these narrow back corridors that resembled a maintenance dump more than anything else. Not even a number marked the hatch to which Kroeger led him. He'd have taken it for a supply closet until the spook palmed open the lock.

As Gregory stepped into Kroeger's den (as Valentina insisted on calling it), he saw Suzannah and the three other pilots of the squad. Zann seemed expectant, Judith, Yuri, and Dustin slightly confused, although they were carefully masked against Kroeger. The place—Gregory glanced about. It looked like more of a clandestine hideaway than the nexus of Intelligence operations for this sector. Everything was battered, scrounged, and mismatched. Idly, Gregory wondered if Kroeger were short on funds, or if he'd had some running argument with the brass.

At Kroeger's gesture, both he and Gregory dropped into the two remaining chairs. There were no papers of any kind on the faded orange plastic table, Gregory saw, and the computer was down. The whir of a white noise generator teased at his awareness. They were protected against eavesdroppers too, then. Whatever was going on was strictly off the record and might not be legal.

Except for Zann, Intelligence operatives made him worry. It was dangerous to work too closely with the gray, the entire Fleet said. Intelligence was . . . well, in addition to the secrets they carried as a matter of course, there seemed to be something . . . there was something around the corners that made even the straightest of them seem dishonest. Maybe it was because they fought with information and schemes rather than the quick cleanliness of lasers.

"Now that I have you all," Kroeger began, "I want to tell you, first, that this comes from the highest level of Operations. You have the right to refuse. Such a refusal will not be held against you, any of you, or prejudice your personnel files. I hope that is quite clear.''

Gregory nodded sharply. There was no need to say anything. He had to stifle an impulse to laugh. This seemed like something he'd picked up in a trash novel or seen on some stupid show when he was in training.

"I have been given authority," Kroeger said, "to task you for an operation in the Mahalir system when we engage the enemy. We have discovered the identity of the saboteur responsible for the accident to that transport. He is to be eliminated.''

Gregory saw the slightest change in Suzannah's eyes, in the set of her shoulders. He practically could hear her thoughts. "Sir," he said to Kroeger, "I am not sure I understand. We're fighter pilots, not Intelligence operatives. There must be more quiet ways you know to accomplish your objective.''

"Quite so," Kroeger replied dryly. "Comm Officer Suzannah has suggested at least three and has volunteered to execute any one of them herself. Though she is too valuable to me to expend, I did consider hers the preferred method. Intelligence, however, sees matters differently. They want this man executed during the battle. Ideally he should appear to have been killed by the enemy. Then we close the dossier on him.''

"I see," Gregory said. "Then I volunteer. I don't mind vaping that traitor-scum in the least. But it's really too clean for him.''

"Agreed on that," Judith spoke up. "I say we draw for it. Whoever takes the task, it's going to reflect on the squad as a whole.''

Yuri and Dustin nodded slowly. Kroeger raised one eyebrow and turned to Zann. "Elucidate.''

"Sir, it is a custom that, with a task such as this, and

several volunteers, chance decides. If you would be so kind as to give the pilots some paper, sir . . .''

Interesting. Knowing Zann, Gregory could guess at Kroeger's reaction as he took the paper, tore it into quarters, and marked one before he folded them carefully into tiny squares. Suzannah mixed them in her hands, then dropped the four identical-seeming squares on the table. Judith drew first, carefully. Yuri picked up the nearest one as casually as if he grabbed the last cookie on a plate. Dustin hesitated momentarily, then drew.

Gregory took the last square, as he'd intended. He could feel Kroeger's eyes boring into him as the pilots opened their papers. Then Yuri laid his flat on the table, the dark X in one corner.

"Who is the target, sir?"

It was Suzannah who spoke. "We've been looking for this one for a long time. In Sejiedi, his name is Aglo. You know him as Lieutenant Commander Haral TreMorion of the Blue Wing."

That Blue! Gregory thought. Lucky Yuri. He wanted TreMorion for himself.

"At four hundred hours tomorrow we leave tau in Mahalir." Kroeger took over. "At approximately five hundred we engage the enemy. TreMorion will be leading his usual flight, near your own. Just make certain he doesn't come back. Dismissed."

CHAPTER 13

When they arrived safely back in White Wing territory, Gregory turned to Suzannah. "I still think they could find a quieter way of taking TreMorion out."

Zann nodded. "At least one. I suggested three of the safest. That civilian operations head wouldn't hear of it."

"What I'd like to know is how you found him out," Judith said softly. "And Zann, if there's anything under-handed about this, shouldn't Val and Joao be here too? They'll be involved if we are."

"The final evidence came from a classified transmission." Suzannah sat down and sighed. "We got it *after* the one Val and Dustin decoded that morning. Narrowing the field down to TreMorion wasn't that hard." She shrugged, and Gregory could sense the weariness in her. It was more than physical fatigue; it almost seemed like defeat. For years, Zann had struggled to keep her squad clear of involvement in her Intelligence work. And now, like it or not, they were in it up to their necks. It would *be* their necks if something went wrong, as it so easily could.

"Only a weaponsmaster rated 5.7 or above would have access to the supplies taken from Ordnance. There are six of them on board. Of those six, one had been in Sick Bay during most of the thefts and at the time when the shuttle had to have been rigged. Two others were on leave at the time at least one of the thefts took place. That left a field of three. We watched them. Now it did occur to me that it was interesting that TreMorion saved Dustin that once. I wondered about that a lot."

"He likes showing off his skills," Judith commented.

"That was part of it. But that's the kind of arrogance one would expect of a Sej. We had other data . . . nothing special by itself, but it added up. The second transmission clinched it."

Dustin winced. Aglo was his senior, his superior in the Service and had acted to save him so that he would live until he got his assignment—betray his squad.

"I'd hate to owe my life to a Sej too." Gregory touched his shoulder sympathetically.

Things were turning over in Dustin's mind, bits and pieces that didn't seem to fit. He didn't like it when he couldn't put them together. The Operations section of Intelligence didn't normally use pilots for executions. At least that was how he always imagined it ought to be. Operations would use subtle, untraceable poisons, or arrange to have someone knifed in a brawl, or found floating face down in the feed vats for the hydropons. Zann probably had suggested any number of good, secret methods of execution. "I still don't like it," he muttered.

There was no way Yuri could make TreMorion's death in combat look accidental. The Sej simply wasn't the kind who'd make a mistake that would get him caught by friendly fire. Novices made that kind of mistake, not aces.

"Did you notice Kroeger didn't promise us immunity?" Gregory asked the others.

Zann lowered her eyes. "I know. I told Valentina and Joao before our little meeting."

"Where are they?" Judith asked again.

"Val's on watch for the break from tau to normal space. And Joao pulled extra duty because there has to be at least one fully qualified physician in Sick Bay at all times and there've been a number of tech-type accidents during overhaul. You *saw* that," Zann replied wearily.

Gregory felt sorry for Zann, who couldn't help remembering and had to endure people who couldn't help forgetting. Ordinarily he'd have said something to cheer her, but something was twisting inside him, something he didn't want to acknowledge, something she'd pulled them into, however reluctantly. There was right, and there was wrong; there was good, and there was evil; and a pilot did what he could for his people and the Wing. Those things should never conflict.

TreMorion, the rotten, stinking Sej, deserved whatever he got. It was just revenge, only not nearly enough, for what he'd done. Gregory knew he'd never forget how the doomed squad had refused help. This was more complicated, more twisted, than a matter of honor or a clean execution. Gregory hesitated. In a moment, he knew he'd have to ask the question that would shatter the certainties he'd always lived by. "Zann, you're holding back on something. Stop trying to spare us and tell us the worst, right now. We may be fighter jocks, but we're not stupid."

Zann closed her eyes. Fatigue hollowed her cheekbones and made her look older than she was. "I was going to tell you," she began slowly. "I know, and Kroeger knows, but not officially, you understand." Her eyes opened and blazed into pure rage, and she slammed a hand down on

the table so hard that Gregory jumped. Zann's control—
that overcontrol eidetics seemed to develop—was legendary in the Wing. He'd never seen her so angry.

"You *know* this stinks like a rotten garbage dump. Why
should Operations order a White Wing squad to eliminate
a Sej plant? Any first-year Intelligence trainee could see
how stupid that is. Kroeger was under direct orders to task
us. I spent six hours trying to wrangle us clear. But the
head of Op's a friend of Abitee's, who's chairing the
Arthan Assembly's Committee on Military Affairs. And
just to make it worse, Abitee is also the League rep on
Fleet appropriations."

"Wait a moment," Dustin broke in. "It always goes
back to the same thing. I mean, the people I spoke to on
Corvynem . . ."

"Get to the point!" Judith snapped at him.

"Arthan. Though Kolatolo's holdings are scattered
League-wide, where's he from? Arthan. And he's the one
who's circulated all that trash against the Earthers and the
Wing. I've seen the Colors in the rec rooms watching his
speeches. Arthan. This makes *bad* sense. Officially Blue
Wing is the Arthan Force. Even if the Colors aren't really
homogeneous in their makeup, since the worlds-minor can
join any one of them, the majority of the Blues are Arthan,
or from Arthan-speaking client worlds."

"Good reasoning, as far as it goes," Zann agreed.
"Now, add this. Abitee's in Kolatolo's pocket. Now the
head of holy operations is playing footsie with the politics
of the Fleet, and Kolatolo's playing along."

"Is there anyone who isn't in Kolatolo's pocket?" Judith asked in disgust.

"Yes," Gregory replied softly. "Us."

"It's a set-up," Dustin said flatly.

Gregory looked carefully at each of them. They had to

execute TreMorion. That squad's murder demanded revenge. But their revenge would undo them before the Fleet, not just their squad, but their entire Wing. Kolatolo would use TreMorion's death to increase anti-Earther prejudice, he realized. That was what he couldn't understand.

"Why does he hate us?" he asked the air.

Judith shrugged off the question. "Will Kroeger try to protect us? He's half-Earth."

"He hates this mess as much as I do," Zann answered. "And he argued for a silent liquidation about as persuasively as anyone could. Surprised me. It was no-go. I think he'll try to the limit of his power, but given what he's up against . . ."

Gregory glanced at Yuri, who hadn't said a word. His face had hardened into the Wing mask. Gregory knew for a fact that the junior ace was no coward, but he had no chance of carrying out this operation without being detected. Yuri was in a bind. If he protested assignment now, nothing Kroeger might try to do wouldn't stop him from being charged with cowardice in the Fleet records . . . and maybe in Wing Command too. It would take more nerve for Yuri to back out than to proceed, but maybe backing out was his best tactic. After all, dammit, they were pilots, not grist for some Arthan's anti-Earther propaganda mill.

Once it had been so easy, Gregory thought. Fight the Sej. Protect the Wing and the family and, incidentally, the League.

"There have to be options," Judith protested. "We could try for an override from Wing Command. If the Old Man himself gave a direct order, we wouldn't have any problem."

"Then we get our funding cut again," Zann said sourly. "Face it, our budget's been reduced for three years running. And now there's another movement to evict us from Wing Moon and throw us someplace else."

Gregory had heard of that exactly once and had nearly broken the jaw of the idiot downworlder who'd spilled it to him. "Now they want it," he sneered. "Now, when we've turned it into prime real estate. It's been the one place we were sure of since . . ." He veered away, as they all did, from the subject of the Destruction of their homeworld. "Well, if they want our Moon back, let's give it to them in the condition they gave it to us. Vape it back to the airless rock the treaty gave us."

Zann smiled grimly. "I think that's what the Old Man told the League Special Committee, only a little more diplomatically. Why do you think they dropped the subject last time? But that's not the point. This is. No matter *what* we do, they're going to use it against us."

"Getting to breathe chlorine or methane instead of air," Dustin spat. "Not what I'd call a real choice."

The words curdled in Gregory's mouth as he spoke. "If we refuse, we're accused of cowardice. Not in so many words, but it'll get circulated through channels, and our appropriations will be cut further. And that will incite more anti-Earther sentiments on the worlds where we have refugees. Most of them are poorer worlds; they've got problems with unemployment, and from what Dustin says, riots already. We can't do that to them.

"Besides, what's our defense? That the League's going to use the death of a Sej traitor against us? That sounds rotten. If the Old Man countermands the task, it sounds worse. Either way, it's lousy. Our only hope lies in the fact that TreMorion's a Sej agent. If we take him, and it goes to a court-martial—which I expect—that's our defense. Yuri didn't murder a Blue Wing flight leader; he took out a Sejiedi spy . . . under orders. If the whole

League knows he was Sej, then we may get some support
. . . won't we? But if we refuse, and they go public on the
fact that we turned down the chance to eliminate a Sej
agent, then we're screwed.''

"I don't have any faith in the court-martial system,"
said Zann. "Not where our Wing's concerned. Not now. I
don't have a lot of faith that the thing will go public.
They'll classify it. I know I would." She spoke slowly,
the strain evident in her voice. "But Kolatolo doesn't own
all the press in the League, Gregory. If I hadn't already
come to your conclusions, I'd have refused to let Kroeger
even suggest this.''

He reached out and squeezed Zann's hand. Her shrewd-
ness always amazed him. He was glad she agreed with
him. If she had suggested another course of action, he
would probably have followed it. Zann knew what worked,
but it hadn't made her dirty, sly like the rest of them. She
was clean.

He glanced at the others. Dustin was staring at his feet
with concentration. The poor guy was probably hating
himself because TreMorion had saved his life. Judith was
biting her lip and twirling a lock of hair that she had
tugged free from the confining braids. She seemed more
thoughtful than gloomy. He hoped that she and Zann could
look after Dustin.

Yuri worried him. He hadn't moved a muscle during the
discussion, and usually he was the most restless member
of the squad. Now he sat as if already under the cold lights
of an interrogation room or facing a full bench, under trial.
And his face was impassive. The steel and arrogance of
the Wing mask wasn't for family. Gregory ached for the
kind of pride that kept Yuri from entering this discussion,
even though he was the one most at risk.

Gregory signaled to Judith with his eyes, then glanced over at Dustin. She nodded almost imperceptibly.

"Yuri, I want to talk with you," he said. Yuri stood and nodded as if he had been given a direct order, then followed Gregory into the privacy of his cabin.

Remembering the time he'd opened the bottle, Gregory poured out a stiff drink of bourbon and handed it to Yuri, who sat on the edge of his chair with his chin propped in his hands. Gregory dropped to the floor beside him, propping his back against his bunk.

"Let me do it, Yuri," he said. "It's not that I think you can't face them. I know you can. If it came to that, I know you'd freeze them to their seats. But I don't want to watch them smear you with the kind of shit that's going to come down the tubes. And I want TreMorion for myself."

Yuri smiled without humor. "You'd really like me to believe that you'd enjoy vaping the bastard more than I would. That's why you're going to wind up being the Old Man one of these years. But I don't believe you."

"After this, for sure I'm not going to get to be the Old Man," Gregory chuckled. It struck him as supremely funny that with this on the squad's record, Yuri still thought he would ever have the chance.

"Don't give me that, Greg," Yuri said. "You want it. You want it so bad you can taste it. That's one of the reasons I can't let you take full responsibility. I'm not the tau-void kid you flew to mass anymore. I can take what they throw at me. But the Wing! That's what hurts." The mask crumbled and revealed an expression somewhere between rage and anguish. "I feel filthy, being *their* pawn against the Wing, against our family, no matter what I do."

Gregory remembered that younger, more innocent Yuri and sighed. After this none of them would ever be innocent again. Zann had tried to shield them as best she could. But it wasn't good for the squads to get involved with Intelligence.

Gregory leaned his head back and looked up at Yuri. "When I was in training, it all seemed very easy. Who needed philosophy? You fought the Sej good and hard. Simple. In some ways, though, it's still simple. You still fight them. You fight the League too, if you can. Only there's no way around the League on this one. At least you can vape that son-of-a-bitch into the hell where he belongs.

"And then we tell the whole League, big and loud, and they'd better swallow it. Classified or not. Zann can take it; she's Wing before she's Intelligence. Our job is to get the Sej. So what if that helps Kolatolo? Every time we fly, it helps him. At least this way you've got a chance to make it clean and tell them all. That might even make things better for all the Earthers."

Gregory let his voice drop. "We're Earthers, you and me, Yuri, and our whole family, all the way back to Earth itself. And we've been bought and sold by people like Kolatolo for the past two hundred years. And who knows what happened before that? Had to be a reason why the whole planet died.

"Either way, they've got us; they've always had us. But if there were no Kolatolo, if there were none of those councils and appropriations committees and all the rest . . . if none of that stuff ever existed, what would you do? Let TreMorion go?"

The younger pilot turned and looked at Gregory, anger flashing across his face. "I'd kill the bastard right now with my bare hands."

"Then that's the right thing to do," Gregory said simply. He waited for the admission Yuri needed to make.

"Yes, you know it, Gregory. I'm scared. I don't want

to stand trial, don't want to end up in some execution chamber. I can't lie about that. But I've done plenty of things that frightened me. That's not the issue. The Wing's the issue. It means more to me than me, or my life, or even all of us. Look what it could do to us. You'd never get to Wing Command. Zann would be torn apart between Intelligence and the Wing. Gregory, if they try to use me to attack the Wing, I don't know if I can live with myself.''

"We can't let their games destroy us," Gregory said. "If we do, we might as well resign our commissions and apply for citizenship tomorrow. Assuming they'd let us. And if that happens, then we've put ourselves exactly where they want us.''

Yuri took a long swallow of the bourbon and set the nearly empty glass on the floor. He shook his head at the offer of a refill, and Gregory saw that his mood had shifted again to sadness. "It's only that . . . well, we were whole again. You, and having Dustin. Things were just starting to be good for the first time since . . .''

"We're still a family. And we're Wing. We're going to fight the Sej and the League on this one.''

Gregory met Yuri's eyes. He was unguarded now and Gregory knew that he understood that no matter what happened, Yuri wouldn't feel he had betrayed the most important things. His glance was even and clear, settled. He looked grim, but he always looked that way before combat.

They had been in normal space less than half an hour, and already the giant hangar-deck airlocks were opening. Surprise, Gregory thought, was the oldest tactic in the book, even better than superior numbers or technology— though those could help. His hands were poised over the control board, waiting to propel the sting into the blackness yawning before him. He could feel the surge in the engines, the smooth flow of energy through the newly cleaned converter, and he smiled humorlessly to himself. The techs had done a good job. He could sense the difference in the sting's performance.

"Flight Fourteen, prepare on the count of three," he spoke into the helmet comm. His fingers touched controls and he was free, hurtling into the void.

About him the flight's cone formed, tight and protected. As a single entity they flew toward the shadow, then veered sharply. The Sejiedi force was shielded from them by Mahalir 4. They curved tight in against the deceptively peaceful-looking rock that hid their presence from the enemy orbiting now on the night side.

"Below" them, Gregory saw a faint glitter of dawn reflecting off the glaciers that covered half the world's surface. As they broke from behind the shield of Mahalir 4 into the full glare of that system's sun, Gregory drew his breath in sharply. Scattered like jewels across the nexus of the system lay a full Sejiedi attack force. Waiting for them. Four cruisers, not the one they'd been led to expect. Four!

Someone had tipped the Sej off. Gregory cursed under his breath and hoped that Yuri realized that only one person could have done this. TreMorion had set the Fleet up for an ambush.

"Keep to their starboard flank," he ordered, giving both his flight and the Colors some warning before he arced out widely, diving straight at the outermost ships. The flight cones widened out and spun. But mobility and the stings' reflective surfaces wouldn't afford much protection from ships' lasers at full power. Only when they were weak, when there was an energy drain somewhere . . . Gregory's mind snapped shut, the full focus of his will and training closing into this single moment. Now the Sej were coming to meet them. The cone behind Gregory opened at the base like a deadly morning glory. The cruisers' hulls were washed a pale lilac by the reflection of high-frequency weapons.

He saw it on the comp grid and let it pass without observation. He had expected as much. From behind came another full flight of Sej, launched from the most distant cruiser.

"Allemand," he said. Six of his flight wheeled in position, forming a spiral that spiked "down." The others mirrored their formation.

The stings were badly outnumbered and, given those four cruisers, heavily outgunned. He already heard the order on open channel for Purple to regroup. Chatter came from some of the Colors and he suppressed an impulse to tell them to shut up and die like pilots. There was no chatter from White Wing, even on their private band, and he was proud.

His flight's spikes flew apart into whirling pairs flying protection for one another. His hands were steady on the fire controls, and he calculated range and target coldly before he released energy into the forward and aft guns. Had to save power. Three Sej came "up" from under him, trying to cut him off from Judith, his partner in this dance. Split them and fight two-on-one: that seemed to be the pattern. Momentarily it confused Gregory. This wasn't usual Sejiedi practice. Never mind, he told himself. However they fought, the bastards always fought to win.

He and Judith clung to one another, moving together to catch the three between them. He saw one Sej turn into a sunburst, then a sprinkle of light. *Good shooting, Jude,* he thought, then fired again.

Over open channel he heard the Green ordered to join

the Purples' strategic retreat. He discounted the order. What the others did wasn't important. White Wing would fight until orders pulled them back to the base ship. If no orders came, they'd fight till they were vaped. They were used to rearguard actions.

His comp showed that the rest of his flight had been scattered. The formation had broken into a series of single combats as the pilots tried to use their agility and fury to combat Sej strength of numbers. "Above" and port, he spotted a Sej coming just barely within range. Willing the other to remain on course, he fired the port stabilizer chamber, emptying it from violet into infrared. The Sej spun, and blew apart. Not a clean kill, but he didn't care. His hands reacted before he thought, and he fired again at the Sej that took the place of the one he'd taken out. He readied the three starboard guns and hoped that the extra fuel he carried would give him enough for a blanket shot. The comp noted another single kill. Dustin's, this time. His ninth. Gregory swore. He hoped Dustin wasn't counting kills, not at a time when they were so badly outnumbered.

No one had time for precision or elegance now. Purple and Green had been recalled. They were never much help, in any case.

"Yellow, regroup and return to Base," came over the comm.

As he watched and fought, his mind divided as it always did. Part of him was the lone fighter in the small sting, coping as best he could with a vastly superior force. The other part was the flight leader, who watched the pattern of his entire flight opening wider and wider until there was nothing at all left of the original tight formation. Gregory noted with satisfaction that Elizabeth was fighting well, had overcome her earlier nervousness.

Yuri had strayed to the edge of the group, was drawing closer to the Blues' field of action.

Debris and chaff littered space for a thousand kilometers, making a mess of Gregory's tracking system. He hoped that the Sej was affected even worse.

"Red, report to Base," came through open channel. So did the Reds' protests and crisp commands to shut up.

Only three of the Wings remained now, with White much smaller than the other two. Gregory gritted his teeth as he spent whatever energy the sting's converter would give him. There were too many ships packed in too tightly for the White to try to outfly them. Besides, he needed the energy for the lasers. No matter how many they killed, more seemed to grow in their places.

Yuri, do it! he prayed. Orange and Blue would be recalled any moment. He could feel sweat dripping down his neck under the tight helmet. His concentration narrowed. Fire. Keep it in the yellow range, not cold enough for them to spin out of it, but not so hot that he drained fuel reserves. Fire again. Move tight, in small bursts of speed, each a little greater than the last. Get some space to maneuver and fight harder.

The Sej were all firing in the violet range, and he couldn't afford to be caught in that; he couldn't spin around it. He dodged about in the small field he had managed to keep control of. Judith too was engaged in her own ring, evading and firing carefully, conserving fuel and slipping between their guns.

"Start to break," he ordered. He wasn't certain if they'd be able to, if they would ever make it back. But if the Sej were going to take out his flight, they'd pay for it, were paying for it now. Another flash lit his screens, and satisfaction filled him. Charles had taken out another. Good work.

Maybe they were stuck here. Given the League, that was possible. Sure, no one had ever sent White Wing squads on a suicide run before, but look at the task they'd set Yuri. He would believe anything now.

Just let Yuri take care of that bastard, and he'd be content to go down fighting . . . almost. At least they'd make the Sej pay ten to one. He swore that on the honor of the Wing.

The breakaway was starting. Yellow was hard to fire. They'd need the fuel to put on the sudden rush, to slip away, and turn back, doubling over their own emissions into the trail of their own fire. It should be scattered by then, targeted or slowed. A risky business; none of them liked it.

Farthest out, with the fewest Sej tailing him, Yuri broke first. Gregory widened his own circle of power, deliberately keeping his speed three degrees below maximum. In a minute, he would surge into max and spray-scatter them. The extra fuel was worth the extra inertial thrust. The Sej fighters built speed with mass-inertia, which gave them less flexibility than the tiny stings, but more power, useful in situations such as these.

The Sej were complacent now, waiting, believing that his energy was low, down to yellow, three steps below max. They might even have hopes of reeling him in. Just let them try! Fury rose as he drew on the reserve power.

"Orange, retreat!" Retreat? This wasn't a retreat, he thought, noting the few surviving Orange ships struggling back home. This was a rout, and all due to TreMorion.

Yuri was diving, spinning in glorious parabolas, as if unaware of the Sej trying to overtake him—until he looped back to surprise one or another of them with a lethal burst of fire. Delaying tactics now while the Blues regrouped, preparing to make their own run for cover. They'd be recalled very shortly. And then it would be the turn of White Wing.

Gregory slammed his left hand onto the board and opened up his reserves to burst through the Sej laser fire.

"Blue Wing, regroup. Return to Base."

Gregory threw his sting into a whirling arc, a wide flyby, his usual signal to gather his flight. It was crazy flying, good for confusing the enemy with the sudden speed and power they'd saved. About him the rest of the flight opened out, dodged, and lifted back into their cone formation. All except Yuri.

Gregory heard Zann's voice coming over the White Wing frequencies, relaying Kroeger's concern that Yuri was backing down. He answered shortly. Zann knew better, and could tell Kroeger what to do with his worries, for all he cared.

Now Blue Wing was retreating as ordered, beaten, weary, but maintaining orderly formations. TreMorion's sting was well to the rear, covering their retreat with his usual bravado. Yuri came blasting behind the Sej, taking two of them who were concentrating on the Blue. The rest of TreMorion's flight was too far away to turn back to cover, and not in the best shape for it. For good measure, Yuri vaped another Sej from behind before he maneuvered a little to starboard, a little "up," and then fired his forward lasers.

It was an elegant kill.

"What the *hell*?"

"Later, Neil," Gregory spoke into the comm. "Let's bring them home."

Pushing his speed past max, past the limits decreed by the test engineers, Gregory raced away from the pack of Sej he'd been fighting to Yuri's position, the rest of the flight following. The Sej weren't pursuing as hard as they might. They knew when they had the Fleet beaten, and they weren't going to risk burning out their own a-gravs for the chance at a few more kills.

"Form on me," Gregory ordered.

The cone formed again, no longer glittering white, but glowing a sullen crimson. But Gregory'd thought too soon. A single flight of Sejiedi raced after them, mass building their speed, bringing them into firing range.

"All units report to Base," he heard. They were being ordered back . . . and about time. The cone spiraled and dove into a loop, the trajectory of which would bring them back to the base ship. The Sej were gaining, and Gregory cursed under his breath.

Violet, pale and ghostly, flickered for a moment, and then died. A white flash blazed on Gregory's screen.

"Neil!" he shouted, breaking his own rule about chatter. Flying with his usual fierce concentration, Neil would never know what had hit him. He'd have been furious at the idea. Gregory sealed off his grief the way he'd had to when Maryam died.

He had them pushing their stings faster than he'd ever dared. Numbers bled together on the boards so fast that his eyes couldn't track them. He had to get the rest of them home.

Now he could see the base ship, the markings, and the dark mouths of the hangar deck. Behind him the Sej wheeled away, reluctant to come within range of the laser cannons, or perhaps appeased by one White Wing death.

Gregory powered down, coming in onto the grating. As the hook line wrenched him to a halt, he let the pain wash over him. Neil was gone. His oldest friend. He'd never imagined that this would happen. There'd be no music anymore. He ached for Glennis and the rest of the squad.

But when he climbed out of the sting, there'd be Colors about, trouble to face. He forced back the tears.

He jumped from the cockpit onto the grating of the flight deck. The cacophony of defeat exploded around him. Medics and corpsmen were sorting the wounded into three groups: those who'd probably die, those who could wait before a physician could treat them, and those who had to be tended right away. Some pilots were already being trundled off on floats, with IVs bobbing over their heads. Whimpers and cries echoed from the hull throughout the cavern of the hangar deck. People bent over and into themselves, mourning wounds or friends' captures, too intent on their own pain to notice his.

Gregory's flight formed around him, standing proud with their helmets held in the angle prescribed by the drill tapes. Maybe they were dead tired. Maybe they'd taken some bruises or minor wounds. But none of the Colors would ever see it in their eyes.

In the middle of the deck, Gregory saw what he'd dreaded—the dark gold of Security, surrounded by a sea of Blues. Security had Joao with them, bloody flecks marring the arms of his coverall. Gregory could hear him arguing that he accepted arrest, and ought to be allowed to tend to his patients, under guard if necessary, but quickly! His voice was almost pleading. Valentina, tiny in the midst of all those Golds, pushed through brutally until she reached Joao's side.

"THREE MINUTES TO TAU . . ."

In drill formation, Gregory's flight marched over to the security guards. Suddenly he felt wetness spatter his cheek. He turned with deliberation. Blues were unworthy of his anger. He met several pairs of eyes, as cold and menacing as the Whites' were supposed to be. Nothing changed the hatred on their faces. One or two stepped back, then surged forward against the barrier formed by the Gold tunics of Security. If the Golds couldn't hold them back, Gregory thought, they might all be torn apart before Yuri had to stand trial.

A senior officer stepped over to Yuri, followed by an assistant who held energy bracelets open. "You're under arrest for the murder of an officer of the Fleet," said the officer, and gestured for the cuffs to be activated.

"Put those things away," Yuri said, his voice tinged with contempt. "I'll come. You have my word."

Gregory drew in a breath, proud of Yuri's disdain. The two security officers glanced at one another.

Again Yuri glared at the energy bracelets. "You have my word," he repeated. His voice lashed at the guards. "On the honor of the Wing."

In two hundred years, the honor of the Wing had never been broken, not by a look, an action (*not even this!* Gregory thought), or a capture. The man put the bracelets aside.

Gregory moved forward to stand between the armed guards at Yuri's side. "He was under my command," he said.

He could see Reds at the edge of the crowd. Some of them looked stunned at what was going on.

"Our orders require us to arrest your entire squad."

Judith and Dustin joined the other pilots, Dustin with composure, Judith with a haughty elegance Gregory might have chuckled at in a more peaceful setting. The dark gold uniforms closed in on them, protecting them from the taunts and spittle of the Blues as they marched from the flight deck. More Golds met them outside. This pack had Zann in tow, but she moved as if they were an honor guard, pulling them with her as she joined the rest of her squad.

"They pulled me right off my board," she said. "But I saw everything."

"The brig?" her guards asked their superior.

Kroeger materialized in the way Gregory found so uncanny and faced the Golds.

"The Captain's ordered them to be taken back to quarters. Someone might decide he didn't want to wait for a full investigation, and the Captain wants to avoid that at all costs."

"Post a guard?" asked Security, almost in protest.

"Certainly," Kroeger replied. "Half from your forces, and half from the Blues'."

Blues in White Wing territory? Gregory looked over at Zann, who nodded at him. "That'll forestall some comment."

A carefully chosen force of Golds and Blues marched them back to quarters. Their door slid shut behind them as it had so many times before. But this time, their quarters were their prison.

CHAPTER 14

"The worst part's that you won't be able to get to Neil's Memorial," Yuri said miserably. "None of us will."

Gregory walked across the wardroom to lay a hand on Yuri's shoulder. "That's not the worst of it, Yuri. But you did what you had to do—and you did a damned fine job."

He wished he could offer the younger man hope or comfort, but he'd never had much hope that this task would turn out well, and there was little enough comfort he could find for himself. Neil was gone, vaped retreating from an ambush that that Sej TreMorion had set up. Neil. They had known each other for as far back as Gregory could remember, had banged each other on the head with model stings in their earliest playgroups. For all the years they had studied together, roomed together, flown together, and fought. Usually they fought at least once a week.

Most people had expected them to marry into the same squad. But Gregory and Neil had known that wouldn't work. There had always been so much competition be-

tween them that their fights had become a running joke
(and spectator sport) among their friends and families.
Gregory was bleakly grateful that this week, at least, he
and Neil hadn't fought. He would have felt Neil's voice-
less recriminations forever. There'd be no fights now, not
anymore, though Gregory suspected that anything that might
remain of Neil's spirit was probably furious that Gregory
would miss his Memorial.

It hurt to keep the feelings bottled up inside, but expressing them would only make Yuri feel worse. Yuri
didn't look as if he could take much more.

"Go lie down, Yuri," Joao came in and ordered. To
Gregory's horror, Yuri obeyed immediately.

Joao padded over to Gregory and sank into a padded
chair. He'd changed into a clean worksuit, and now he sat
rubbing his hands against his bare forearms. "I told those
Golds that they needed me on the flight deck or in Sick
Bay. I told them! They wouldn't listen." Gregory knew
that Joao hated being pulled away from the casualties.
Then Joao sighed. "Probably, they wouldn't have let me
treat them anyhow. Not after what they saw."

"The others?" Gregory asked. Without waiting for Joao's
answer, he got up to investigate. Zann was in her quarters,
deep in that trancelike state that she called concentration.
Valentina was sorting chips into various containers. Judith
and Dustin passed him in the corridor, Judith quiet, Dustin
watchful.

"Yuri's out cold, thank God," Judith told Gregory.

So much for checking up on his squad. He returned to
his seat beside Joao. He wished he could talk to Zann. She
might have some idea whether Kroeger could do anything
to spring them out of this trap. She'd said that the gray civ
hadn't liked matters any better than she had, and she was
usually right about such things. Perhaps Kroeger was trying

to be useful, pay them back a little. Maybe he would talk to Command and try to set an investigation going in which he could spill all his precious data and Intelligence orders all over the Captain's databases before his own chief gagged him.

"You know," Joao spoke into the silence, "I warned Zann about this order. I told her to let me take care of it. No mess, no trouble. I could've made it look like a heart attack. Easy. No problems with drugs either. Hell, I wouldn't have been surprised if TreMorion already had high blood pressure. He was a classic type A."

"We might as well know the worst of it," Dustin said. He reached for computer controls. "Hmm. Val's usual passwords are blocked. She's not going to like this. Let's see if we can hook into the viewing systems."

Gregory grunted. The screen blanked, then resolved into a shot of a press briefing, a mob scene of important, rushed-looking men and women badgering another man with questions. He was very tall, this man, and a classic Arthan type, light-eyed, with the pale hair starting to gray at the sides and the carefully groomed sweep across his brow. His clothes were conservative, drab even, but the effect was one of solidity and reassurance. Even as Gregory watched, the man on the screen sighed, rubbed his hands across his temples, then rolled up his sleeves: the image of a pained, conscientious man attending to a dirty business. But this was no careworn official; this was something far more hostile to them and, because less hedged in by restrictions, far more powerful than any member of the League's civilian Assembly.

"Oh my God," Gregory muttered. "It *would* have to be Kolatolo. Do you really want to watch this? He'll mop the decks with what went on today."

"We have to know," Dustin persisted, and turned on a recorder. "Zann will need it too."

They listened in silence to Kolatolo being shocked and saddened by the loss of so many ships. He went on to call the Mahalir action ill-conceived, and Dustin reacted. "Damned straight. And poorly funded."

"We were set up!" Judith said. "In more ways than one."

By the time Kolatolo, his long face pinching with disdain and sorrow, got to the part about "wanton murder of an Arthan national, one of Blue Wing's most illustrious . . ." Joao exploded.

"What about that squad he killed? What about all the pilots who got killed today—or captured?"

What about Neil's life? Or Yuri's career? If the audience reaction was anything to judge by, they'd all be lucky to escape execution. Dishonorable discharge might be the best they could hope for, Gregory thought.

"They move fast," Dustin observed in an undertone. "Wait till you hear what he's probably got saved to call us!"

In a low monotone, Judith was swearing without rage, originality, or relief.

" . . . see no other course but to demand the suspension from the Fleet of the League of Known Worlds the unit of refugee auxiliaries known as White Wing . . ."

"What the hell's going on?" Yuri muttered sleepily from the door.

"The Ag Kolatolo show. Public indignation at our expense," Gregory said. Auxiliaries! The Wing had the best damned record in the Fleet.

" . . . pending a thorough investigation into their activities and their loyalty."

Valentina emerged from her cabin and shouted with

incredulous rage at that one. Zann came in and sat beside Gregory, taking his hand.

"This should be brilliant," she observed, with reluctant admiration. "Watch him. So concerned, so . . . saddened by what's happened. If I were in his boots, I'd probably stress the fact we're noncitizens, that our Treaty restricts access to the Wing Moon . . ."

Historians showing archived tapes of the arrival of the orphaned Earthers, of the treaty negotiations which admitted them to League Service. Political analysts. News commentators, showing anti-Earther riots on at least ten worlds they'd heard of, including Corvynem. And now that the damage was done, officials of the League.

"How long do we have to watch this shit?" Gregory asked. The strain around Yuri's mouth was forming brackets, and his eyes were glazing.

"We might as well," Yuri said morosely. "We're going to have a lot of time to pass. You know, you shouldn't have insisted on standing by me like that. Maybe they'd be content with just one victim."

"Not this time, Yuri," Zann said. "They're not out to make a little trouble. This is a full-fledged witch-hunt. League-wide."

"God help all those Earther civs down there," Dustin murmured. He thought of the people he'd met on Corvynem, of their pride and their vulnerability, and winced. He had no way to check up on them. What would be the point? Hundreds of thousands were in the same situation.

"You kicking us out of our own quarters, Yuri?" Joao managed a good facsimile of a chuckle.

They kept the viewer on out of a kind of morbid fascination. Kolatolo's voice, then a host of others, provided background chatter for Yuri's desultory work on the squad's books.

"We're really going to be broke," he pointed out. "Naturally we forfeit combat pay as long as we're under arrest . . ." He fell silent again, gloomily contemplating the spreadsheets. After a time, he turned away from them.

"That's the Old Man!" Valentina shouted, and brought them running to the viewer. Zann and Gregory exchanged glances. If this mess had brought the Wing Commander from the Wing Moon to the Assembly . . . the military governor almost never left his post.

"They won't let him speak," Zann predicted. "They'll shout him down."

"He looks furious," said Gregory. "How's he manage it, keeping his face so calm yet making people know he's ready to start swinging?"

"Look in a mirror sometime," Dustin commented.

Gregory as Old Man? Hell, they'd be lucky if they weren't torn apart. He had little faith in the abilities of Security to hold back an angry mob, and none at all in the Blues who stood guard with them.

Time dragged by. Gregory slept, or dozed. Two meals were brought in, Joao scanning each one in case a Blue or anyone else had bright ideas about bagging some White Wingers. Except for the coffee, the food wasn't too bad. Arrest was arrest, sure. But at least they were confined to quarters, not thrown into the brig, where they'd have been split up.

Voices woke him from a nap he hadn't expected to take. Joao was talking to someone . . . he knew that soft, precise voice. Kroeger.

"Suzannah's resting now," Joao told the civ. "If this is an emergency, I will wake her. Otherwise . . . I may be under arrest, but I'm still a qualified physician. Yes, certainly, you can sit down. Sorry there's no coffee to offer you.

"No, I have no idea what's going to happen to us," Joao went on, his bass rumble easier to pick up than Kroeger's lighter tones. "The 'casts don't look good. The squad? Thanks for asking. Neil's squad's probably halfway to Wing Moon by now. That's right, there's always a Memorial service. We're suspended. That leaves Anna as senior pilot. Probably she'll elect to join two sib squads. She ought to make a good flight leader."

Gregory heard something about casualties. "In the past year," Joao's voice went on, "we've lost three: John, Maryam, and now Neil. Twenty-five percent." Another murmur from Kroeger.

"Yes," Joao said, his voice heavy, "I know that figure's low for the rest of the Fleet. But given our overall population . . ."

A long, long silence. Gregory could imagine the medic wishing Kroeger gone while Kroeger thought up ways of keeping Joao talking. "Sure, there's something I need," Joao said. "I need to have my squad's name cleared. I need to get to Sick Bay. Do you know the burn-out rate among medics in the Fleet these days?"

Gregory heard a figure, then the snort that meant Joao was refusing to admit he was amused. "I ought to be there. Yes, I appreciate you're doing the best you can. I'll tell Suzannah that you will be in contact, then. Thank you for stopping by."

"Rise and shine, White Wingers!" A security guard walked into the wardroom, his eyes sweeping it curiously.

Yuri rose to his feet. "Where do you want us to go?"

"*I* frankly couldn't care less. Neither, it seems, does the Captain. The brass seems to have decided to set you free."

Gregory lowered his feet to the floor, and sat bolt

upright. "Would you please repeat that? Slowly, this time, and with details."

The guard sighed. "Never heard of such a short investigation in my life. What kind of friends do you White Wingers have in high places? Doesn't matter; the order for your release just came through. You've all been cleared. Beats me."

"Where's Federico Hashrahh Kroeger?" Zann demanded, striding toward the guard.

"Recovered, I see," Kroeger observed dryly. "My congratulations. It appears that the Captain's recent investigations have exonerated Yuri and the rest of you."

"What investigations?" Gregory whispered to Dustin.

"In any case, I'd advise you to be careful in what you say. The entire proceedings of this inquest have been classified. In fact, you'd best not refer to this incident again."

"Request transcript," Zann said.

"You're not cleared for it."

She stared at him and held out her hand. After a moment, he handed her a gray plaque. She raised her eyebrows. "Destroy upon readout? Serious. Thank you, sir." She turned and headed for her quarters and her reader there.

When she emerged, Greogry ran over to her and hugged her. "How'd Kroeger pull it off?" He kissed her, laughing against her face at their narrow escape.

Zann laughed and rubbed her cheek against his shoulder. "He went to the Captain while we were in tau and spilled everything. Everything. Of course, he had to do it while we were in tau. Otherwise he'd have had to consult with the Chief's office, and they'd have shut us down for good. But it worked."

Valentina had logged on and was calling up data furiously. "We're still too late," she said, looking up. "We emerged from tau at oh-eight-hundred to transfer wounded to the base hospital at Coberous. Neil's squad got transport to Wing Moon there."

Well, Gregory hadn't expected to get to Neil's Memorial. Still, it was a blow. "Where are we headed now?"

"Subiat," Valentina replied heavily. "Not exactly a good place for White Wingers to go on shore leave."

Gregory nodded. Any White Wingers on the ship would be virtual prisoners on board the base ship. Subiat, one of the Arthan worlds-minor, was heavily settled, heavily industrialized, and heavily indebted to the Arthan Assembly, which no doubt told it how to vote.

The hunger pummeled Bikmat awake. It couldn't be. It was too soon after the last time, far too soon. What could they want with him on Subiat?

Beside him, Valentina murmured and stole more of the sheet. Bikmat had a sudden urge to wake her, to bury his face against her soft shoulder and to confess everything. Valentina looked so innocent, so incapable of the fury he knew she would display if she knew what he was. She mumbled something and he stroked her cheek gently.

In the dark, the hunger washed over him like a vast tide. It tore into him, demanding, abrasive.

Against the sheets, Valentina looked so fragile, her beautifully molded fingers curled gently like a child's against her cheek. The sight of her lying there made him want to fight again, to fight harder than he had on Corvynem, and even before that.

No operative has ever changed sides. Many have died— honor to their names—but none has ever betrayed us. The words rang in his head, circling in the throbbing at his temples. They had never been betrayed? Bikmat would see about that. He would see. He had other things now, more important things, that he dared not betray.

Silently he slipped from the bunk, careful not to disturb Valentina's rest. Covering her with the rest of the sheet, he bent and kissed her tenderly.

Without turning on the light, he slipped into a work uniform and softly padded through the wardroom and out into the corridor.

He would need clothes before anything else, he knew. This was the ship's night cycle, and there was only a skeleton crew on duty. He made his way deep into the bowels of the ship, down near Kroeger's den near Maintenance. The supply closet near the Intelligence operative's hideaway was lucky for him. Bikmat was able to find a heavy dark green maintenance coverall, something that one of the lowest-rank Greens might wear for dirty work. It hung on him, a good thing, since he'd be able to fit clothes on underneath it.

He didn't plan to look like a maintenance tech downworld. He didn't want to be distinguished as military at all. Adjusting his posture and walk to fit the uniform he wore, he made his way down to the ship's stores.

It wasn't difficult to palm the lock open. He had learned more ways of breaking into locked rooms than he would ever use. He found only a very small selection of off-duty wear, mostly things people might want to replace during a long tour of duty or something they might want to borrow for a day's shore leave. Bikmat pulled a sports shirt from a shelf and dug out a pair of casual slacks that weren't a terrible fit. He stripped and put on the civvies, adding socks and gym shoes from Athletic Supplies, which was stocked almost creditably. Over this clothing he pulled the baggy maintenance worksuit.

He rummaged through his discarded white uniform for

whatever cash he had left from his last round of bets on simulation games and for the lucky handkerchief he always carried. Once more he checked the pockets to make certain they were empty, then stuffed the uniform into the nearest recycling chute. In a few seconds it would be broken down into component atoms, indistinguishable from scrap metal, last night's dinner, or anything else that got dumped to be used for the ship's drive. Then he headed down toward Cargo Transport.

Good. There were no low-rating Greens among the crew readying three ships to head downworld. Bikmat glanced at the checklist, then walked over to the enlisted woman at the desk.

"I'm supposed to accompany shipment 11975," Bikmat told her. She raised her eyes wearily and waved him through.

Bikmat strapped down into one of the uncomfortable seats that made cargo transports notorious in the Fleet. This time, unlike his trip to Corvynem, he didn't have to feign sleep. He didn't have to worry about being polite to seatmates. He thought briefly of worrying that the transport's pilot had only an enlistment rating, and put it out of his head.

They reached the cargo port at Subiat early in the planet's business day. Bikmat grunted to the pilot and went to the nearest food booth. As he hoped, his meal came in a large plastic bag, brightly colored, and with strong handles. He munched on some of the food, hoping to stave off the hunger for a few moments more. Then he headed for the restroom. Once inside, he stripped off the green coverall and stuffed it into the bag, then arranged the rest of the food to cover it.

Clothes not only didn't make the man, he had learned from his Sejiedi instructors, they didn't make the disguise either. A shuffling, surly Maintenance man had entered the washroom. A jaunty, whistling tourist in sports clothes came out. It was all in the walk, the turn of the head. Clothes simply made the act easier to pull off.

He took the tube into the city. Seeing the other passengers absorbed in newspads or the holographic ads flickering on the car's walls, Bikmat stuffed the bag under his seat. It galled him to throw away the food, but he didn't want to be linked with that uniform now. Subiat was a well-run place. Doubtless the bag would be found and turned in. He could always claim it later when he needed to get back to the base ship.

The hunger washed over him again, turning him dizzy and sick with a craving that had nothing to do with the food he'd eaten earlier, and everything to do with the potent hathoti pulp with which his system had been saturated when he was a child. The hunger and his hatred of it warred with each other. Once again, the hunger won. The hypnoreels deep in his unconscious took over again. But this time the anger was stronger than it had ever been. This time he knew what the Sej wanted. This time, they wouldn't be satisfied with innocuous reports on the Wing. They wanted Gregory.

Well, they couldn't have him. Gregory was his, just like the rest of the squad. For the first time, even the horror of isolation, of knowing what he was, abated. Bikmat breathed slowly, trying to still the churning in his mind. If he could slow down, he could think of something, could avoid being herded to his contact by the hunger. There was no way he was going to obey the Sej. Not this time. Not ever again.

He let his eyes glance at the tube holos. The Sej had made sure he knew Arthan as well as most of the rest of the worlds' major languages. One ad caught his eye. That would do it. Carefully, he memorized the address of the music shop offering lessons and instruments from most of the Known World.

Debarking at City Station, Bikmat headed for the large map in the central hall. His guess paid off. A shop that could pay for that ad would have a good location, close to the station. He could walk.

The human clerk—another touch of class—sold him a set of guitar strings without turning up her nose at the mention of the Earther instrument. After all, it wasn't all that different from its Arthan counterpart.

Three doors down was a stationer's. Bikmat purchased a 30cm ruler made of heavy polished wood with patterns cut in it. The hunger beat at him again, more and more insistent. He stuffed his purchases into his shirt and followed the codes that had been ingrained in him so long ago. The pattern was the same as Corvynem: the small shop, the purchase, the capsule.

He wandered toward a sunny bench in a plaza and sat down to open the capsule. No one would question a tourist who chose to rest in the sun for a while and here, out in the open, it would be impossible to be shadowed. It was always best to stay in the open.

For a moment, he studied the contents of the capsule, then crushed it between his palms. Taking out the bags with his purchases, he pulled the low E string, a heavy thing wrapped in silver wire, from its packet and dropped it in the bag with the ruler. Then he discarded both the capsule and the rest of the strings.

He studied the ruler he'd bought for a moment. It was an ugly, sturdy thing, its thick, hard wood pierced with the name of the city and its symbol. Excellent.

Stuffing string and ruler into his clothing, he closed his eyes as if napping and counted slowly to fifty. Then he left the park, heading from the business district into the more fashionable residential areas.

He had been a tourist long enough, he decided. It was time to change. The last of his cash bought him fairly decent casual separates at a store dealing in "nearly new" merchandise. Ten minutes later, a quick foray into a cleaning establishment allowed him to replace his sports outfit with a fine-quality jacket and jumpsuit cut in the Arthan style. Now he could walk unnoticed into the best part of the city.

He braced himself. Unlike his previous meetings with contacts, the person he was going to meet now was no illegal but a courier on a full round of business. He found the address contained in the capsule, and raised one eyebrow at the hotel's quality. The concierge was human, not robotic, and smiled at the prosperous Arthan as he gave him the room number he'd been ordered to seek. Ignoring the tubes, Dustin took the nearest stairs two at a time. Once outside the courier's suite, he rapped twice heavily, paused, then knocked again three times in rapid succession. Then he placed himself so that the courier could study his face before admitting him.

By the time the door finally opened, the hunger nearly had him dizzy. He felt weak, but there was no way he would show it before the courier, a tall black-eyed woman—a true Sej trained in every art of subterfuge.

"Bikmat," she said and stared him up and down.

He glanced up sharply. The courier hadn't used the recognition codes. Suddenly he understood why she hadn't, and why she was the one they had decided he should report to.

Her eyes went hard. "What was the name of the third in our field survival test group?" she demanded.

"Idris." The name of the boy he'd had to kill came in a

whisper. He had once wondered what had happened to Aramin. A courier. She'd come fast and far. Couriers were the aristocrats of the trade. The Aramin he remembered had been lanky and intense. This one was tall, beautiful, with a carefully groomed sweep of russet hair brushing her shoulders, bared by the halter cut of her expensive white tunic and trouser outfit. White, no less. In his honor? The Aramin he remembered liked to set little traps. A large, almost violet baroque pearl glistened in the ear not covered by her long hair.

Hunger pulsed through him. For all his attempts to hold himself straight, he knew Aramin could see it. He felt as if he were candy melting in the sun.

"Why didn't you encourage Gregory to eliminate Aglo, instead of permitting your other squadmate the task?" she asked harshly. "It is necessary to discredit Gregory as quickly as possible, do you understand? I wonder about you, Bikmat. You were reluctant enough to kill Idris. Have you gone soft?"

"Gregory volunteered. He was overruled. How would you like me to discredit Gregory? Shall I blow my cover?" He matched her tone.

"That would indeed discredit Gregory and the entire Wing," she replied. "But it would render you incapable of further service." She paused, weighing options. "If you cannot think of another means of discrediting the Wing, reveal yourself. Whatever you do must occur within the next thirty days."

"May I ask why?"

"Orders."

"Aramin," Bikmat said quietly. "This is me. Bikmat. From training. You know you can trust me. Not like the others. I want to function well, and I need more information if I'm to do so." He let himself waver perceptibly.

"And this hunger . . . could you give me at least one of the ration cakes now?"

She appraised him for a moment, while he reached out to grasp the back of a chair. Then, deliberately, she unwrapped one of the pungent squares, placed it on a delicately painted plate, and laid it on a table as if it were the last course in an academy banquet. Bikmat ate slowly, with attention to his manners. His thinking cleared as the hunger ebbed. Aramin wasn't the sort to trust people, but she knew him and perhaps he could count on that a little. They had trained together, and she'd decided, years ago, that he was soft. He noticed that unlike the fat man on Corvynem, she felt no need to keep a weapon trained on him.

Jarred and reeling from the hunger, his mind read something in her face. Her expression was gloating. She knew something, something he didn't, and he wanted to—for the welfare of his squad and Wing.

The one ration had taken the edge off his hunger, not enough to comfort him, but enough to let him concentrate. He would have at least half an hour before the hathoti pulp hit him hard enough to make him sick. The fact she'd allowed him to have it before he'd made his report let him know that she and the Sej in general had no particular suspicions about him.

"Why was I called in? I reported on Corvynem."

"The time frame here is highly important," she said haughtily. "Actually I wasn't scheduled to meet with you at all, but my superiors deemed it important in light of my overall mission in this sector. And it was easy enough to arrange." She glanced over to the closet, and Bikmat felt his chest tighten.

Either she had made a mistake, or was deliberately misleading him. When he had known Aramin as an Intelligence trainee, she wasn't the type to make mistakes. She was too close to the hungry packs for that. But now she was lavishly dressed, had grown into a beautiful woman who used her beauty as one of many weapons in her arsenal. She was obviously trusted with extremely important messages. Maybe she had grown careless, arrogant with success. It was a failing of the warrior-born with whom Aramin identified. But he wouldn't want to lay any money on Aramin's having it.

He could feel the guitar string and ruler in his pocket. Suddenly he wished he faced the fat, dangerous illegal on Corvynem. It would be easier to kill him than someone like her. Odd: he wouldn't have thought he'd be reluctant to kill a woman. Fighting sting-to-sting, you never knew if the pilot you battled was male or female. Somehow, this was different.

Aramin had turned her back on him, but there was no trust in that gesture. She was looking into a mirror, watching him speculatively.

Hands out from his sides, he moved toward her. He could see printouts and tapes stacked on nearby tables . . . something about commodities. He forced himself to concentrate only on Aramin. "This is better than Nahi, when we had to huddle together to keep warm," he said. "You've done well." He let admiration shade his voice. When she didn't reply or object, he came up behind her carefully and began to stroke her shoulder.

She chuckled. "I always did think you liked me," she said.

"You were right." He nuzzled deep into her heavy russet hair. The scent of a very expensive Arthan perfume enveloped him. The touch and smell of her hair reminded him of Judith's favorite scent. Suddenly he found Aramin revolting. He told her she was beautiful.

He felt her relax slightly, leaning against him the way Zann had done the first time they were together. He put that out of his mind. Zann was family, and he loved her. Aramin had ambitions to link with the warrior-born. In that case, what was he to her? An operative to brief, an old comrade to bully, a diversion to while away the time in the boring restrictions of a small city until she could take up her real mission again. The Sej lower classes were taught to think that they were honored if a warrior-born noticed them, and privileged if they submitted to be used.

Clearly Aramin had adopted that mind-set. Well, the news was always full of stories of beautiful, ruthless women who'd mistaken a nasty piece of rough trade for a sexual plaything and paid for their mistakes with their lives.

He wasn't an entertainment; he was Dustin, White Wing pilot, a member of a family. His right hand flashed to the string he'd bought. Before she had noticed the movement, he had it around her neck, ends slipped neatly through the ruler which he twisted for leverage.

Aramin clawed at the wire and his hands behind her neck. He arched his body away from hers, his feet planted well to the sides, as she tried to jab an elbow back into his ribs, to stamp on his instep with the sharp heels of her sandals. He had been taught the same moves; he expected them. And he was a pilot, his faster-than-normal reflexes trained to a high pitch.

Aramin sank down, the wire crushing her larynx into her throat. Bikmat was glad he couldn't see her face. He knew what strangulation looked like: the silent gasping scream, and finally the narrow ribbons of blood that oozed from the eyesockets and mouth. He held the ruler tightly as her struggles weakened, then stopped. Even then, he didn't let go. He glanced down at his wristcomp and watched the seconds flash by on the chrono, sweating and willing them to pass faster. He gave it ten minutes, then pulled the string loose.

If that's all you valued your life, Aramin, he told the crumpled, white-clad body, *why should I value it for you?*

He pulled the handkerchief from his pocket and carefully wiped the ruler, the door, any other surface he had touched. Wrapping his right hand, he went to the closet. Several very expensive garments hung there, and a light suitcase lay on the floor.

He dragged it into the room, opened it, and found it empty. Well, he'd expected that. He went through the various catches for a false bottom and wasn't surprised to discover an irregularity in the lining. He touched it gently and a hidden part of the case opened. It was easy with Aramin. They had been trained alike.

At the bottom of the case weren't the documents or weapons he had hoped for but jewelry. She *had* misled him, and he began to sweat. Hathoti reaction started to make the room swing in lazy arcs about him. He rose to his feet and began to search in earnest. What was her cover? Commodities trader? It made sense; people expected them to be far-traveling, high-living . . . he pulled open drawers and found nothing, then headed for the suite's kitchen. In the cooler lay a spray of flowers, the sort of thing that a woman like Aramin had impersonated might give or send to someone important to her. In the center of the bunch lay one of the most beautiful flowers he had ever seen. Royal purple at the base of the petals paled to crimson at the fluted edges. The long stamen was a soft, pale yellow. Akharti hathoti, he recognized the flower, most potent, most expensive, and most difficult to procure of all the drug lilies. Usually the Sej reserved it for the highest echelons of Sejiedi society, or for the very few they wished to addict and buy.

Who were they buying with this one?

Bikmat went to Aramin's cosmetics and searched quickly. No chip in the little silken bag, no credit slips. Then he smiled. Aramin posed as a civilian woman, and civilian women carried bags. Hers lay on the floor near the closet. An envelope of credit slips lay within. There was a magnetic tape across each slip. One of those tapes would contain data far more important to them both than purchasing limits and bank numbers. As he riffled through them, a slip of paper with a comm code scribbled on it dropped out. Bikmat clicked his tongue. Aramin had indeed become very careless. She'd have been beaten for this stunt if she'd pulled it in training. They'd all been drilled to memorize just such numbers; it totally violated regulations to write down and keep anything like this. But then, it had also been severely against all training for her to let him within arm's reach. As the drillmasters had always said, errors were invariably fatal. He grinned, mirthlessly.

Now he could feel the hathoti pulp working in him. He walked to the bathroom and was sick. Then he returned to the room and sat down. He had the call code memorized. He had the lily and all of Aramin's credit slips. And he had the records of her commodity-trader persona. Somewhere in this data he'd find information about his assignment to turn on Gregory and, through him, the entire Wing. He had options, choices.

Only one option was gone now, completely and forever. He had killed his contact. He was the very first operative ever to betray the Sej.

Time to leave, he thought. The concierge would be on the prowl, gossipy like all his breed. He found a shopping bag in the closet and let out a low whistle at the name printed on it. Even White Wing pilots could recognize that one. What a shame it was that this Sej spy could afford such things while the women in his squad . . . never mind that. He put the lily in the shopping bag, then took one of Aramin's dresses and laid it over the deadly flower.

Then he took one of Aramin's cards over to the messager unit, debiting her account for the call.

The other line chimed only once. "Aramin? How's my lovely lady?" Bikmat froze, then broke the connection. He knew that voice, had heard it, plausible and injured, when he sat with his squad, under arrest, not knowing if they'd face disgrace and execution. Kolatolo. He gasped. As a commodities trader, Aramin might well be expected to come into contact with the financier. And she was—had been—beautiful. The flower was for him then, a gift or a payoff from Ag Kolatolo's secret, Sejiedi mistress, herself another reward for his efforts to sell out the League . . . and destroy the Wing.

Bikmat scooped Aramin's jewelry from the false bottom of the suitcase and dropped it into the shopping bag. It was elaborate, expensive stuff. Even if one piece could be traded to Kolatolo . . . he staggered, knocking over a chair, then deliberately pulled out drawers and knocked over a second. Then he lifted the last chair in Aramin's study and broke it over the desk.

The newspads would be full of the shocking story of the beautiful woman with the glamorous career and important contacts, the woman too arrogant or too foolish to resist picking up a young man who robbed and killed her. If they found out about the hathoti, it didn't matter: she'd picked up a man of her own class and he'd killed her for it. Bikmat was covered.

Suddenly he started to tremble. Wing training/Sej training. Stand up. Leave . . . unseen. Go to the nearest bar. Without thinking, he chose a back booth that com-

manded a view both of a window and the door, and sat
down. He ordered a drink and sat rigidly.

It was all over now. It had to be. He could go back and
pretend that he knew nothing. He could try to forget the
lily, the call code designed for only one person's access.
He could know nothing, could simply, finally, be Pilot
Dustin, part of his family, the only thing he'd ever wanted
to be.

But he remembered Yuri's face, grim and determined as
he learned about the set-up he had to carry out, of his
dignity during arrest, how he had been prepared to face
court-martial and execution.

Dustin/Bikmat was a pilot too. It was his job to protect
his family, his Wing, and all Earthers. Kolatolo worked
for the Sej. If Aramin meant the flower for him, he was
certainly a hathoti addict. Dustin had evidence: the tapes,
the jewelry, and the lily itself. Once that was laid before
the League, Kolatolo would be no threat to the League, to
Earthers at large, or to the Wing Moon and its appropriations. The people he'd bought would scuttle him to save
their own futures.

He saw other bar patrons stare at him enviously: a
fair-haired, well-groomed man sipping an expensive drink
as he rested one hand on a bag, a gift, doubtless, for some
equally well-groomed and prosperous woman. They saw a
success.

His family would see a traitor. At the very least they'd
divorce him. He'd be brainstripped for certain, probably
executed as a Sej spy, not that his mind would be in any
shape for him to know about it. Just as well. He didn't
know if he could live with Gregory's hatred, with Yuri
calling him scum, worse than TreMorion, with having
Judith recoil from him.

On the other hand, he knew he couldn't live in the same

universe with Kolatolo, free and in power. First, last, and always, he was Wing. He had a duty to perform. And so he would. But only the discipline of his years among the Colors kept the tears from spilling over.

Careful to remain in character, he savored the last sip of his drink. Then he took out Aramin's card and called for a portable messager. Why not? She wouldn't need the credit.

"Base ship? Pilot Dustin, White Wing, here, requesting input to Deputy Director of Intelligence Federico Hashrahh Kroeger . . .

"Sir? Dustin here . . . I'm downworld . . . request permission to report . . ."

CHAPTER 15

I might not have known him, Zann compelled herself to admit as she caught up to Kroeger and his companion outside the hangar reserved for visiting high-rank civilians. Her hands began to sweat and twist in the fabric of the uniform she'd brought along with her for Dustin.

She was scared, and she'd been scared since Kroeger's call came through.

"Dustin called me from downworld. He's coming in to make a full report." Knowing Kroeger as well as she did, Zann guessed at the rest of the message. She should have guessed long ago. The clues had been there all along for anyone, let alone an Intelligence-trained eidetic, to put together. TreMorion had saved Dustin's life, and TreMorion was a Sej. Dustin was a little too astute politically for a fighter jock—and a lot too lucky at codes. If she wanted to bother, she could calculate the odds against that much luck, that many important breakthroughs in less than six months. Her initial hope had been that Valentina might have broken a fragment of a message in that time. But they'd needed results, and the spectacular success Val and Dustin enjoyed lulled them all.

I didn't want to think about it, Zann reproached herself. *I still don't want to believe it.* She glanced at Kroeger, unwilling to look at his companion, impeccably tailored in a gray and buff suit that any prosperous Arthan might have been glad to own. It hurt too much, and she envied Kroeger, who could concern himself only with the report he was about to hear. Kroeger never mixed data and emotion. He was an eidetic, pure and simple. But damned-fool Zann had tried her whole life long to be human, too, and look what it had gotten her. A Sejiedi squadmate. She should have known. In refusing to know, in allowing herself to be drawn in, she'd jeopardized the family she cherished.

"My assistant." Kroeger introduced her to Dustin for the benefit of passersby who must only see a high-placed Arthan visiting the base ship.

Dustin raised his eyebrows, as if surprised at the Earther company that Kroeger kept. Then he shrugged.

Zann raised her chin and stiffened her back before she nodded slightly. No White Winger would grant an Arthan civ more than bare recognition.

"Shall we go, sir?" Kroeger invited. Dustin gestured with the bag he carried, indicating that he was at Kroeger's disposal. Zann recognized the name printed on it. In another time—another universe, she mourned inwardly—she'd have waited till they got back to quarters, then accused Dustin of pillage and plunder. But she'd have to abandon that dream. It belonged to a Zann whose squadmate wasn't a Sejiedi operative she'd been tracking for months, too stupid . . . too distracted to realize just how close he'd been to her all along.

The two men turned toward the tubes. Zann walked

behind them, playing military escort. She noted that Dustin retained enough awareness of her that he didn't automatically fall into step with her. She felt an incongruous pang of admiration at his skill. He looked like any one of the Arthans she'd seen in the 'casts of the Assembly, trying to legislate her Wing out of existence. Dustin was good at disguises. Yesterday he'd looked exactly like a White Wing pilot, a man who'd told her he loved her.

That hurt worst of all. Not being taken in, but knowing what he was, and knowing that his outstanding gift for Intelligence was one of the things that had made him so deeply attractive to her. She'd found him easy to talk to. He understood just how she felt. Why shouldn't he? They both did the same job. It would be easier if she could hate him, turn on him the way Gregory would, Gregory who counted on her, who'd probably be ready to kill her too.

She clutched the uniform she'd brought him. Had the rest of it been a lie? Before she'd met Joao, and then Gregory, she'd have had to answer yes. An eidetic squadmate—there weren't that many functioning anywhere in the League. Automatically her mind supplied the figures: twenty-seven eidetics fully functional. She knew of only one other White Winger, and the boy hadn't been commissioned yet. Some of her classmates had seen an eidetic squadmate as a quick road to visibility and promotion. Hurt and bewildered by that attitude, Zann had resigned herself to life as a solo. *Just like Dustin*. And then she'd found the others. And Dustin.

She forced detachment on herself, rebuked herself for jumping to conclusions with inadequate data, and thanked God she'd been alone when the call from Kroeger came.

None of them spoke as the tube took them down to Maintenance, as they walked the dingy corridors to Kroeger's office. She followed Kroeger and Dustin in. As the door locked behind them, Dustin placed the shopping bag on Kroeger's dreadful orange table and dropped the facade.

"Evidence," he said quietly.

"I'll open it," Zann said. At that moment she hardly cared if it were rigged or not. God, how was she going to break this to the others? She spilled the bag's contents out across the table and stepped back. Heavy jewelry rang and tumbled out into the fine silk of an amber gown. One ring bounced over across a pack of credit slips and rolled until it came to rest against a spray of carefully wrapped flowers.

She bent closer, then took a too-rapid step back.

"Akharti hathoti," she said, amazed that she could speak at all.

She glanced at Kroeger. "Bikmat has apparently found a destination for this particular shipment."

Bikmat. From the moment Kroeger had called her, she'd known who Dustin had to be. Hearing the name straight out simply turned the knife.

"Indeed?" Zann asked, and sat down, not waiting for Kroeger to sit first.

Dustin remained on his feet.

"Sit down, Dustin," she said, trying to keep her voice level.

He took a chair opposite the two eidetics and sat rigidly on the edge of the seat. He placed his hands flat, palms down, on the table.

"Where did you get this?" Zann asked.

"Let him present a full report, Suzannah. When Bikmat contacted me, he told me he had a great deal of information for us, not just on this . . . particular trove, but on Sejiedi policy and the rationale behind it in general."

Dustin glanced about quickly. Zann interpreted the question. "Neither of us needs recorders."

He glanced at her and Kroeger, and nodded sharply.

"You may wish to note that my statement is completely voluntary. I have no reason to conceal anything. My elimination today of the Sejiedi courier Aramin . . ."

Kroeger gestured, and Suzannah tapped computer memory for information on that name, then for any information linked to the credit records before them. Aramin, the courier Dustin had killed—*she was beautiful*, Zann thought.

". . . makes me a traitor to the Sejiedi state. To the best of my conscious knowledge, I am the first Sejiedi operative to break conditioning."

Zann's nostrils wrinkled at the heady scent rising from the folds of amber silk. "Might Aramin have concealed other information in this dress's seams?" she asked. She drew a tiny knife from a pocket and slashed the seams open. The sound and feel of ripping silk satisfied an urge she decided not to put a name to.

"Do you have any idea," Kroeger inquired, "of how much money that gown you've just torn to shreds must have cost?"

"Two months' pay," Suzannah replied. "Combat supplement."

Where did this Aramin . . . that was foolish. Aramin had been an illegal, working a high-paid profession. Zann glanced over the jewelry speculatively. She didn't think that a commodity trader's credit ran to that impressive a collection. What other trade did the dead spy work?

"Excuse me." She rose and dumped the shreds of silk into the recycler, then wiped her hands down her coverall to remove lingering traces of the Sej's perfume from them.

She heard Dustin's quiet, dispassionate voice explaining his day's activities.

"Before we move on to the late Aramin's connection with Ag Kolatolo, it might be best if Bikmat supplied us with some background on the principal Sejiedi worlds. Don't you agree?'' Kroeger asked her.

She'd better agree. He was eyeing her too closely for it to be anything but the beginning of curiosity about her actions. Zann returned to her seat.

''To the best of my conscious knowledge, I am the only Sejiedi operative of Earth ancestry in that Intelligence network. I am told that I was born of Earther parents who died in space when I was three. I was jettisoned in a bubble which the Sejiedi retrieved. From then on, I lived on Nahi II, one of three central worlds, until my training was complete and I was placed in the White Wing academy.''

I'd love to know how they pulled that off, Zann thought and promised herself that before too long she would.

''The other trainees at my school all came from the Sejiedi underclass.''

''Later,'' Kroeger ordered. ''Tell us about the Sejiedi core worlds. Location first.''

His eyes were shining, his face intent and almost terrible as he bent toward Dustin slightly and drew the information from him. It was a hunger, Zann thought, before she surrendered to it herself. She pitied Dustin's having to submit to two eidetics' eagerness for data. This was an extraordinary source, another part of her mind exulted. Finally, finally, there might be enough information even for her.

''The systems are identified on League star charts as ML-519, MR-106, and MR-107.''

''R-class stars are unstable,'' Suzannah recited from a text she'd scanned once. ''The triple digits of their numbers indicate that fluctuations occur only once in several centuries.''

''Is this the reason for the Sejiedi incursions?'' Kroeger

demanded. "Not just world-stealing, but desperation? Yes, that makes sense."

"Yes, sir," Dustin replied. "The MRs are known among the Sejiedi as Nahi and Naricot. They are the major agricultural, industrial, and population centers of the state. ML-519 is known as Neyss. It is the only star possessing nine habitable planets in that particular octant. Most of the warrior-born—the Sejiedi aristocracy—and high-ranking administrators maintain homes on Neyss-S100a, a small world unfit for agriculture.

"For at least three hundred Earth years, or two hundred seventy-nine Nahi II years, the Sejiedi have known that the stars are unstable. Scientists have devoted much energy to the prediction of radiation and temperature fluctuations that would render the worlds mentioned uninhabitable.

"In addition, the agricultural worlds have suffered soil depletion. Throughout the Sejiedi systems, the most valuable item is food. The population is relatively large, too large for its food supply. In order to eat, much of the underclass becomes slave labor to grow both edible plants and hathoti.

"There are five basic Sejiedi classes. Only three are of any real concern. The highest class consists of the warrior-born, high-ranking military families. Below it is an administrative class. Like the warrior-born, this class is largely hereditary. The next two classes consist of middle- to low-level fighters and bureaucrats, as well as merchants. These classes often intermarry, are difficult to distinguish from one another, and are of little concern.

"The lowest class comprises nearly eighty percent of the population. Since such a large reserve of human labor is available, since mechanization, given current conditions, is expensive and difficult, many of this class are laborers in the fields, as I said, or in factories producing

war matériel. The majority of both field and factory workers are at least partially addicted to hathoti pulp. The pulp
dulls both hunger and reflexes, thus rendering this population easy to control.''

"They *need* planets," Zann said. "It's not just glory."
Then why destroy our Earth? It was such a rich, beautiful
world. She saw curiosity in Kroeger's eyes too. Then both
túrned their attention back to Dustin.

"I appear to have developed an allergy to hathoti
sometime around puberty. This is, I suspect, all that enabled me to break as much of my conditioning as I have
done.''

Suzannah narrowed her eyes and called to mind what
she had once learned of Sejiedi conditioning: the training
by hunger, hypnotapes, and the realization that bad as
things were, they could get far worse. Worst of all might
be the fear that fighting conditioning could kill; it had been
that fear, she suspected, that killed Astun Koda. Why
hadn't it mastered Dustin? Surely not because of his allergy to hathoti.

"At present the major focus of Sejiedi activity is the
war effort. Undoubtedly other planets exist that might be
discovered and colonized, but the time that might take and
the uncertainty factor make search a less attractive option
than conquest. It is simple to locate planets already sup-
porting human populations.''

But not always so easy to take them, Zann thought,
remembering Earth. Something in Dustin's report bothered
her. The Sej fought for living space. Why would they
destroy Earth? It didn't make sense . . . or perhaps it did.
Perhaps they had deliberately expended one world to convince the others that they meant business. Somehow, given
what Dustin had just told them, that didn't seem a strong
enough rationale.

"Codework," Kroeger snapped. "What code information do you have? Begin with military codes."

"I have already passed on such data to Engineering Officer Valentina. To the best of my conscious knowledge, I have no further information."

" 'To the best of your conscious knowledge' . . . you use that phrase repeatedly. Do you think you might be conditioned against revealing secrets of that nature?" Kroeger asked.

Under the rigid discipline Dustin maintained, Zann could sense the fear in him.

"Yes, sir," he said evenly, glancing quickly at Zann, then back to Kroeger.

He feared her too, she realized in that moment, and something died in her.

"Why did you surrender yourself, Bikmat?"

Dustin's face turned ashen at Kroeger's repeated use of his Sejiedi name.

"Sir, I found evidence that Ag Kolatolo of Arthan has been bought by the Sejiedi. You have the evidence"—he started to gesture at the table, then replaced his hands, palms down—"in the form of the akharti hathoti, Aramin's credit slips, and the call code that gives immediate access to Kolatolo. How many people would possess such a code? Trace the jewelry. I'm certain you could discover that he had it purchased for her."

"This Aramin," Zann dared to ask, "what was she to you?"

"A classmate," Dustin said. "We took field-survival training together. She made me kill a friend."

"None of that answers my question," Kroeger snapped in Sej.

"I am a man of Earth," Dustin replied in Standard. "The people Kolatolo attempts to destroy are my own. It is my duty as a member of the White Wing to protect them and the League we serve.''

"And that's why you renounced your loyalty to the Sejiedi," Zann said softly.

Dustin met her eyes, and she thought she caught a glimpse of pleading, a hope that she might understand.

"It was never a loyalty worthy of the name. And I renounced it when I received my commission," he said slowly.

"You think you renounced it," Kroeger persisted.

"I have no idea how deep my conditioning goes. To my knowledge, no one has ever tried to break free."

"Why didn't you come forward before?" Zann asked. If only she'd known, or Joao, or any of them, there might have been something they could have done to spare him this agony, this exposure. She tried to signal him behind the expressionless masks both had assumed that she was on his side. No matter what he *had* been, he was Wing, and he'd brought them Kolatolo. She couldn't call that a traitor's action. No matter how Dustin had been trained, he'd fought well for the Wing.

Would the others see it that way? Would Gregory? She suppressed a shudder.

"I had nothing of importance to tell," Dustin answered simply. "I was tasked only recently."

"What was your task?"

"I was aimed against a flight leader of the White Wing, which the Sejiedi regard as their major antagonist. This is one reason why Kolatolo has conducted such a virulent campaign against Earthers in general, and the Wing in particular. I was to provide evidence by discrediting this flight leader. Insistence—from *your* own service—that the Wing eliminate the operative called Aglo was also intended to provide evidence that Earthers were dangerous and untrustworthy.''

Gregory, Zann mourned. Knowing Dustin as well as she did, she could hear the strain in his voice. In a moment Kroeger would be able to detect it too. It was the strain that convinced her, more than anything else, that she was right. Dustin idolized Gregory. Of course he would. Gregory had all the traits that the Sej, as well as the Wing, admired, and something of the Sejiedi training still lingered about Dustin. His fanatical adherence to duty, for one thing. Fanatical? She thought about her choice of word for a few milliseconds, checking her assumptions. She had regarded the Wing's concerns with duty and honor as reasonable and praiseworthy, while those of the Sej were obsessive and inhuman. Perhaps they were about even.

Perhaps, she thought, people in the League suspected that. It could account for much of the suspicion against Earthers. She marked that line of thought for future consideration and went back to her main idea. By either code, Gregory measured up. Given Sejiedi training and lacking the allergic reaction to hathoti that had enabled Dustin to free himself, what would Gregory be? Her conclusion came fast and hit hard. Gregory's counterpart among the Sej would be Haral TreMorion.

"You were tasked, Bikmat. What have you done?" Kroeger snapped.

Dustin looked back coolly, pride in the set of his shoulders, the lift of his head.

"Nothing."

"Can you give us any more information, Bikmat?" Kroeger asked.

"None that I am aware of.''

Federico Hashrahh Kroeger sighed, as if reluctant to wake from deep sleep.

"However, I will subject myself to full interrogation," Dustin went on.

"You'd *voluntarily* undergo brainstripping?" Kroeger interrupted, his whole body taut with the excitement of possibility.

Dustin jerked his chin up.

"Absolutely not," Zann said. "The technique is clumsy, unreliable. Look what happened to Astun Koda; a cerebral hemorrhage, and who knows how much more information conventional interrogation might have gotten? Dustin is of more value to us alive and coherent."

She could hear how her voice strained and raised in pitch. So, obviously, could Kroeger. She forced herself to breathe deeply. She winced at the thought of Dustin strapped to the tables of the interrogation staff, with their soft voices and the inexorable probe of the stripper homing in on encephalographic peaks and smoothing them, removing data, sapping the will to resist, and, most likely, intelligence.

"It would be a waste," she said with a show of reason. "Dustin is a pilot. His reflexes are faster, more sensitive than normal . . . and the Wing has invested a great deal of money in his training. I have an obligation not to see that money wasted. Sir, I'll fight you on this one all the way to Wing Command."

Kroeger paused and Zann could read his thought processes. Brainstripping was a technique unpopular in the League presses. If what Dustin had told them was true, then as soon as Kolatolo was exposed, top-echelon Intelligence was going to be equally unpopular because of its ties to him. Zann was also banking on the value Kroeger placed on her as an ally.

"I want Dustin's conditioning broken," she continued. "I want the information he may be withholding as much as you do. But I say that if anyone's interrogating him, it's going to be Joao, who has access to all of his medical records and who knows him.''

Kroeger stared at her for a long time and she held her breath. Then he nodded. ''You're right, Suzannah. He is of more value to us fully functional. In fact''—he smiled thinly, pleased with a sudden thought—''should his conditioning be broken successfully, I see little reason why he could not be used as a weapon against the Sej. He's been functioning for years as a highly effective double agent, it seems.

''Pilot Dustin, you'll let us know immediately if you feel this hunger that you've described.'' Dustin nodded.

Kroeger paused. ''I want to relay this information to Central immediately . . . and get these things''—he gestured at the deadly flower, the credit tapes, Aramin's jewelry—''processed and stored. Will you be all right?''

Zann stared at him. Then, an instant later, incongruous realization hit her. Kroeger was concerned about leaving her alone in an isolated part of the ship with Dustin. Why? Because he'd killed one woman that day? Extraordinary.

''I've known Dustin for years.''

''So have the Sej,'' Kroeger retorted, gathering up what lay on the table. The jewelry clattered as it tumbled into the bag.

Even after Kroeger left, Dustin kept silent, closing himself off from her.

''I brought you a uniform,'' Zann said and tossed it onto the table. ''You can't go into White Wing territory looking like that.''

Dustin reached out a hand and touched the uniform with one finger. Then quickly, before she could change her mind, he pulled it to him and began to change. Lowering her eyes, Zann watched him through her lashes. Her mouth went dry.

"Where'd you get the clothes?" she asked to take her mind off the sight of him.

"Stole them."

Dustin sealed the uniform at the throat and bundled up the Arthan garments, then stuffed them down the recycler. Something drifted unnoticed to the floor.

"Destructive, aren't we?" Zann made herself ask lightly. "First I shred that dress, then you discard an expensive suit. We'll probably never be able to buy anything like that for ourselves, you know."

"And thank God for it." Dustin's voice was hoarse.

They had made an object of him, Zann thought with sudden remorse, debating the merits of drugs over brain-stripping while he sat there. He hadn't protested. She realized that from the moment Dustin decided to kill his contact, he expected to die. He'd fought, he'd brought them precious information, and neither she nor Kroeger had taken time to consider that he might be exhausted, frightened, and still suffering a reaction to the hathoti that Aramin had made him eat. Zann brought a cup of water over to where he stood by the chute, his back toward her.

She touched his shoulder to get his attention, and he recoiled. Had she driven him away by being what she was? Faulty logic, her training told her. Dustin feared that she would no longer love him.

"Don't, Dustin," she said. She laid her hand on his arm and made him turn around before she handed him the water. He drank thirstily, but avoided her eyes.

What do I do now? Zann asked herself. She wished she had Joao's compassion or Judith's sure touch with people. She glanced about. Catching sight of whatever it was that had dropped from Dustin's civilian outfit, she bent to retrieve it.

Why would Dustin hang onto a handkerchief, large,

worn, and with the palest hint of stains still rusty at its center?

In a sudden gestalten flicker, she remembered: *They'd been at the Blue Angel. There'd been a fight, and Joao was muttering about the pitiful waste of good spirits, bandaging Dustin's hand with the stupid, anachronistic cloth he invariably carried, while Dustin sat watching, his eyes lowered, the way they were now.*

"What are you going to do with me?" he asked and sank down into a chair. His shoulders were bowed.

She crumpled it in her hand, then, gently, smoothed it. Many pilots carried charms. So this was the lucky piece Dustin carried—and he'd carried it all this time? He hadn't been tasked then, hadn't known them. And then Judith's impulse to pull him out of a fight had brought them into his life . . . it wasn't all a lie, Zann concluded rapidly. For once she blessed her memory which enabled her to know that whatever else Dustin was, he was theirs.

"What am I going to do with you?" Zann echoed. She knelt in front of him, trying to get him to meet her eyes. Lifting his hands from his knees, she cradled them warmly beneath her chin.

"I'm going to get you back to quarters and find you something to eat," she told him and took a deep breath. "Then I'm going to take you to bed and make sure you're in shape to fly tomorrow."

When he didn't answer and didn't meet her eyes, Zann felt like dying a little. What if she'd made him hate her? It had taken almost all the courage she'd had left to say what she'd just said to him.

"It's all right," she said faintly. "The others . . . they know I have secrets to keep." She squeezed his hands, and pushed the handkerchief into them. "You dropped this. I didn't know you had kept it. You're still ours. That much hasn't changed, has it?''

Dustin freed his hands, but only to gather her close against him. His head went down on her shoulder, and she could feel him shake. When he finally released her, she raised a hand to touch his face. His eyes were wet. Taking the handkerchief from his fingers, Suzannah dried the tears, and Dustin smiled.

"I guess nothing's changed," he said. "It's still bringing me luck."

CHAPTER 16

Dustin ignored Hangar Deck Control's eagerness to have him get the shuttle out of the launch bay and checked its systems one last time.

"No bombs, I assume," commented Federico Hashrahh Kroeger, who occupied a seat that should have been reserved for a medic or copilot. The whine of launch devoured his voice, and Dustin was glad. He had already heard too much chatter from the Yellow Wingers who were escorting their Wingmates downworld. They had been furious that Kroeger had pulled rank to squeeze himself on board one of the first Subiat-bound shuttles that morning.

"That's one less spot!" the Yellow Wing's chief flight surgeon had protested. "I meant to send another corpsman down." She'd sounded a good bit like Joao, Dustin remembered.

"I'll see that he helps your Wingmates get settled," Dustin had offered the surgeon, and seen her eyes flash with astonishment. "Give him some real work to do."

Then, before she could reply, he had turned to assist a man limping over to the shuttle.

Now, as Dustin eased the ship into its assigned trajectory, he felt Kroeger's eyes on him. *He doesn't trust me*, he thought, and considered whether or not he should be insulted. He had given his word, after all. It was Kroeger who suggested Dustin be considered part of Counterintelligence. Dustin owed him, and he knew why the civ had to get downworld early.

There was a body to be found—Aramin's. Kroeger had to be there first, to arrange the evidence for maximum effect, calibrate the fact of her murder, and aim it all the way to Arthan.

Once the shrieking whine of takeoff subsided, Kroeger leaned over toward Dustin again. "I've tapped Subiat comm," he said. "No news yet. Time lag to Arthan's a good eight hours, so if the news breaks here by mid-morning, it should hit Arthan—"

"Evening 'casts," Dustin cut in. That would be a fine time to confront Kolatolo with the news about Aramin and watch him do his "shocked and saddened" routine.

Subiat loomed ripe and beautiful in the shuttle's screens. The ice at its polar caps glinted, reminding him of Mahalir before the battle.

His hands moved steadily over the board. He was amazed at their steadiness, but they'd been steady, too, as he'd twisted a guitar string . . . he refused to think of that now. He was Wing again, safe, assured of his place despite how resigned he'd been to denunciation and arrest. He was Wing, and he was within twenty minutes of landing on Base with a work-schedule input into his wristcomp.

"What do you want me to watch for?" he asked Kroeger.

"Stick to the Base," Federico Hashrahh Kroeger ordered. "And keep monitoring the news. You should be listening right now, in fact. I just learned that your Wing Commander has been granted permission to address the Committee on Appropriations.''

A tyro might have made the shuttle jerk in that instant.

"When?" Dustin asked, and corrected course, smoothing his angle of descent. Below, the nightside of Subiat rolled past, lights gleaming like thermal holographs through a tracery of a cloud.

"Entering atmosphere, five minutes," he warned the passenger compartment.

"During lift," Kroeger said. "Thirty days from now that committee adjourns for elections.'' The civ's gray eyes narrowed. Aramin had ordered that Gregory be discredited in thirty days. They'd have been the last thirty days of Dustin's life. The Sej had been very clever, very thorough— and now Zann and Kroeger were taking the chance of their lives on him.

"I'll watch," Dustin told Kroeger grimly. He wanted to offer to assume some of Zann's tasks for Kroeger, but feared the eidetic's curiosity. He might suspect that Dustin felt obliged to her for the way she'd protected him, or that he wanted to prove himself to a new master. But he must never suspect that the real reason was something simpler: Zann already had spent at least a day and a half's schedule just squabbling over supplies, and that went without mentioning her other tasks of helping Ground Comm direct the hundreds of ships in the traffic above Subiat today, and of assisting Kroeger.

She really had been magnificent as she fought with Kroeger over Dustin's life. The line about Wing Command's investing a fortune in his reflexes, for God's sake!

"Did I sound heartless enough?" she'd asked him, laughing.

"You gave it your best try," he had told her.

As he steepened the angle of descent, he bent over his console to conceal a smile from Kroeger. No complaints came through in-ship communications. Most of the Yellows Dustin was flying downworld were either walking wounded or heavily sedated. That was bad enough. By tradition, the flight leaders drew the real heartbreak rides, including burn victims and burnout cases. Joao and Gregory were teamed on such a flight later that day.

"Subiat Base?" Dustin made verbal contact, hoping Zann would be at comm already. The voice answering him was male, though, and with an unmistakable Arthan accent. He switched to that language and identified his ship.

The man let contact slip into a minor squall of static, and Dustin sighed imperceptibly. Of course his no-rank was a giveaway. Again he informed Subiat Base that Pilot Dustin requested clearance for immediate landing for a Yellow Wing medical transport, and repeated himself at least three more times. He was proud that he wasn't swearing under his breath in front of Kroeger.

"Trouble?" Kroeger stretched himself.

"No more than usual." Dustin shrugged. "The locals get wind of a White Winger and 'no speak the language.' Or lose clearances or test systems. Minor annoyances. We'd be second-class citizens, if we were citizens at all," he added lightly.

Kroeger reached for the comm. Dustin shook his head. "No need. He's had his fun now." Clearance numbers flashed across the screen, and the disembodied Arthan voice reeled off approach vectors and landing instructions. Clouds and then the crimson of Subiat's violent dawn surged around the shuttle as Dustin set it down gently on the landing slick.

The Yellow Wing senior surgeon was waiting at the

ramp as Dustin assisted the wounded and their escorts, one
to each person, to the waiting Rehab van.

"There's two left over," she said and glared at Kroeger.

"I'll take one, and I'll inform Federico Hashrahh Kroeger
that there's no such thing as a free ride. Want me to?" The
Yellow medic almost grinned at him, and Dustin turned
back to inform Kroeger of his unlikely duty assignment.

*How long would it take for him to steer someone to the
van, anyhow?* Dustin thought. Aramin could wait. She
wasn't going anywhere.

"What do I do?" Kroeger asked the flight surgeon.

Hadn't he ever had to help out on anything before?
From what Zann had told him of her own training, no one
had ever excused her from any task the Wing required.
Kroeger must have beem pampered for his freak talent. If
that were the case, it hadn't done him much good.

"Walk with him," the surgeon instructed. "If he slows
down, you slow down. If he stops, you stop—and call
me."

"Shouldn't you get a float?"

"Jared's going in for therapy under real-G. He has to
walk."

Gingerly Kroeger slipped his hand under the injured
tech's elbow. The man looked as if he'd rather stumble
along by himself than have the White Wing's personal
curse as his escort.

Dustin stifled a grin at Kroeger's discomfort.

"Take the next one," ordered the medic. She gestured
at a lean young man whose eyes were heavily shadowed
and whose neck was encased in an enormous foam collar.
Dustin winced. Judging from the injury, the man was a
pilot. Even fighting harness wasn't proof against neutrino
buffeting and nonlethal direct hits. A neck injury could put
you out of action for months while the medics coaxed

vertebrae into healing well enough for you to pass med boards again . . . assuming you ever could. There wasn't a pilot alive who didn't fear this kind of injury.

"What's it take to bribe a Yellow flight medic?" Dustin asked.

The injured pilot shrugged, then concentrated on walking straight.

What could Dustin say, pilot to pilot, to this man? His career might be over right now, all because of a tiny bone shaking itself free in the inner ear. Dustin had heard lectures and seen a demonstration of a new harness that allegedly cut down on the risk of this kind of injury. He didn't believe it. Neither did any other pilot, except maybe Judith, who always tried such things out.

"Let's go," he muttered to the Yellow. "Pretend you're coming in at dawn from a really good bar-crawl. If you're very lucky, and you walk really straight, the sentry'll just wave you through and you won't get put on report." Gregory would call this needless chatter, but he had to say something.

The Yellow pilot's hand dug into Dustin's arm as he lurched to one side.

"You suppose they'll give me a fake ear?"

"You really want to grow up to be a cyborg?" Cybernetic implants—pilots detested them too. A fluctuation in magnetic field, or a shock, or a medic in a mean mood, and there you were, grounded.

The man looked up too fast, then swore at the sudden nauseating movement. "I'm not going to be sick," he said. "She wouldn't let me have breakfast."

"Damn all medics!" Dustin agreed. "Wouldn't you think that by the time we're commissioned, they'd realize we're toilet-trained?"

"They say White Wingers have vacuum in their veins," the Yellow commented. "You seem all right."

"I could be the pilot wearing that collar," Dustin muttered, embarrassed by the compliment. "Do me a favor, will you? *Don't* tell the Blues. I hear they've got money riding on it."

The injured man laughed. Dustin could hear the whispers starting up behind him. Had these Yellows really expected a White Winger simply to stalk off, leaving wounded stranded on the landing slick?

The sun felt good on Dustin's back as he walked toward Admin to pick up his lock code. Temp quarters were right behind Admin. Seeing them, Dustin wanted to grimace. He couldn't say he was surprised. The rooms were depressing. Thin ochre walls and paneling coming loose made him remember the projects on Nahi. Probably they were going to tear the place down soon and build something else. At least he hoped so. The only things that made the place look marginally decent were Valentina's terminal and a heap of newspads.

Then Dustin smiled. Zann sat near the scratched commscreen, her hair tangled and ruddy in the early light. Her eyes flickered over the readout faster than he could possibly follow.

Curious, Dustin glanced at the newspads. He hoped he wouldn't see a picture of Aramin. If news of her death were out now, it would mean that someone had discovered her body before Kroeger had had a chance to work his sinister magic in the downworld Intelligence community.

"Nothing yet," Zann muttered without looking away from the screen. "Relax" Without slowing the speed of the readouts, she split the screen. There were comm plugs in her ears, and Dustin would have bet each was turned to a different frequency. "Ahh, wait now . . ."

Zann slowed the screen, and Aramin's image flashed vividly onto it and remained. As the dead woman's black eyes met his challengingly, Dustin found himself shivering. How many men couldn't meet that challenge? he wondered. Kolatolo, for one. Aramin had been deadly, and now she was dead.

He could hear the announcer sketching in details of Aramin's cover as a commodities trader . . . "three times she rejected a vice-presidency from which, ten years ago, another financier consolidated a successful takeover of the multiplanetary holding company . . ." Yes, Dustin knew all about Kolatolo, including some things this announcer didn't. "Now we switch you to Arthan. One of our affiliates has asked Ag Kolatolo for a statement . . ."

"This should be interesting," Zann commented. She set the screen on "record," then reached for a caffeine tablet. Dustin frowned at her, but she only shrugged.

"What're you two watching?" asked Judith, coming in quietly.

Dustin gestured her to silence. She sat, saw Zann's caffeine tabs and scowled at her. "She's always like this downworld," she told Dustin. "Does two people's work, and then caves in for eighteen hours. I wonder if Joao knows she's got these."

"Not *now*," Zann hissed.

Kolatolo's face appeared on the screen. His wavy hair was disarranged slightly, his tunic opened at the collar about three cm as if to indicate that he was a busy man who forced himself to take time out from a very crowded schedule "in order to pay tribute to one of the brightest, most promising young women"—his voice started to go husky—"with whom it's ever been my pleasure to work."

"Some work," quipped Zann.

"I am deeply shocked," Kolatolo continued solemnly, "and I will demand a full investigation into Aramin HaLoren's tragic death . . . and into Subiat security procedures."

Imperceptibly Zann's shoulders shook. "A full investigation," she repeated. "You don't know what you just said, mister. You're going to get the fullest investigation—"

"What's going on?" Judith interrupted plaintively. "Some pickup murder a civ? *Why* don't these people learn to defend themselves, anyway?" She sighed. "Now I suppose that everyone downworld's going to be chattering about it. Sex, money, and violence. Damn! I was looking forward to getting some *news*."

"The Old Man's scheduled to speak before the Appropriations Committee," said Dustin. "How's that for news?"

Judith brightened. "Before they adjourn for elections? Is that good for us, Zann?"

Zann nodded.

Not if I'd broken cover, it wouldn't have been, Dustin thought. He could just imagine. Statisticians were already weighting the elections in favor of candidates who favored cuts to military appropriations—all military appropriations. If anyone even suspected that White Wing had been infiltrated . . . he didn't want to think about that. It didn't matter that moles had turned up in Yellow and Blue Wings; Trassians and Arthans were citizens with full voting rights. They could protect themselves. But the discovery of a Sejiedi operative in White Wing would probably finish them.

Zann shuddered, disengaged herself from the terminal, and stretched, rousing herself from concentration.

"I'd better get to the quartermaster," she said. "Dustin, want to come with me? Your Arthan's better than mine."

"Not according to this morning's controller," he retorted.

"Typical," said Gregory. "Any of you others going to be in a position where you need really fluent language? No? All right, Zann, you can have him. We'd all better move fast. We've got some day lined up."

"Remember to be back by eighteen-hundred," warned Yuri. "I meant what I said about dinner at the Officers' Club. Why else did we pack dress uniforms?"

"Excess credit burning a hole in your pocket?" Valentina asked sweetly.

"No. Ship's ration burning a hole in my gut. We're about due for a decent meal, don't you think?"

Naturally, you couldn't expect to find coffee in a drinks dispenser on an Arthan world-minor, Dustin thought half a day later. Just as well, seeing as Zann had used her fruit juice to wash down another caffeine tablet. She held up a hand to forestall criticism.

"Don't you have your own checklist to cover?" she asked.

"Yuri said he'd take care of it. We're pretty much duplicating effort anyhow. I'm more useful here." Dustin looked about. "I liked your idea of calling that last office. You sound like a high-up civ, and that got us what we needed without the usual back-chat."

Zann glanced at her wristcomp. "I'd better check in." She left him sitting in a tiny lounge, so new that the plastic of its chairs still smelled of factory, rather than stale drinks and recycled air. Idly he leafed through discarded printouts and listened to the buzz of gossip around him. He heard Aramin's name come up repeatedly. Good. He'd created just the scandal he'd hoped for. He would have liked to have gone over and talked to some of the civs and enlisted ratings clustering by the dispensers, but he knew that his white coverall would shut them up. He'd tried it before.

"The only one of us who's lucky with that is Valentina," Suzannah had reassured him once. "She plays sims with all comers, and there's a lot of chatter. Oh yes . . ." Her eyes went far away for an instant. "And Maryam. People used to say she wasn't like a White Winger at all. She'd drink . . . oh, she never let them get too close, but they didn't know that." Zann had sighed and been quiet for a long time.

As she reentered the lounge, she glanced at the viewer, nodded minutely in satisfaction, and raised a thumb at Dustin.

"Before we meet Joao, we should watch this."

Kroeger again, Dustin concluded, raising an eyebrow. He went over to adjust the volume. A man in a Green tech's uniform joined him with some idea of switching to an entertainment channel. One glance made him abandon his plan. Muttering something about officers, he sank down into a chair.

The familiar, hateful facade of Aramin's hotel appeared on the screen, melting away to reveal the carefully manufactured vandalism of her study. At least they'd removed her body, Dustin thought in relief.

"Medical investigation disclosed a new detail in what now appears to be more than a simple case of murder. A routine blood test revealed a heavy concentration of hathoti—"

"That consummate *bastard!*" Zann whispered with keen appreciation. Now the reporter was interviewing a security officer who demonstrated how a suitcase with a false bottom might appear ordinary but all the while be concealing contraband such as hathoti. "He rigged it. He didn't tell me that he'd gotten in there with hathoti and set her up.''

Dustin leaned forward, using the cover of the hoots and comments rising about them to ask, "Now what?"

"You heard Kolatolo calling for an investigation," she whispered back. "Well, he'll get one. *Our* people will call for a full autopsy. Just the suspicion of hathoti addiction's enough to justify it."

Dustin suppressed an urge to whistle. A complete autopsy included somatic scan and chromosome analysis. Unless someone sneaked past Kroeger to tamper with medical records, there was no way to hide the fact that Aramin was genetically Sejiedi.

"The hunt's up," Dustin whispered. "Either way we win. If Kolatolo didn't know she was Sej, he's a fool. And if he did . . ."

"Precisely." Zann smiled. Her teeth were white and sharp.

The Green switched to an Arthan broadcast. The screen darkened. It was night on the capital world. Commcrews had tracked Kolatolo down as he came out of a private club the name of which made a few Subiat civs whistle. A woman of his own age, with patrician features, walked beside him.

"Trying to brazen it out," Zann muttered.

As the commcrews rushed him, Kolatolo's face twisted with dismay for an instant before a mask as good as the Wing's covered it.

"Did you know she was an addict?" asked one reporter.

"What do you think of recent reports that she was trading with the Sej?" Someone else interrupted to ask if he would run for the Assembly.

Kolatolo's eyelids drooped haughtily as he glared at the crews. "I am appalled by this crime. I am also revolted by the irresponsible behavior of the media and the investigators. I have no further comment."

"Did you catch the Kolatolo act?" the Green asked two newcomers. "Irresponsible media, my ass."

Dustin watched out of the corner of his eye as an Orange tried to hush the tech.

"I still say they've had a rotten deal," insisted the tech. "You were at Mahalir. If the White hadn't held out, maybe none of ours would have made it back. And none of those Blues, either."

Suzannah yawned, pretending to nap.

"Of course I know Famne got put on report for sounding off about that investigation," the tech continued. "That's what makes me suspect the whole thing. Sure, White Wing's trouble. But trouble or not, they're still being set up."

"We've got what we need," Suzannah murmured. "Shouldn't let him talk himself into any more trouble."

As if he were just now overhearing, Dustin lifted his head and caught the Green tech's eyes. Minutes later he and Zann had the lounge to themselves.

"I have to go now, Dustin," Zann said. "Do me a favor? Check the prices of grain futures on Arthan. And stocks in any companies Kolatolo controls. Fine! See you back in the rooms."

Suzannah was the last of the squad to arrive in their temporary quarters. She looked wasted, Dustin thought. Her hair was tousled from her favorite gesture of running fingers through it while she thought, and her hazel eyes were reddened and strained. She smiled quickly at him, perhaps reassuring him that whatever tricks she and Kroeger had planned were going to work. Then she manufactured a wide grin that she turned on the entire squad.

"Did you see the news, Gregory? You're famous."

Gregory grunted and lowered his eyes. "That's the last thing I need, to hear the Subiat news services dissect me."

"I want to see," Valentina decided. She scrolled until she discovered the story Zann must have meant. Dustin leaned over her shoulder and scanned the feature about White Wing Command. It included profiles of the Old Man and his surviving squadmates, even capsule biographies of the officers considered most likely to be promoted into Command. "There you are, Greg!" Valentina said, clearly pleased.

"And I'll just bet it says plenty about TreMorion—"

"That's classified," Zann cut in.

"Well, what does it say, then?" Gregory asked grudgingly.

"About your record," Val supplied amiably, "and when you made ace, and then flight leader." She winced. "When asked about the Mercy of the Wing, the Commander observed that Flight Leader Gregory's action was in accordance with the highest traditions of the Wing and refused further comment."

"More balanced reporting than I'd have expected," Joao said. He walked over to Suzannah. "You look worn out, Zann. Sit down. And give me back those caffeine tablets. Now."

Zann sank into a deep chair and sprawled out. Though the vial she handed Joao was a third empty, she held out a rock-steady hand in response to his disapproving headshake.

"I know you've got a lot of control, Zann. Too much, maybe. Stop trying to fool me."

"Come on, Joao." She looked at him pleadingly. "Don't scold right now. That last interview . . . stupid quartermaster's assistant pretended not to understand me till I warned her that impaired hearing could get her dropped from the Service. Val, quick! Isn't it time to switch to Arthan morning news?''

Valentina cued the screen. "There are no new developments on the murder of commodities trader Aramin HaLoren pending completion of an autopsy. When reporters tried to contact Ag Kolatolo, his staff informed them that he was unavailable at that time.''

"Not available for comment?'' asked Valentina. "When he's talking about us, you can't shut him off!''

Dustin remembered the lean, controlled face and wondered idly how long it would take before withdrawal symptoms set in. Akharti hathoti was potent stuff. Zann had said she'd like to take the people who sabotaged that transport, addict them to hathoti, then deprive them of it. It looked like she was getting just what she wanted.

Zann stretched in her chair. "Yuri, are you still set on the Officers' Club for dinner?''

"Why not?'' he asked. "Looks like we've even got something to celebrate.''

"The rest of you go,'' Zann said. "I'd be just as happy to grab something from a machine and turn in early. Really I would. And I look even worse than usual.''

"Come on, Zann.'' Judith walked over. "You'll feel better after you change. I'll make you up so no one'll know how tired you are. If you don't come, the rest of us won't enjoy it.''

"Did Joao put you up to this?''

"Come *on*, stupid.'' Judith tugged at Zann, trying to get her on her feet.

Zann started to chuckle. "That's right. Stupidest eidetic in the Fleet. If I had to think about it, I'd probably forget how to breathe.'' Laughing, Zann let Judith tow her from the room.

"Did you make reservations?'' Joao asked Yuri.

"Let me," Dustin offered. "My Arthan's better." He used his most prosperous voice on the Officers' Club. It was the one he'd turned on the hotel concierge, the one he'd used in the bar near Aramin's hotel. Again it worked. A table would be waiting at nineteen hundred hours.

"You only gave them a room number," Valentina observed with a small, wicked smile. "No name. I wonder if they like surprises."

Subiat Base Officers' Club served an enormous group on one of the most prosperous worlds-minor, and it looked it. Tall bush-purple fronds lined the lounge and discreet bar and quivered against the shimmering lightwalls that closed off the two main dining rooms with electronic rainbows that were never the same for more than a millisecond.

"I saw another White Wing squad go into the room on the left," Judith said softly. "I hope they put us in there too."

"Let's see if they honor our reservation first." Valentina beckoned the rest of the squad to follow Dustin forward. Their room number gleamed on the reservations monitor. Dustin almost choked as the stiffly formal attendant's face colored momentarily with surprise and chagrin.

"They'll have to seat us right away," said Joao. "We're on time, and there's our room number. They can't say they lost it."

"I bet they dump us by a service hatch," Valentina groused.

"Are you looking for a fight already, Val? Or can we just have dinner?" Zann asked. Dustin looked over at her. Judith had concealed most of her fatigue with makeup and managed to brush her hair sleek. "I don't care where we sit just so long as we do it soon. I'm hungry. The rest of you can drink. All I want is coffee.''

Dustin spoke quickly and arrogantly to the attendant, borrowing tones he had heard Arthans—and the warrior-born of his childhood—use to outsiders.

"Not bad." Judith raised her eyebrows. Their table was located against a wall and separated from much of the room by holographic panels of snowflakes that twisted silver/white/blue/almost ultraviolet. From this vantage point, the squad could see most of the room, yet manage to keep some privacy.

"Tactful," Zann observed. She glanced down at the old-fashioned leather-bound menu set by her place. "They've got coffee here, but wouldn't you know they'd camouflage it with liqueurs? I'll wait."

Dustin gave his own order to the human waiter, who seemed to have passed almost miraculously through the delicate holographic blizzard. Now that they were seated, Yuri's idea seemed better and better. It would have been stupid to lurk in those depressing rooms and eat stale synthetic protein concentrates just as if White Wingers didn't dare go where they pleased on a Base of the Fleet. The other squad was nowhere in sight.

"Crowded tonight," observed Joao.

"It just got too crowded," muttered Gregory. "See that man in Orange, the one with gold collar tabs and an ace's scarf? He led a flight during the scramble at Capra 6."

"You waxed his tail over a couple of Sej, didn't you?" Valentina laughed softly. "Well, here he comes. You can wax it again."

As the Orange flight leader approached their table, talk died down and then rose again in a rustle of malicious speculation. Gregory rose and nodded.

The Orange flight leader held out his hand, compelling

Gregory to shake it. "I see your recent celebrity hasn't made you more aloof," the intruder observed.

Gregory raised an eyebrow.

"You do know about the article in which you're listed as a possible successor to your Wing Commander?"

"Do you always read civilian sources with such attention, Lieutenant Commander?" Zann asked.

"My squad's communications officer," Gregory volunteered. "May I present the others?"

"Please don't trouble yourself. Another time, perhaps. I see that there have been some changes among the pilots." The unfamiliar ace nodded at Yuri and Judith, and stared at Dustin. "More celebrities or, let's say, notorieties? We followed the battle at Mahalir, Gregory."

His words were louder, deliberately challenging, as if he were trying to incite every other officer in the room.

"Resourceful of you," Zann remarked, "seeing as how the investigation afterward was classified. Or does Orange have its own Intelligence sources?" She looked up at the flight leader, and Dustin knew that the man had to be remembering every rumor he'd ever heard about the squad. He smelled something savory coming their way and stifled a sigh. If this damned Orange decided to stand here and play games all evening, dinner would cool, and he was starving.

"Gregory"—Judith leaned over—"we're either keeping this gentleman from his own party or else being terribly rude in not asking him to join us. Shall I call for another chair?" she asked in her huskiest, most charming tones.

They waited until the man had stammered some excuse before exchanging brief nods of approval. Then they settled into their dinners and ate in appreciative silence.

"Coffee," Zann said after the table was cleared. "Anyone else?"

"I'm for another bottle of wine," Joao said. "How're the finances, Yuri?"

"Holding out. I'll join you."

Dustin opted for coffee. He glanced over at Suzannah, as he had done repeatedly throughout the evening. She sat with her head against the high, padded back of their booth. Clearly she was trying to rest without spoiling everyone's mood. *Too many demands,* Dustin thought. It was too much for her. First the dual work load, and now the terrible responsibility of knowing who Bikmat was and having to protect him. Dustin was used to it. The chance to share it last night had somehow made it that much easier to bear. He hoped Zann wouldn't blame herself that she hadn't guessed before. Under the table he reached down and squeezed her hand. He had never dreamed of the trust, love, and acceptance she had given him.

The waiter returned and served their drinks with just the slightest edge of carelessness to indicate his dislike of White Wingers. He set coffee in front of Dustin, and the pilot's nostrils flared. Suddenly he was dizzy. Though he'd just eaten a lavish dinner, he was fiercely hungry. He drew a deep, shuddering breath. He sat in the middle of his squad. He was in superb health. He'd killed his contact. There was no reason for . . . the hunger struck again, a terrible wave. This time the scent of hathoti, masked by the spices and pungent sweet alcohol in the coffee, filtered through more sharply.

The Sej never gave up, Dustin thought in a black rage. And they were everywhere. He knew they wanted him to break cover or do something equally devastating so that the Old Man's invitation to speak to the Committee would be withdrawn, so that the scandal involving Aramin and Kolatolo could be indecently buried. And they wanted revenge on the first operative ever to betray them.

From here, Dustin saw too clearly, all courses of action led to the same end. *They knew their Bikmat*, he thought. Threaten his squad and he'd blow cover to protect them, even if he destroyed himself.

Dustin could drink the coffee. Though he'd have the dry heaves and one hell of a hangover, he'd live. But Zann, tired as she was, and with the alcohol and caffeine fighting it out in her system . . . the hathoti would kill her. Even if Joao could pump her out as soon as they got out of here, she'd be in grave danger. Dustin couldn't allow that.

When she and Kroeger had offered him the chance to hide Bikmat forever in the files of Counterintelligence and to be Dustin, for real, it had seemed like one of the hallucinations that some hathoti addicts raved over. He should have known better than to believe in it. Here were choices he could believe in. Keep silent and let Zann die. Or take the cup from her and create such a scandal that his cover might get blown as high as the base ship.

Zann blew playfully at the streaming coffee, then lifted the cup. Leaning over, Dustin caught her hand, forcing it down onto the table. The coffee slopped over, leaving a dark stain on the white cloth.

"Don't drink it, Zann," he cautioned softly. "I smell something. Joao?"

"What's wrong?" mouthed Joao. With his eyes he warned the others to go on talking.

"Check this," Dustin said. "It's been poisoned. Lethal dose of hathoti, I'd say."

Joao dipped a finger in the cup, sniffed, and then, very cautiously, licked at it. "Hathoti," he said, and his green eyes chilled. "Enough to kill us all. Yours too?"

"Mine too."

"Gregory," Joao said in an undertone, "we have to get out of here. Now. Pay up, will you?"

Zann sat without moving. Her eyes closed, then flickered open to meet Dustin's. He caught a single blaze of sorrow before she closed them once again. She knew what this would cost him. And her too.

"I'd like to know," Joao remarked to Dustin in a mild tone that everyone in the Wing distrusted, "just how you spotted that."

Here it came. *Gregory, I'm sorry,* Dustin thought.

Dustin bowed his head. It hurt worse than any nightmare of pain or betrayal he'd ever had. "I think we'd better get back to the ship first. And someone ought to contact Federico Hashrahh Kroeger."

CHAPTER 17

Kroeger smiled grimly at the lists of shipping manifests racing across his screen. Commodity traders tried to avoid taking delivery, but Aramin had been different. Here were the records of deliveries accepted, titles transferred to any one of three Kolatolo-owned enterprises, and cargo transported. At this point someone had tampered with computer memory, wiping or altering destinations. This was a minor annoyance. In an hour more Kroeger knew that he could check fuel, maintenance, and itineraries for the ships involved and pinpoint the grain's ultimate destination: Sejiedi worlds. Bikmat had told him that they were desperate for food.

Aramin had been very good, but she'd made two mistakes. She had underestimated her enemies, never thinking Bikmat could break conditioning or that League Intelligence might turn the case over to an eidetic; and she had dealt with a traitorous fool. If only for being so easily manipulated, Kolatolo deserved whatever he was about to get . . . and Kroeger was going to make certain he got it.

Someone thrust a spool into his hand. "Not *now,
Dorvic,*" he snapped at the young civ. Any of Suzannah's
squad would have known not to disturb him. And Suzannah
herself would have known how to interrupt without shattering his concentration.

"It's from some White Wing pilot, a man called Dustin,"
Dorvic replied, avoiding Kroeger's eyes.

If Bikmat had left a message for him, it had to be
urgent. Kroeger slipped the spool into his console and
waved Dorvic away. A Sejiedi ambush detected, perhaps,
or an attack on Bikmat through what was left of his
conditioning. He would have to be tested, possibly using
the brainstripper, possibly to destruction. Suzannah would
object, of course, but in all prudence, he'd yielded to her
protests as much as he dared. He slipped on a headset. *Any*
communication from this source was highly confidential.

"This is Dustin. Can you report back to the base ship
immediately? There's been an attempt on Suzannah's life,
and mine, with a lethal dose of hathoti. We'll be expecting
you."

Kroeger swore in three languages and was out of his
chair so fast that his long legs kicked it over. Printouts
flew wildly as he plundered them for the special ones,
the ones destined to be leaked to the media, and the ones
to be sent to Center, printouts damning Kolatolo not just
for hathoti addiction but for collaborating with a Sejiedi
agent to sell grain to the League's enemy. How Kroeger
had looked forward to presenting them himself and watching the Director of Intelligence and that imbecile Abitee
squirm. There'd be resignations right and left, and he had
to be there. But now he thrust the evidence into Dorvic's
hands and outlined, in clear detail, how it was to be
handled.

If it weren't so disconcerting, it would have been intriguing, Kroeger thought. He seemed to be splitting into two people: the clinical, dispassionate Intelligence chief who could observe that his hands were sweating at the same time he briefed his staff, and the wretched character who barely had time to order his plans implemented before he commandeered a shuttle up to the base ship. *Someone had tried to kill his prize operatives,* Kroeger thought. He was astounded at his own fury. He was going to get a lot of information. And then someone was going to get very, very dead.

Deep in White Wing territory, outside the doors of the squad he had come to regard as his personal property, Kroeger straightened his Arthan-style tunic and announced himself.

The physician met him at the door. "Hathoti tincture." He greeted Kroeger with the most important fact first. Suzannah had trained him well. "Someone tried to dope Suzannah's coffee. It was pretty heavily laced with liqueur and spices, but Dustin sniffed it out. I don't know how he smelled it—"

"Later," Kroeger said. He tried to push by the man, but Joao outweighed him by at least thirty kilos and wasn't moving.

"*Later,*" the medic said softly, "we're going to demand some answers for ourselves. From Subiat Base, and from you."

"Is that Federico Hashrahh Kroeger yet?" Suzannah's voice sounded strained. Kroeger had only heard that note in it once before, during the interminable arguments with Center when her squad was tasked to eliminate Aglo. "Let him come in, Joao."

Joao ran his eyes over Kroeger—*as if he thinks I need treatment*—critically. "Suzannah needs to see you in control of yourself," he said, still in that soft voice Kroeger found himself distrusting. "Afterward, if you want to tear some people apart, I'll help. But before I let you see her, calm down."

Kroeger bit back a protest. That he'd started to object was a sign of how overwrought he must have been. *Regard the attempt on Suzannah and Bikmat as data,* he cautioned himself and followed Joao into the bare wardroom. Suzannah sat in the center of it, the rest of the squad around her. Bikmat stood behind her, one hand on the back of her chair. Gregory glared at Kroeger's entrance, but Kroeger ignored the flight leader's usual hostility to concentrate on his Intelligence officer. Incongruous blotches of cosmetics streaked her pale, drawn face. He hadn't known she ever used them.

"I'm alive," she said flatly. "Somebody get Federico Hashrahh Kroeger a chair."

Behind them, Bikmat stirred. "I knew it wouldn't work. Tell them," he ordered coldly.

"Tell us *what?*" Gregory asked.

Kroeger forced his attention from Suzannah to the rest of her squad. Judith, seated beside her, patted her hand reassuringly. Yuri was watching Gregory. Joao exchanged a glance with Valentina, then looked over at the man they knew as Dustin.

"I'll be in my quarters," Dustin said, a little too rapidly. "I don't have to hear it. I can spare myself that much."

The big medic watched him leave, then turned to Kroeger. "I told you we want answers," he said carefully. "Suzannah's worn out with two people's work—hers and Intelligence's. We went to the Officers' Club for dinner, to relax. She ordered coffee. So did Dustin. When it came, he sniffed it and told her not to drink. He said it was hathoti. I tested it, and he's right. There was enough in those cups to kill two people my size. Then he insisted we return to the ship and he left that message for you. Now, why don't you tell all of us what's going on?''

Kroeger stopped himself from leaning over and taking Suzannah's hands between his own. She leaned back against her chair, trembling. A simple assassination attempt, even combined with overwork, shouldn't have shaken her this much.

"Tell them," she said and closed her eyes.

"You remember that we identified the Sejiedi operative called Aglo as Haral TreMorion. He was one of two Sejiedi we knew were operating in the Fleet. Recently, we have had some assistance from the second, the one called Bikmat.''

As Kroeger spoke, he looked around. Suzannah might have provided as detailed a report, but she seemed too exhausted to do more than stare at the others and shrink into herself as their faces changed. As Kroeger told the squad of Bikmat's attack on his contact and how he had turned himself in, amazement colored his voice.

Judith's face twisted, and she reached over to squeeze Suzannah's shoulder. Valentina shook her head and whispered to Yuri, "That poor, brave bastard, sneaking out on me like that. He could have told me."

This wasn't possible, Kroeger thought and continued his summary. "Your Commander addresses the Committee on Appropriations before the Assembly adjourns thirty days from now. Clearly, the attempt on Suzannah's and Bikmat's'' —Yuri's eyes flamed and Kroeger corrected himself— "Dustin's lives had to be made, both as punishment for what the Sej would regard as treason and as a final attempt at discrediting the Wing. If Dustin had allowed Suzannah to drink that coffee, which would have killed her, they

WHITE WING   271

could have used that information against you. But, frankly, I suspect they judged he would intervene. That would have been even more satisfactory from their point of view. Dustin would have broken cover, discrediting himself, providing his own punishment and, incidentally, completing his task. That he saved Suzannah's life without creating a bigger scandal than I can silence is a tribute to him.''

"That son-of-a-bitch!" Yuri burst out, grinning. "He brought us TreMorion, and now he's bagged Kolatolo. Good for him!"

"He's a *Sej*!" Gregory shouted. "A rotten, stinking Sej. And we're flying with him."

Kroeger's fingers tightened on the arms of his chair. In all the years of the Wing's existence, no outsider had ever seen one of them lose control. Excitement raced through him as bits of information correlated, meshing into a larger whole. A few more and he could crack the enigma of the White Wing.

Yuri's face went gray at Gregory's words. "I don't think I can take another execution."

Judith narrowed her shoulders, hugging herself into a tight, protective knot. "You wouldn't have to. Gregory gave Maryam the Mercy. You vaped TreMorion, Aglo, whatever he was. This time it would be my turn . . . oh, God, and I brought him in!"

"You knew, Zann." Gregory bent over the comm officer. "How long have you known? Since he came in and reported?"

She shook her head wordlessly. The makeup looked like bruises on her skin.

"And you spent last night with him anyhow?" Gregory went on. "With a *Sej*?"

Even Kroeger could feel the revulsion in Gregory's voice. The emotion became a catalyst, and he knew he was very, very near to his solution . . . but Gregory's harsh voice pierced Kroeger's concentration again.

"Years, Suzannah, it's been twelve years. And still I don't understand you at all. *I don't know you, Zann!* How could you do this? How can the rest of you just sit there and talk about it as if Dustin—*Bikmat*—pulled some prize stunt on the Blues? He's as bad as TreMorion. Worse. Is this what we trusted? Is this what we—"

He turned on his heel, away from the squad, and headed for the door.

"Where are you going, Greg?" Suzannah was on her feet, her voice pleading. "Gregory, please."

"I'm going to get drunk," he retorted coldly, "with strangers I *don't* know."

As the door hissed shut, the stunning, elegant solution hit Kroeger, shocking him with its simplicity. The White Wing's refusal to use rank wasn't an affectation designed to confound the Colors. They didn't need rank within the squads, and with their sibs . . . siblings? If Kroeger had been a man for a family, he might have seen it sooner. Gregory, he remembered, had lost a friend at Mahalir. Then Kroeger's thoughts turned quickly. Maryam. The Mercy. Gregory had killed Maryam, and she was his— wife. And now Dustin. No wonder Suzannah was distraught.

"It all makes sense now," he muttered.

"You're not telling Central about this too," Suzannah said and leapt at him. Her hands twisted out to claw or grapple.

Kroeger didn't want to fight her. As he stepped back, Joao caught her by the arm and pulled her against him, wrapping his arms about her to trap and to comfort.

"That won't help, Zann."

Briefly Suzannah struggled against him, then started to sob. Against the physician's immense height, she looked small and fragile. Joao stroked her hair with one hand and whispered to her before he raised his head and met Kroeger's eyes.

"So now you know," he said.

Kroeger nodded. The knowledge was satisfaction enough. He knew he would not report this new information. Because now he understood, and in understanding, he also realized why the White Wing had such a passion for guarding itself. The strength of its squads was also their greatest weakness. What would Gregory do if someone kidnapped or captured one of the others? Enemies within the League would try to disrupt its efficiency by isolating or attacking a single member of a flight. No wonder the Wing Commander had been accompanied to Arthan by his squad. At a time like this, he'd want his family about him. Even Kroeger could see that.

Joao studied him, unblinking. A terrible compassion in the medic's eyes forced Kroeger to his next conclusion.

He had respected Suzannah, admired her, enjoyed working with her. And he'd been a fool not to realize that the exhilaration he had derived from it wasn't based just on competence, or even fellow-feeling for another eidetic. As far as he'd been concerned, eidetics didn't have fellow-feelings. He had never been lonely around her. For that matter, he'd never felt lonely around the rest of the squad. They might dislike him, but they had accepted him for himself. Not as a gifted child to be trained for the greater fortune and status of his clan, not as a too-bright student threatening his teachers, not as an operative or administrator to be used hard and jeered at behind his back for his theories and his Earther blood.

Blood called to blood. He'd read that once, when fiction still held some attraction for him. What if he had followed his Earther blood and entered the Wing? His proud citizen family had decreed that would be unacceptable and self-destructive. But if he had, he would have known Suzannah. He would have worked with her. Now that he saw her with her squad, her family, about her, he realized that he too might have had such a squad. He might have had someone like her . . . *might have had her*.

He had loved without knowing, and so his love was without hope or jealousy.

Joao nodded. For the first time in Kroeger's life, he wanted to hide from someone else's knowledge.

Abruptly he thought back to that evening at the Blue Angel. The squad had been grieving over Maryam's death, but it had obeyed orders. That evening he had realized that Gregory disliked him, that Valentina taunted him, that Judith just wanted him to go away. A new experience for him, he told himself, the first time he'd been disliked for himself, not his ancestry or his intelligence or his politics. Suzannah had tolerated him, had taken time to answer his questions. Why had the bartender given them free drinks? Because that was a kindness so tactfully expressed it could be accepted. The Earther refugees were proud of their Wing.

He was Earther too. And he, too, was proud. It was something more to hold onto than his tenuous clan loyalties back on Reykskjoldar or the intrigues at Center.

Gently he reached out and touched Suzannah's hair. At this moment Gregory's rage, Dustin's dual identity, the next battle, didn't matter. He just didn't want Suzannah to hate him.

"Gregory is a bad drunk," Joao told him. "I'd go after him, but I want to get Suzannah comfortable."

"I'll arrange for someone to watch out for him," Kroeger offered. It gave him an excuse to leave. They'd be glad to be rid of him.

"Thanks, Federico," Joao said, and the door closed behind him.

Gregory was rather proud of himself. Did Joao really think he couldn't go out drinking without a keeper? He'd spent the entire evening among other White Wingers, among a few Reds, even a sprinkling of other Colors, and he hadn't gotten into one single fight. Now he was headed back to quarters and was even quite steady on his feet. A very occasional lurch sideways didn't count.

"They ought to service these lifts more often," he solemnly told the civs who shared this one with him, and they agreed. Sensible people, not like his squad. But he wouldn't think about that. He was a long, long way from quarters, and the corridors took a lot of complicated turns. The civs seemed headed in the right direction, so he followed them.

"You can't come in here," he told them outside the corridor leading to White Wing country.

They shrugged and walked away, almost as impassive as Wingers. Neil would have thought that was funny. Neil had always loved jokes. Back on Wing Moon, when he'd gone drinking with Neil, they had always gotten into fights or contests. He missed Neil. He didn't want to go home, but there wasn't any other place to go at this hour. There was something back in quarters, something dreadful, something he knew he didn't want to think about.

The something was seated in the wardroom with the rest of his family. Dustin-who-was-Bikmat. The spy.

"What's *he* doing here?" Gregory demanded. Funny, he'd asked that once before, and there'd been a terrible fight.

"Where do you want him to go, Gregory?" asked Joao. "The brig?"

Abruptly the warm comfort of the drinks he'd had was gone. "I want him to go to hell! Where's Suzannah?"

Joao's face was like rock. "I put her out. Nepenthine, no less."

"She's not a burned-out pilot," Gregory protested feebly.

"You rejected her pretty thoroughly. She was hysterical." Gregory had never heard such condemnation in Joao's voice.

Why were they condemning him? *He* wasn't a Sejiedi spy, *he* hadn't sneaked and snaked his way into a squad until he could tear it apart from the inside. He strode over to where Dustin was sitting. Bikmat. Dustin. The hell with it. The damned little traitor rose and met Gregory's eyes.

"Send me the divorce decree," Dustin said heavily. "I'll 'print anything you want."

Gregory growled, then backhanded him across the face. Dustin went skidding into a chair and came up in a crouch, his eyes flashing. Blood dripped from his mouth onto his flightsuit. Then the anger in his eyes turned to ash, and he stood, hands spread to his sides, waiting for whatever else Gregory might do to him.

"You rotten bastard!" Gregory shouted. "I'm going to—" He started to lunge at Dustin, but Judith and Yuri had him by the arms. He didn't want to fight with them. He knew them. They were honest pilots, good squadmates. Family. Not like that Sej.

The pattern of red drops down the breast of Dustin's uniform troubled Gregory. They shouldn't be there. It was wrong. He wavered between wanting to wipe the blood from Dustin's face and wanting to strangle him.

"I'm glad Neil's dead," he said harshly. "The shame would have killed him. And I'd like to kill you."

"I'll save you the trouble."

"You're bluffing!"

Dustin had started to leave the wardroom. Now he jerked around and smeared his hand across his bloody mouth. "I am Sej and I am Wing. And we do not bluff."

"He might as well stay alive," Gregory muttered as Dustin left. "He can sleep with Zann. Zann likes sleeping with him."

"Sit down and shut up," Joao said. "You've been vicious enough for one night."

"Why'd *we* get so lucky?" Gregory rambled. "Why us?"

"Blame me," Judith said. "I brought him over to the table at the Blue Angel, remember?"

They were watching him. Yuri looked sorrowful, and Judith was almost crying with anger. Joao was watching with the cold rage Gregory preferred not to provoke.

Valentina walked in. "Suzannah's resting easy now," she reported to Joao. Then her eyes lit on Gregory.

"Why'd we get stuck with a Sej?" he appealed to her. Val was smart, almost as smart as Zann.

"They wanted to discredit the Wing," she snapped at him. "And guess who they wanted to start with?"

Her words were sobering him up, and he knew he'd give a month's pay not to hear her next comment.

"He was *aimed*, Gregory. Would you care to speculate just *who* he was aimed at? You can thank God he's the man he is."

Dustin had been aimed at them? No, that wasn't entirely accurate. The article Val had read him only a few hours ago. A possible candidate for command of a Wing already hated and feared, one already notorious in the League for giving a squadmate the Mercy, a man with a kill record even the Blues admired . . . the man in the article was a perfect target for the Sej.

Dustin had been aimed at him. Realization hit him like a

hot rush of bile to his mouth, and he staggered against the wall.

"Somebody else make him stick his finger down his throat," Joao ordered. "I don't have time. I didn't like the way Dustin was talking at all."

Divorce . . . suicide . . . a spy . . . it was more scandal than Gregory could imagine. Dustin was Sej and Dustin was Wing. He might murder somebody, but he'd never dishonor the Wing . . . or his squad.

Gregory knew he was going to be very sick. For the next interminable half-hour he repeatedly and earnestly cursed himself, Dustin, and all the liquor he'd consumed.

Gregory rinsed his mouth, spat, and splashed cold water on his face. He was considerably more sober, but no less confused. Between spasms of vomiting, he'd heard voices arguing, criticizing, condemning. Now everything was muted, surreal, unfamiliar, and he badly needed something or someone to hold onto.

He stumbled back into the wardroom. Yuri handed him a mug. Steam rose from it and Gregory waited for the nausea to start again.

"Drink it slowly." Yuri collapsed into a corner and stared intently into his own cup.

Gregory sipped the broth slowly. As the hot liquid worked its way down, he began to feel more guilty than bewildered. He had hurt Zann, hurt her unforgivably. No wonder Joao was furious. Usually Zann was so strong, so right, that Gregory forgot how vulnerable she was. All the time he'd been acting crazy after Maryam died, Zann had been the one person who could make him see reason. And now he had turned on her, hurt her in the way that only someone she loved beyond reason could hurt her. And Kroeger had taken it all in.

"Can I see her?" he asked humbly.

"Joao's still talking to Dustin," Val said. "I suppose it can't hurt. But Gregory, if you wake her, Joao'll skin us both."

Valentina hadn't forgiven him yet. He didn't know if he'd ever forgive himself.

Suzannah's room was dark. He moved quietly, careful not to bump into the stacks of reports and references she kept about. As his eyes adapted, he moved more surely and sat beside her bunk. The blanket Joao had put on her had slipped down to her waist, and Gregory smoothed it around her shoulders again.

Zann whimpered a little in her sleep, then sighed and nestled into the warmth. She flung out one hand, and Gregory took it, cupping it against his face for an instant.

He remembered when he had first met her. He had just made ace and was back on Wing Moon, on leave, but still keeping his flying hours up. What was that man's name? Ulf? Ulf's computer had crashed, nearly taking his sting with them, and Gregory had volunteered to shepherd him in. Comm officer that day had been a woman he'd heard of but never met. Instinctively he had liked the low, melodious voice which instructed and reassured the blind flier.

"You should make visual contact with Pilot Gregory in fifteen seconds. He'll lead you in," she had told him.

"Are you certain?"

As Gregory remembered, Suzannah had laughed. "Of course! My calculations are never wrong."

Gregory had waited around until her watch was over, then offered to buy her dinner. Joao had come with them that time and other times too. The hulking medic seemed to have appointed himself Zann's personal bodyguard.

"You watch it, mister," Joao had told him. "People

have tried to exploit her, and she isn't too good at protecting herself. It's very simple, Gregory. If you hurt her, I'll hurt you, and I don't care if they court-martial me for it.''

He had been immediately attracted to Zann. It had taken him far longer to appreciate Joao's integrity and humanity the way he had later learned to prize Yuri's courage or Judith's stability.

Tonight was the first time Suzannah's calculations had been wrong. Dustin's proving to be a Sej must have shaken her confidence, but she'd snapped back long enough to try to save him. She'd fought with the kind of guts any pilot would envy. And then he'd had to tear into her till she cracked, right in front of Kroeger.

"Forgive me," he murmured into her palm. "You know I really do love you." He set her hand down gently. She murmured and stretched out.

Somewhat comforted, Gregory started for his own cabin, but a square of light against the darkened corridor made him pause near the open door.

"You haven't let anyone down yet, Dustin," he heard Joao say. "Think about it. You've never let the Wing down, and you turned on the Sej, even though they raised you."

"I've thought about it. That allergy to hathoti was just a lucky break. But there's still the conditioning. They're going to call me in, Joao, and I don't know if I can fight it."

Gregory knew he shouldn't listen, but he felt compelled, welded to the place just outside that bright square of light.

"You've fought it before," Joao replied.

"Not well enough," Dustin said. "Joao, my decision isn't open to debate. Once I killed Aramin, I knew it was over for me."

"Why do you think you have to throw it all away?"

"Come on, Joao. There's no way Gregory will ever trust me again. Everyone's falling to pieces. Besides, you're evading the issue. Can you fix me up with something, some kind of tooth with poison or something? No one in the Wing's ever been taken prisoner!"

"I'm not going to be responsible for your suicide," Joao replied harshly.

"I'm not asking you to. Combat's clean. It won't be hard to make a mistake, and take a few more Sej with me. I don't think I'll mind too much. But I don't want to be taken, Joao. Maybe there won't be anyone around to help me. Or maybe it won't be in combat. Don't forget, I know how Operations works. I don't know if I'd have time to take a pill or something."

"Let me think about it," Joao said slowly. "It might take me some time to get the supplies I need. Promise to stick around until then?"

"Do you want me to promise on the honor of the Wing?" Dustin's voice was heavy.

"Your word's good enough for me." There was a long pause, and Gregory started to breathe again. Then Joao broke the silence.

"Are you sure you don't want something to help you sleep? Maybe you shouldn't be alone, either."

"I'll be fine, Joao. Thanks. Get back to Zann."

The glowing rectangle darkened as Dustin closed his door. Joao padded noiselessly to Zann's cabin, and Gregory waited for him.

"She's sleeping peacefully," he reported. "I didn't wake her."

Joao examined him in the half-light. "You overheard what Dustin and I were saying. What are you going to do about it?"

"What can I do?" Gregory said. "He's right. I don't know if I can trust him anymore, especially not in a fight. I was thinking that maybe he could go on sick call, and we'd get in a solo—"

"Think *straight* for once, Gregory!" Joao glanced into Zann's room and lowered his voice. "What happens if some Green medic examines him and says he's fit to fly? I can't guarantee I'd be the duty officer. That would raise some pretty questions, wouldn't it? Besides, if anything would destroy him, that would. And I don't think you really want to kill him."

"What about you?" Gregory replied. "You're going along with that tooth idea of his."

"Of course I am. It buys me some time. And once I've got it ready, I'll say I have to knock him out in order to put it in. If you think all I'll be doing is dental work, you're a bigger fool than I take you for."

"To quote Val, not possible." Gregory wanted very much for Joao to laugh.

"You're no fool, Gregory. The problem is, you don't think. I hope that right now you're upset enough to try and *think* about something, not just react. Listen. If anyone asked you what was the most important thing in your life, you'd say it was the squad, right? But who hurt everyone even more after Maryam died? Who kept pushing Dustin away until Yuri raised hell? Who ignored Judith and Yuri— and who drove Zann nearly crazy tonight? I've never seen her that bad, Gregory. You're loyal to the squad, but your loyalty's been what's hurting us, every time, down the line. You can't be this rigid, Greg. You're killing all of us."

"What do you want me to do? Do you want me to go in there and tell him—"

"I want you to think about it," Joao said firmly. "Maybe he's Sej. But just maybe he's our Dustin, and you can trust him after all. You've got to decide for yourself, Gregory. Otherwise I don't know what we're all going to do."

CHAPTER 18

The sting's a-gravs strained toward the tau that would blow them, past red into crimson. Lasers blasted at him, still faster than he could flee—and he was flying blind, headed back to a base ship that seemed like a pin-point even smaller than the indifferent stars so many light years away. His comms were dead, and the Sej were tracking him. He couldn't call for help, or the Mercy. And then he saw White stings. He wanted to laugh and greet them, but that was chatter. He couldn't allow it. He tried to slow, but the controls were frozen. The White stings swooped by him, daring tau. He almost thought he could see the pilots' faces . . . his squadmates? Was the one headed straight at him Kroeger, or just a grinning skull? He might have punched controls, pleaded for more speed, but the emergency lights were on, were glowing amber, then red, and the alarm was buzzing, buzzing, buzzing . . .

The harsh buzz rose, piercing, then shattering the dream. Before Gregory was even able to think clearly, he found himself two-thirds dressed. Two flights should be patrol-

ling. There'd be six others on watch in the ready-room.
They'd be engaged already.

As he emerged from his cabin, Judith, Yuri, and Dustin
fell into step behind him. They ran into the corridor, where
Charles, Anna, Elizabeth, and Michael appeared. Footsteps pounded behind them, as Glennis, Vlad, and Alan
joined them. For a moment, Gregory hesitated. Neil was
missing. Then he winced. No time to remember that. No
time to make his peace with Suzannah. She ran by the
pilots to her own duty station.

As they crowded into the tube, Gregory shook his head
clear, listening to the exclamations. Subiat? No one expected an attack this far inside the League. How could the
Sej have penetrated the system's perimeter defenses? Don't
ask that, just fight.

Then he remembered Dustin, and his face tightened.
With Neil gone, they were flying one man short. Fine.
One man short, and a Sej at his back.

Zann had sworn that Dustin hadn't told the Sej anything, that he was loyal to the Wing and the squad, that
he'd turned double agent, and had brought them Kolatolo.
None of that mattered. Maybe the Sej had been telling the
truth last night. Maybe he wouldn't turn on them, and just
maybe, the way he'd promised, he'd fly out ahead and get
himself vaped.

As soon as the tube opened, they sprinted across the
hangar deck and leapt into the waiting stings. Seconds
later, the giant wall slammed down and the depressuriza-
tion locks snapped into place. Then the blast came, and
they accelerated into the battle zone.

The familiar clean fury poured into Gregory. The cone
of stings stayed tight. He could hear garbled chatter from
the open channel and discounted it. The Wing frequency
was silent. His scopes showed him what was happening.

There were two Sejiedi cruisers out there, each carrying twenty-five flights. Only fifteen showed now. The Sej were holding back.

Counting the seven flights of White Wing, the League had fifteen flights out—their seven, the six on watch, and two on patrol. No, make that seventeen. A Red and a Blue flight had reacted quickly enough to get out this fast.

Gregory eyed the scopes again. He wondered bleakly how much support they could expect from Subiat Base. Whatever it was, it would almost certainly come too late for them. The base ship held only thirty-five full flights. If Subiat Base didn't support them, they were badly outnumbered.

Below them Subiat's seas and the lights of its cities gleamed. This was no outpost, but a fully settled world. Had Earth looked like this?

As they closed in on the Sej, Gregory spoke to his flight. "Hedgehog," he ordered crisply. "Without heroics."

The cone bulged and turned, converting itself into a bristling sphere with all primary lasers pointing outward.

"Roll," Gregory commanded. The sphere danced and began to spin into the swam of Sejiedi stings surrounding one of the cruisers. Even if they were outnumbered, they were covered, Gregory thought. And then, just when the Sej had them down as an easy target, just so long as they evaded the cruisers' heavy cannon lasers, then . . .

A sudden burst of a language he didn't recognize came over the open channel. He ignored it, and maintained his position in the ball, watchful both of his own and the others' firing ranges. When a Sej came into his scope, he fired in yellow band, Judith joining him. The fighter blew jaggedly. A bad kill, not even near clean. Careful. Hold your fire till it's in your scope. He had said that a million times to Maryam, to Yuri, to the youngsters on Wing

Moon. He chanted it again and again to himself. It was a litany he understood only too well, something to keep him cold and firmly directed.

The strange language came again, a long babble of it.

Before Gregory could contact Battle Op, he heard Zann's voice: "Dustin, stay in formation. Close up." Gregory scowled. The Sej was already a problem.

He scanned Dustin's position. He was definitely moving away from the formation.

Damn him, Gregory thought, *why can't he just go play hero and get killed like he promised?*

"Gregory, this is Suzannah." The familiar low voice came over the Wing frequency. "Watch Dustin. What you just heard was a command statement in Sejiedi. I've reason to believe it's keyed to a hypnotic sequence. They've ordered him in."

Gregory switched off the general frequency communications, then he swore. "Specify," he told Zann.

"Dustin has been ordered to report in to the Sejiedi cruiser 200–40–97."

Gregory's fingers froze momentarily on the board. He watched as Dustin's sting held position for precious seconds longer, then jerked slightly out of formation.

"Dustin, get back," Gregory told him.

"I can't." Dustin's voice was ragged. "I won't let them . . ." The sting jolted again, moving closer to the cruiser that hovered "above" their present position. And held there. For long moments the lone sting held, blasting against the single Sej in the area who wasn't attacking. As if contemptuous of the battle around it, the ship hovered. Its winglights pulsed sullenly, dull, red, keyed to the rhythm of a man's heart.

A shepherd, Gregory thought, *waiting to bring him in. What would they do to him once they had him?*

"Gregory, this is Dustin." The voice was shaky, but quite clear. "I'm still trying . . . no, the conditioning . . . it's too deep . . ."

"Hold him, Gregory," said Zann. Her voice sounded flat and he knew she'd activated her board's privacy zones. "I'm getting Kroeger. He's been researching this."

Fine, Gregory thought. *Subiat may blow up like Earth, and Kroeger's on another data-hunt.*

Gregory's scopes showed Dustin's sting wavering. It wandered a few kilometers closer to the formation, away from the Sej cruiser. Then, as if caught in a tractor beam, it jerked back to its previous position. The single Sej, the shepherd, was still carving great loops between the Wing sphere and Dustin's sting. Gregory was a breath away from ordering his flight out to take it. But TreMorion had ambushed them at Mahalir. This could be another trap.

"I've tried self-destruct." Dustin's breathing was ragged. "I can't. I want to, but my hands won't . . . Gregory, I know I don't deserve it, but for the Wing, for the honor of the Wing, please don't let them take me."

His sting bobbed forward, yawing. Dustin had always been such a crisp flier. The Sej would get him, and it would look like they'd taken a White Winger, for the first time in two hundred years.

Time yawned open before Gregory. He could still see the brilliant lasers flashing around him, but now they moved as slowly as if they were the long, lazy arcs of sunset. He saw an explosion of purple-white, heard a blast of chatter, and ignored it. The single Sej ship was still out there, waiting for Dustin.

Zann had told him. So had Joao, and all the others, but he hadn't seen the whole picture before, not completely, not with this clarity. *Think about it,* Joao had pleaded. But it was so simple, so fundamental, that he didn't need to obscure it by anything as complex as thought.

Maryam. The Sej had had a tractor beam on Maryam. She hadn't asked for it; she'd fought it to the best of her ability. Now they had what amounted to the same thing on Dustin. They'd had it on him for years. Like Maryam, he'd fought it, fought harder than he'd ever have to in any scramble, yet never betrayed the Wing, not by so much as a glance. He had never surrendered anything to the Sej. What was more, he'd delivered Kolatolo to Kroeger and by doing so, had saved Wing Moon, and all of them. And all the while, he was only afraid of one thing: that the people he fought to save would hate him.

Dustin's sting was heading forward, toward the dark shepherd, when the full realization hit Gregory.

"Hold on, Dusty, just hold on," he said.

"Anna, I'm going after him. Take the flight. Zann, get Joao! Where's your damned Kroeger? Dustin, hold on. Put your hands on your head and recite as many prime numbers of three or more digits as you can think of. Hurry up, Zann."

"Gregory, I don't know if I can fight it . . ." Dustin's voice was husky.

"Just a little longer, Dustin," Zann broke in. "Gregory, try something else, Kroeger's on his way here."

For the first time, fear hit Gregory. He had wanted Dustin dead, and now he didn't. But he was unsure, and the fear felt small and cold and hard, tightening his throat, and numbing his mind. If it came to that, he'd willingly be obligated to Kroeger. This was his sort of game. But it was Gregory who was alone out here with Dustin, who couldn't control what he was doing.

Another burst of Sej in his comm. Dustin's sting seemed to flinch. Would he turn on Gregory? He never had, even when Gregory had struck him. The Sejiedi swooped closer, sure it was almost done waiting.

Prime numbers weren't much help, it seemed. Gregory tried testing Dustin on cube roots. He could hear Dustin's breathing, harsh and panting. Cube roots were failing too.

"Dusty?" he made his voice gentle. "Please don't leave us. You're Wing, Dustin. You're Earther, and you're Wing . . . and you're a part of my family."

"A few hours ago you were ready to kill me," came the chilly reply. "Who says I'm Wing? Everyone says I'm Sej. Seems like I am, too. And now they're bringing me home." His voice was bitterness itself, and it broke on the last word.

Gregory couldn't hide from that kind of pain. "You belong with us! Joao says you're Earther to the core," he yelled.

"Bikmat is a Sejiedi spy." Dustin's voice sounded dead, beaten.

Another spate of Sejiedi came over the Wing channel. Gergory tensed. Before he was even aware of it, his hand went to his armscomp. One way or another, that Sej wasn't getting Dustin. He glanced up, dimly aware that a battle was going on about him, but his real attention was riveted on that one sting. It came to a complete standstill, quivering between the flight and the Sej cruiser. Then he heard a choking whimper, and Dustin mumbling something in the same language.

"What?" Had they lost him? He tensed, ready to fire.

On the scope Dustin's sting slowly began a long, looping maneuver, around and back. "I'm coming back," he heard Dustin say. His voice was very weak. "Cover me. And, Gregory, no matter what, *don't let them take me.*"

No time for curiosity or chatter. Gregory whipped his fighter around, trying to match Dustin's trajectory, to cover

his back as he made the long sweep home from enemy
space. But here came the shepherd, furious at losing Dustin,
firing in heavy bursts of violet and blue and yellow,
interspersed with deep orange. It was like his dream.
Gregory whipped the sting, pushing the a-gravs the way he
always did, to their limit and a little beyond it, and then a
little farther. His alarm was buzzing. He didn't notice it.
He only had one goal now. Get Dustin back to White
Wing territory, get him back into the flight. There was no
thrill in this, no tau-void abandonment to heroics. Neces-
sity, not joy, drove him to this. Lights burst in his path,
and his sting shook. If he didn't get out of here fast,
neutrino buffeting could get so bad it would tear him apart.

Now he was in visual contact with Dustin's sting. He
could identify it from the colors it threw off and its size
and speed. As he raced toward intercept, he swept the area
for possible targets. He was coming in low, beneath Dustin.
He adjusted slightly to bring his own flight path closer to
the other's.

Then the Sej watcher lunged forward. A furious bril-
liance erupted. Damn. Must have packed full thrust into
that laser, he thought. His eyes watered, and he blinked
ferociously. He had to see. Dustin . . . what had happened
. . . by now he must be a million billion subelementary
particles drifting . . .

He realized that Zann was demanding answers of him,
that another voice was backing her up, but he had nothing
to say. He had to see. He wouldn't permit himself to think
yet. They'd lost too many. He'd fought too hard to understand to bear losing Dustin too. Not now. Not just when
they were on the verge of winning, of breaking the Sej
conditioning.

It wouldn't be much comfort to know he'd died free.

"Dustin?" he asked softly, wondering if there would be

no answer. The laser cannon were immensely powerful, but sometimes . . . he couldn't let himself hope. He wasn't entitled to hope. He had thought of Dustin so vehemently as the enemy. Fifteen hours ago he would have given anything to kill the man with his bare hands. Now he only waited, suspended between ally and enemy, praying for a reply.

"My port stabilizer is gone." Dustin's voice was interrupted by static. "No speed, either. They didn't connect because they want me alive. Now they'll come back for both of us. Gregory, please, for God's sake, give me the Mercy and get out of here."

"How are you?" Gregory asked.

"A little banged up," Dustin replied. "Greg, here comes that ship. I can't evade—"

"You're coming home with me," Gregory told him flatly. "Anna, get the flight over here. We'll need all the firepower we've got to cover. Dustin, change course to 0–91–M812. Back to the base ship. I'm coming up behind you."

"Not the whole flight, Gregory! I'm not worth the risk!"

"No more chatter. That's an order!" Gregory snapped. He matched Dustin's turn precisely, covering the crippled sting's tail. Dustin would have some firepower left in his starboard and forward lasers. Then Gregory caught a Sej diving at him from behind and well below. He waited grimly, calculating range and priming his guns. Then the Sej was only a burst of light and slight flecks of cooling orange, and he still hadn't fired.

"Battle Op, mark it down. Single kill—Elizabeth's first."

It was Charles' voice. Something in Gregory smiled. Just out of laser range now, he saw the entire flight, strung out between himself and Dustin and the Sejiedi ship. They moved out into a hemisphere, covering Dustin and each other.

The Sej were coming in fast, true to form, trying to split the globe up into single ships. That was their style. The flight stuck together, assisting, covering for each other, keeping the Sej at a distance. It was for all of them, for Maryam and John and Neil and all the other pilots who flew out to die in the eternal morning of deep space. They would not lose another, not this time. A Sej came between the crossfire of Judith's and Michael's guns.

Something else, something strange, came up on his scope. A phalanx of Reds were closing in on the flight from the opposite direction, were forming into a sphere, a prefect defensive grouping. Then his scope blossomed with color, as Orange, Green and Yellow joined the Red, creating a thicker ring of defense. One lone Purple even flew on Dustin's blind portside. The Fleet was escorting them home. Gregory cleared his throat and opened Fleetwide communications. He listened to agitated reports. As his flight retreated—just for a moment!—a thousand kilometers away, other flights were harassing the Sejiedi stings, drawing their fire to permit this almost stately retreat, this honor guard for a lone, crippled White Wing craft.

Brother, I hope you're watching this! Gregory wished at Dustin.

Once they were well out of enemy space, practically back in the shadow of the base ship, Gregory opened Wing communications again. "Zann, what turned Dustin around out there?"

"Kroeger," she said. "He told Dustin, as Bikmat, that he had to obey his first loyalty. That was part of the conditioning. But he also gave Dustin the facts of his capture, his parents' names, even his own birth-name. So it was clear that his first loyalty had to be Earther."

Zann's voice went a little faint and Gregory concluded she was speaking to someone else. "Request . . ." She faltered and he heard her try again. "Request permission . . ."

Kroeger's voice, crisp but underlaid with warmth, came through to Gregory and the rest of his flight. "Request granted, Suzannah. Go and get Gregory's report."

As the great airlock of the hangar deck closed and cycled around them, Gregory had to remind himself not to smile.

CHAPTER 19

When Gregory climbed out of his sting, he saw that Joao had pushed forward through the cluster of techs and was waiting, one hand behind his back, concealing a hypo. The other stings of his flight surrounded Dustin's, protecting it from the other pilots who leapt from their stings and closed in. The scavengers! He remembered how they'd circled in after he gave Maryam the Mercy, practically shoving one another to see if the Wing would crack. Perhaps this time they were concerned as well as curious. He hated to admit it, but he'd needed their support. Without it, neither he nor Dustin might have made it back to the base ship.

Now all the pilots milled around, waiting for Dustin to lift the canopy of his sting. When it finally swung back, Gregory clenched his jaw, trying hard to keep his mask on. Dustin looked like he had lost a brawl in a garbage dump. His eyes didn't track, and his face looked rubbed raw. His left sleeve was filthy, streaked with rust. Gregory realized that he had tried to clean himself up before facing the Colors.

He hesitated before climbing out of the ship, as if gauging distances and whatever reserve energy he had left. Joao moved closer. Several Red pilots blocked his path. Gregory beckoned him in. Now that Dustin was out of his ship, Gregory could see how much it had cost him to break that conditioning. On top of that, Dustin had taken a beating when the Sej blasted his stabilizer. His lip was bitten, and a drop of crimson glistened at the swollen corner of his mouth. Bright streaks matted his hair. Buffeting. If Joao wanted to put him out of action, Gregory decided that for the first time in his life, he'd probably side with the medic against a pilot. Dustin was barely in shape to move, let alone to fly.

Rousing himself from what seemed to be a stupor, Dustin crouched, then jumped down to the deck. He steadied himself and looked around blearily.

"I don't need you, Joao," he said loudly. "I have to go back out there."

Gregory moved in. Joao flashed Dustin one of those serious doctor-looks that Gregory had always found so discouraging and brushed by the Reds. He wouldn't have overlooked the way Dustin's eyes were glazed or the angle at which he held his right arm. Gregory doubted that the younger pilot had enough of his wits about him to try to hide it.

Joao shook his head, and Gregory knew what that meant. Before even examining Dustin, he was prepared to certify him unfit to fly. Gregory wondered. Dustin looked bad, sure enough. But was he really only a little bruised, a candidate for collagen packing and a facewash, or was there real damage there? He couldn't tell. Joao could, and he took no chances. Not with any pilot, and certainly not with the pilots of his own squad.

Seeing Joao approach, Dustin backed off. "Hey," he

shouted hoarsely to the crowd, "I need another sting. This one's busted. Sorry. Just get him out of here and give me another sting."

"Dustin," Joao began persuasively, "you have to let me look at you. When the Sej hit, you may have suffered some injury you're not aware of. Unless I examine you, I can't certify that you're fit for duty." He started to bring his hand out from behind his back.

Leaning against his sting, Dustin didn't move. A cocky expression played across his face momentarily before the Wing mask was back in place. He surveyed the group, a rainbow collection of pilots who'd brought him in. Gregory already knew what he was going to say, and suppressed a sigh. Prudence and his responsibility as flight leader should have compelled him to back Joao but there was no way around this. Even a medic who stood shoulders taller than anyone else on deck couldn't do anything against this assembled crew. They'd mob him. The Reds who'd blocked Joao before were grinning. It was always pleasant to see a pilot get around a medic.

"Examination, my ass!" Dustin told Joao and the rest of the hangar deck. "He's got a hypo behind his back, and he's got nepenthine in it. And you all know it. Come on. There's a lot of Sej crawling around outside, just begging for it, and all I need to make ace is one. Is that so much to ask? One rotten Sej out of two cruisers full? Just one tiny single kill."

Joao glared. In all these years he'd heard enough pilots talking to know what he was up against. Every pilot on the deck, many wearing ace's scarves over their colored flightsuits, knew exactly how Dustin felt and would back him.

Gregory felt Dustin's eyes on him, found himself facing the whole crowd. Just possibly, he could order Dustin to stay behind. But it would hurt him, maybe make him think that Gregory still didn't trust him. He couldn't allow Dustin to feel like an outsider for an instant longer, not even if it got him killed.

"All this chatter's a waste of time," Gregory said. He met Joao's eyes aggressively. "There's a battle on outside. Give the man another sting, and let's get going."

Hoots and laughter trailed after Dustin as a reserve sting was brought forward. The hoots were derisive, aimed not at Dustin, not at the Wing, but against any medic who tried to ground a pilot. That feud had been going on longer than the war with the Sej, even.

Gregory climbed back into his sting and waited for launch. Joao was going to give them real hell when they got back. But that wasn't worth thinking about when there were so many Sej out there. As Dustin said, they were just begging for it.

As the flight headed toward the silent, lethal lights of battle, Gregory glanced about. There were more League flights out there than the base ship carried. So Subiat Base had managed to provide some support. With luck, it would be veteran pilots in state-of-the-art ships. Without luck, it was likely to be kids right out of training flying veteran stings.

Before he could resolve what kind of ships ground base had sent up, the Sej were on them. The flight held position around him, their cone flaring outward and blazing. The usual chatter came through on the open band.

Around him, the Colors who'd escorted Dustin peeled away to rejoin their own flights. The Sej flew to intercept them. Those Colors were owed something. "Assist," Gregory barked at his flight.

The cone broke into squads, each squad trailing one of the Colored flights. Gregory led Dustin, Yuri, and Judith

after the Red flight that had been first to come to their aid.
He knew the flight leader. If she weren't White Wing, she
fought like she was trying to earn the title. And she'd
certainly earned some help.

They formed on the defensive Red cone, protecting its
flanks. Suddenly, the Sej were swarming about, and it was
one-on-one. They were almost evenly matched. Gregory
slid easily into the reactions he'd known for a lifetime.
This was ease, simplicity, his mind and fingers flying in
conjunction, his thoughts cold, pure analysis. Target. Aim.
Shoot. Almost without conscious knowledge, his hands
played across the board. He glanced at his screens. It was
instinct for a flight leader to keep his pilots in sight. He
noted with some concern that Judith's mark was drawing
her out, away from the group. The ship was larger than
most stings. It looked like . . . yes, he thought it was the
Sej who'd tried to bring Dustin in.

"Judith," he said. Just her name. It ought to be enough
warning for her.

Then another Sej showed up close, coming in from
under his tail. He'd be vulnerable. Flashing back to his
own board, he began the tight series of jumps and turns
that would shake the Sej's aim and move him into position
to blast the larger ship with his own violet beam.

Judith knew she was being drawn too far. Gregory's
voice simply reminded her. But she couldn't help it. This
one was good. *Too good*, she thought again. Every time
she opened fire, it slipped just a bit aside, always waiting
till after her calculations were made and she'd committed
herself to the attack. This was risky. The hair on the back
of her neck prickled, and she drew a deep breath. She
didn't have time for anger or for anything except the

cunning and economy her enemy showed. This one would never let a mistake slip by.

She was so intent on tracking him that her mistake came before she knew it. It was almost too late to correct . . . no, it was too late, for sure. The Sej seemed to disappear into a shadow. Suddenly Judith realized what the shadow was. A Sej cruiser.

They were playing this one dirty, she thought, very dirty. Anger flared in her, and she felt like even her eyelashes could send out sparks. She realized what the Sej were trying to do. If they couldn't take Dustin, they'd settle for any White Winger they thought they could get. Like her. The ship had danced and cajoled and teased her right up into range for that cruiser and . . .

As Judith felt the first quiver of the tractor beam, she froze. Time stopped for her. *Back on Wing Moon they were sitting on the living-room floor, reams of specs that Zann had "brought home" gleefully spread out. Maryam, her face flushed and her eyes wide, was plotting how to take out a cruiser again. Engineering specs ran in front of Judith's eyes. She could almost see them, dancing on the gleaming consoles of her ship.*

It took a while for tractor beams to build up to full power. She remembered how long it had taken before the Sej had started hauling Maryam in. What was it she'd done wrong? Fly with it? Try to break free? Judith knew she wasn't as fast as Maryam had been. She couldn't rely on speed, on evasive tactics.

Then, in a single, perfect gestalt, she knew. She knew what Maryam had done wrong, and she knew how to take this revelation and those engineering specs, and make things come out right. She'd have sworn at the risk, but between trying it and the certainty of a tractor beam, she had no choice. Before she could waste time on second thoughts, she cut all thrust and channeled full power, even deflector power, to her forward lasers. She was wide open for any shot a Sej cared to take. They'd kill her for that when she got back to the ship. When. If. Damn. Furious at the risk, she blasted and blasted at the cruiser, even as it dragged her toward it.

As the shadowy violet spread on the cruiser's hull, she realized what was going to happen. "Oh shit!" She was furious at the cruiser and even more so with herself. It was the others who did crazy, dangerous things. It was the others who planned to take out cruisers. Judith was the one with mass, the safe one, the one who covered everyone else's stupid moves and never, never made stupid moves of her own.

It took only seconds for the violet energy to burn through to the cruiser's power ganglia. Judith darkened her screens. As if trying to rival Subiat's sun, the cruiser exploded, slowly, majestically, and in utter silence. The tractor beam released, and her sting careened away from the explosion. Safe in her harness, Judith fought her sting back onto a safe course and watched the cruiser die.

"Oh shit," she said again, almost reverently. Leaning forward to check her damage control readout, she noticed that her comms were on. Both of them. This time she managed not to swear aloud. Her face felt slightly cooler than the fragments of Sej cruiser whirling around out there, but not much. Every ship in that Fleet had heard her swear, had heard a White Winger let down defenses. She could have cried with rage.

Then the Sej who had danced her out this far to where she had had to do such un-Judith-like things had doubled around and was back, "up" and ten degrees off her starboard stabilizer, just where the stings were laser-blind.

He was very good, she had to admit. But it wasn't fair

to kill a cruiser and then get yourself vaped by one puny sting. She began evasive action, trying to buy enough time to turn and fight. She could see Dustin racing in to cover her, and wanted to spare enough time to order him back. She heard his heavy breathing . . . "Can't let . . ."

She wasn't going to make it, she thought, but kept trying anyway. At any second, she expected to feel . . . *when you get vaporized, do you know what hit you? Why didn't the bastard shoot already?*

Just as she tightened her muscles against the inevitable blast, the Sej fighter turned into a fall of dust.

"Damned near burned my a-gravs out on that one," she heard Dustin say.

"Thanks, and good shooting," she said. Then it hit her. "Dustin?" she asked. "Was that ten?"

No answer.

On the Wing frequency, a whoop pierced her eardrum. After seeing Dustin on the flight deck, she didn't think he'd have the energy for that kind of howl. Maybe he looked in worse shape than he actually was in, or maybe it was adrenaline. She'd put her money on adrenaline. The howl came again. Not Dustin. Yuri. Where had he come from?

"Good shooting, cruiser-killer!" he shouted. "Oh shit, did you ever take out a cruiser. Oh shit, are we ever going to hear about this."

She supposed she had it coming.

"Cut the chatter," came Gregory's usual command. "You glory-riders can come back with the rest of us and clean up. I don't suppose you've noticed that the Sej are retreating."

Even through Judith's embarrassment, she heard his voice change then. "Dustin," he added softly. "Come on back. Congratulations."

"Judith's safe," said Dustin.

On the Wing frequency Judith could hear Suzannah's voice, explaining what had just happened to Kroeger. She called him Federico? Well, Joao had started doing that last night. They'd probably be the first squad in the Wing to have such a weird sib. Maybe it would take people's minds off her.

A slow smile stitched itself across her face as she scanned the area. If the Sej were retreating, despite the firepower they'd brought to Subiat, it must be partly because they hadn't planned to make do with only one cruiser.

Gregory was profoundly grateful that they hadn't lost anyone in the flight. He'd had his worries about Judith, of all people, and he was still concerned about Dustin. He hadn't looked good enough to finish out the scramble. And it was strange that he hadn't even remembered that the Sej he'd taken out was his tenth kill.

Gregory sighed, letting himself sag back into his seat. He was glad to be back in the base ship. Through the darkness of his helmet's blastshield, he saw that the entire hangar deck was its usual chaotic mess. Zann and Val and Kroeger were standing by the flight monitors, and Joao was waiting in front of the stings again. He closed his eyes momentarily. The high reflective coating of the shields would hide him. He wanted to sleep. A hundred years sounded about right.

He sensed that the Colors were crowding around again. Not twice in one day, dear God, not twice. It wasn't fair. But there they were, and he couldn't do anything about it. He wondered how Dustin would manage to navigate the expanse of deck between his sting and the corridor. If *he* felt this wrung out trying to talk Dustin in and fight a battle, how must the other feel, breaking Sej conditioning, having a sting shot out from under him, and then making ace and probably taking some of the impact of Judith's cruiser-kill as well? If he didn't have a concussion from all that buffeting, and maybe a few broken ribs, Gregory would be surprised.

And then he'd have to talk to Judith, who was probably mortified about letting the entire Fleet and probably anyone listening in from Subiat Base hear a White Winger in distress or shock. Serve her right. Judith had always insisted—and been obnoxious about it—that she hoped *never* to make ace. And now she'd joined the smallest and greatest of elites, those with a cruiser-kill. Serve the little bitch right.

For once, it was Yuri who'd had the mass. Of all the people. That crazy squad. Slowly he keyed the unlock sequence and waited while the canopy swung back, adjusting his face to expressionlessness, much good that that was going to do now.

One by one, his flight left their stings and formed a ring about Dustin's. Its canopy stayed firmly shut. Gregory worried, reading the microcues of fear and anxiety through the harshness of his squadmates' attitudes as well.

"I'll put money on it that he can't make it ten meters across the deck."

"I'll take you, and I'll also bet that they show *something . . .*"

Gregory identified the gamblers from the corner of his eye. Reds. Of course. He started to be annoyed, then decided to forget about it. Maybe the Reds were being friendly in some perverse way. Or maybe they were just working off tensions of their own. It was none of his business. But then Dustin's condition was none of theirs.

The canopy of Dustin's sting cracked somewhat. Gregory tensed, ready to go and assist Dustin out if need be.

He hoped not. It would shame Dustin to ask for or receive aid. Joao was near. This time he even had a float half-hidden by Valentina. Medic or not, Joao would be just as upset as the rest of them if he had to use it.

Slowly Dustin hauled himself out of the fighter. His eyes were wild. If he'd had trouble focusing the last time he set foot on deck, it was doubled now. Fresh blood streaked his hair and the collar of his uniform. The hangar deck was quiet, as if everyone knew that one loud noise might bowl Dustin over.

But he had rubbed his face to cleanliness, or some imitation of it. Though he was shaky, he made it out of the sting on his own.

Then Gregory was at his shoulder, Joao on the other side. Yuri moved to stand in front of him, and Judith closed in behind. The rest of the squad, then the flight, joined them, escorting Dustin as he'd been escorted in the limping sting. One step at a time, so slowly that the expense of the deck seemed to multiply, they moved. Gregory calculated each step, watching Dustin list to one side, then to the other. He wondered each time if he could manage the next step, and then the one after that.

Come on, Dustin, come on.

He could feel eyes on him. The Colors were watching as they always did. No, not quite as they always did. And they didn't know about Dustin and Bikmat. They only saw what they knew, the Wing taking pride that a pilot as badly battered as Dustin could still walk away. He felt no hostility from the Colors, no resentment that the White Wing had just acquired another ace. It might be grudging, but it was respect that Gregory saw in those eyes above the colored flightsuits.

Now he didn't have time to think about the Colors. Every bit of his remaining energy had to focus on Dustin, to will him to walk, to stay upright. In the shape Dustin was in, it wouldn't be a disgrace if he couldn't, but Gregory knew how he'd feel about it. The honor of the Wing—what had Dustin said? He was Wing and he was Sej, never bluffing, always doing more than anyone could expect, and never giving away what it cost by so much as a look.

Finally, they made it to the door. The familiar gray shadow dislodged itself from its contemplation of the holoboards and resolved itself into Federico Hashrahh Kroeger. Gregory was even glad to see him. Just as well, since he supposed he was stuck with him as a sib now.

"I'm surprised he can walk," Kroeger murmured to Gregory.

"Why shouldn't he?" Gregory snapped. "That's *our* Dustin."

Dustin looked up. Maybe his eyes weren't tracking, but they shone.

Mercifully, the corridor was empty. Dustin glanced around as if making certain no one but his squad could see him, then gratefully let himself collapse against Joao, who eased him down onto the float.

Joao peeled back one eyelid, then brushed his matted hair back from his face.

"Is it just concussion?" Zann asked.

"I'll have to test him," Joao said. "You saw how he was reeling about. Just observing his general disorientation, I can't rule out the possibility of inner-ear damage as well."

Judith clapped her hand to her mouth.

"No," Gregory croaked. "God, no, not now." His voice was breaking. Dustin had survived so much, he'd just made ace.

He felt Dustin fumble after his hand, and knelt beside

the float. "Doesn't matter . . . I'm *home*." Gregory bent his head.

"Told you." He heard an amused, sardonic voice. "They're really human after all, with feelings and everything. Now pay me."

He whipped to his feet and turned around. Three tall pilots in Red flightsuits lounged in the doorway. One of them even dared to wink. *Brawling under battle conditions would net him a week in the brig,* Gregory thought, and he didn't want to be away from Dustin that long. Besides, he was too damned tired to fight anyhow.

CHAPTER 20

Outside Wing Moon's slick seven, Zann waited nervously. Several people glanced briefly at her. One or two smiled. She glanced at her wristcomp again. Six minutes, and then Kroeger would disembark.

She wondered what he'd think of Wing Moon, if he would find the flowers and the comfortable houses much different from anything he had expected. Granted, when the squad had issued the invitation, she had warned him that the Moon wasn't what people imagined. He had only smiled curiously, inquiring.

Now she had second thoughts about the invitation, about being out of uniform, and, at that, in a casual tunic that left her long legs bare, and about everything else. How would Kroeger react to the rest of her squad, to the rest of the Wing, all relaxed and at home, and unmasked, around him? He'd be gathering data faster than the new Battle Op computer they were experimenting on in the labs.

He knew he was the first outsider ever to be permitted access to Wing Moon. You couldn't very well keep a sib out of your home, could you? She remembered the moment when she realized what had happened. Kroeger had been watching the boards in the Hanger Deck, waiting for Gregory and the others to bring Dustin in, when Peter, an engineer from a squad she barely knew, had leaned over. "It's a strange sib you've brought us," he'd said, and she had shrugged.

Did Kroeger really understand what being a White Wing sib meant? He couldn't possibly understand, not without living it. It was a good thing that he learned fast.

Suddenly the terminal filled with people coming in off the transport. Behind them she caught sight of a gray shadow waiting at the back. Observing.

"Federico!" she shouted and waved vigorously.

He looked up, caught sight of her, and started forward. She grinned at the astonishment on his face as he realized that she was out of uniform, and her face was alive. Granted, he'd seen emotion on her face before, but that was strain, not nature. He slid through the crowd, which parted for him, scrutinizing him with the same curiosity he had for everything around him: the chairs, the holos depicting the Escape, the Founding of Wing Moon, and every stage in its terraforming since then.

"Su . . . Zann?" he asked tentatively. After all, she had called him by his first name.

"That's right, Federico," she said. "Zann." She thought of hugging him, and settled for linking arms as she led him out of the building.

"I've got a flier over to the left. Our place is out a ways from the Center," she said, talking a little too rapidly from nervousness. "Of course you're staying with us. Much easier for everyone, since we don't have any tourist accommodations. You'd have to stay with the Old Man, and . . ."

She let her voice trail off. She didn't think either of them would appreciate that arrangement.

"How is he?" As usual, Kroeger asked the question that pierced to the heart of the matter.

"Almost fully recovered now." Zann shivered, remembering the long nightmare of Dustin's convalescence and final freedom from Sej conditioning.

As they left the terminal and entered the dome, with its elaborate filters that made it resemble a sunny blue sky, Kroeger let out a low whistle.

"Precisely," Zann agreed with him. "We had no intention of being forced out of our home."

The flier, one of three that her squad had the use of, was old and battered. She hadn't noticed before. Too bad.

They climbed in, and Zann took off with the casual flourish she'd learned from Yuri. She amused herself by playing native guide. "We're on the perimeter now. As we fly, I'll point out the chapel, and the schools, and the Club. Probably we'll eat there one night. But everyone's waiting for you now, so we haven't time for a whole tour."

As she swooped low to point out the park where the Memorial stones rested, her comm lights flashes, and Kroeger clenched one hand against the seat.

"Suzannah here," she replied to the signal.

"I know it. Had to be Gregory's tame spy holding things up. Stop thinking and fly, will you? You want to get cited?"

"Too much chatter." Zann laughed and signed off.

"Recklessness?" Kroeger tried to sound casual.

"No. Too slow. I usually am." She gained speed and altitude with the disdain for passengers' comfort that the pilots generally showed, then realized that Kroeger wouldn't be used to it and slowed again.

From the park she headed away across a more closely built area, then into what seemed to be another park, this one dotted with sprawling houses. Glancing over at her passenger, she saw how he was studying it. She hadn't seen such enthusiasm in him since they had absorbed all that data from Dustin. She hoped he had brought her the transcripts of the investigations she had requested.

"They weren't joking about prime real estate, were they?" he asked no one in particular.

"We made it," Zann said. "And, partially thanks to you and Dustin, now we get to keep it."

She sent the flier spiraling down in front of the house and gestured. "Home."

Kroeger sat where he was and stared at her. "I'm really the first outsider you've brought here?"

"The first anyone has ever brought," she assured him and climbed out quickly.

Kroeger picked up his case and followed her. She hoped that the place wasn't its usual comfortable shambles, and that someone had remembered to clean dishes off the table. She felt very shy suddenly, not just because of what Joao had told her, but because Kroeger didn't know what to expect. They had all decided that he would be treated like any other sib, but she wasn't certain if he'd known he was being honored by getting the same treatment as one of their own.

Come off it, she told herself. *Kroeger isn't stupid. But I just wish he didn't look so . . .* fascinated *by everything. We tried to explain that we were quite normal when we were at home. But that's it. He doesn't know what normal is. Not for him, and not for us.*

She could smell coffee. *Not surprising,* she thought, as Yuri came out with a pot in one hand, mugs in the other.

"Want some coffee?"

Kroeger smiled. "You know, I've decided that no one except Earthers can brew a decent pot of coffee. The others can't even *code* the stuff right."

They all laughed a little too loudly. "Where's Gregory? I brought what he asked me for," Kroeger said.

Yuri shouted, and Gregory came up from the side of the house. He was wearing his brightest shirt and carrying a plant.

"You garden by hand?" Kroeger asked, amazed.

"Not always." Gregory smiled. "But around individual quarters . . . Most of our money goes to really heavy-duty terraforming technology, so we don't have the funds to invest in a lot of small equipment. Joao says it's relaxing. The rest of us just swear at him."

Kroeger was digesting the information far more readily than he was adjusting to the turquoise, green, and yellow shirt Gregory had chosen. Zann pitied him; at least she'd had the entire day to get used to the thing. Tearing his eyes away from it, he reached into his case and pulled out a small, plainly wrapped package. "I hope this is right," he said. "Besides, I want to talk to the whole squad, well, family, before anyone else comes."

Gregory took the package, checked it quickly, then disappeared inside.

"Does he know yet?" Kroeger asked.

"Dustin?" said Yuri. "Judith saw him wander out to the garden and followed him there, with her hairbrush and her friendliest smile. She'll keep him busy."

Zann chuckled. Then Valentina appeared. "You'd better hurry," she advised Zann. "If Judith's . . . diversionary tactics are any more effective, we could get in trouble for creating a public nuisance. Oh, hello, Kroeger."

Zann just knew that Kroeger was going to ask her to elucidate. When he didn't, she almost kissed him. Finally

Val took pity on him. "You've never seen Judith when she's off duty, have you?"

"I've never seen any of you off duty."

"We never really are, away from here. Come on."

Astoundingly, Valentina took Kroeger's hand and led him to the garden where, apparently, Judith was keeping Dustin busy. There was Dustin, seated with his back against a tree, and Judith leaning against him as he brushed her astonishingly long, dark hair. The squad slowed, and Kroeger slowed with them.

Dustin and Judith seemed unaware of their presence. Dustin stroked Judith's hair, buried his hands in it, and then kissed her. Judith flung her arms around him, and they overbalanced, to sprawl on the grass. Their kiss deepened.

"It's good that he's responding," Joao said, emerging from the house with Gregory.

"Responding?" Gregory asked. "He'd have to be dead not to."

Yuri coughed. "We've got company," he said, moving forward to nudge at Dustin with one toe.

He disengaged himself, and held out a hand to Judith, who smiled up at Kroeger. He started forward, half-embarrassed. There had been such tenderness in that kiss! He didn't know where to look. Certainly not at Suzannah, but then he had never hoped that she might respond to him that way. The pilot Judith's shoulders were distractingly white and rounded above the bright wrapped garment she wore. As if enjoying his confusion, she hitched it slightly higher over her breasts and smiled.

"Hello, Federico. Different, aren't I?"

Behind him, he heard Zann laugh again.

"Yes," Kroeger said. "Very different indeed. But I like it."

He eased himself down onto the ground and looked at Dustin. He was tanned from hours in the open air, but Kroeger could see the marks of his long fight back to health still on him. His expression, especially when he looked at Kroeger, was uncertain, and his temples slightly sunken. He had lost a great deal of weight.

Dustin met his eyes, prepared to endure anything Kroeger might say. He had made the young pilot fear him, and he hadn't really meant to. "I understand that you'll fly again," he said.

Dustin nodded. "I want to thank you for your offer of an instructorship in the War College at Central. I hope you understood why I couldn't accept it, even if I couldn't have flown again."

Kroeger waited for him to continue.

"The others—they'd have to go back on duty, and it was too far from anyplace they'd be. If Joao couldn't have cleared me, I'd have gone into Comm work or something."

Kroeger raised an eyebrow. It was such a waste. Intelligence would have profited from Dustin's experience. It still would, he thought, as Zann lounged beside him on the grass. Dustin might hate the idea of a second Intelligence career, this one for the League, but he'd help Suzannah.

"I'm glad you'll fly again," he told the pilot and was pleased when he relaxed. "But that isn't what I came to talk about. I have some information for you all, something I think is important. You must be the judges of how to use it, however."

"I have some information for you, too," Joao said. "Very probably this should be kept secret, but it's of general interest to us of the Wing."

"What is it?" Kroeger leaned forward. Seeing the others grin at one another, he smiled wryly and shrugged. He would always demand more information than he gave, he realized; he couldn't help it. But at least there was no condemnation in their expressions. His information could wait.

Joao nodded. "I was interested in what Dustin called his allergy to hathoti, so I ran several tests. Then I reran them with as many samples as I could. In fact . . ." He eyed Kroeger speculatively.

"You can't outfight him," Valentina said. "If you start running right now, though, he won't be able to catch you with his needles."

"You want to test me too?" Kroeger asked. "You will have my fullest cooperation, providing you explain what your tests are."

"The biochemistry is intriguing, far more interesting than gardening or lecturing to medical trainees. As far as any of the researchers on the Moon can tell, Dustin's reaction to hathoti isn't an allergy. Let's examine the facts. While the human populations in the League tend to have similar phenotypes, their body chemistries have marked, though subtle, differences."

"Come on, Joao, you're lecturing," Valentina interrupted again. "Give him the good stuff."

"It seems clear from the research that several of my colleagues and I have done that hathoti and Earther hormones are antipathetic. Before puberty the effect is negligible. But during it, when production both of pituitary hormones and either estrogen or testosterone are stopped up, any Earther will display a violent reaction to the drug."

Kroeger smiled slowly. "In other words, we are the only humanoids in the League incapable of hathoti addiction. Which in turn means that we are the only people who cannot be suspected of selling out as Kolatolo did. Very interesting indeed.''

"You said 'us,' Federico," Zann observed quietly.

Kroeger looked at her. Perhaps one day he'd find someone . . . not Zann, but someone who could mean to him what these people meant to her. She would be happy for him on that day. "Of course I said 'us.' I'm here, aren't I? And you showed me once that Earthers are proud of their Wing. All the League whispers and propaganda to the contrary, I have found something here to be proud of.''

He let himself grin. "Besides, I'm sure you'll agree that a lot of that data came from a profoundly biased source which any sensible person would discount." Zann laughed, and he was delighted.

"But I said I had information for you. Some of it must be restricted to Suzannah, but for the rest . . . you probably know that four days ago, Kolatolo was found dead in his garden.''

Suzannah nodded. Dustin looked shocked.

"We didn't want to upset you." Judith laid her head briefly against his shoulder.

"The autopsy disclosed that he died from an overdose of hathoti. He must have had reserves hidden away and when the investigation into Aramin's death exposed him—"

"He had no choice," Dustin said. "It wasn't fear of hathoti withdrawal, not if he had supplies stored away or could get more. There wasn't anything else he could do. It would be the only decent choice.''

"For us." Zann nodded. "Or, let's be frank, for the Sej. Maybe for an Arthan, there are other options, though he didn't choose them.''

"In any case," Valentina said, waving the discussion away, "I'd bet things will change a lot. There aren't going to be more riots, and the League Special Committee's going to conveniently forget it wanted to appropriate our Moon. I'll lay next month's combat bonus on it. Any takers?''

"Try one of the Colors," Yuri cautioned her. "We know a sure thing when we hear it."

"There's one more thing," said Kroeger slowly. "I've heard people in the Wing get angry at the Special Committee for threatening your possession of the Moon. 'Vape it back to the airless rock they gave us,' '' he quoted. "Not that I blame you. But I want to caution all of you against using that phrase."

Zann nodded. "I think I know what you're about to tell us."

Kroeger might have expected that. Suzannah hadn't been cleared for the full story, but she could deduce it from clues. And he wasn't sure that it was good to keep the information from the Wing. "About Earth," he began. "One reason the League hates you—hates us—is that it's afraid. Afraid because of the rumors that perhaps it wasn't the Sej who destroyed Earth. I started some private research of my own and I must report that the rumors are correct." He threw a disk down in front of Dustin.

"I needn't tell you just how eyes-only this is. You might call it my gift to you. It's the record of the last few days of Earth. When the Earthers were faced with a choice of surrender or destruction, they loaded all the children and as many other people as they could on board every ship capable of tau. Those who remained behind . . . blew all the arms on the planet."

The squad exchanged glances, the impassivity of the Wing flickering momentarily across their faces. "We should have known it from military history," Yuri said softly.

"What would we do in that situation?" Gregory asked. "I like to think we'd make the same choice."

Kroeger tightened his lips. He had been proud of this squad, his squad, before. And now . . . he shut his eyes, thinking of the Earther history he'd absorbed in between investigations of Kolatolo and Intelligence scandals on Central that might just land him with a directorship. Three hundred men dying at a pass with a strange name. A mud brick fortress filled with enemies—and corpses. A divine wind of pilots who resembled Yuri, who sat here with his eyes shining. And beside him, Gregory, Dustin, and Judith, all the descendants of people who might die, but who would never surrender. He brushed his hand across his face. The disk lying before Dustin seemed to glisten.

The whine of fliers coming in for a landing brought Kroeger from his meditation into a half-crouch.

"It's not a scramble," Gregory assured him, slapping him on the arm. "Here come the rest of the sibs!"

"Do we have everything ready?" Judith asked. "Oh, I knew I should have gone in earlier!"

The garden was full of sibs, including one very young girl, clinging to the hand of a trainee, who burst through to hug Dustin.

"You made it, Gwen!" he said happily. "I thought you would."

Kroeger recognized some of the people—members of their flight, other pilots, and what looked like half the population of the Wing Moon. Many carried bottles or lavish platters of food.

Despite the knowing smiles of the people around him, Dustin still looked confused.

"We were counting on Kroeger's help," Gregory explained to him. "We were in such a hurry to get you home that there wasn't time . . . in any case, we did want to wait till we knew Joao could clear you for active duty.

And now that he has, well, there's no reason why we shouldn't celebrate.''

Kroeger and Joao hoisted Dustin to his feet, then stepped aside. ''Yuri?'' Gregory asked. ''Will you join me? Judith, I'm afraid you'll have to wait till you take out another cruiser.''

Everyone laughed, then fell silent as Gregory walked over to Dustin.

A doubled length of white silk glistened across Gregory's hands, and he displayed it to the people gathered about. Then Yuri came over to join him. Together they draped the scarf of an ace pilot around Dustin's neck.

THE DRAGON REBORN

Sequel to *The Great Hunt*

Book Three
of
The Wheel of Time

by

Robert Jordan

Praise for *Eye of the World*

"A powerful vision of good and evil...fascinating people moving through a rich and interesting world."   —Orson Scott Card

"Richly detailed...fully realized, complex adventure."
—*Library Journal*

"A combination of Robin Hood and Stephen King that is hard to resist...Jordan makes the reader care about these characters as though they were old friends."   —*Milwaukee Sentinel*

Praise for *The Great Hunt*

"Jordan can spin as rich a world and as event-filled a tale as [Tolkien]...will not be easy to put down."   —*ALA Booklist*

"Worth re-reading a time or two."   —*Locus*

"This is good stuff...Splendidly characterized and cleverly plotted...The Great Hunt is a good book which will always be a good book. I shall certainly [line up] for the third volume."
—*Interzone*

The Dragon Reborn
coming in hardcover in August, 1991